Praise for *USA TODAY* bestselling author Lynne Graham

"Graham makes this episode in the Marshall Sisters series exciting, intense and full of humor. Her explosive couple—he's arrogant, she's sassy— are great together and the love scenes are award-winning quality."
—*RT Book Reviews* on *The Billionaire's Trophy*

"[An] engaging romance featuring terrific characters, searing love scenes and a superb story."
—*RT Book Reviews* on *A Deal at the Altar;* Top Pick!

"The romance was filled with seductions, interesting conversations, secrets, confrontations and sizzling sexual tension. There was never a dull moment in the book because something was always happening."
—*HarlequinJunkie.com* on *Challenging Dante*

"I love second chance romances and this one was amazing as only Lynne Graham can pen."
—*ThePinkHeartSocietyReviews.ca* on *Virgin on Her Wedding Night*

LYNNE GRAHAM

Born of Irish/Scottish parentage, Lynne Graham
has lived in Northern Ireland all her life. She grew
up in a seaside village and now lives in a country
house surrounded by a woodland garden, which is
wonderfully private.

Lynne first met her husband when she was fourteen;
they married after she completed a degree at
Edinburgh University. Lynne wrote her first book
at fifteen—it was rejected everywhere. She started
writing again when she was at home with her
first child. It took several attempts before she was
published and she has never forgotten the delight of
seeing that book for sale at the local newsagents.

Lynne always wanted a large family, and she now
has five children. Her eldest, her only natural child,
is in her twenties and is a university graduate. Her
other children, who are every bit as dear to her
heart, are adopted: two from Sri Lanka and two
from Guatemala. In Lynne's home, there is a rich
and diverse cultural mix, which adds a whole extra
dimension of interest and discovery to family life.

Lynne loves gardening and cooking, collects
everything from old toys to rock specimens, and is
crazy about every aspect of Christmas.

USA TODAY Bestselling Author

LYNNE GRAHAM

A
CONVENIENT
ARRANGEMENT

HARLEQUIN® FEATURE AUTHOR

Recycling programs
for this product may
not exist in your area.

ISBN-13: 978-0-373-60662-7

A CONVENIENT ARRANGEMENT
Copyright © 2010 by Harlequin Books S.A.

The publisher acknowledges the copyright holder
of the individual works as follows:

THE ITALIAN'S WIFE
Copyright © 2001 by Lynne Graham

THE SPANISH GROOM
Copyright © 1999 by Lynne Graham

Printed in U.S.A.

CONTENTS

THE ITALIAN'S WIFE

CHAPTER ONE

WHEN RIO LOMBARDI finally heard the apartment door open, his handsome mouth quirked and he sprang upright. Christabel was in for a surprise.

A breathless series of giggles and an urgent whisper which he didn't catch sounded from the hall, making him frown. Evidently, his fiancée had a friend in tow. That was the trouble with surprises, Rio acknowledged in exasperation: their very nature made them unreliable. He should've warned her that he might make it back to London a day early. Surrendering his fantasy of sweeping Christabel straight off to bed for a passionate reunion, Rio crossed the spacious lounge to announce his presence and make polite social chitchat instead.

But the hall was already empty. A pair of kitten-heeled turquoise shoes and a pair of diamanté-studded black satin mules lay abandoned on the carpet. Frowning a little at the suspicion that his fiancée might not be sober again, and now also wondering if he was about to break in on some cosy girly get-together, Rio strolled down the corridor to the bedroom. He'd intended to knock on the door but it was wide open and the sight which met his eyes was so shocking, so utterly unbelievable to him, that his lean hand froze in mid-air.

Halfway out of her dress, Christabel was kissing... another woman, also half out of her dress. Paralysed to the threshold, Rio stared, his dark-as-midnight eyes totally refusing to accept what he was seeing. They were drunk, fooling about, he started to tell himself; maybe they had realised he was in the apartment and were playing some stupid tasteless joke on him. But they were locked together, breast to breast, hip to hip, Christabel's glossy blonde hair mingling with the brunette's darker tresses as they touched each other with the unmistakable eagerness of lovers. He was so revolted by that acknowledgement that for an instant he felt physically ill. Christabel, *his* woman, *his* lover, *his* bride-to-be...

Christabel drew back with a husky, sexy laugh, her fabulous face flushed with excitement, and only then did the two women realise that they had an audience poised in the doorway. Rio recognised the brunette as one of Christabel's friends: Tammy something or other, another fashion model, also another man's wife.

For a split-second nobody moved or spoke. Aghast, Christabel and Tammy gaped at him, and then the brunette loosed a strangled moan of horror and fled into the connecting bathroom, noisily slamming and locking the door behind her.

'H-heavens...what a fright you gave me...' Christabel faltered, frantically yanking up her dress to cover her bare breasts, her face now pale and stiff as marble, her wonderful green eyes glittering with fearful anxiety. 'Please...you mustn't misunderstand what you just saw, Rio—'

'Misunderstand?' Rio could never recall it taking more effort to speak one word levelly. Initial shock and disbelief were giving way to rage and an unfamiliar

sense of appalled bewilderment that only stoked the rage higher.

'We were just mucking around. Don't be old-fashioned about this...' Christabel urged in the charged silence as she moved closer and made a little pleading movement with her manicured hands.

Rio could not take his eyes off her. Christabel Kent, the world-famous supermodel and media darling who wore his engagement ring, her Nordic fairness and endless legs a legend in the fashion and beauty market. Perfect face, perfect body.

'OK...I'll come clean,' Christabel continued feverishly. 'So I was missing you dreadfully and I like a change occasionally—'

'A change? You make it sound like it's nothing—'

'It isn't...it's just *sex*!' his fiancée interrupted, reaching for the lean, powerful hands coiled into fierce fists of self-restraint by his sides. 'Nothing for you to worry about or even think about, because if you don't like it I swear it won't *ever* happen again!'

Rio backed out of her reach. In his mind's eye he could still only see one image: Christabel wrapped half-naked and excited round another woman. Just sex? He felt betrayed. He felt incredulous. He felt something he wasn't used to feeling: foolish.

'All right...you're shocked and furious and I understand and I'm really sorry!' Christabel was panicking at his lack of response. 'I'll make it up to you—'

'What with? An offer to *join* the two of you?' Rio derided between clenched white teeth.

Christabel looked up at him, green eyes gleaming with sudden relief lightened by a shard of seductive amusement. 'Would you like that, darling?'

Violence coursed through Rio in a molten wave and a shudder of angry revulsion passed through him. If she hadn't been a woman he would have knocked her through the wall and if that was an old-fashioned reaction, tough! Yet her stupidity in assuming that his contemptuous question might have been a serious hint that all would be forgiven if he got a piece of the same action freed him from that first binding shock.

'I'll give you time to move out of here,' Rio breathed with raw clarity. 'I'll deal with cancelling the wedding arrangements—'

'You *can't* be serious!' Christabel gasped in stricken horror. 'We're perfect together!'

Rio swung on his heel and strode back down the corridor, Christabel pursuing him every step of the way, pleading with him to calm down and think again. In the hall, she shot between him and the front door to prevent his departure.

'If you tell people about this, my career will be ruined!'

Christabel's career had been built on her clean, wholesome image. No risqué lingerie assignments, no media coverage of Christabel whooping it up in the clubs, no bad-ass boyfriends. Christabel liked to pose for off-the-record interviews with fluffy animals and talk about how mad she was about children, not to mention how crazy she was about the man she was to marry and how much she was looking forward to giving up work to be a full-time wife and mother...

Rio reached out and lifted her bodily out of his path. '*Dio mio*...I won't be talking—'

That fear overcome, Christabel cried in desperation. 'Then *why* can't you forgive me? Tammy means nothing to me. It's not like she was another man or I'm in love with her. I love *you*, Rio—'

She loved him? Had she *ever* loved him? Or had she loved his enormous wealth most of all? His sculpted mouth tightening, he recalled that Christabel had expensive tastes that far outran even her own healthy earning power. Within a week of his marriage proposal she had confessed to a string of outstanding bills and had told him how hopeless she was with money. Impressed by her honesty, he had felt hugely protective towards her and had cleared her debts without even thinking about what he was doing.

Yanking himself free of her clinging hands in growing disgust at what her every reckless word revealed about her character, Rio left the apartment and made it into the elevator. He raised one of his hands and watched it shake in disbelieving outrage. Balling his fingers back into an aggressive fist, he punched the steel wall with the full force of the rage and the pain splintering through him, the savage pain he had been struggling to deny. He had loved her, he had *really* loved her and wanted to marry her.

Santo cielo, he might have given his children a mother who thought three-in-a-bed sex was a wonderful thrill! A woman who had contrived to hide her true nature from him so successfully that the sheer shock value of what he had witnessed and heard would linger with him for a very long time.

Just sex? Hadn't he been enough for her? Obviously not. As his bodyguards reared up from their seats in the ground-floor reception area, their surprise at his unexpected reappearance patent, Rio was blind to them, his darkly handsome features rigid and ashen pale. Outside, he drank in deep of the frosty night air before crossing the street to his limo. Had Christabel been lying back and thinking about other *women* in his bed? Had even her pleasure been faked? Had the eager desire she had shown for his lovemaking all been part of one giant con to ensnare a very rich husband? How could he have known so little about a woman he had been with for almost two years?

'Your hand's bleeding, boss. Are you OK?'

Rio angled a cursory glance down at his bruised and bleeding knuckles before meeting the troubled dark eyes of Ezio. The stockily built older man had been on his security team since Rio was a student and knew him too well.

'*Sì*...' But right at that moment Rio did not know when he was ever going to feel normal again. Like Saverio Lombardi, billionaire head of one of the proudest, oldest families in Italy and the driving force behind Lombardi Industries, one of the biggest, most successful companies in the world. He felt humiliated, sick and less than a man for the first time in twenty-nine years of existence.

How was he to explain this fiasco in acceptable terms to his vulnerable mother? Alice Lombardi was literally counting the days to her son's wedding and was pitifully eager to cradle her first grandchild in her arms. She was a sick woman, crippled by arthritis, further weakened by a series of debilitating illnesses. Every week she survived was a literal gift from God and her poor health permitted her precious few pleasures in life. Now there would be no wedding, no prospect of a baby to fill the empty nursery, no bright and chatty daughter-in-law to occasionally enliven her dull, pain-filled days…

He had never openly acknowledged the reality before but he *needed* a wife.

'Tammy means nothing to me…it's not like she was another man.' The insidious and seductive echo of Christabel's husky voice made Rio's hands clench into ferocious fists. No, he could not, would not forgive her, not for the sake of his own powerful libido, not even for the sake of the mother he adored. Christabel, the woman he had loved beyond belief, was a total sham. What did that say about *his* judgement? He had believed he knew his fiancée through and through, yet he had not even penetrated the surface of that calculating immoral mind of hers. He could not have chosen worse had he decided to marry a total stranger. He might as well stop and ask the first woman he met to be his bride…

With a harsh and bitter laugh at that insane idea, Rio Lombardi poured himself a large brandy from the bar in the back of the limo.

Holly was cold, hungry and scared.

It was barely one in the morning and the whole of the rest of the night hours still stretched ahead of her. For how long had she been walking? Her back and her legs ached and her vision was blurring with exhaustion but where could she possibly stop for the night that she would be safe? She had sat around in a train station for most of the day, moving seats every so often, striving not to attract the attention of anyone official, until the crude heckling of two youths had forced her to take refuge in the restroom. While she had been trying to freshen up there, her jacket, which had had her purse in the inside pocket, had been stolen. Her *own* fault for taking her jacket off, leaving it carelessly draped over Timmie's stroller and turning her attention away for a minute.

No point approaching a policeman, not when awkward questions would be asked and an address requested. Her purse, which had had her last few pounds in it, was gone and that was that. Like so much else that had happened to Holly since her arrival in London so full of naïve hopes seven months earlier, it was just one more kick when she was down, one more piece of bad luck in a run of bad luck that seemed endless.

As she paused to check that her eight-month-old son was still wrapped up snug against the chilly air, she shivered violently and fingered the two battered carrier bags that now contained all that she possessed in the world. She had to be the ultimate loser and failure, she decided wretchedly. Useless at everything, not even able to put the shabbiest roof over Timmie's head and look after him as he deserved. Here she was out on the street, homeless and penniless, next door to being a beggar...

Yet just twenty-four hours earlier she really had tried so hard to pick up her sagging courage and get a grip on her problems. She had gone to the Social Security office to report that her landlord had tried to break into her room twice during the night and that she was terrified of him.

'We've never had any complaints about him before,' the woman behind the protective barrier had said, coolly unimpressed, not even trying to hide her suspicion that Holly was simply trying to get her accommodation upgraded. 'If you don't return to the lodgings we arranged for you, you will be deemed to have made yourself in-

tentionally homeless. I advise you to think long and
hard before you make that mistake, as you have a young
child to consider. I'll inform your social worker that
you're having problems—'

'No…please don't do that,' Holly had begged, in terror of what such an interview might mean where Timmie was concerned. Her baby might be taken away from
her and put into foster care. The last social worker she
had spoken to had started out sympathetic but had lost
patience when Holly refused to name the father of her
child. But Jeff had said that if she dared to tell anyone
that he was Timmie's dad he would make her sorry that
she had *ever* been born…

Well, she was sorry enough herself about that fact,
Holly conceded miserably. She had devastated her parents by giving birth to a baby outside marriage. When
she had finally admitted that she was pregnant her father had cried. As long as Holly lived she knew she
would never, ever forget the sight of her father crying…
or her own sick sense of guilt and bitter shame.

Her eyes swimming with tears at that painful recollection, and lost as she was in her own thoughts, Holly
did not even notice that she was approaching an inter-
section. Staring blankly ahead of her, accustomed to
the noisy flow of traffic down the main road as a background, she was equally unaware of the lights of a car
coming from her right.

The sudden steep drop of the pavement down onto
the road took her by surprise and sent the overladen
stroller lurching off-balance. As she made a frantic effort to right it, the scream of car tires striving to brake
to a halt alerted her to the danger that she and Timmie
were in. In the split-second at her disposal Holly thrust

Timmie's stroller away from her with all her might in the desperate hope that it would carry him out of the car's path to safety. But her own shaken attempt to make it back up onto the pavement was doomed as her heels hit the curb and she lost her footing. Falling backwards, she felt a sickening explosion of pain at the base of her skull and then blackness folded in and she knew no more.

Rio Lombardi leapt out of the limousine. 'Did we hit her?' he demanded.

'No!' Ezio, who could move at the speed of light when required, was already retrieving the stroller and drawing it back from the other side of the road to a safer resting place.

'I didn't hit her…I *saw* her; I was already slowing down. But she walked out into the road without looking and just fell over!' Rio's chauffeur exclaimed over the top of the driver's door, his attention lodged in horror on the still figure lying in the path of the headlights.

'Call an ambulance…a private one from the foundation hospital; it'll be faster,' Rio instructed harshly, his tone of command pronounced to steady his companions.

He crouched down on the road and lifted a limp wrist to feel for a pulse, drawing in a slow deep breath of relief when he found what he sought. Although her skin felt frighteningly cold to his touch, she was alive. 'She's not dead…' Springing upright again, he peeled off his suit jacket and bent down to carefully drape it over her, surveying the face of the unconscious victim for the first time. '*Dio mio*…she's a young woman!'

A very pretty young woman too, Rio found himself conceding, scanning that delicate bone-structure and the mass of bronze-coloured ringlets rioting round her small head, their vibrant colour only serving to accentuate her pallor. 'What is she doing out with a baby at this hour? Did you see what she did for the baby? She was ready to sacrifice her own life to give it a chance—'

'She's probably its mother, boss,' Ezio suggested, lowering his cell phone, having made the requested call for immediate medical attendance at the scene. 'It's depressing, but kids are giving birth to kids all the time these days.'

Rio found himself strangely reluctant to accept that opinion. After a second, lengthier appraisal, he was prepared to concede that the girl could possibly be seventeen or eighteen years old. But she looked so innocent and untouched, and he had already noticed that she wore no rings. Ezio stooped to retrieve his employer's jacket.

'What are you *doing*?' Rio demanded.

'I got your overcoat from the car, boss. It'll keep her warmer. There's no point you catching pneumonia.' Ezio had to pitch his voice higher to be heard above the noisy sobs now emanating from the depths of the covers heaped on the stroller.

'I'm OK. I wish we could risk moving her into the limo. Giovanni…you're a family man; comfort the child,' Rio urged his other bodyguard as he accepted the overcoat from Ezio but chose to lay it gently over the top of his suit jacket to provide an extra layer of warmth for the girl. 'She's frozen through.'

'Timmie…?' Her head pounding fit to burst, Holly surfaced and with a heroic effort raised her head, reacting to the sound of her son's cries. Not a pain cry though, only an anxious cry, she recognised in instant relief. 'My baby?'

Rio gazed down into huge anxious eyes as disconcertingly blue as a Tuscan midsummer sky. 'Your baby's fine. Lie still. An ambulance is on its way—'

'I can't go to hospital…I've got Timmie to take care of!' Initially bemused by that deep dark drawl with its unexpected liquid foreign accent larding every syllable, Holly was startled when the man dropped down on a level with her and pressed on her shoulder to prevent her from lifting herself higher.

Mouth running dry, she stared up at him just as he turned his arrogant dark head away, presenting her with his bold profile and the impossibly smooth, proud lines of a high cheekbone to address someone else out of her view. 'Have you contacted the police yet?'

'No police…*please*,' Holly broke in shakily. 'Are you the bloke that was in the car?'

In silent response, he turned back to nod in confirmation, regarding her with dramatic dark golden eyes which could have turned a saint into a sinner overnight.

Shaken by that abstracted thought, Holly said, 'We don't need the police or an ambulance. I'm all right. I tripped and knocked myself out for a second…that's all—'

'Have you any family…a boyfriend I can contact on your behalf?' he prompted, very much as if she hadn't spoken.

Even though it hurt, she turned her head away in self-protection. 'Nobody.'

'There's got to be somebody. A friend, a relative, surely?' he persisted.

'Well, maybe you're coming down with them but I've got nobody,' she muttered in a voice that wobbled in spite of all her efforts to control it.

Rio studied her in frustration. She wasn't a Londoner. She had a pronounced country brogue with rounded vowel sounds but he could not place it, although he had a vague recollection of once hearing an exaggerated version of a similar accent in a stage comedy. First things first, he reminded himself. 'What age are you?'

'Twenty. I don't want the police...do you *hear* me?' Fear made her strident and she began to sit up in spite of the sick whirling sensation that engulfed her the moment she moved. If she went into hospital, the police would call in the authorities to take charge of Timmie and he would be put in a foster home.

When she swayed backwards, Rio shot a supportive arm round her narrow spine. 'You must have medical attention. I promise you that you will not be parted from your child.'

'How? *How* can you promise that?' she gasped.

The ambulance pulled in, all flashing lights and efficiency, and the paramedics took over, forcing him into retreat.

'Timmie!' Holly exclaimed in panic as she was moved onto the stretcher.

Rio strode forward. 'I'll follow you to the hospital with him—'

Holly realised that he was asking her to trust him with her son. 'I don't *know* you—'

'But *we* know him.' For some reason, the paramedic who had spoken chuckled with decided amusement. 'Don't worry, love. Your kid will be safe as houses with this gentleman.'

Exhausted by the effort she had expended, and trembling, Holly mumbled her agreement.

As the ambulance drove off Ezio passed his employer

his jacket and said, 'We've got the name and address of a witness and we should make a statement to the police just to be on the safe side.'

'Per meraviglia...' Somewhat bemused at the offer he had found himself making to placate the girl's fear on her child's behalf, Rio strode over to stare down into the stroller. In the nest of bedding and beneath the bobble-topped woolly hat, all that could be seen was a pair of big, scared blue eyes full of tearful anxiety and a tiny upturned pink nose. 'You see to the statement. I'll take...Timmie the timid to the hospital—'

'I could take care of that and the statement,' the older man pointed out quietly. 'You haven't slept more than a hour since you left New York.'

Nor had he been planning to *sleep* for what remained of the night, Rio recalled, his strong jawline clenching hard as he registered that he had contrived to momentarily forget the climax of his unannounced visit to Christabel. Closing his mind to that grim awareness, he stooped to remove the baby from its concealing layers of bedding. Timmie emerged rigid as a stick of rock, if possible his fearful eyes growing even larger to encompass the tall, dark, powerful man cradling him with surprising dexterity.

'I'm a push-over for babies...especially scared ones.' Climbing into the limo, Rio watched as the rest of the baby's possessions were piled in, including the two worn carrier bags, one of which spilled over and let a feeding bottle roll out.

Timmie let out a squeal and stretched out a hopeful hand in the direction of the bottle, little feet kicking with eagerness.

'You're hungry...OK.' Rio rooted through the bags

and discovered a packet of baby cookies but nothing of a liquid persuasion. Timmie wasn't picky. He had no manners either. He snatched at the rusk and lodged his two tiny front teeth into it, got them stuck and then let out a mournful wail.

Rio was kept fully occupied all the way to the hospital. He discovered that affectionately handling one of his friend's babies while a fond mother hovered within reach to take care of all the necessities was a far different affair from actually trying to handle a real live squirming and complaining baby all on his own. With the aid of a glass tumbler and a bottle of mineral water from the built-in bar, however, he managed to quench Timmie's thirst—but not without soaking Timmie and himself into the bargain.

He emerged from the limo at the entrance to the hospital looking something less than his usual sartorially splendid self, with rusk crumbs scattered all over him and clinging to the damp patches. He was also for the first time feeling the effects of too little sleep on top of a severe attack of jet lag.

Ezio attempted to relieve his employer of his baby burden but Timmie wasn't impressed and lodged two frantic hands in Rio's hair and screamed in naked panic.

'If you don't smile at him, he doesn't like you,' Rio shared wearily, rearranging Timmie in a somewhat unconventional drape over one broad shoulder, where the baby hung like a limp but relaxed sack, one large masculine hand pinned to his spine. 'He's a real little bag of nerves.'

Greeted like visiting royalty by the receptionist, Rio was ushered into his friend's comfortable private office to wait and a nurse arrived at speed to remove Timmie.

'He needs to be fed…and other things,' Rio warned, wincing as Timmie tried to cling to his protector and then bawled blue murder at being detached from him. The high note of fear he could hear in the baby's cry was traumatic to listen to, Rio reflected, riven with discomfiture at the child's distress.

It was an hour before John Coulter, the senior physician at the hospital, came to join him and report back on his most recent patient.

'I think you just saved a life tonight, Rio,' the older man announced in his usual cheerful manner. 'That young woman is suffering from the early stages of hypothermia. Falling in front of your car was the best thing that could've happened to her. She and that child might have been dead by morning—'

'I noticed she had no coat on, but presumably she would've made it home before hypothermia got a grip on her,' Rio slotted in, his tone one of casual dismissal.

'But she was planning to spend the night walking round the streets…she's homeless, didn't you realise that?'

Rio frowned in surprise.

'I'll have to call in the duty social worker. I'll feel a heel doing it, though,' Dr. Coulter confided ruefully. 'She's terrified that her baby will be put in foster care, and even though that is very unlikely, as Social Services work to keep mother and child together, I wasn't able to convince her of that.'

'How are they?'

'The baby's in fine form. But the mother's another matter…skin and bone, needs feeding up and looking after, but there's no sign of drug or alcohol abuse, which is something in her favour. That accent too…deepest Somerset,' the older man remarked with a wry smile.

'Somerset?'

'*Cider with Rosie* and all that,' John Coulter quipped, referring to the classic book set in a rural area. 'Although, come to think of it, that wasn't Somerset. I think it's based on Gloucestershire—'

'John,' Rio groaned. 'Never mind the book.'

The older man sighed. 'Holly's a country girl and hasn't a clue how to go on in a city like London. I imagine that's why she's in such a fix—'

'Holly? That's her name? Can I see her?'

'This *is* your hospital—'

'It belongs to the Lombardi Foundation, not to me personally,' Rio said drily.

Holly lay in her comfortable bed, scanning the elegant and luxurious layout of her private room and feeling as though she had dreamt it all up. But no, Timmie lay just feet away in the cot that had been provided. The kindly nurse had rustled up a proper feed for him, changed him and tucked him in. Her son was asleep now, snug and secure with a full tummy. Her eyes prickled with weak tears of shame over her own inadequacy. Timmie had a *right* to be snug and secure *all* the time.

The obvious solution to their predicament had been staring her in the face for many weeks now but she had been too much of a coward to confront it. She was not scared of social workers but she *was* scared of being made to look head-on at her own failings when set next to Timmie's needs. Timmie had to come first. She had been horribly selfish. What kind of mother love put a baby on the streets in the middle of the night? She was twenty years old, and she might have left school early but she was not stupid. She knew right from wrong and she was finally accepting that all along her mother had known exactly what she was talking about...

'If you give the baby up for adoption you can come home to us afterwards,' her mother had promised with red-rimmed eyes full of strain and regret. 'I won't let you put your father through any more pain, Holly. You did what you shouldn't have done and you're paying the cost of it now. If you try to keep the kiddy there'll be nothing but grief ahead of you.'

Over the past months Holly had learned the truth of words that had seemed so harsh to her at the time she had listened to them. Then she had still been foolish enough to hope that Jeff was making a home for them both in London, that he would want their child as much as she did and that he would go ahead and marry her just as he had promised. But Jeff had not made a home for them, had been outraged that she should've dared to give birth to a baby he did not want, and had never, ever had the smallest true intention of marrying her.

Timmie would be much better off adopted, Holly forced herself to concede. It would break her heart but it was cruel of her to keep him when she could not provide for him as he deserved. Her eyes stung with hot, prickling tears. There *was* no other choice available to her. She couldn't earn enough in the employment market to pay for childcare or a proper home. Even living off the state in recent weeks, as she had been forced to do after a spate of ill health had seen her sacked from her last job, she had managed no better. Everything she had once owned had either been sold for cash or stolen. She now literally owned only what she stood up in. It was time to do the right thing for Timmie. He would have two caring parents and a decent home. How could she stand in her son's way when she herself had so little to offer him?

The nurse bustled back in with a wide smile. 'Mr. Lombardi is planning to come and see you...now, aren't you the lucky one?'

'Mr...*who*?'

'Saverio Lombardi. The man whose limousine you almost dented!'

'A limousine...Lombardi? Isn't that the same name as this hospital?' Holly queried in confusion. Had he been in a limousine? He had certainly been travelling with an awful lot of people, she recalled dimly.

'This hospital is run by the Lombardi Foundation. It's a charitable trust set up by Mr. Lombardi. We only take in local patients on emergency,' the nurse explained. 'People come here from all over the world for surgery that they can't get in their home countries. The foundation covers the costs. Mr. Lombardi is a very well-known philanthropist...surely you've heard of him?'

'No...I didn't notice the limo either.' The nurse was talking about underprivileged people from less developed countries, Holly gathered in some discomfiture, charity cases. Although she had been taken aback by her luxurious surroundings, she had not realised that the hospital was private. Indeed, she had assumed that the hospital was simply brand-new and that she had got her own room either by sheer good fortune or because Timmie's initial crying would have disturbed other patients. But now it was obvious that luck and Timmie's lungs had had nothing to do with it. *She* was a charity case too.

'Maybe you were too busy looking at those scorch-

ing tawny eyes of his,' the other woman teased. 'Not
to mention the rest of him. Rio Lombardi is drop-dead
gorgeous, and so fanciable you could kidnap him.'

On the other side of the ajar door, Rio hesitated in
receipt of that unsought accolade and raised his brows
in exasperation. Then, strong jawline squaring, he entered with a light warning knock on the door.

Holly jerked in dismay, her pale skin taking on instant discomfited colour as if she had been the one talking out of turn, while the night nurse scurried out with a
bent head. But after just one look at the very tall, powerfully built dark male coming to a halt at the foot of
her bed, Holly was challenged even to recall what had
briefly embarrassed her. In all her life she had never
seen a more breathtakingly handsome male and, no
matter how hard she tried, she could not stop staring.

Drop-dead gorgeous had been no exaggeration. That
lean, taut bone-structure, composed of flaring dark
brows, proud cheekbones, wide narrow mouth and as-
sertive jawline, was the very essence of raw masculinity. As she encountered his stunning dark golden eyes
her mouth ran dry, and without any good reason at all
she was suddenly very conscious that she was naked beneath the thin hospital gown she wore, suddenly hugely
aware of her own female body. Her breasts seemed to
ache and heat flickered deep in her pelvis, an oddly
charged heat that drew her every muscle so taut that
she could hardly breathe as he studied her.

Luxuriant black lashes screened his gaze as his attention lingered on her soft full mouth. In that quick
upward glance he made to connect with her scrutiny
again, she met the flashburn effect of those intense

eyes of his and was appalled to find herself wondering how that beautiful male mouth would feel on her own.

'How are you feeling?' Rio Lombardi asked quietly.

'F-f-fine,' Holly stammered helplessly, aghast at a mind that could throw up such inappropriate thoughts, terrified that he might somehow suspect the effect he was having on her. 'But I've got concussion.'

'I know…' As Rio Lombardi strolled over to the cot to gaze down at her son, Holly, her face burning like a bonfire, struggled to get a grip on herself. But it was no use, for she could not drag her magnetised attention from him. He was well over six feet tall, his impressive physique lean and muscular, and in spite of his size he moved with extraordinary grace. 'Timmie looks happy, though.'

'Yeah…nice cosy cot,' Holly mumbled, feeling like an idiot as soon as the inane words escaped her.

Rio Lombardi glanced up from his scrutiny of Timmie's slumbering and peaceful little face, a faint smile still softening the hard line of his sculpted lips. 'You shouldn't have been on the streets with him,' he remarked with quiet assurance.

'I…I *know*,' Holly stressed jerkily, her dilated gaze clinging to the mesmeric tawny hold of his, her heart jumping as if she had just leapt off a cliff, pounding inside her so hard she could hardly squeeze the words out.

She was still blushing as fierily as a schoolgirl, Rio registered with reluctant amusement. He had switched his attention to Timmie to give her a moment in which to compose herself but his subtlety had been wasted. He turned her on and she couldn't hide it. Yet there was something strangely touching about her lack of artifice, her total inability to conceal what she was feeling and thinking. Those big blue eyes were like windows and that lush pink mouth betrayed her tension.

Her slight, slender body barely made a decent impression in the bed. She had the most amazing hair, though, Rio acknowledged. Released from whatever had held it in temporary subjection, her hair now cascaded in snaking corkscrew ringlets halfway to her waist, catching the light like rich, gleaming bronze. His attention strayed lower and momentarily lingered on the surprising fullness of the rounded swells pushing against the hospital-issue gown as she sat forward, the prominence of her taut nipples visible even through the barrier of starched cotton. Nice breasts, he found himself thinking, and he was startled when he felt himself hardening in urgent response, startled that even exhaustion and stress could not stifle his most basic urges.

'I'm going to sort me and Timmie out...I r-really am,' Holly swore earnestly in the charged silence, desperate to make him think better of her. 'When can I get out of here?'

'You need a couple of days of R & R,' Rio responded, recognising the naïvety of that question when she was free to walk out the door any time she wished. But he was relieved by it and did nothing to disabuse her of her notion that she had to pay heed to some superior authority.

'R & R?'

'Rest and recuperation. A lady is coming to see you tomorrow.' Recognising the flash of instant panic in her wide eyes, Rio gave her a bland smile of reassurance. 'Nobody is going to make any arrangements against your will, but I think you'll agree that you need some professional advice and support right now.'

Holly's tummy muscles contracted in a sickening spasm of alarm, her thin shoulders hunching as she lost colour. At last, she gained the strength to take her eyes from him, but only because fear and deep shame over her own failure to give her son a proper home made it impossible for her to continue meeting his level gaze.

'You'll both be fine,' Rio asserted in conclusion, strolling back to the door.

For an instant he hesitated as he remembered that crazy thought he had had only a few minutes before Holly fell in front of his limo. She was, indisputably, the very first woman he had met since walking out on Christabel.

Just as well he wasn't insane enough to marry a complete stranger, he told himself with grim amusement. After all, Holly Sansom might be green as grass but she was still an unmarried mother. While he was a male who prided himself on his open mind, his family background and traditional Italian upbringing had imbued him with certain values and expectations.

CHAPTER TWO

PALE AS DEATH, Holly flopped back against the pillows, feeling as weak as water and trembling.

She had gawped at Rio Lombardi like a bedazzled kid and had severely embarrassed herself. Since she had never felt that way around a man before, not even around Jeff, she could only put her behaviour down to the effects of concussion and total exhaustion. Fortunately a guy like Rio Lombardi, so rich and so important and so utterly above her in every way, wouldn't have noticed how awkward and silly she had been, she told herself. In any case, she had a lot more to worry about than the poor impression she had made on some bloke she was never likely to see again!

From her bed she stared at her sleeping son, tears stinging her strained eyes in a blinding surge. She adored Timmie; she could not begin to imagine her life without him. But tomorrow authority, with all its unlimited power, was coming in the guise of that lady Rio Lombardi had smoothly mentioned. Why hadn't she had the strength to get up and walk away after her fall in that street? Once officialdom became involved, the die would be cast.

Rio Lombardi had sworn that no arrangements would

be made without her agreement. Did he really think that she was that stupid? She had had her baby out in the middle of the night. She had no home to go to and that doctor would confirm that she had been betraying signs of hypothermia. Those three facts were like three big extra nails being hammered into her coffin. The powers-that-be would decide that she was an unfit mother and would lose no time in removing Timmie from such inadequate care.

Just half an hour ago she had been telling herself that it was her duty to give Timmie up for adoption, but when it came to the crunch she could feel herself tearing apart inside at the prospect of never, ever again having the right to hold his sweet, trusting weight in her arms. Surely she could do better? Surely she had enough backbone to pull herself up out of the mess she was in and provide for her own child?

Couldn't she allow herself one more chance? Was that so selfish? Tears streaming down her guilty face, she studied Timmie in despair. He was all she had, all the family she was ever likely to have. She would go to a shelter for the homeless, one of those places from which advice came without the price of remorseless, grinding officialdom. If it killed her, she would find them somewhere to live. Only if she was faced with another night on the streets would she acknowledge defeat and accept that adoption was the only solution. That was the pact she made with herself, the promise she knew she had to make for her son's sake.

But she had to get out of the hospital before that lady came to call in a few hours' time, she told herself frantically. However, Timmie needed his sleep and she still felt too dizzy to walk, so she had to be sensible and stay in her bed as long as possible.

On his way to a business meeting at eight that morning, Rio found the memory of Holly Sansom's frightened face continually flashing up between him and the figures he was scrutinising.

In one of the snap decisions that invariably threw his employees off-balance, Rio swept up the phone to communicate with his chauffeur and told him to head for the hospital instead of the Lombardi Industries building. Impatience tightening his sculpted mouth as he checked his watch, he questioned his sense of responsibility. He had done all that he could reasonably do. However, he should have kept quiet about the social worker's visit. Forewarning Holly had been careless, and he had only made that mistake because he had gone without sleep for too long.

The limo drew to a halt in the busy car park of the foundation hospital. Waiting with a sigh for his chauffeur to walk round the bonnet in his usual dignified fashion, which he knew was simply a ploy to ensure that his security team alighted from their car behind in advance of himself, Rio caught a glimpse of a bright bronze head moving behind the line of cars parked about forty feet away. In a sudden movement, a vicious swear word impelled from his lips, Rio thrust the door of his limo open for himself and sprang out to stride in the same direction.

'Holly!'

Hearing that shout just when she had believed she was free and clear of having attracted any adverse notice almost gave Holly a heart attack. Her blood literally chilling in her veins with fright, she spun round, her arms automatically tightening round her child.

Rio Lombardi stepped up onto the pavement ahead of her. 'Where the blazes do you think you're going?'

He was the very last person she had expected to see, and for the first time she was facing him upright and he was an incredibly intimidating figure. She was five feet four but he had to be almost twelve inches taller, and he had shoulders like a rugby player that even his fancy dark business suit could not conceal. He also looked… *livid*, shimmering dark golden eyes flaming over her, telegraphing anger and strong censure.

'I…I'm g-going to find a shelter for the homeless—'

'Like bloody hell you are!' Rio interrupted, lean strong face set in steely lines as he closed the distance between them in a couple of strides. 'Where's his push-chair?'

'I c-couldn't find it—'

Holly was trembling, her own guilty conflict over her decision to give herself one more chance intensified by the disapproval Rio Lombardi was emanating in powerful waves. Just twenty-four hours, only twenty-four hours, that was all she had wanted.

'Give Timmie to me…' he demanded.

And, so shaken and ashamed was Holly as she stood there with tears filling her anguished eyes, she found herself instinctively obeying that authoritarian note of absolute command. As Rio Lombardi reached out she let him take her son from her. A split-second later she could not credit what she had done and she stared up at Rio Lombardi in dismay, her distraught face pale as parchment. 'Give him back to me!'

'Not until you agree to go back inside and wait to

see the social worker, who is going to *help* you,' Rio stressed, watching her begin to tremble and recognising her fear. Striving not to feel like a bully, he reminded himself that he was doing the best thing for both mother and child.

'I can't *do* that!' Holly suddenly sobbed.

As Rio removed his frustrated attention from her he caught a glimpse of Ezio's face. His security chief was positioned about twenty feet away, watching him in frank astonishment. Rio's high cheekbones fired with a slight rise of colour.

'You must be sensible about this…' Rio stated as the baby in his arms went all stiff and loosed an anxious little moan of fright at the sound of his mother's distress. Timmie was just about to blow. Indeed, any moment now, mass hysteria was going to break out and spread like a disease, Rio recognised with a very male sense of discomfiture. *Dio mio*, they were in a public place and he didn't know what had got into him. He could only recall the savage jolt of pure rage he had felt at the sight of Holly trying to sneak away from the safety of the hospital.

'*Please*…give him back!' Holly cried.

An older man unlocking his car just yards away had now halted the activity to openly stare, his expression already that of someone thinking that perhaps he ought to intervene. Rio threw his proud head back and murmured in a tone calculated to soothe, 'My car's just over there. We'll discuss this calmly in private.'

Holly was totally disconcerted when Rio just strode away from her. But she raced after him in a panic. As the chauffeur yanked open the door of the gleaming silver limousine Rio broke the habit of a lifetime and, instead of standing back politely to allow Holly first access, climbed in ahead of her, thereby forestalling any possibility of further debate in public.

Holly shot in after him like a mouse in stricken pursuit of a cat. The passenger door closed on her. Rio Lombardi had her son clasped under one arm while he spoke to someone in his own language on the car phone.

In a daze of confusion, Holly absorbed the startling sight of Timmie smiling up at Rio. Timmie, who never smiled at anyone but her! Her head ached even more. She felt clammy and sick and scared. 'Please give him back to me…'

'Look, I haven't got time for this right now. I have a very important meeting to get to,' Rio imparted, leaning forward to make some curious adjustment to the rear of the leather seat facing them. Before her bemused eyes, a child's travelling seat complete with safety restraint folded down out of the once flat surface.

'Mr. Lombardi—er—?'

'You can stay at my home for a few days until you feel stronger,' Rio cut in flatly. 'You're in no fit state to make decisions right now. It'll give you a breathing space.'

'Your…*home*?' Holly was so taken aback by that offer coming at her out of the blue that she could only stare at his bold bronzed profile with wide shaken eyes.

Rio settled Timmie into the baby seat. After tightening everything up, he snapped the harness into place with a definite air of satisfaction at his own efficiency.

'Your home?' Holly watched his manoeuvres in bewildered stillness, quite unable to react with any greater volubility. Her head was pounding fit to burst and her brain felt like mush, for she had had little sleep during what had remained of the night hours while she fretted and waited for an opportunity to steal out of the hospital without being noticed.

'Why not?' Suppressing the faint suspicion that once again he was reacting in an impulsive manner that was quite unlike him, Rio told himself that rescuing Holly would be his good deed for the year and he warmed to the concept at similar speed. He would soon get them sorted out. He might have given millions to humanitarian causes but when had he *ever* become personally involved in someone else's problems? But intervention was definitely required. Without a helping hand, there was an all too real possibility that Holly Sansom would end up selling her body for the price of her next meal. A pervert would spot her from a distance of a hundred yards, Rio reflected with distaste. She had victim written all over her. As for Timmie…well, Timmie was already measuring up to follow faithfully in his mother's footsteps.

'Why…not?' Holly echoed, pressing a weak hand to the bruising that still throbbed at the back of her skull. 'Because people don't do stuff like that for people they don't know.'

Rio settled brilliant, dark, deep-set eyes on her. 'Make your mind up.'

Holly tensed at that demand. He was offering them a lifeline. A roof, a bed, no worries about food or the future for a few days. He was an incredible guy. He was just so kind. She could not believe how kind he was being when he had been so furious with her only minutes earlier. 'OK.'

'I'll make the arrangements.' Rio swept up the phone and watched Ezio answer from the front seat. At one point during that conversation, Ezio twisted round to frown in amazement through the glass panel separating him from his employer. Rio ignored that pointed reaction.

That deep, dark, sexy drawl of his just seemed to shimmy down her spine, Holly thought absently. She *loved* his voice even though she hadn't a clue what he was saying. Catching herself up on that mortifying train of thought, Holly reddened fierily.

'As soon as I've been dropped off for my meeting, my security chief will take you to my town house. Any problems, speak to Ezio. He speaks English but most of my household staff don't,' Rio warned her.

Holly nodded uncertainly, momentarily attempting to picture the kind of world where a person had household staff, and then watching the gold in Rio's eyes reflect the light, her mouth running dry and her breath catching in her throat.

Rio sprang out of the limo outside Lombardi Industries.

Ezio cleared his throat. 'Miss Kent won't like another woman in the house, boss.'

Rio froze. 'The wedding's off, Ezio.'

Leaving the older man gazing after him in consternation, Rio strode on into the building, inclining his proud dark head in acknowledgement of the doorman's respectful greeting and concentrating his mind on the challenging business meeting ahead with considerable relief.

The limo nosed its way with all the arrogant assurance of its owner back into the flow of traffic. Holly breathed in slowly and deeply and then pinched the back of her hand. The stinging sensation of that small hurt convinced her that she was not dreaming. She was really and truly sitting in Rio Lombardi's fabulous limousine. For potentially the next forty-eight hours she could stop worrying. He had taken pity on her.

Inwardly, Holly squirmed, the self-esteem that had been battered to ground-level in recent months burning at the wretched awareness that she was just a charity case to a male like Rio Lombardi. Well, she had never let anyone do her favours for free. She would make herself useful round his house, repaying his generosity the only way she could. But at that moment the simple knowledge that she needed to worry neither about food nor shelter in the immediate future was like a giant weight rolling off her shoulders.

Just *how* had she contrived to sink so low that she was prepared to accept such charity? It had happened by degrees, she conceded. But undoubtedly her biggest and worst mistake had been getting involved with Jeff Danby...

Holly had grown up on a hill farm on Exmoor where her father was the tenant farmer. Her parents had married late in life and her mother had been forty when Holly was born. That her mother never conceived again had been a source of deep disappointment to her parents, for it had meant that there would be no son to help out when her father became too old to cope alone with the harsh winters and the lambing season and that eventually he would have to give up the tenancy.

She had had a happy childhood and she had enjoyed school. But possibly, as an only and much loved child, she had been a little spoilt, she conceded with pained hindsight. For, while her parents had urged her to aim at a college education, Holly had been more eager to find a job so that she could have her own money and spend more time with her friends who lived in the nearest town.

Working in a dead-end job that hadn't struck her as a dead-end job had been fine the first couple of years when all that had been in her head was buying the latest cheap fashions and finding a boyfriend. But, although boys had made her plenty of offers, they had all come with the price tag of casual sex attached. And, for all that she had liked to pretend to be as cool in her outlook as her peers, Holly had been raised in a home where that kind of behaviour was just not acceptable and had shrunk from doing anything likely to distress her parents.

And then Jeff had come along in her eighteenth year, Jeff, with his ancient sports car and cheeky grin and impressive aura of sophistication. He had been a pool attendant at the local leisure centre, much admired by all her friends and seven years older. So she had been thrilled when he had asked her out and infatuated by the end of the first week, but not so foolish as to jump into bed with him. In any case, if she was honest, the sex side of things had never appealed to her much, even with Jeff. She had liked the romantic stuff better, holding hands, just listening to him talk about his plans to become an instructor at some trendy fitness club in London and admiring the fact that he had a goal and ambition.

'He's too flash,' her mother had said when she'd finally met Jeff.

'He's a big-head,' her father had sighed. 'He's a lot older than you are too. You'd be better off with a boy your own age.'

Jeff had ditched her a couple of times and gone off with other girls. Each time he'd come back to her, and she had been so grateful she'd repressed her hurt and forgiven him. Then he had got the job he had always wanted in London and, struggling to conceal her breaking heart, she had gone out with him and his friends for a last-night celebration. The drinks had been lined up in front of her and Jeff had kept on urging her not to be a killjoy and drink up. He had talked about how she was 'his' girl and how he would send for her once he got a place of his own. Hearing him talk like that, including her in his lofty plans, she had almost cried with relief.

'I really do care about you, Holly,' he had said fondly. 'You're the girl I want to marry, so surely you can come home with me tonight.'

And she had, and she had gritted her teeth in the darkness, tears running down her face at the roughness, embarrassment and pain of the experience. She had wanted to please him, had so wanted to prove that she was not the silly little girl still tied to parental dictums he had often accused her of being but a real adult woman capable of loving her man and being loved.

True to his word, Jeff had phoned her while city life was still strange to him. She had written great, long, adoring screeds to him and had been four months pregnant before she'd even realised that she had conceived. During his final phone call, she had begged him to visit for a weekend. She had needed to see him face-to-face to share her news. But he had complained that it would cost too much and he had not phoned again. Weeks afterwards, when she had been climbing the walls with panic over his silence and trying to conceal her changing shape from her parents, one of her many letters had been returned to her with 'Not known at this address' written across it. She had not seen Jeff again until she'd finally tracked him down in London many months later.

Emerging from those unwelcome memories, Holly felt cool air on her face and only then realised that the passenger door was open. The chauffeur was waiting for her to vacate the limo.

The most enormous house lay before her. It had a gravel turning circle in front and tall shaped evergreen trees in fancy metal troughs.

'Miss Sansom…I'm Ezio Farretti.'

Holly focused shyly on the heavily built older man with his steady dark eyes. 'Nice to meet you.'

Ezio engaged the employee positioned at the front door in a flood of foreign speech, and motioned Holly into the house. Feeling like a third wheel, Holly followed him inside and skimmed an intimidated glance round the huge hall, the fantastic staircase and the big pictures adorning the walls.

'Come this way, Miss Sansom,' Ezio urged.

'What's that language you speak?' she asked to fill the silence.

'Italian.'

He showed her into what appeared to be a drawing room. Well, she adjusted, what she would call a drawing room, because the opulent sofas and marble fireplace were way too grand to belong in a humble sitting room. A fire glowed in the iron grate. Holly had not seen a real fire since leaving home, and without warning her eyes smarted as she pictured the cosy farmhouse kitchen where her parents sat by the fire on cold nights.

Ezio extended a notepad and pen. 'Will you make a list of supplies for you and your son?'

'Supplies?'

'Anything you require.'

She reddened to the roots of her hair. 'I don't have any money.'

'That's not a problem.'

The waiting silence that followed embarrassed her into making up a list. Diapers, a feeding cup and baby juice were really all she *had* to have. She was down on her luck but she was not a freeloader, and she was sure to get the chance to wash their clothes.

'You should put down a few more things.' Ezio's voice was gruff.

Holly shook her head. Having to put down even the necessities had hurt. Rio Lombardi was putting them up and he would be feeding them as well. The very last thing she wanted to do was *cost* him money into the bargain.

Ezio led her up the imposing staircase. The magnificent landing was adorned with gilded furniture that looked as if it belonged in a palace. But then, Rio Lombardi's home *was* just like a palace, Holly conceded in a daze. She was shown into a fabulous guest room, complete with an adjoining bathroom, and then into the smaller room next door which contained a cot. The cot, which contained several very new-looking toys, surprised her. Belatedly it occurred to her that perhaps Rio Lombardi was or had been married and had children. Tensing, tummy suddenly feeling hollow, she asked Ezio right out.

'The boss is…single,' the older man stated after a slight hesitation. 'But he often has relatives with kiddies to stay. The Lombardis are a big family and very close.'

As Ezio departed Holly glimpsed her reflection in

a mirror and a mortified gasp left her lips. The backside of her jeans was filthy, probably from the road the night before. Fetching a couple of the toys from the cot, she took Timmie into the bathroom, set him down with them on a bathtowel and then stripped down to her skin. Everything she wore went into the bath to steep in hot water. She stepped into the separate shower cubicle but could only run the water in bursts because she couldn't close the door properly while she watched over Timmie. Her son could not yet crawl but he could cover a surprising amount of distance by rolling.

It was such bliss, such *utter* bliss to feel truly scrubbed clean again. Making use of the luxury toiletries in the corner shower compartment, she shampooed her hair and then conditioned it for the first time in many months. Having pounded her clothes back to cleanliness with soap, she then realised in dismay that there were no radiators in which to dry them. At that point, a knock sounded on the bedroom door.

Wrapped in a towel, she peered round the edge of the door. It was Ezio Farretti and he had a large cotton sack in his arms.

'Where are the radiators?' she queried.

'There aren't any. The heating is under the floor.'

'Oh…'

'This bag is full of clothes left behind by other guests,' Ezio continued. 'There might be something which will fit you or Timmie.'

'I can't wear someone else's things…they'd be furious—'

'These are very rich people. They don't miss what they overlook; they just buy *more*,' the older man told her gently. 'I'll leave the bag outside the door.'

There was a horrid thickness in her throat. 'Thanks, Ezio.'

'No problem.' He cleared his throat. 'But, if you don't mind a spot of advice, give the boss a wide berth. Off the record, he's just not himself right now and you don't want to get your feelings hurt.'

Not just himself? Her feelings hurt? What on earth was that supposed to mean? Holly's face burned up scarlet. Oh, my goodness, had Ezio noticed her blushing and getting on like a teenager with a bad crush around Rio Lombardi? Was he warning her off? What else could he possibly be doing?

CHAPTER THREE

'HOLLY'S DOING...*what*?' Rio ground out with rampant incredulity.

'Almost finished cleaning the kitchen floor, boss,' Ezio repeated with reluctance. 'She's been dusting and scrubbing and polishing all day and, short of physically restraining her, there was nothing I could do about it. She's got a lot of grit but she's on the brink of a collapse—'

'The kitchen floor...' Rio seethed, striding through the door that led down to the basement where all the household utilities were situated. His mood was not improved when he went through the wrong door on the lower floor and found himself in some sort of boiler room because it had been a very long time since he had visited the kitchen quarters.

When he finally located his own kitchen, the first sight that met his eyes was Timmie strapped into a high chair, slumped over fast asleep, curly dark head down on the tray, a feeding cup dangling from one tiny hand. He looked rather like a miniature drunken sailor, his little legs and feet clad in white...*tights*? And what was that frilly thing round his almost non-existent neck? *Dio mio*, Timmie was wearing a little girl's woollen dress with a lace collar! Rio was truly appalled by that discovery.

He strode round the protruding unit to gaze down the length of a kitchen that stretched more than forty feet in depth. He settled his outraged gaze on the female behind weaving from side to side as Holly knelt on the floor with her bucket and scrubbed like a Victorian housemaid. He stilled, attention entrapped by the wholly feminine fullness of that derrière, every line defined by the fine fabric shaping its delicious curves.

Without warning, an attack of such powerful lust assailed Rio that his every muscle clenched in shaken resistance. Four weeks without sex and he was turning into an animal, ready to jump anything female, he decided in even darker fury. His lean hands clenched into fists as he willed the throb of his aching sex to dwindle to manageable proportions.

'Get the hell up off that floor!' Rio launched with wrathful bite.

Dredged from her concentrated efforts to deny her exhaustion until she had completed her work, Holly swivelled round on her knees in fright, collided with the bucket and tipped it noisily over. Her soft mouth opening in dismay, she gasped strickenly, '*Now* look what you've made me do!'

'How *dare* you come here and start cleaning my floors?' Rio demanded with savage censure.

Very slowly, Holly picked herself up, the over-large green dress with its wide neckline lurching off one bare white shoulder. But that shade was incredible against that fair skin of hers, Rio noted before he registered that she was swaying and literally grey with pallor.

Holly focused on him, butterflies breaking loose in

her tummy. Snatching in a stark breath, she met his stunning golden eyes and felt the burn of reaction deep down in her pelvis, an enervating sensation that made her weld her slender thighs together in fierce embarrassment. 'I'm sorry, I thought—'

Rio strode through the grimy flood that had spilled from the bucket and lifted her off her feet before she fainted in front of him. 'How could you be so foolish? Do you think I invited you here to slave for me?'

'I only wanted to make myself useful…' Holly drank in the scent of him that clung to the jacket beneath her cheekbone, her nostrils flaring with helpless eagerness on that fresh familiarity.

Holding her that close was doing nothing for Rio's rampant arousal. He was furious with himself, furious with her. Lack of control was not a sensation he was accustomed to suffering around a woman. But he was hugely tempted to tell her that if she wanted to make herself useful he had a whole catalog of undomestic distractions to offer, not one of which, he was ashamed to admit, would have been thwarted by a wet floor, a child within hearing distance or even a fire alarm. He had seen her susceptibility in her eyes, in the way she held her slender, shapely body and in the mood he was in, a don't-give-a-damn-about-anything mood of intense bitterness, that awareness inflamed his libido even more.

Ezio was positioned by Timmie's sleeping form when Rio strode for the kitchen exit. 'Bring Timmie upstairs and get him out of that stupid dress,' he instructed the older man.

'I only put it on him to keep him warm until his own clothes dried. *He* doesn't know it's a dress,' Holly protested. 'It was all that was available—'

'You could be damaging his sexual identity for life!' Rio condemned fiercely.

'Do you think so?' she questioned, aghast, as Rio carried her into a lift that she had not known existed until that moment.

He set her down and hit the buttons, choosing not to wait for Ezio. The door buzzed shut. She slumped back against the cool wall. 'The floor's in a *real* mess now,' she lamented. 'I can't leave it like that.'

'Shut up.' Rio closed his eyes and breathed in deep and slow. He had had one hell of a day, barring calls from Christabel, putting his social secretary in charge of cancelling the elaborate wedding arrangements, watching the slow ripple of awareness pass round his personal staff one by one, recognising the amazed speculation in the eyes of those too stupid to hide their curiosity. Rio Lombardi and Christabel Kent, the *golden* couple, had broken up. All his life he had been a private individual, who hated others to breach his reserve. Now he was a mass of raw emotion and seething bitterness and, to crown his intense sense of raging humiliation at being *put* in such a position, all he could think about was the wild, savage oblivion of sex!

Holly shut up while the silence charged up. Rio opened eyes as bright as golden sunlight and dazzled her. The atmosphere was fraught, full of vibrations that skimmed along her nerve-endings, filling her with the strangest excitement in spite of her weary bewilderment. He was smouldering like a powder keg, she registered. She had no idea *why* but she had never been so aware of the potent magnetism of powerful masculinity.

In fact, she finally admitted, she was so hopelessly attracted to Rio Lombardi she could barely think straight, and that was a major shock to her system and her knowledge of herself. Jeff had never made her tremble just by looking at her. Jeff had never made her crave his touch. So, doubtless her ex-boyfriend had had good reason to call her a 'lousy lay'. That humiliating recollection from the past steadied her and cooled her as nothing else could have done and made her drop her eyes from Rio Lombardi's lean, strong face in shame.

'I'm sorry I spoke to you like that,' Rio murmured curtly as he stood back for her to precede him out of the lift.

She nodded with a bowed head.

'Go to bed and rest,' Rio advised harshly, stopping dead on the threshold of her bedroom but going not one step further. 'I'll have a supper tray sent up.'

'I'm not hungry,' Holly whispered shakily, no longer able to look at him. She listened to him walk away, feeling the loss of his vibrant energy and despising herself for that sensitised awareness.

A bloke like Rio Lombardi would never look twice at her, which was just as well, she conceded dully. She was useless in bed. *Frigid as a corpse.* She stilled a shiver of revulsion at that unforgettable description of her less than adequate performance: Jeff had spelt out exactly why he had lost interest in her. She might not have enjoyed that single session of physical intimacy that had none-the-less resulted in Timmie's conception, but Jeff had made it clear that he had enjoyed it even less. How could she have actually believed his drunken assertion that she was the girl he wanted to marry? That had just been a standard line to get her between the sheets.

'Why the hell didn't you get an abortion, you stupid cow?' Jeff had railed at her before he'd hit her smack in the face with his fist. He'd knocked her right off her feet in his rage almost five months back and had terrified her with his violence. 'If you think I'm forking out my hard-earned cash to keep you and your little bastard, you'd better think again! If you try to hang him round my neck, I'll make you sorry you were ever born...'

She was sorriest of all that she had been so unforgivably stupid as not to see through Jeff's superficial charm to the user and abuser of women that he was. He had slept with those girls he'd dumped her for twice over. He had lied about that, and in her heart of hearts she had always suspected that truth but had blindly refused to face the fact that a man who treated her that way could have no caring feelings for her. Jeff was the kind of creep whose ego could not bear female rejection. The instant he had taken her virginity, he had begun losing interest.

So she had got her punishment for being a silly, credulous doormat, dreaming of white dresses and the 'Bridal March'. What she could not stand was that her parents, and now Timmie, seemed to be sharing that ongoing punishment with her. For of course her parents would be missing her, but she could never go home as long as she had her son and no ring on her finger. Farming communities were not liberal. An unwed daughter and fatherless grandchild would shame and mortify her parents.

As Holly slumped down on the bed, slight shoulders sagging, Ezio appeared in the doorway, clutching Timmie. 'I got his clothes out of the drier but I'm afraid you'll have to change him.'

'Thanks...' she said chokily, getting up to reclaim her son.

Ezio hovered on the threshold. 'The boss is on a pretty short fuse at present. I did try to warn you.'

She was just no good at listening. Her stubborn pride had offended Rio Lombardi. She had slighted the one person who had tried to be kind to her in countless months of indifference. A rich, good-looking guy of Rio's calibre could not have any ulterior motive in helping her and she was ashamed of the reality that she wished that he *had*, ashamed that she reacted as she did around him.

The phone ringing by the bed woke her the next morning.

It was Rio. 'I'm taking you shopping and I don't want to hear any arguments. The sight of you running round dressed like a bag lady embarrasses me.'

Holly was poleaxed. *'But—'*

'I've hired a nanny to take care of Timmie. You got to sleep in because she's already here. He's now playing in the garden. As soon as you've had breakfast, I want you downstairs.'

Click went the phone as Rio cut the connection. Even as Holly replaced the receiver in sleepy, shell-shocked bewilderment, a manservant was knocking on the door and entering with the promised breakfast. A nanny had been hired just to take care of her Timmie? For goodness' sake, had Rio Lombardi gone mad? She could not possibly allow him to buy her clothes! It was out of the question.

However, hunger made her succumb first to the tempting dishes on the beautifully arranged bed tray. She explored the bruising at the base of her skull. The spot was still tender but she felt fine after a really good night of sleep. As soon as she had eaten she had a quick shower. Dressing in her clean jeans and shirt, she pulled on the man's sweater that she had found at the very foot of the pretty-much useless bag of clothing which Ezio had brought to her.

Her bronze ringlets fanning wildly round her narrow shoulders after a too vigorous and impatient brushing, she hurried down the stairs. Rio was pacing the hall floor and her first glimpse of him just took her breath away. His superb tailored suit in palest grey set off his exotic darkness and bronzed skin to perfection. His black hair gleamed in the light coming through the windows and was so temptingly touchable to her dilated gaze that her fingertips actually tingled.

'I can't let you take me shopping,' she told him unevenly.

A curious expression tensed Rio's darkly handsome features and his strong jawline hardened, his gorgeous dark golden eyes almost bleak. 'I need a distraction today. You're *it*. You'll be doing me a favour.'

So disconcerted was Holly by the roughened sincerity patent in that unexpected response that she was halfway into the limo before she recalled that she had not yet seen her son. 'Just two minutes, Rio.' She said his name for the first time and then reddened with self-consciousness.

The nanny was a really nice young woman. She looked like the sort of nanny that might be hired by royalty and Timmie, propped up in an incredibly impractical but imposing coachbuilt pram, might even have aspired to being a little prince, had it not been for his shabby clothing.

'Satisfied, *cara*?' Rio asked as Holly got into the limo. 'Timmie seems happy enough—'

'You should ditch the Timmie and call him Timothy,' Rio informed her just as she glimpsed Ezio's unusually grim expression before the older man turned away to swing into the front passenger seat.

'Why?'

'He's timid. Give him a name he can grow into, not one that makes him sound like a pet pooch.'

Holly flushed but she said nothing. She was over-whelmed by the sensation that she was being carried away by a very forceful personality on a trip she did not understand. 'Is…is there something wrong today? I mean,' she muttered awkwardly, 'that you feel you need a distraction?'

His lean, powerful face tautened, brilliant eyes veiling. He had the most extraordinary long, inky dark lashes, Holly noted, studying his classic profile with helpless fascination.

'Everything's right. Everything is as it ought to be,' Rio stated in a cold tone that contrived to chill her to the marrow.

The uneasy silence dragged.

Holly made a frantic effort to redress the apparent damage she had caused. 'So you're not working today?'

'No.'

'And you taking me out shopping is just a whim… the sort of thing rich people do when they're bored?'

The taut line of his sensual mouth eased and he flashed her a glittering glance that sent her heart racing like an express train. 'You could put it that way. Or maybe I want to spoil you because you don't *ask* for anything and I'm not used to that with a woman.'

'I'm not used to blokes buying me stuff,' Holly shared in a sudden rush of confidence. 'Jeff used to borrow money off me all the time. He was always running out. I've always paid my own way…well, until recently.'

'Jeff…Timothy's absent father? He sounds a treat,' Rio breathed with perceptible scorn. 'Where is he?'

Holly repressed a shiver and studied her tightly linked hands. 'Don't know…don't want to know,' she admitted shakily. 'He thumped me last time I saw him—'

'I beg your pardon?' Rio curved lean, strong fingers round her slight shoulder to turn her back to face him.

'Me and my big mouth,' Holly muttered, for she had never intended to tell anyone that.

Rio raked her strained face with flaring golden eyes. 'He *hit* you?'

'It was my own fault—'

'How *could* it have been?' Rio demanded.

'I came up to London with Timmie to find Jeff. It took time because he had changed jobs and moved on from his last address,' Holly explained heavily. 'I was stupid. After all, he *always* knew how to get in touch with me, but I couldn't accept that what we'd had had fizzled out—'

'You had a child. Naturally you didn't want to accept it. Did he *know* you were pregnant when he abandoned you?'

'Abandoned', she reflected, made what Jeff had done sound dramatically worse than it had been. All he had actually done was stop phoning, and had she had the wit to leave it at that she might never have sunk as low. Following Jeff up to London and searching for him had been her second biggest mistake, she conceded. With a child in tow she had found it impossible to make ends meet in so expensive a city, but she had had nowhere else to go and neither friends nor family to fall back on for support.

'No. I was a bit slow on the uptake when it came to realising that I was pregnant myself,' she confided in some discomfiture on that subject.

'So what happened when you traced him?'

'He was living in Notting Hill in a very smart flat,' she faltered, her mind taking her back to that ghastly day of awakening to the discovery that the father of her child was a creep of the lowest order and, worst of all, a *weak* one. 'I had Timmie with me because I had nowhere else to leave him. Jeff opened the door…'

'And?' Rio prompted impatiently.

'He said he had a friend visiting and he sort of yanked me into the kitchen,' Holly whispered shakily. 'I told him that he was a father and he just went berserk. Then his girlfriend came in…that was worse than being hit because she felt sorry for me.'

Rio expelled his breath in a slow, measured hiss.

'It was her flat and she threw him out to cool off. She was dead sophisticated, much older than me and not at all embarrassed by the situation,' Holly gulped. 'She even made me a cup of tea while she told me that chasing after Jeff with a baby was really dumb. She said Jeff had lost his head because I had cornered him when she was home and he was desperate to get rid of me without her finding out that my baby was his.'

'Charming.'

'She was right.' Holly swallowed hard and raised her sleeve, intending to wipe her eyes. 'I was just too scared to face up to the fact that I was on my own, so I clung to this stupid dream that it would all work out once he saw…Timothy,' she pronounced with precision.

Releasing a groan, Rio Lombardi tilted up her chin to dry her damp eyes with a fine lawn handkerchief. 'Jeff was no loss. You're lucky that you and your son escaped a man so quick to use his fists in a crisis.'

Her drowning blue eyes gazed up into glittering gold and Jeff went out of her mind so fast he might never have existed. She tried and failed to swallow. Rio was so close that breathing was no longer an option. Lashes lowered, she focused on that wide, sensual mouth of his and the tip of her tongue snaked out to moisten her dry lower lip. Never in all her life had she been so desperate, so shamelessly eager to feel a man's mouth on hers. The craving was almost unbearably strong.

His fabulous bone-structure taut, proud cheekbones prominent beneath smooth bronzed skin, Rio murmured with a fracturing edge to his thickened drawl, 'It's not my fists you have to fear. I'm much more inventive but probably more dangerous.'

Please, please, kiss me, I don't care, was running through her mind as he set her back from him and turned to answer his cell phone. She had not even heard it buzzing and she sank back into her corner again like a boneless doll, registering that she had just glanced into potent contact with a male far more sexually charged than Jeff had ever been. It had been there in the atmosphere between them, an instant, surging awareness that shook her to her very depths.

Rio took her to an exclusive salon to get her hair done first.

'Cut it *short*?' Rio repeated on a rising note of disbelief when the retro-clad stylist made that laconic suggestion after poking through Holly's hair much as though it was beyond all human intervention. Closing one hand over hers, Rio dragged her back out of the leather chair and headed for the exit.

'What are you doing?' Holly gasped in embarrassment, horribly aware of every head in the place turning in their direction.

'I'm not leaving you at the mercy of a scissor-happy lunatic, *cara*—'

'*Rio!*' A female voice intervened.

Rio halted, his lean, strong features tensing.

A stunning brunette with cat-like eyes and vampish burgundy lips surged up to them, but, for all her elegant cool, she was exuding a definable air of panic. 'That stupid lump on the desk didn't recognise you, did she? You walking out of my salon with a big frown is very bad for business, Rio.'

'Your top stylist wants to chop off her crowning glory!' Rio delivered.

Cheeks burning, Holly stood there while the brunette's shrewd gaze flicked from Holly's cascading ringlets back to Rio. 'Obviously a guy with no imagination. I'll do it. She just needs some shaping round her face. One of your tribe of little cousins over from Italy?' she asked, as if Holly were mute.

'She speaks hardly any English,' Holly heard Rio state and, at that startling announcement, she shot him a wide-eyed glance of incredulity, barely able to credit her hearing.

'But I presume she has a name. I'm Sly.' The brunette extended a manicured hand to Holly. 'And *you're*—'

'Fiammetta,' Rio slotted in with a perfectly straight face. 'She's unbelievably shy. I'd like her made up as well—'

'What age is she?' Sly enquired of him with a cloying

smile, both of them now talking over the top of Holly's head as if she were a very small child.

'Old enough to look like a woman,' Rio quipped huskily.

'Then I presume you're planning to do something about the clothes she's wearing as well,' the salon owner remarked with a speaking little giggle.

Fifteen minutes later, Holly was seated in front of a mirror while Sly cut her hair with exaggerated care. 'What Rio wants, Rio always gets…'

Since Holly had not one Italian word at her disposal and did not trust herself to emulate an accent, she compressed her lips and concealed her discomfiture. When she got her hands on Rio in private, she was going to scream at him for doing this to her. Why, though? Why deprive her of the ability to talk?

'I do wish I spoke Italian,' Sly sighed. 'I bet you have the inside track on the whole story, and I would *give* my right arm to hear every dirty detail on the fall of Christabel. The rumours are just *so* intriguing.'

Who was Christabel? Some ex-girlfriend of Rio's? Or possibly just a not very popular mutual acquaintance, Holly allowed, someone who had suffered some kind of disappointment. Gritting her teeth, she sat through the styling session and then through the incredibly tickly and painstaking experience of having cosmetics professionally applied. She wasn't able to see herself until the very last moment and then she simply stared in disbelief at her own transformed appearance.

'I'm the best in my field even though I say it myself,' Sly drawled with amusement.

Smoky shadow had been smoothed round Holly's eyes, giving them dramatic depth and enhancing their colour. She had cheekbones now like a model in a magazine and a mouth as ripe and pink and lush as a peach.

Rio was pacing the waiting area, talking in staccato Italian on his cell phone, the cynosure of interest for every female in the vicinity. He lowered his phone, tawny eyes welding to her with gleaming intensity, a faint and wicked smile curling at the corners of his beautiful mouth. '*Bella*, Fiammetta...' he drawled with lazy amusement.

And in that same moment, Holly knew beyond all doubt that she had fallen passionately in love. Riveted to the spot by his unashamed appreciation, she could feel herself glowing inside like a megawatt light bulb suddenly connected to an electric current. *He* was the source of the current. He was redefining her in her own eyes, making her feel good about herself for the first time in almost two years.

Resting a casual hand on her spine, he urged her back out to the limo.

'Why did you tell Sly that crazy story about me being Italian?' Holly prompted, trying to muster her former fury but finding it strangely absent.

'She's the biggest gossip in town and not nicknamed "Sly" for nothing. She could have bared your soul for you in the first five minutes,' Rio mocked.

'I couldn't open my mouth! I don't know a single word of Italian!'

'I know. Class act, aren't I?' Rio teased. 'It was as good as gagging the two of you. Sly was seething with frustration.'

Holly mock-punched him in the ribs and then jerked her hand back, afraid that she had been too familiar. But he gave her a slanting grin of answering amusement that turned her heart inside-out. Nobody was ever going to accuse Rio Lombardi of being a charisma-free zone, Holly thought dizzily in receipt of that smile while she struggled to get mental feet back safely on the ground again. Only the ground had vanished. Every time he looked at her she felt as if she was flying.

The next stop on the shopping trip was a high-fashion outlet of such size and style that the deeper they got into it the more Holly tried to hide behind him, cringing at her own shabbiness.

'Who would you like to be here? Daughter of an eccentric billionaire?' Rio murmured, inclining his dark head down to hers, making her tremble at his proximity. 'Minor European royalty, travelling incognito?'

'I think I'll just be me, but you get to do all the talking,' Holly said apprehensively as a smiling, terrifyingly svelte female began to move in their direction.

'All these people care about is the colour of my money,' Rio breathed, his dark drawl hard-edged with what sounded remarkably like bitterness. 'And the richer you are, the more they grovel.'

'I wouldn't know a lot about that but I hope you're not going to be rude,' Holly whispered back worriedly.

Unexpectedly, he laughed.

He sent her off alone to the lingerie department. Ignoring the bountiful advice of a saleswoman keen to flog her a hundred of every item, not to mention undergarments that Holly had not until then known even existed, Holly settled for several sets of bras and briefs. No, she did not need nightwear. There had been a nightie in Ezio's sack that had done her fine the night before and she was no spendthrift. What she was doing was *wrong*, her conscience warned her. Letting Rio

Lombardi spend his money on her could not be right. But it was making him smile, it was making him tease her. He could buy her a series of numbered fertiliser sacks if he liked.

'Now I get in on the act,' Rio announced when she was led back to him to find him seated on a tall stool at a mini-bar in a spacious room that contained a small stage and catwalk. 'Champagne?'

With difficulty, she made it up onto the stool beside him and accepted a moisture-beaded glass. 'What happens in here?'

'The models parade the product. We pick what we like. Then you try it on.'

'You've done this before.' The champagne bubbles tickled her nose but she didn't laugh. She did not like the idea that he had sat in that exact same spot with other women but he knew the form too well for her to doubt it.

'But never before without being asked or set up or cajoled,' Rio confided darkly.

'If you felt like that, you should just have said no,' Holly muttered uncomfortably, quite at a loss on how to comment on the behaviour of women capable of being that bold about their greed. 'I mean…this wasn't my idea and it doesn't seem to be amusing you any more, so let's just leave it here…*please*—'

Lean fingers tugged at a ringlet of her bronze hair, curving her heart-shaped face round to his. 'But I don't want to leave it. I want to see you look beautiful…'

Her breath feathered in her throat, her clear blue eyes betraying her confusion. 'I can't be what I'm not—'

'You can be whatever you want to be, *cara*.'

She gazed into lustrous eyes shaded with burning gold and her heart was racing. The sense of caution

taught by the hard lessons of recent experience strove
to keep her grounded, though. What he was doing for
her was like a fairy tale but she knew fairy tales didn't
happen in real life: there was always a catch. As she
parted her lips to snatch in much needed oxygen to
sustain her, Rio bent his head lower and let his tongue
delve in a subtle flicker into the moist interior of her
mouth. It lasted only a second, but in that second she
was electrified by the instantaneous, stormy response
of her own body, the surge of enervating heat that inflamed her every sense. Indeed, so great was the erotic
hit of that sudden sexual foray she jerked, and if he
hadn't shot a steadying arm round her she would have
fallen off the stool.

'Relax,' Rio urged with husky clarity.

He lounged back from her again in perfect balance,
the easy, indolent grace of his lean, muscular length
in striking contrast to her trembling state of near-
devastation.

Holly was in shock, mental shock, sensual, bodily
shock. Maybe that had been a trifling bit of flirtation
on his terms, but her quivering body was on fire with
sensations it had never known before and she wanted
to emulate his cool but found it impossible. What did
he want from her? Surely not the obvious? Was he out
trawling for a cut-price mistress or something? What
did they have in common? Yes, *what* did they have in
common? Well, they were both human.

'Sorry…I couldn't resist it,' Rio admitted in his
smooth accented drawl.

'I bet you can resist me just fine,' Holly heard herself snap in her unease at not knowing what was likely
to happen next. 'Don't play games with me!'

'Then stop giving me the green light,' Rio traded quick as a flash, plunging her into such mortified discomfiture that she went weak with relief when an older woman took up position at a speaker's stand. The curtains glided back and the first model strolled out, looking impossibly haughty and superior until she espied Rio and flashed up a seductive smile instead.

From that first moment Holly was entranced. She had never been to a fashion show before and the knowledge that the display was being put on for an audience of two just blew her mind. The descriptions of the various outfits were foreign to her, but every item struck her as the ultimate in colour and design. She was totally undiscriminating, for she could not imagine actually wearing such elaborate garments. She was learning what women who had pots of money and little to do but look good wore and it was an education.

'You enjoyed that...' Rio was watching her intently as the curtains finally glided shut.

'Yes...thanks,' she sighed, her slow smile breaking out like sudden sunlight.

'So now you go and try on all the selections I made.'

'But why? I'm never going to wear stuff like that in *my* life!' Holly protested in honest bemusement. 'I'm much more downmarket than that and quite happy to be. Where on earth would I wear suits and long dresses?'

Disregarding that argument, Rio lifted her down from the stool and sent her in the direction of the saleswoman awaiting her. She was taken into a room where she became the centre of a throng of eager helpers. A whole selection of shoes and handbags were already standing by. She was whisked into outfit after outfit and marched out onto the catwalk.

At first she was self-conscious and she stood there like a plum with Rio telling her to move about, but then someone put on background music with a dance beat and Holly got into the spirit of the occasion. She began to pose, eyes wide in a pretence of haughtiness, shoulders thrown back in what she hoped was a model-like manner. Every time he laughed she clowned a little more, answering amusement sparkling in her eyes, but her greatest pleasure derived from his.

'Put on the green dress,' Rio told her when her own personal show was at an end.

He could buy her *one* outfit. That was OK, Holly thought in considerable relief. He really wasn't a very practical bloke. A couple of skirts and tops and new trousers from a chain store would have been much more sensible, and heaven only knew what even just one designer 'ensemble', as the saleswomen called them, cost in such a fancy place!

The dress bared her shoulders and rejoiced in a fabulous boned velvet bodice and a flirty skirt that came to her knees. She absolutely loved it. In the mirror, she saw a fashionable stranger, a young woman who just might have been a high-society party girl without a care in the world. It was just an illusion, she *knew* that, but it had been so much fun and she would never, ever forget the experience. She walked out to rejoin him, conscious of the unfamiliar height of the heels on her shoes, and with her entire attention pinned as though magnetised to his darkly handsome face.

'You look gorgeous, *cara*.' Rio lifted something furry from a nearby chair and draped it round her shoulders. 'And now you look like a queen.'

There were mirrors everywhere. Now she studied

their twinned reflection, the impossibly smooth and rich pale blonde fake-fur falling to mid-calf, the raised collar providing a glamorous contrast to the vivid fall of her hair. His proud head above her own, his tall, dark, powerful figure backing her slighter build. 'Do you flog dreams for a living?' she asked unsteadily, shaken by that view of them together, committing it to memory, knowing that dreams didn't last. 'You ought to.'

'The day's not over yet.'

But it was already evening. She had not realised how late it had got until they were ushered from the building and she saw the fading light. 'Does that place always stay open to this time?'

'They stayed open just for us,' Rio informed her lazily. 'We'll dine now.'

Ezio Farretti straightened from his lounging position against the bonnet of the limo. He stared at Holly and his whole face tightened and he turned away.

'Why did Ezio look at me like that?' she whispered in dismay.

'Ezio shouldn't be looking at you in any particular way,' Rio pronounced, a cool, hard edge to his dark, deep voice that made her tense.

He took her to a restaurant which appeared to be the very last word in exclusivity. The head waiter surged to greet Rio. He took the attention as his due and it was obvious that he was a regular customer. As Rio strolled between the tables the low buzz of conversation died and a kind of unearthly hush fell. Every head in the room seemed to be swivelling in their direction. Several people addressed Rio, but, with only a word of acknowledgement or a cool inclination of his dark head Rio kept on moving.

Holly dropped down into the seat spun out for her occupation by an attentive waiter. 'Why do I get the feeling that everyone's staring at us?'

Rio lifted one broad shoulder in a slight fluid shrug that was the very essence of supreme cool. 'They're staring at you—'

'Me?' Holly exclaimed in lively astonishment.

'Speculating on your identity. You *do* look incredible in that dress.'

Locked to the brilliance of his tawny appraisal, she felt her heart race like crazy behind her ribs and she smiled. She didn't believe that anybody had the slightest interest in her but she liked the compliment. However, she went on to study her enormous menu in growing dismay. At first glance the menu seemed to be in English, but what was a sorbet? A croustade? A coulis?

When the waiter reappeared, perspiration beaded Holly's short upper lip, because she was still looking frantically for a dish she could recognise.

'I'd recommend the sorbet,' Rio murmured.

'OK, yes…I'd like that,' Holly hastened to confirm with relief.

Rio was being a very entertaining companion when something that resembled a pudding in a tall glass was set in front of her. She tried not to seem surprised and just ignored it, because she couldn't work out which of the many items of cutlery she was supposed to use to eat it and Rio had confounded her by ordering soup. She would have loved soup but she hadn't seen it anywhere on the menu.

'I'm not really that hungry,' she said as the sorbet was borne off, but in truth her stomach was meeting her backbone and she felt on the brink of starvation.

'I love salad,' she dared when it came to the next course, and then inwardly cringed when it seemed that that was actually a special order and there was such a carry-on about what *kind* of salad she wanted. Just shove some lettuce on a plate, she wanted to scream.

She knew she used the wrong knife and fork for the salad because as she picked them up the waiter was trying to remove them, but she braved it out as if she hadn't noticed that. At least she got to eat and, although dining out with Rio was an enervating challenge, he did not appear to notice her silent agonies of indecision.

She triumphed, or thought she did, when it came to the dessert course. *'Chocolat' had* to be chocolate. But the menu won all over again when her selection arrived. A sparkly cobweb thing covered a shell containing a mixture which she couldn't get at and a lot of leaves and tiny red berries were scattered round the edges. The latter tasted poisonously bad and put her right off the rest of it.

'You should be eating more,' Rio scolded, ignoring the greenery on his own plate and heading straight for his mouthwatering meringue concoction with a fork. A *fork*?

Suddenly, Holly was very grateful that she had pushed her own plate away. Hunger was better than public embarrassment, and as soon as everyone had gone to bed she would raid his kitchen fridge.

At the door, Rio draped the gorgeous coat round her shoulders. That personal attention made her feel ten feet tall. At the same hour just two nights back she had been walking the city streets, cold and scared, and already that seemed a lifetime ago, she conceded, sobered by that reflection. Yet the world she was now inhabiting felt far less real to her than the one she had so recently left behind. But then, it was Rio's world, not hers.

That fleeting kiss that had set her on fire earlier had only been a tease, Holly told herself. He was a very sexy guy and he had been flirting with her, that was all. Settling back into the limo, she thought about her son. Timmie, who was not high-class enough to aim at being Timothy, was *her* real world, along with bedsits, creepy landlords and dead-end, boring jobs, she reminded herself doggedly.

But still she found herself watching Rio, storing up images for the future. It wasn't just his sleek, dark goodlooks, his innate elegance and grace; he had an incredible aura of self-assurance that made her feel safe. It was a challenge to credit that anything could go wrong while he was around. Was it possible to fall in love so fast? Well, whether it was or not, she would *have* to get over her silly notions. Cocooned in her glorious fakefur, she took advantage of the shifting play of light and shadow as the limo travelled through the quiet streets to study him from all angles in search of a physical flaw. But he defeated her. He remained drop-dead gorgeous and no mistake.

'You don't need to restrict yourself to just looking. You can touch as well, *cara*,' Rio murmured in indolent invitation.

In sharp bewilderment, Holly froze. Agonised hot colour flooded her face. He might as well have stripped her naked and turned her out in front of an amused audience. Beneath the appraisal of those glittering golden eyes that saw far too much for her comfort she felt like a butterfly caught on a pin. He *knew* how he could make her feel but she had never made a physical advance to a man and she was not about to break that habit, she told herself fiercely, her small hands closing in on themselves. She had enough problems; she had made enough mistakes. Diving into bed for a casual one-night stand with Rio Lombardi would be the ultimate of mistakes. Not only would she fail to deliver what he expected, but she would also despise herself for being so cheap afterwards.

'Is that why you gave me the fairy-tale day out?' Holly heard herself accuse.

In the flickering lights, his lean, strong face clenched. 'Of course not.'

'But you got a kick out of dressing me up like some toy doll, trying to make me fit the blueprint of what presumably you like.' Holly was fighting so hard to keep the sob rising inside her from surfacing that her voice shook. 'But I'm still me, and I may not be anything that special, but if Jeff taught me anything he taught me that I need to have more respect for myself.'

'Right now, I do not want to hear about your abusive boyfriend,' Rio responded with sizzling bite. 'But, believe me, I've never had to bribe a woman into my bed!'

Holly did believe him, but she also knew that if she spoke again she would start crying and make an even bigger fool of herself. When the limo arrived at the house she jumped out, practically raced past Ezio and was indoors and up the stairs most probably before Rio had even made his own front step. Out of breath she went straight into Timmie's room and crept over to his cot. Her son was sound asleep, little face flushed and peaceful. Tomorrow she was going out to look for a job, and she would tackle the Social Security office again. Tomorrow was the beginning of another day.

Under the shower, she let her pent-up tears flow. How could she have been tempted? But then, how could she not have been? She was *mesmerised* by Rio Lombardi. It had been a magical day and she shouldn't have taken offence, for she had not objected to being kissed. Rio was no different from any other single oversexed male: he was programmed by his hormones to take advantage of willing women. If only she had had the wit to respond with a light-hearted negative, rather than getting upset and preaching and condemning. The memory of her own clumsy lack of tact made her cringe.

She slid into the silky white nightie she had worn the night before. Taken from the bag of clothing Ezio had given her, the garment was about a size too small in the bosom department, and rather revealing, but then she wasn't planning to walk down the street in it. She got into bed and tossed and turned for ages while telling herself that it was hunger that was keeping her awake. Then she heard a faint cry from Timmie's room and scrambled out of bed to check on him.

Timmie was still asleep. She straightened his bedding and assured herself that he was breathing normally and not too warm. Maybe he had had a bad dream. Slipping out of his room again, she stopped dead at the sight of Rio standing in the corridor, wearing only a pair of black boxer shorts.

CHAPTER FOUR

'I HEARD TIMOTHY crying...is he OK?' Rio prompted.

'Yes, he's still asleep,' Holly told him in a rush.

His ebony hair was tousled, his strong jawline blue-shadowed and his eyes were bright in his lean, bronzed face. He looked like a very sexy buccaneer, all elemental male and rippling muscles. Welded to the spot, Holly gazed at him, her soft lips parting. If she had found it impossible not to stare when he was clothed, she was even more challenged to deny that temptation when he was half-naked. And, although she knew she should not be looking and she was embarrassed by her own fascination, she couldn't stop.

Her heartbeat felt as if it was thumping in her constricted throat. He was magnificent. Her dilated gaze ran from his wide, smooth brown shoulders down over the black curls liberally sprinkling his muscular torso to his tight, flat stomach, and about there, where the band of his boxer shorts encircled his lean hips and challenged all further curiosity, Holly stopped dead in horror at herself.

Eyes shimmering hot gold, Rio strolled closer and, barefoot as he was, he made hardly a sound. The quiet had become a silence that buzzed, a silence alive with dangerous vibrations. Rio dealt her a slow-burning smile of appreciation. Only then did it occur to Holly that her scanty nightdress was scarcely adequate covering in which to parade herself before any red-blooded male. Her cheeks burning fierily, she raised her arms and began to fold them protectively over herself.

'Equal rights, *cara*.' Rio snapped long fingers round her wrists and held her still for a lingering physical appraisal.

Her breath snarled up in her throat, for she knew what he was seeing, her full breasts shamelessly delineated by the sheer, tight bodice. She felt the burn of her own mortification right down to the soles of her feet and was duly punished.

Rio made a husky sound low and deep in his throat. He just reached for her, hauling her up to him, his lean hands curving round her hips to crush her feminine mound into connection with the full, hard force of his arousal as he lifted her up against him.

'I hope you're in the mood to satisfy one very hungry guy, *bella mia*,' Rio growled before he brought his mouth crashing down on hers with devouring heat.

It was their first true kiss and it blew Holly away. Crushed to the hard male strength of his big, powerful physique, she was conscious of his virility with every fibre of her being. His mouth was hard and hot and carnal and nobody had ever kissed her that way before. Prying her soft lips apart, he plundered the tender moist interior with his tongue in a very sexual onslaught. He made her want more, he made her want so *much* more that she trembled and gasped under the raw, forceful passion he unleashed on her.

His strong hands moulded her to him and he swept

her right off her feet and up into his arms. Her shaken eyes opened just as he shouldered shut a door behind him. Tall lamps burned on each side of an enormous antique bed. The great carved headboard was topped by a fabulous canopy from which elaborate drapes fell to lie in opulent folds on the floor.

'I've been hot as hell for you all day,' Rio muttered harshly above her head.

'Honestly…?' Holly mumbled shyly into a sleek bare brown shoulder, marvelling that she could have incited his desire, feeling his entire body flaming for need of his but terrified that she would be a disappointment. The option of saying no did not even occur to her.

'I'm as hard as a rock, or haven't you noticed that yet?'

That earthy assurance drenched her cheeks with colour.

Rio sank down on the edge of the bed with her still locked in his hold. One hand anchoring into a fistful of ringlets, he turned her hot face up to meet his searching scrutiny. 'How does an unmarried mother contrive to blush like a furnace every five minutes?'

'I don't know…' He hurt Holly with that question, for to her mind it suggested that he believed she'd slept around before she'd fallen pregnant, which was very far from being the truth. Yet he had only to settle those brilliant, beautiful eyes on her and she was lost without any hope of reclaim. This was the *only* way she would ever get even temporarily close to a male like him, a little voice whispered inside her head. This was not the start of a relationship. Blokes like Rio Lombardi didn't have relationships with ordinary girls like her. In fact she couldn't work out what miracle had occurred to make her seem attractive to him.

Rio set her down onto her own feet so that she stood between his spread thighs and reached up to the slender straps on her slight shoulders. 'I want to look at you,' he told her, and before she could even guess his intention he had tugged the straps down her arms and let the nightdress fall to her ankles.

'Please...' Naked in front of a man for the first time in her life, Holly trembled, the flush on her face now feeling as if it was enveloping her entire body, and it was with the greatest difficulty that she resisted the urge to try to cover herself. A coil of heat burned low in her pelvis as his intent gaze scorched over pert breasts crowned by prominent rosy peaks and the cluster of bronze curls at the apex of her slim thighs. She felt as if she was burning alive with shame on a slave block.

Rio scooped her back into his arms as if she was the size and weight of a toy. 'You're shaking...and I haven't even touched you yet.'

'Yes...' Her teeth were almost chattering together in the wake of an enervating wave of apprehension, shame at her own weakness and the most desperate physical longing.

He closed his hand into her tumbling bronze curls to tug her head back and arch her spine, so that he had better access to her shivering body. 'Your skin is so fair against mine,' he husked, letting his hand splay over her slender, taut ribcage, listening to her suck in a gasping breath before he finally let his lean fingers rise to the jutting swell of her breasts to play with her throbbing nipples. 'You have gorgeous breasts...'

Her head was falling back now of its own volition

and she was gasping out loud, helplessly thrusting her aching flesh against his palms, white-hot heat snaking up from the very heart of her. He lowered his dark head and let his mouth engulf a distended bud and she cried out loud, shattered at the strength of her own response but helpless to control it.

His teeth teased at her tender flesh and then the tip of his tongue lashed the sensitised tips, sending tremors like lightning sizzling through her trembling length. She had not known that she could *feel* with such intensity, and the whole time he was touching her she was in shock at the twisting ache of sheer pleasure that jerked her every muscle tight.

Rio gathered her up and rose to bring her down across the bed. He leant over her, rearranging her to his own satisfaction, his control absolute. She connected with his burning golden eyes and felt herself melt like honey on the boil. Lying there so exposed, she had never been more conscious of her own body. Her nipples were swollen and glistening from his attentions and the private place between her thighs was embarrassingly moist. Her nails dug into the bedspread beneath her as she struggled to get a grip on herself, dredge herself from the unfamiliar world of what felt like an erotic fantasy, and as soon as she did she felt wildly out of her depth and as nervous as she had a mere second earlier been thrilled about what might be coming next.

'Could you put the lights out?' Holly whispered shakily.

'No…I want to *watch* you,' Rio asserted thickly, lean, strong face set with primal male determination, his sexual hunger unconcealed.

'W-watch me?' Holly stammered in dismay, utterly overpowered by that statement, that very concept.

'You don't hide anything. You *can't*,' Rio pronounced with almost grim satisfaction. 'I like that. I really get off on the fact that just about everything you feel you show me.'

'Do...I?' Holly dropped her eyes, gripped by intense mortification.

'Look at me...'

Holly shut her eyes tight.

'*Holly*...if you want me, look at me.'

For an instant she felt like a wind-up toy that he controlled. Her eyes smarted and opened and he came down on the bed on one knee, all domineering male but absolutely gorgeous, and she looked, of course she looked, was literally nailed to the spot by the sheer power of those scorching golden eyes holding hers.

With a roughened laugh of satisfaction, he let the tip of his tongue tease the tremulous line of her reddened lips and then slide between and delve in an erotic flicker that made her heart hammer and her pulses race.

Levering himself back, Rio stripped off his boxer shorts. Holly turned scarlet. Eyes widening, mouth running dry, surprise and dismay making her jerk. She had never seen a male in that state before, hadn't ever wanted to, but there he was, his sex fully aroused, and there was a great deal more of him than she had naïvely expected.

'What's wrong?' Rio noticed there was something wrong immediately.

'Nothing...' The denial emerged all shaky. She was already resigning herself to the prospect of pain but consoling herself with the thought that what she had once assumed would be the main event hardly lasted a minute.

Rio came over her with all the nerve-racking cool and grace of a predator. He toyed with her mouth again, let a knowing hand curve to a pouting breast and rolled the rigid pink peak straining for his attention between his fingers. All the breath that apprehension had made her hold in was driven from her on a long moaning sigh as her hips rose off the bed in an instinctive movement old as time itself.

'I want to torture you with pleasure, *bella mia...*'

He slid a fingertip between her parted lips and she sucked on it instinctively, the knot of hunger low in the pit of her stomach tightening.

'I want you begging,' Rio confided, shifting with fluid strength against her thigh to let her feel the hard, potent force of his arousal. 'Mindless...it's going to be a very long night.'

Shock gripped her at those words of sensual threat. She was melting again, she was enslaved by just the sound of his smoky drawl, the warm male scent of him and the incredibly seductive feel of that big, powerful, hair-roughened body in contact with hers. She lifted her hand and touched one high, proud cheekbone, letting her fingers stroke down the side of his face, loving the feel of him, loving the right to touch him, totally hooked on her connection with his liquid dark golden eyes, and enthralled.

He turned his head and entrapped one of her fingers between his lips, and suddenly she was snatching away her hand and reaching up in desperation to find that taunting mouth again for herself. She buried her fingers deep in his black silky hair, a moan dredged from her as he ravished her mouth with hard, hungry heat. She was aching for him, aching where she had never ached before, wanting what she had never wanted before with the most wanton craving.

'Rio, *please*...' she gasped, twisting under him.

'You don't want me enough yet,' he assured her thickly, letting his hand splay against her quivering tummy muscles and then stilling to trace the fine scar he had discovered. 'What's that?'

Holly tensed at his reference to that imperfection. 'I had to have a Caesarean when Timmie was born.'

'It's beautiful.' Moving on, Rio let his fingertips flirt with the damp curls below and laughed with earthy satisfaction as she automatically parted her thighs.

Locating the tiny bud beneath her downy mound, he proceeded to slowly drive her wild. Excitement just exploded in her and she writhed as the throb of need centred at the very heart of her rose to unbearable proportions. And she was mindless, beyond thought, speech, everything, reduced to one gigantic, all too sensitive ache of screaming need. But when she thrashed about, instinctively reaching for a fulfilment she had never known before, he stilled and let her slide down again, withholding what she most craved. And every time it happened she became just a little bit more frantic, clinging to him, almost in tears of frustration, utterly at a loss as to what was happening to her own body.

'Please...I want you now,' she begged strickenly.

Rio traced the swollen moist cleft between her legs, let an expert finger penetrate her once, twice until she cried out, beyond all shame and control. 'You're hot and wet and gloriously tight, *amore*.'

He settled his hands beneath her squirming hips and

thrust a pillow under her to raise her. Then there was a pause and she realised he was donning protection. But before she could even process that awareness Rio came over her like a Viking attack force, tipping her up to receive him at an angle that startled her, and then he drove into her in one long, deep thrust that put being startled right out of her mind. Indeed, *everything* went out of her mind. One moment she was almost sobbing with impatience, and the next she was plunged into the most wild physical excitement she had ever experienced.

'*Santo cielo...how* I want you,' he groaned. 'You feel *so* good...'

The intensity of her own excitement drove her crazy. He slammed into her with rhythmic force and she was on fire, gasping and sobbing for air, overwhelmed by the sheer raw pleasure of his every powerful plunge into her tender sheath. Blind and oblivious as she was to everything but the ongoing thunder of her own heartbeat and the plundering glory of his dominant possession, she was completely out of control. He sent her hurtling to the peak of ecstasy and a climax so strong that she felt as if she was shattering into a million pieces.

Letting her quivering weak body settle back down onto the support of the bed, Rio absorbed the shattered look of pleasure she wore. She collided dizzily with his searching gaze and her heart turned over at the sizzling smile of very male satisfaction he gave her. 'I never knew...' she mumbled in a total daze. 'I just never knew...I could feel like that—'

'Again...and again...and again, *bella mia*,' Rio husked, reaching down and lifting her to flip her over onto her stomach before she had the remotest idea of what he was doing. 'Let me show you.'

'Rio?' she cried in total bewilderment as he tugged her up onto her knees.

He slid into her again and she was so sensitised and so shaken by both sensation and shock at the position he had put her in, she let out a startled yelp.

'Am I hurting you?'

'No...' She shut her eyes in shame. *I'm not doing this, I'm not.* And she could not believe the pleasure that surged through her again, was seduced afresh within seconds, beyond caring about anything. She was a creature enslaved by sensation, totally wanton in her responses. Explosive excitement had her in a stranglehold and he controlled her, he controlled her so completely she was incapable of thought or reaction. And the second time that glorious joy racked her she didn't recognise the sobs and moans he dragged from her. The experience was all the more heightened by the feel of him shuddering over her and the groan of savage release he vented as he finally reached his own climax.

In the aftermath, Holly just collapsed, every piece of energy expended. Rio turned her over, flipped back the covers and brought her down on a cool linen sheet. Sprawling down beside her, he curved her back into his arms. He was hot and damp and the scent of him was so familiar now she pressed her lips against a smooth brown shoulder, glorying in that physical closeness. The silence didn't bother her. What she had just shared with him had been a revelation to her, and the languorous relaxation of her own satiation was so new to her she could not yet shake off the effects.

'You're not very experienced, are you?' Rio asked above her head, and for the first time she registered the tension in his lean, muscular length.

'No,' she whispered, suddenly wondering with a deep inner chill of fear if he had found her less than adequate.

Rio rolled her back against the pillows so that she could no longer evade his scrutiny. 'So when did you last indulge?'

Her wide, vulnerable eyes settled on his lean, dark features and the probing gold of his intent gaze and her eyes slewed from his in dismay. 'It's been a long time—'

'*How*...long?'

Feeling foolish, Holly worried at her lower lip before muttering with cast-down eyes, 'Not since the night I got pregnant.'

'Not since the night you...?' Long fingers curved round her delicate jawbone and tugged her back beneath his searching appraisal.

'It was my first time,' Holly told him with mortified defensiveness.

'You got pregnant the *first* time you had sex?' Rio ground out in visible shock.

'It does happen, you know,' she mumbled, unable to work out quite what interest he could have in such a subject and embarrassed, but at the same time needing him to know that she was not promiscuous.

With a seemingly idle hand Rio brushed a stray corkscrew curl back from her brow and she noticed that there was a slight tremor in his fingers. His stunning dark golden eyes were trained to her with intensity, his blue-shadowed jawline clenched hard. 'Are you taking any current precautions against pregnancy?'

In surprise Holly shook her head.

'I didn't think you would be, *cara*.' His keen gaze

screened by his luxuriant dark lashes, Rio released his breath in a long-drawn-out sigh. 'You were almost a virgin. No wonder my every move seemed to shock you so much. You hadn't a bloody clue—'

'No, I—'

'*Still* don't have a clue,' Rio contradicted with a raw edge to his deep, dark drawl, his accent very thick.

'I do!' Holly protested feverishly. 'Maybe I didn't before but I do *now.* I thought sex was awful until to-night...what did I do wrong?'

Above her, Rio closed his eyes, his expression pained, dark colour scoring his fabulous cheekbones. He threw himself back against the tumbled pillows with a very male groan. 'You didn't do anything wrong. I did it *all.* The condom broke...'

As those three words sank in Holly stilled, her face tightening in shock. As she processed that admission and registered the potential consequences her complexion paled to the colour of milk.

Springing off the bed with lithe ease, Rio strode in the direction of the bathroom. 'Come on,' he urged with wry mockery. 'Let's drown our sorrows in the shower!'

'In a minute...' As he vanished from her view she almost fell off the bed in her haste to vacate it. Struggling back into her nightie, she fled to her own room, driven by the kind of panic and shame that wanted no witnesses.

CHAPTER FIVE

EMERGING FROM A restive sleep, conscious that she had still been awake at dawn, Holly sat up in bed slowly. With every movement, a telling series of aches in certain private places reminded her of her abandoned behaviour with Rio the night before and her shadowed eyes filled with anguished regret.

Last night she had locked her bedroom door. Rio had followed her and, quiet though he had kept his demands that she open the door, she had sensed his angry impatience even through the solid thickness of wood separating them. When, minutes later, the bedside phone had rung she had rushed to unplug it from the socket.

She was *so* ashamed of how stupid and reckless she had been. It was her fault that the whole situation had developed in the first place. She fully believed that it had been her obvious attraction to Rio which had first incited *his* interest, was convinced that without that sexual spur and provocation it would not even have occurred to Rio to touch her. Her feelings, her weakness, her reactions had drawn him.

But at least Rio had thought of precautions. Such a sensible consideration had not crossed her mind once and he was hardly to be blamed for the reality that misfortune had struck. Misfortune was her middle name, Holly reflected, a shuddering sob hurtling up from her constricted lungs. Hadn't she learnt anything from Timothy's birth? Was she still irresponsible and naïve and foolish?

What on earth had got into her? Another sob quivered through her slender frame. She wiped at her eyes but the tears kept coming. How could she ever face Rio again? He had been so kind to her and she had had a magical time with him earlier in the day. Even last night, when she assumed other less well-bred males would have been cursing furiously over such an accident, Rio had maintained his cool courtesy. In fact he had proved himself a guy worthy of being loved.

But she had behaved like a slut, she told herself wretchedly; she deserved everything she had coming to her, but no baby deserved an inadequate mother. For the first time she glanced at the clock by the bed and her eyes flew wide in horror because it was already after ten and Timmie always woke up around seven!

Holly leapt out of the bed and unlocked the door. Pausing for an instant, she then stopped and grabbed up the luxurious fake-fur she had worn to the restaurant and dug her arms into the sleeves before hurtling into the room next door to check on her child. In an almost all-male household she needed to be careful to cover up and perhaps, had she been more sensible the night before, nothing would have happened between her and Rio.

In Timmie's room the nanny, Sarah, looked up with a smile. She was in the midst of dressing Timmie. Holly was startled, for she had assumed that the nanny had only been brought in to look after her son for just the one day.

'Good morning, Miss Sansom. Aren't these clothes beautiful?' Sarah said chattily as if there was nothing odd about Holly choosing to wear a fake-fur coat over her nightie. She held up a tiny navy jacket embroidered with a Scottie dog motif and a pair of miniature checked trousers for Holly's inspection. 'Mr. Lombardi had a whole selection of outfits for Timothy delivered this morning.'

The 'Timothy' tag had spread, Holly noted in a daze. Rio had had clothing purchased for her son? Was there no end to his generosity? Or her own indebtedness? Didn't he understand how hard it was to continually receive gifts when she was in no position to reciprocate? Although she was longing to hold her baby in her arms, she backed to the door again. 'I'll just go and get dressed.'

But her attempt to re-enter her own room was forestalled by the reality that there was a giant heap of boxes and bags now sitting on her bed and two manservants were engaged in opening them. A frown of bemusement on her brow, she stared. What was going on?

'I'm glad you put the coat on, *bella mia*,' a dark, deep drawl remarked from behind her. 'I wouldn't like anyone but me to see you in that nightdress.'

Holly whirled round. 'For goodness' sake, what are those blokes doing?'

'Unpacking your new wardrobe…what else?'

'Wh-what new wardrobe?' A band of tension was tightening like a vice round Holly's temples. It was as if she had woken up in another world where everything was slightly different from what it ought to have been.

But she had still to look any higher than the level of Rio's gold silk tie.

'What we bought yesterday.'

'Are you telling me…there was *more* than that dress I wore out and the coat?' Holly gasped, appalled by that news.

'*Dio mio,* of course there was more. You had nothing but what you stood up in,' Rio pointed out rather drily.

'But I can't let—'

'Excuse me…' Striding past her, Rio snapped his fingers to alert his staff's attention and addressed them in Italian. The two men immediately abandoned their task and filed out. Closing his fingers over hers, Rio drew her into the bedroom and pushed the door closed. 'Right now we have something rather more important to worry about—'

Holly was gazing aghast at the huge heap of shopping strewn across the bed. 'You can't *do* this, Rio… it's not right, it's totally wrong—'

'Holly,' Rio slotted in grimly, 'in fifteen minutes a Miss Elliott will be calling to see us and you need to get dressed. I suggest you wear one of your new outfits.'

Her brow indented. 'Who's Miss Elliott?'

'The social worker whom you would have seen had you remained in hospital.'

Holly had turned a sickly shade. 'But how did she find out I was here in your house?'

Rio's wide, sensual mouth compressed. 'I informed Dr. Coulter, who's a friend of mine, that I had brought you here—'

Holly was trying very hard not to burst into tears. 'Some friend…shopping me to the authorities!'

'*Per meraviglia!* Will you stop talking as though

you are a criminal? You and Timothy are both all right now, but naturally enquiries have to be made to establish that fact.'

'They'll t-take him away from me…' Holly sobbed, backing away from him in her distress.

Rio gripped her by the shoulders, dark-as-midnight eyes level. 'Nobody is going to take him away from you. I promise you that. Now pull yourself together and come downstairs—'

'I *can't*—'

'You're talking like a child.' Rio dealt her a hard look of censure, lean, dark features set in impatient lines. 'This matter will be easily resolved. Once I inform the woman that I intend to marry you, she will see that neither you nor your son are in need of further support.'

As he released his hold on her Holly fell back from him, thunderstruck by that statement. 'You're going to tell her that we're getting…*married*?'

'And the less you say on the subject the better…OK?' Rio breathed, striding back to the door and flipping it shut in his wake.

In a daze, Holly blinked as comprehension slowly sank in. Yet she was amazed that Rio was willing to tell such a whopping lie on her behalf. However, that fiction would indeed satisfy any concerns as to her son's future well-being. Rio Lombardi was rich, respectable and a noted philanthropist, she reminded herself dizzily. He was the fake husband-to-be from heaven, only lacking an actual halo. He was also very clever. She was really touched that he was prepared to spout such a story purely for her benefit. Not that he was exactly looking forward to the prospect, she conceded, shame assailing her. Rio had had a bleak, grim aspect new to her experience of him. Most probably he wished he had never met her and never got involved.

But the least she could do to back up his story was look the part of a woman on the brink of marriage to a very wealthy man. She lifted a turquoise dress and jacket from the bed and rooted about until she found the matching shoes. Imagine him spending such a huge amount of money on her! So crazy too! He really and truly had no concept of the life she led or of her level in society compared with his own. Where the heck did he think she would wear designer suits and fancy evening outfits?

Neither Timmie nor his nanny were in his room when she emerged from her own. Holly descended the stairs, taking careful steps in the high heels. Her heart was beating so fast with fear and nerves she felt sick. She dawdled in the hall, scanning her reflection, once again barely recognising herself. Who was that slender figure in the beautifully cut jacket that just screamed class and expense?

A door swung open off the hall. 'Holly…hurry up,' Rio urged with controlled exasperation.

Even talking like that, he was just so beautiful, Holly thought painfully. And fear was unknown to him. Of course, he could not understand or sympathise with her distress. Of course, her terror struck him as being exaggerated and illogical. He had probably never been in a situation he could not control. He did not know what it was to feel powerless and at the mercy of others. Good and well-meaning people those other parties might be, but sometimes they took terrifying and merciless decisions.

A blonde older woman with cool blue eyes and a distinct air of efficiency was seated in the drawing room and immediately addressed her. 'Miss Holly Sansom?' she queried, scanning Holly's appearance with dubious brows raised like question marks.

'Yes…I'm Holly.'

Timmie was sitting on the rug with some toys and he chortled and held out his arms when he saw his mother. In his fancy clothes, he looked not only like a baby who had swallowed a silver spoon at birth but a baby who might well have swallowed an entire silver service. Scooping her son up, Holly sat down with him on her lap and hugged him tight, her chin resting on his sweet-smelling fluffy dark curls.

'Dr. Coulter informed me that you're living here for the present, Miss Sansom,' the blonde woman commented. 'Is that true?'

'Holly and I are getting married,' Rio imparted with the utmost casualness.

And that was just about that, bar a few minor comments. The blonde was taken aback, but then she consulted the file in her lap and lifted her gaze to study Timmie. Last of all, she directed her attention in a discreet flicker at Rio and a faint smile flickered at the corner of her lips. 'I'm so pleased that the situation has been sorted out. Timmie looks very content.'

'I hope to adopt Timothy as my son,' Rio remarked.

The other woman nodded slowly but now looked slightly bemused before finally wishing them all well and rising to leave.

Leaving Rio to take care of the courtesies, Holly just flopped where she sat.

Rio strode back through the door again, lean, strong

face taut. 'Miss Elliott just assumed that Timothy was *my* child.'

Holly flushed to the roots of her hair and sat up with a start, corkscrew curls bouncing. That possibility had not occurred to her, but as soon as Rio suggested it she recalled the way the social worker had behaved. 'Honestly? Did she say something on her way out?'

'She didn't need to. It was written all over her face. I suppose Timothy has quite dark hair and that possible explanation for our marital plans made the most sense to her. But I don't like anyone believing that I would treat the mother of my child as you were treated by your son's father. That's why I referred to my wish to adopt Timothy.' Having given her that frank assurance and made her stiffen with embarrassed discomfiture, Rio crossed the room to hunker down and survey her son, whose big blue eyes were drowsy. 'He's *amazing*. He spends half the morning getting fed and bathed and dressed and no sooner is he up and about than he's ready for his cot again!'

Grateful for that distraction, Holly burbled, 'He's always slept a lot. He's a good baby. You were really wonderful with Miss Elliott, Rio.' She nibbled awkwardly at her lower lip as she thanked him for his support. 'Very convincing. I know you couldn't have enjoyed saying *that* about you and me...but I'm very grateful and, no matter what happens, I'll never, ever take a risk like that with my son again.'

Rio surveyed her strained expression with narrowed dark, glittering eyes and frowned. 'I do believe we've been talking at cross purposes. We'll discuss that after you've taken Timothy up for his nap.'

Cross purposes? What cross purposes? And how

come she was only now noticing how domineering his powerful personality could make Rio seem? He came off with commands as if it was his birthright. But then, she supposed he *had* been born to that sort of stuff, she reflected forgivingly, feeling truly guilty and ungrateful for thinking on such lines after all he had done to help her.

What if you conceive again? a little voice sniped in the back of her mind. Are you going to think of that as help too? Her tummy churned. She adored her son but knew she could not in her present circumstances cope with a second child. But then Rio was already letting her know that he would not abandon her, wasn't he? How come she had not immediately recognised *why* he had made that speech about how he would not treat the mother of his child in the manner that her ex-boyfriend had treated her?

But there was so much tension between them now. He was no longer relaxed with her. That was what that reckless bout of lovemaking had done. It had spoilt things, she reflected wretchedly, and cringed at the intimate images teeming in her memory banks. Not once even yet had she managed to look Rio directly in the face. Last night she had sobbed and begged and pleaded for him to make love to her. There was no forgetting that. She had been out of control, totally out of control *and* out of her depth, but even she knew that men preferred a challenge to a push-over. Rio Lombardi was hardly the sort of male who needed an adoring slave to massage his ego. Women had to be falling in the aisles around him, so he would want and expect more.

Nervous as a cat walking over hot coals, Holly returned to the drawing room.

Rio swung round from the window, tall, dark and immaculate in his tailored business suit. 'When I said that we were getting married, it wasn't some crazy story, *cara*.'

Not understanding his meaning, Holly stilled with a frown of confusion. 'Then—er—what was it?'

'The truth of what we're going to do. I can't say that I feel flattered that you should assume that I would lie about something that important,' Rio continued with a level cool that only made her own astonishment feel all that more intense. 'We'll be married just as soon as I can get a special licence arranged.'

Her knees felt as if they were fashioned out of cotton wool and wobbled under her. She was finally looking at him for the first time that day and only because she was reeling with shock. Blue eyes very wide, she whispered unsteadily, 'You're not having me on?'

'You might be pregnant. I took advantage of you last night,' Rio breathed, aggressive jawline clenched hard. 'You were very vulnerable and I should have kept my distance. I took you to bed because I wanted—'

'That's OK. That's not taking advantage!' Holly protested with feverish relief at what she assumed he was about to tell her.

'Sex. I wanted sex. It was as primitive as that.' His superb bone-structure fiercely taut, Rio made an admission that slaughtered Holly where she stood, for she had believed when she interrupted him that he had been telling her that it was her, personally, that he had wanted. Only that was not the case, was it? The truth was much more painful. When a bloke said he had just wanted sex, it was like saying that she had only been a convenient body, Holly reflected in agony.

Deeply hurt by that confession, wishing he had thought enough of her feelings not to have voiced it, Holly dropped heavily down onto the nearest sofa, no longer trusting her weak legs to hold her upright. 'I wanted you…just you,' she heard herself mumble like a foolish child, digging herself into an even more embarrassing hole.

'I know…' That confirmation just splintered through her shrinking, shaking body like the cruellest of knives, tearing tender flesh wherever it touched. 'I must be honest with you, *cara*—'

'Don't call me that…whatever it means. You use it like it means something and it *doesn't*.' Holly squeezed out that condemnation in a voice that was far from level. 'So why are you talking about marrying me…feeling like you do?'

'I like you, Holly. I like Timothy too. I believe I could become fond of you.'

Holly wanted to die where she sat. Fond? She curved her arms round herself, appalled at the emotional hurt he was inflicting on her in the name of honesty. Even Jeff with his abuse had not wounded her as much as Rio wounded her at that moment. Rio was ripping apart everything, every naïve and harmless belief, every tiny inner hope. He *liked* her, well, whoopy-do! So she felt even more pathetic to be sitting there thinking that she loved him while he hammered the self-esteem he had rescued for her back into the ground again.

'Until relatively recently, I was engaged to another woman.'

That startling admission hung there like another giant slap in the face just waiting for her to lift her cheek to receive it. But something stronger than she was, the most powerful curiosity, forced Holly to lift her head again. The brilliant flare of anger lightening his gaze in the aftermath of that acknowledgement did not match her expectations. There was none of the regret or emotion that she had feared that she would see. In fact, his darkly handsome features were set hard in stone.

'Engaged?' she prompted uneasily.

'I finished it. That's over and done with and in the past.' Beautifully shaped mouth curling, glittering golden eyes resting on her, Rio murmured, 'I only mentioned it because while I was engaged I got used to the idea of being married, and I do still need a wife.'

'What for?' It sounded inane but Holly couldn't help it. But then, she was weak with relief at the finality with which he had pronounced that his engagement was over. It must have ended quite some time back, Holly assumed, or he would hardly have been saying that it was in the past.

Rio spread his lean brown hands in a fluid expressive movement. 'Some day I want a family of my own.'

'Oh...'

'I also need a wife to oversee my domestic arrangements and entertain friends and family. A wife who will try to be a daughter to my mother, who suffers a lot of ill-health,' Rio enumerated, very much more relaxed now that he was getting to talk practicalities. 'A wife to make *me* more comfortable, for I have got beyond the stage where I enjoy spending my time, indeed, often *wasting* my time with a variety of different women.'

And he wanted superwoman as a wife. He had huge expectations, Holly thought heavily, knowing she could never, ever measure up to such requirements, and marvelling that he had not immediately realised that fact.

'You could *learn* to be the wife that I want,' Rio informed her confidently.

But it sounded as if lifelong training would be necessary. She had been stymied by one trip to a fancy restaurant. A near-hysterical giggle bubbled in her aching throat but she had never been further from laughter.

'You need to know that I've good reason *other* than the risk that you may already be pregnant to talk of marriage,' he continued in his dark, deep drawl that flowed like honey even now down her sensitive spine.

'But we're probably worrying about nothing —'

'Are we? You're young and fertile and I would prefer not to wait for proof one way or the other.' Rio expelled his breath in a measured hiss. 'If we wait and a child is eventually born there will be those who believe that I was *forced* to marry you. That would be humiliating for you.'

He really did expect the worst. He really did believe that there was a very strong chance that he might have impregnated her. His certainty scared her. But how could she marry a man who felt nothing for her? Did that mean that she was considering his offer? Of course she was. Dredging her attention from his lean, strong face, she knew she did not even have to take her own feelings for him into account to make that decision. She had nothing to offer Timmie, who would no doubt thrive as Timothy. If she married Rio her baby would want for nothing. He would have a home, love and security and a bloke who was willing to be his adoptive father. Rio liked kids. He liked her son already. In fact she had pretty much hit the equivalent of the jackpot falling in front of his limo, she acknowledged guiltily, feeling that *she* would very much be taking advantage of *him*.

She linked her trembling hands together, hugely worked up but trying so hard to emulate his calm and logical approach. 'When did you start thinking of all this?'

'Ten minutes after you fled from my room last night,' Rio admitted, bringing her bright head up again. 'I have never felt so guilty in my whole life.'

'Thanks…' Her voice wobbled again and she pushed her lips together hard, striving to will back the tears threatening behind her eyes.

'I'll look after you and your son. You need me. I like to be needed. I'm *used* to being needed,' Rio completed with a shrug of arrogant acceptance.

He was so volatile. So very, very volatile and until now she had not even recognised that reality. He had seemed so controlled and reserved at their first proper meeting at the hospital, only to overturn that impression with his angry, intimidating reaction when he had found her trying to sneak away from the Lombardi hospital. Ever since then he had alternated between fiery heat and indolent cool. He could switch from one mood to the other within seconds. He fascinated her.

'You might go and fall madly in love with someone else…' she heard herself say, although it was an effort to make herself say that.

'You must be joking,' Rio said in a tone of icy derision.

He was so sure of himself, so sure he knew everything there was to know. Recalling all the awful anxiety she had suffered just struggling to survive, she felt reassured by that infinite confidence of his. So how could she hold his patent belief that she would *snatch* at his offer of marriage against him?

After all, here she was, dead keen on him and incapable of hiding it, not to mention homeless and broke. Had he pretended a little uncertainty as to his reception it wouldn't really have been convincing, she told herself. He was incredibly good-looking and sexy and a huge catch for someone like her. But he was also feeling guilty as hell over taking her to bed, she reminded herself reluctantly. She really *ought* to be turning him down flat. Wasn't it wrong to let him make such a massive mistake? He didn't love her, he hardly knew her, and in time he might even come to despise her for the mistakes she would make trying to fit into his world. But he was right, she could learn, and a part of her that she wasn't very proud of desperately wanted that chance.

'I shouldn't say yes to this,' Holly breathed unevenly.

'But you will.' Rio leant down and closed his hands round hers to pull her up to him. His sudden flashing smile as her cheeks blossomed with self-conscious colour made her tummy somersault with excitement. The warm, intrinsically familiar scent of him made her ache. The mere fact that he was only inches away reduced her to quivering, melting compliancy and, guilty as hell aside, she could see that he liked that, he *liked* that very much. That she did not mistake.

He gave her the kind of brief kiss that he excelled at, provocative, intimate, intensely erotic. Then he set her free again when she was desperate to cling and every nerve-ending craved the heat of his passion.

'We'll be very uncool and wait for our wedding night,' Rio decreed, soft and husky and boundlessly sure, it seemed, of his welcome.

And for the very first time Holly realised that she could crave him like an addict and still want to scream at him.

CHAPTER SIX

THREE DAYS LATER Holly climbed into the limousine that would ferry her to the wedding that had been arranged and the ceremony that would make her Rio Lombardi's wife.

Ezio Farretti beamed at her in flattering admiration of her bridal regalia but it felt so very strange to be alone, with neither friends nor family for support, indeed none of the more personal trappings Holly had once naïvely assumed would be part and parcel of such an event.

She had thought of phoning her parents and telling them that she was getting married but had given up on the idea when it occurred to her that naturally her parents would want to know all about her relationship with Rio. How on earth could she admit that she was marrying a man she had known for less than a week? She would have to wait until her marriage was already an established fact before meeting up with her parents again.

For three solid days she had done little but shop, first for her gown and then for clothes for both her and Timothy that would suit a warmer climate. That last instruction from Rio had actually caused a panic when it had emerged that he was planning to take them abroad after the wedding and she had confided that neither she nor her son had a passport. Fortunately it had proved possible to redress that oversight, but Rio's incredulity that anybody should be without a passport had reminded her all over again of how different her world was from his, for her parents had never been abroad in their entire lives.

Emerging from that recollection, Holly rearranged the skirt of her dress, fearful of creasing the delicate folds before she arrived at the church, desperately wanting to look the very best she could for Rio. She had fallen in love with her ivory and gold wedding gown at first sight, but Rio had told her to pick something traditional and a dress strongly reminiscent of a medieval bride might not fit the bill, she reflected anxiously.

Long pointed sleeves ornamented the boned V-shaped silk bodice which was decorated with exquisite gold embroidery and laced tight at her tiny waist, and the skirt was long and elegant. A fabulous sapphire and diamond tiara was lodged in her bronze curls and she wore a matching and equally impressive necklace and drop earrings. The set was Lombardi family jewellery sent from Tuscany by special courier and Rio had requested that she wear the items. She had had to tie on the earrings with thread because her ears were not pierced and, terrified of losing the earrings, she checked that they were still in place every few minutes.

In fact, nerves were eating Holly alive, for Rio had been abroad and she had only spoken to him on the phone in recent days. Indeed, at one stage she had honestly believed that the wedding might have to be cancelled. The same day that she had agreed to marry him Rio had flown out to Stockholm on business before travelling on to Florence to call on his mother. Rio had hoped to bring the older woman back to London with him to attend their wedding but Alice Lombardi had felt too weak to make the trip.

'I *was* going to fly you out for the day so that you could meet,' Rio had informed Holly on the phone twenty-four hours earlier before he explained why he could not return that evening as he had hoped. 'But she had palpitations and I had to call her doctor in. He prescribed complete bedrest.'

Holly had repressed the troubled suspicion that her future mother-in-law might have been felled by sheer horror that her only son was about to wed a stranger who was not only an unmarried mother but also a young woman from a background that in no way matched their own. Since that possibility did not appear to have occurred to Rio, she had not liked to mention it.

'What's Mrs. Lombardi like?' she had asked Ezio.

'A fine woman,' he had responded. 'But a martyr to ill-health.'

'Maybe the wedding will have to be put off.' Holly had felt horribly guilty at the dismay which had filled her at that prospect.

'Mrs. Lombardi has a remarkable ability to pull back from death's door,' Ezio had asserted bracingly. 'In fact, I wouldn't be surprised if the lady outlives all of us.'

As the limousine turned off the road Holly was amazed to see that the church appeared to be buried in a sea of parked cars and that there were a lot of people standing outside the iron railings bounding the car park. Had there been a wedding booked before their own and had it run on late? Or was she arriving too early?

Leaning forward, she lifted the car phone to ask Ezio.

'They're all here for *your* wedding,' the older man informed her, his astonishment at her question audible.

All those cars? Holly was aghast. She had assumed that there would be no guests, had believed that their wedding would be a very quiet and private affair. True, Rio had not said that, but he *had* told her to leave Timothy at home with Sarah, and in the time frame concerned and with him out of the country who on earth could have made arrangements for so many people to attend?

As she emerged shakily from the car a seething crowd seemed to come out of nowhere at her. Security guards held back the crush while aggressive men with cameras shouted and urged her to look up. In the midst of that fracas, she was seized by a shock and fear so profound that had Ezio not seized her elbow and hurried her on into the church she would have shot back into the limousine and screamed at the chauffeur to drive off again.

In the church porch, she shivered and stared at Ezio in incomprehension. 'What's going on? Who *are* those people?'

'The press.'

'But why would they be interested in our wedding?'

'Rio getting married is news,' the older man advanced. 'Nobody knows who you are either, and that was sure to whip up a storm.'

At that point the double doors near by were opened wide from the other side and organ music flooded out from the main body of the church.

Holly gazed in horror at the packed pews she could now see, the swivelling heads of those keen to see the bride, and she backed out of sight again at speed. 'I can't *do* this!' she gasped in genuine panic. 'Not walk down that aisle on my own without my dad or any bridesmaids. Why didn't Rio *warn* me it would be like this?'

'He probably didn't think. You'll be fine,' Ezio Farretti soothed.

Holly liked and trusted the older man. She scanned his smart appearance in his well-cut suit and mustered the courage to make a special request. '*You* could give me away...' A note of entreaty underlined her strained voice. 'That way I wouldn't look so odd and I wouldn't be alone.'

Ezio dealt her a startled look and then absorbed the fact that she was still backing in the direction of the exit. With a slow smile, he straightened his shoulders and extended his arm. 'I would be honoured. But remember that this was your idea, not mine,' he warned her gently.

However, if Rio was taken aback to see her approach the altar in tandem with his security chief, Holly was too enervated to notice. No sooner had she arrived than the priest began to speak, and as she looked at Rio and met his brilliant dark eyes her heartbeat just went haywire. The instant the ring went on her finger was so precious to her but it also made her regret that she had not thought to ask him if he would have liked to receive a ring too.

But then, he would have had to buy that for himself as well, Holly realised with a stab of mortification. She wondered how it was that when life had been normal she had never worried quite so much about money nor felt so much of a pauper. It hurt her pride that not a shred she wore even on her own wedding day had been paid for with her own money, for she had nothing that he had not given her.

'You look really stunning in that gown.' Rio flashed her an appreciative smile while they stood on the church steps being filmed and photographed.

His smile filled her with warmth and security. Without him by her side, Holly knew she would have bolted for cover. Never before had she been the target of so many speculative stares and she had never dreamt even in her wildest fantasies that she would ever marry a male likely to attract such enormous attention from the media. She fingered the slender band of gold on her wedding finger as if it was a talisman that might yet make her feel that she was really and truly Rio Lombardi's bride. But just then, regardless of the winging sense of happiness strengthening her, it still felt like a crazy daydream.

As a limousine whisked them away from the church she turned to him, her lovely face betraying her continuing strain. 'Why didn't you tell me that there would be so many people coming?'

Rio elevated a smooth ebony brow and responded with his own question. 'Why would you have thought otherwise?'

'You told me to leave Timothy at home—'

'I thought that that would be more relaxing for you,' Rio slotted in smoothly. 'Nor would Timothy enjoy being deprived of his mother and surrounded by strangers.'

Both statements were indisputably correct but Holly could not help wondering if her son's exclusion might also have been linked to a certain unwillingness on Rio's part to brandish the fact that his bride was already a parent, and to a child who was not his.

Rio rested knowing dark golden eyes on her. 'You're *wrong.*'

Holly flushed. 'I didn't say anything!'

'You don't need to. I also once sat through a wedding during which a baby screamed continuously. It left a lasting impression on me,' Rio mocked, reaching for the taut fingers coiled on her lap and closing his hand over hers in reassurance. 'I will look on Timothy as my son and treat him accordingly. Didn't I promise you that?'

'Yes...' Holly's throat had thickened with tears because she was ashamed that her own insecurity had made her doubt him.

'If I kiss you now I'll wreck your make-up,' Rio teased.

'To heck with that...' she muttered in a wobbly undertone.

With a husky masculine laugh, Rio laced indolent fingers into the bright fall of her hair and crushed her soft mouth under his own with a hunger that sent miniature lightning bolts stabbing to every sensitive spot in her quivering body. 'Enough,' he groaned, setting her back from him. 'We still have a reception to get through, although I'm not planning on a lengthy stay.'

Holly tensed. 'A reception?'

'Feeding one's guests is an inescapable duty,' Rio quipped. 'Sometimes I wonder if we grew up on the same planet, *cara.*'

At that crack, Holly paled and said defensively, 'I just didn't know we were going to have a proper wedding.'

'What else could we have had?' Rio regarded her in polite bewilderment. 'What did you expect?'

'Just us.'

'Just *us*?' Rio stressed in patent astonishment at the

idea. 'Don't you think that would have looked very odd? In the circumstances, the very last thing I would wish is the suggestion that there is anything odd about our marriage.'

'So who arranged all this stuff, then?'

'My staff. I have an extensive staff,' Rio pointed out gently.

Her mouth still tingling from the smouldering contact of his, Holly nodded hurriedly in receipt of that information and strove not to look as if her own ignorance was embarrassing her when indeed it was.

In the grand and exclusive hotel where the reception was staged, she shook hands with a countless number of people and later recalled not a single face or name. Rio's relations, his business connections and personal friends got all mixed up inside her buzzing head. During the superb meal that was served, a lot of the conversation around her kept on switching from English into Italian and she tried not to feel excluded and tried not to seem conscious of the enormous curiosity behind the lingering appraisals she received. Obviously learning to speak Italian was going to be one of her first challenges, she told herself, but it was something of a shock to meet with that language barrier and to sit there feeling like the quietest bride that had ever existed.

She angled her head closer to Rio's and whispered, 'I'm just going to find a phone to ring Timothy.'

Rio interrupted his conversation to turn questioning eyes on her. 'Ring…Timothy?'

Holly reddened. 'Yes. Sarah can hold the phone to his ear so that I can talk to him.'

Rio eased a hand into his pocket and withdrew his cell phone. 'Be my guest.'

'I don't know how to use it—'

'It's *simple*.'

Accepting the phone, Holly slipped away from the table to find a quiet spot in the foyer, but no matter how many buttons she stabbed she couldn't work out how to use the darned thing and got nothing but words coming up on the tiny screen. Peering down at it in frustration, she only then noticed that the same words seemed to be going round and round: 'I love u. Call me.'

A chill ran down her sensitive spine. As she stood there by the wall, two women engaged in animated conversation strolled out of the crowded function room. 'Well, all I can say is…if the *baby* bride stole Rio from Christabel, there's hope for all of us!'

'Did you hear that hilarious accent of hers? I almost burst out laughing! She talks like a hayseed— '

'I could practically see Rio wincing. He is *so* refined. And she obviously doesn't have a single presentable relative because I know *everyone* here.'

'Poor Christabel,' the first woman said with mocking sympathy. 'Just imagine the agony of being that beautiful and being replaced by a creature with red hair like an electrified ragdoll! What did you think of her wedding dress?'

'If you're that skinny, you should hide it, not flaunt it!'

'It was so cheap-and-nasty-looking too. Bargain basement. You could tell *he* hadn't paid for it.'

Her back pinned to the wall, her tummy churning at those comments, and trembling, Holly waited until the women had moved out of sight before setting off without even knowing where she was going. She just wanted to hide somewhere. Rio was getting love messages on his phone and everybody was laughing at her. In an archway, she stumbled as her gown caught on her heel and she had to pause to free the hem. When she looked up she realised that she was in a bar and that people were looking at her. Spying the restroom at the far end, she began to walk fast towards it, head held as high as she could manage.

'I'm *telling* you...' a loud, very upper-class male voice proclaimed full of amusement just as she moved past the bar. 'I'll lay you a grand that I'm right. Rio's bride is preggers. He's been playing away behind Christabel's back and then *bang*...his perfect life just went up in smoke!'

Holly stopped dead behind the tall blond man in full flood. 'If that's what you think, why did you come to our wedding? Guests are supposed to want to wish the bridal couple well...fat chance!' Holly snapped with stinging disgust, her charged voice falling into a deathly silence that she was quite beyond noticing. 'The likes of you are too nasty to wish anybody well!'

The young blond man swung round. Warm colour flooding his fair, open face, he stared down at her with appalled blue eyes. 'Oh, no...I am *so* sorry!'

Holly only dimly recalled him from the long procession of guests she had been forced to greet. But, without another word, she headed on into the restroom. She wondered dismally if she could brick herself up in one of the cubicles and stay there for ever undiscovered. She studied her 'electrified ragdoll' hair and her 'cheap' dress, which she had believed was so lovely, and tears started streaming down her face. On her terms the gown had been quite expensive enough for something that would only be worn once, but probably by rich people's standards it *had* been bargain basement.

Yet all she could really think about at that moment was the woman sending 'I love you' text messages to Rio on his phone. A woman called Christabel, the same name that the beauty-salon owner, Sly, had mentioned that day she trimmed Holly's hair. Christabel, who was so obviously Rio's former fiancée. *Beautiful* Christabel, whom Rio had evidently dumped and yet nobody seemed to have the slightest idea why. Unless it was because he had got Holly pregnant behind Christabel's back.

But only time would take care of that kind of spite and, knowing her own luck in the fertility stakes, time might yet convince people that their suspicions had been entirely correct. Furthermore, Rio had married her but he didn't love her and she had better get used to that reality. How could she demand the same boundaries as any other new bride? It was not a normal marriage. Mopping her damp face dry, powdering her shiny nose and repairing her lipstick, Holly headed back into the fray.

As she recrossed the bar, looking to neither left nor right, the young blond man fell into step beside her. 'Go away,' she spat out of the corner of her mouth.

'I don't think you even know who I am. I'm Jeremy, from the English side of the Lombardi clan—'

'Didn't know there *was* an English side—'

'But Rio's mother, Alice, is English…she's also my mother's sister,' Jeremy remarked, his surprise at her ignorance unconcealed.

Holly walked away from him. Unable to face returning to the function room until she had got a better grip on her overtaxed emotions, she picked one of the sofas in the seating area just off the main foyer. Her unwanted companion infuriated her by throwing himself down beside her and reaching for her hand.

'Look, I'm willing to grovel. What I said was utterly indefensible but I was sounding off for a laugh,' Jeremy asserted earnestly. 'I would sooner have cut off my right arm than hurt you like that—'

'It's not too late. Go ahead,' Holly told him.

Amused respect flared in Jeremy's eyes. 'All right, so I was laying on the syrup a bit thick.'

Without the smallest warning, Rio strode into the alcove. His sudden appearance made Holly jerk in dismay, and Jeremy hurriedly removed his hand from hers. His devastatingly handsome features set like steel, Rio flashed scorching golden eyes over the two of them and then settled his hard gaze on Holly with intimidating force. 'Where have you been all this time? Sitting out here flirting with my layabout cousin?'

Jeremy shot upright, visibly disconcerted by the speed with which that accusation had emerged from the bridegroom. 'I was trying to make a grovelling apology to Holly—'

'What were you apologising *for*?' Rio demanded of the younger man.

'Oh, leave it, for goodness' sake!' Attempting to reclaim some dignity, Holly got up. 'I still have to ring Timothy.'

Jeremy had already started to speak to Rio in a low-pitched flood of Italian. It was just as though she wasn't there, and she had had enough of that throughout that endless meal. She had married an Italian, she reminded herself ruefully. Had she really thought that his family would talk in English just for her benefit? What was she…stupid or something?

She located the public phones and called the town house. However, Timothy was having a nap. Sarah offered to wake him but Holly told her not to be daft and just to leave him sleeping. Even so, denied even the small comfort of talking to her baby, Holly felt tears sting her eyes afresh. She had never felt so alone in her life.

'Holly…Jeremy told me what happened.'

It was Rio's dark, rich drawl, his hand coming to rest on her taut shoulder, and Holly gulped, fighting for composure before she could turn round. 'It doesn't matter—'

'It *does* matter—'

Holly spun round. 'Just before that, I heard another couple of your charming guests talking about my cheap dress, my hilarious accent and my *electrified* ragdoll hair—'

'Who the hell—?' Rio growled after a shaken pause at that outburst of confidence.

'They're all the same…horrible!' Holly was feeling so alienated from him that she was in no mood to accept sympathy. 'You know, *my* friends, had they been invited, might have drunk too much and laughed a lot louder, but they wouldn't have attended only to pull the bride or the groom to shreds. Where I come from, weddings are *happy* occasions. I've had more fun at a wake than I've had today!'

'Really?' Rio breathed glacially.

Finally, Holly thrust his phone back at him. 'I don't know how to get rid of that stupid message going round and round,' she framed jaggedly. 'But either you're making a mockery of me or you're being too *refined* to tell her where to get off!'

His dense black lashes screened his gaze as he studied his phone. With a fingertip he jabbed a button and the screen went blank. Even the ease with which he did that annoyed her, for she had hit every tiny button on that even tinier panel in her frustration and got nowhere. She stared up at him, saw the faint rise of dark blood scoring his cheekbones.

'You shouldn't have accessed my messages,' Rio drawled with freezing cool.

Holly could not credit the level of sheer rage that blasted through her at that facetious response, that unjust attempt to turn the blame back on her. 'Well, your simple phone wasn't *simple* enough and I couldn't get rid of the blasted thing. And what's more,' Holly snapped, truly lathered up into a steaming temper, 'you're just trying to sidestep the whole subject and I'm not so stupid that I can't see that!'

'If you raise your voice once more, I'm going to cart you out to the limo like a sack of coal,' Rio murmured with a smouldering smile full of threat.

Holly sucked in a deep, charged breath. She felt as though the top of her head might fly off with the force of unvented anger still blazing up inside her.

'So go upstairs now and get changed and we will say our goodbyes,' Rio completed in full command mode.

'Get changed into…what?' Holly queried helplessly.

'Into your going-away outfit—'

'I haven't got one,' Holly told him. 'You told me we weren't going abroad until tomorrow. It's about the only thing you *did* tell me. I mean, you didn't mention the two hundred guests, the press or the hotel reception either.'

'I can't believe you didn't pack anything.' Rio was impervious to that blatant invitation to take their argument into a new and fresh dimension. 'But I presume you want to throw your bouquet.'

'You must be joking. Waste my lovely flowers on this crowd?' Holly shrugged a rigid shoulder not very successfully and stuck her nose in the air.

Fifteen minutes later they were in the limousine and seated in silence. Indeed, the silence went on and on and on until it seemed to howl in her ears like a gathering storm, clawing at her nerves.

'You have gorgeous hair,' Rio murmured in a gritty tone. 'If you heard anyone comparing that glorious mane of yours to a ragdoll's, it was pure bitchiness. As for your gown, it looks wonderful, and if it was cheap it was the find of the century. Your accent's cute, it's you. I can't imagine you without it.'

Holly snatched in a shuddering breath but said nothing

'Jeremy was drunk and he is very sorry but, let's face it, he wasn't to know the bride would be in the public bar. I don't like what he said and I'm angry that you should've been hurt but I really don't give a damn what people say!'

'Like Rhett Butler…?' she squeezed out shakily.

'He walked away. I'm not about to…*not* on my wedding night,' Rio purred like a predatory tiger on the prowl, his earthy intonation sending a quiver of helpless awareness down her sensitive spine. 'As for the text message you saw. It was an old message. I wasn't aware it was still stored and it's now been deleted.'

'People think you got me pregnant and that that's why you broke up with your fiancée. I don't like being stuck with the blame.'

'It's a five-day wonder, not worth worrying about.'

'Was…*she*?'

The silence hummed as if she had turned on a turbo switch. She could literally feel his rising tension.

'At one time I thought so, and then I realised that she wasn't.'

'I'd kind of like to know what went wrong,' Holly admitted, but only after a long pause to see if he added anything more.

'I don't want to discuss that. It happened before I met you and has nothing to do with you,' Rio countered with cool emphasis.

In receipt of that snub, Holly felt flags of pink mortification unfurl in her cheeks. Well, he hadn't missed and hit the wall there, had he? Christabel was not to be talked about. Only at that point did Holly notice that they appeared to be leaving the city behind them. 'Where are we going?'

'We're spending the night at my country house and flying out to the Maldives tomorrow.'

She had never even heard of the Maldives and once again felt crucified by her own ignorance. All those hazy schooldays she had sat daydreaming and looking out of windows, giggling at notes passed between her friends, never, ever appreciating that some day she might regret not taking school seriously. *He* probably had a university degree, she thought with a sinking heart. Every time she opened her mouth she was at risk of dropping herself into a big black hole of embarrassment.

'I've asked for your cases to be sent down to the Priory. I assume you can get by without Timothy until tomorrow when we all meet up at the airport.'

Holly swallowed hard and nodded in reluctant silence. It had not been a great wedding. She had been too nervous and her self-esteem was still too low for her to feel confident in such exalted company. She so much wanted their marriage to work but she could not feel she had made much of a start.

'Are you *still* in love with her?' Holly hadn't even known that she was about to ask that question, but even as the anxious words escaped her lips she saw that that was what she most feared: that every moment he spent with her he might be fighting the desire to be with the unknown Christabel.

Rio did not pretend to misunderstand. 'No.'

Slowly she breathed again and her tension eased. Obviously something pretty serious must have happened for him to break off his engagement to Christabel. She did not feel he was a here today, gone tomorrow sort of bloke. So she had nothing to worry about and it would be very foolish of her to risk spoiling the early days of their marriage with pointless regret and envy that *she* did not have his love. She would just have to make herself lovable, which meant finding out where the Maldives were and learning Italian and trying to put him first rather than Timothy.

Some time later, at the end of the long, winding, wooded drive that the limo had traversed, an enormous Gothic pile in mellow stone met Holly's stunned gaze. Against a backdrop of mature trees and smooth green lawns, the house looked magnificent.

'How old is it?' Holly's attention lingered on the innumerable diamond-paned windows and turrets and the hotpotch of different roof levels.

'The earliest part of the building has been dated to the twelfth century but the main building works took place four hundred years later, although, of course, it has been altered in many ways since then. Marchmont Priory was my mother's family home.' Rio assisted her out of the limo. 'She stays here in the warmer months of the year.'

Old words were carved into the weathered stone lintel above the heavy oak door. Elizabethan English, welcoming all to the Priory, Rio explained before sweeping his curious bride up into his arms and carrying her in traditional style over the threshold. There was no sign even of who had opened the door and she commented on that.

'The staff are engaged in tactful invisibility,' Rio informed her.

Laughing at that explanation, Holly let her admiring gaze roam over the worn flagstone floor and the inviting fire burning in the giant stone fireplace. There was a wonderful atmosphere of peace and comfort.

'It's just beautiful,' she told him.

Rio set her down and tugged her face up so that he could gaze down into her eyes. 'So you don't think it's a little shabby and outdated?'

'No, it's glorious…it feels like a proper home, you know, not all perfect and fancy like the town house.'

Rio sent her an appreciative smile that made her heart lurch inside her. 'I confess that I've always loved it just as it is. As a kid, I used to run wild here with my English cousins.'

'What were you like as a kid?' Holly was smiling,

happiness enclosing her in a protective cocoon, all her earlier uncertainties set behind her and forgotten. She loved him. It might kind of embarrass her that she felt that strongly after so short a time but just then she felt that there was absolutely nothing that she would not do to make him happy.

'Spoilt rotten. Only-child syndrome. Got everything I ever wanted and more, *cara mia*…ah, forgot, terms of endearment are on the forbidden list,' Rio mocked.

'Not now we're married,' Holly hastened to assure him as his hand settled on her spine to draw her closer and her pulses began racing.

'Makes a difference, does it?'

Holly nodded.

He let caressing fingers toy with her ringlets, watched her arch towards him in instinctive response, seeking out the hard heat of his lean, strong body. His stunning dark golden eyes flamed and he bent his head and brought his mouth swooping down on hers with an irresistible passion that she felt right down to her curling toes.

When Holly emerged from that scorching first move she was being carried up the big carved staircase and she was weak with the strength of her own longing.

Shouldering open a door, Rio glanced down at her with a look of amusement. 'I'll close the curtains for you if you like…'

It was only early evening and she blushed and shook her bright head, taking the opportunity to scan the big wood-panelled room and the oak four-poster bed, resplendent in dark red brocade drapes that glowed in the fading light. A beautiful arrangement of white lilies adorned a table near the burning fire. A fire in a bedroom. She could hardly believe the luxury of it.

Rio lowered her to the floor and began removing her jewellery piece by piece. When he realised that her earrings were tied on, he surveyed her in wonderment.

'I need to get my ears pierced…it's just I'm a bit squeamish about that sort of thing,' Holly admitted ruefully.

She followed him to the doorway of the most incredible Victorian bathroom that also rejoiced in its own fire and watched him locate a pair of scissors. He was so beautiful, she thought with an inner ache of possessiveness that seemed to squeeze at her very heart. Daylight picked up the blue-black tint of his luxuriant hair, already ruffled by her disrespectful fingertips. She studied that bold, vibrant profile with consuming fascination that he was *her* husband. That against all the odds someone like her should have ended up with someone like him. He cut the thread with which she had attached the earrings and smoothed a finger over the tiny red score marks left behind.

'Why did you hurt yourself like that?'

'I didn't want to lose them.' That he had asked her to wear them went unspoken.

He removed his tie, undid his collar and tossed his jacket down onto a chair. Suddenly she felt shy, shy as she had been before the revelation of that first experience with him. But now there was a wicked burn beneath the shyness, a tingling expectation she could not repress. She just looked at him and she wanted him. It was that simple and it had been that way from the first moment for her.

'I'm glad you couldn't get changed, *bella mia*,' Rio

confided lazily, scorching golden eyes flaring over her slender figure. 'I spent half the day fantasising about undoing those very provocative laces.'

'Did you?' Beneath the tight bodice, her breasts were stirring and lifting, the tender peaks straining to taut points. Momentarily she was embarrassed by her own susceptibility to a certain look, a certain tone in that dark, deep drawl. He just generated the most impossible level of excitement inside her and he did it without even trying.

'I love the way you watch me. Like there is no other guy in the world for you.'

Well, there wasn't for her, but it was no longer a sentiment she wanted to brandish, not for the benefit of a male who had informed her that he thought he could get *fond* of her. If he had to think about it too much, the likelihood was that he would never get beyond lust and liking. And she wanted a lot more, knew it in that instant, saw it as clear as day. She wanted him to love her, *really* love her, the way he must have loved his ex-girlfriend

'You're all warmth and promise and desire...' Rio drew her back against him, brushed her bronze-coloured hair out of his path and let his mouth press against a taut, slim shoulder. 'And it fires me up every time I look at you.'

'Oh...' A slight sound was wrenched from Holly as she trembled in reaction to the heat of his knowing mouth against her cooler skin. He knew exactly where to touch her. Her head tipped back against his muscular chest, throat extending as she struggled to breathe again, eyes sliding languorously shut. She felt as if the very blood in her veins was turning liquid with longing.

'You match this room. I ought to be wearing a Tudor doublet and a plumed hat,' Rio teased thickly, his proud dark head bent over hers as she opened her eyes and saw them etched together in the carved mirror adorning the table set in front of the tall windows. She watched long brown fingers pluck loose the laces with studied slowness and her heart raced. She pushed helplessly back against him, already aroused beyond belief just by the contact of his big, powerful body against hers.

'The Tudor bridegroom was probably a pig,' Holly mumbled, recalling that much from her history lessons on the subservient role of women through the ages.

'Not necessarily. There are love letters and diaries stored in the library downstairs that tell a very different story.' Rio loosened the laces level by level until her anticipation was at such screaming pitch that she was ashamed of herself.

He released his breath in a soft, sexy hiss as he discovered that she was not wearing a bra. Embarrassed, she mumbled, 'My bra showed through the silk at the back and I took it off again—'

'Don't apologise for what I like, *cara*.' He eased down the dress from her shoulders and shimmied the soft fabric down her arms so that it fell to her hips, baring her full breasts to his view and attention. Her breath caught audibly in her throat as he let his expert fingers roam over her achingly sensitive nipples, catching the swollen buds between thumb and forefinger.

He might as well have set a torch to kindling inside her, for the strength in her lower limbs just dissolved, legs shaking under her as she fell back against him, the whole of her consumed by the power of her own almost agonised response. With a husky laugh he gathered her up with easy strength and laid her down on the big bed.

Rio gazed down at her, lean, strong face intent. 'Your response to me is the biggest erotic buzz I have ever had.'

Odd how that assurance seemed to both reassure and undermine, she reflected as the wave of weakness lessened while he plucked off her shoes and began to tug her gown from beneath her hips. On the one hand, it did not say much for his intimate experiences with other women, which delighted her, but on the other hand, it suggested all over again that it was her longing for him which was her strongest attraction, and that was humiliating.

'*Dio mio...*' Rio backed off a step, the better to appreciate the sheer stockings, diminutive briefs and the blue garter his bride wore. His shimmering scrutiny lit on her hot self-conscious face and he flashed her a wolfish smile. 'Full marks for surprising me.'

'What do I have to do to get a ten?' she heard herself whisper.

'Just lie there. I'm in a very uncritical mood,' Rio murmured with considerable amusement. 'And during the next couple of weeks I intend to teach you everything I want you to know, *bella mia*.'

She watched him peel off his shirt with scant ceremony and dispense with his well-cut trousers. Watching him thrilled her, she decided, so she could hardly blame him for enjoying her visual attention. He was all bronzed, hair-roughened skin and taut, strong muscles with not an ounce of superfluous flesh on his athletic frame. She couldn't tear her gaze from him or unlock herself from the mesmeric hold of those dark golden eyes. It had barely been four days since he had first made love to her but her body was behaving as if it had been denied for months.

He came down over her, teasing fingers flirting with the garter. 'An old-fashioned girl?'

'Yeah...'

'So what was old?'

'That jewellery you loaned me.'

'It's not on loan and that set is only a small part of it,' Rio informed her, running an unsettling hand in an exploring motion down over a slim stockinged thigh as he stared down at her. 'It's all yours. I'm the head of my family and you are my wife.'

And then he kissed her and it was different from the last time in a way she could not identify. Then within seconds she lost the ability to discriminate and to think. A kind of slow, drugging heat began to warm her in secret places and she speared her fingers into his thick, silky hair, raising herself to him, unable to restrain her own hungry impatience.

Rio settled her hands back to the bed and lifted his head, heavily lidded eyes narrowed to a glint of hot, determined gold. 'We've got all night...I want this to last—'

'I don't want to beg...' she mumbled shakily before she could think better of that admission, for every time she remembered how she had behaved the last time not even a recollection of the ecstasy could wipe out the sense that she had demeaned herself and been something less than she should have been.

Slight colour burnished the sudden taut angle of his fabulous cheekbones. 'It won't *be* like that again.'

He framed her face with his hands and claimed her

lips again, and it was so sweet but so intense that she could feel the burst of heat low in her stomach, the quivering readiness of her own wretched body, and it crossed her mind then that he did not need to *make* her beg. He turned her on so much she might well end up begging all on her own. He eased himself down over her and found her swollen nipples with his mouth, suckling her tender flesh, sending arrows of arousal right to the very heart of her so that her hips shifted and squirmed against the mattress. He drifted on down, skimming her panties away in a motion so smooth that she only noticed the cool of the air hitting her where she was warm and damp.

'Relax...' Rio urged thickly as she tensed instinctively.

She could not comprehend such an instruction when he was doing things to her that made relaxation a total impossibility. She shut her eyes, panting for breath and restraint, striving to be what he wanted without even knowing quite what that was but dimly suspecting that greater control was what it was all about. But keeping still, preventing her hands from rising to his broad shoulders and clinging, was the most dreadful challenge when she was trembling and hot and far too eager for his every move.

He let his lips travel down over her flexing tummy and her spine arched of its own volition, the burning tingle in her pelvis already starting to torment her. 'Stop it...' he told her raggedly.

And then he roved in a direction that was entirely unexpected and her startled eyes flew wide. 'What are you *doing*?' she gasped in dismay.

'What do you think?' Rio angled a dark, wicked

smile up at her and eased her thighs apart, his intent unhidden.

Her face burned. She wrestled with fierce embarrassment, curiosity and secret craving, and while she was engaged in that massive inner struggle he splayed his hands beneath her slim hips and just did what he wanted to do. And the chorus of urgent complaint she'd believed to be on her lips remained unspoken, because the instant that he made contact with the most sensitive spot in her whole shivering body was the same moment that any idea of her staying in control was vanquished.

Never had she ever imagined that level of sensation, so it was like one glorious shock piled onto another, so that she lurched mindless and wordless from one splintering wave of excitement into the next, and all the time the tormenting hunger was notching up higher inside her. She moaned, she sobbed and she jerked in a wild response beyond any denial, and when she was within what felt like touching distance of the satisfaction she craved with every sense he settled himself between her thighs and surged into her with measured force and cool.

And suddenly she was snatched up into the eye of the storm. The feel of his hot, hard fullness stretching the slick, wet centre of her inner heat just exploded through her in a cascade of multicoloured, blinding sensation and she hit a peak of ecstasy that burned through her in an explosive flood of pleasure.

'Good?' Rio tugged her head up and kissed her breathless in the aftermath, male satisfaction and fire in his smouldering gaze as he looked down at her and started to move again, slowly, almost teasingly, allowing her shaken still trembling body a little time for recovery.

'Unbelievable…' Holly muttered shakily.

'Oh, you can believe, *bella mia*,' Rio asserted in ragged promise, sending a reawakening surge of excitement through her with a subtle encircling motion of his lean hips. 'We're going to have an incredible honeymoon.'

Getting out of bed the next morning was something of a challenge for Holly and she was pretty much shell-shocked by the amount of raw energy Rio had and his ability to spring out of bed as though he had had a full eight hours' sleep.

Yet the urgency with which she longed to hold Timothy in her arms again would have sent her to the airport at dawn, had that been an option. As Rio had promised, her cases had been brought down to the Priory. She dressed at speed but had to sit through a long breakfast while Rio behaved as though they had all the time in the world.

Her baby was not *his* baby, Holly reminded herself. They were only having one night away from Timothy, which was very, very reasonable of him. How many blokes wanted to drag a nanny and a baby off on their honeymoon? But he had not even mentioned the option of leaving Timothy behind.

At the airport, the minute Timothy laid anxious eyes on his mother he went frantic, waving his arms and legs in excitement and relief. Sarah confided that Holly's son had had a rather unsettled night. Holly's eyes stung with tears and she got Timothy out of his seat restraint so fast there might have been a fire alarm howling. Clasping his warm, cuddly little body to her, she hugged him tight, only becoming conscious of her husband's scrutiny some minutes later.

Rio looked grim. 'Don't you ever let me *do* that to you again,' he breathed in a driven undertone of reproof.

Holly turned pale. 'Do…what?'

'Timothy spent the night fretting for you and you couldn't get here fast enough this morning because you missed him so much,' he spelt out flatly. 'I didn't know I was doing that to you. Why didn't you say something?'

Too many frank words hovered on her lips. Timothy was not his son and there had to be limits to even his tolerance at this stage of their marriage, she thought fearfully. The very last thing she wanted was to turn him off with the downside of parenting. He was used to complete freedom of choice and he was not used to the restrictions of being with a woman with a child either.

'It was only one night. I just didn't want to spoil things—'

'You just *did*,' Rio drawled ruefully. 'Sarah told me he was inconsolable and she called the doctor out to check him just in case there was something else wrong. Timothy isn't secure enough to do without you for very long.'

Holly was ashamed of that truth.

'But I couldn't have done without you last night either, *bella mia*.' Rio slanted her a sudden flashing smile of forgiveness that turned her heart over inside her tight chest. 'Maybe we're going to have to work out some way of dividing you in two.'

CHAPTER SEVEN

Two DAYS LATER, lying on the sun-deck that overhung the lagoon, Holly trailed idle fingertips in the crystal-clear water below. She could see every rise and dip of the soft sand below, each tiny multicoloured fish darting beneath the sparkling sunlit surface.

She thought the Maldives were a paradise on earth. The lagoon was ringed by lush green palms and vegetation. The sky was a deep, dense cloudless blue and the white sand on the beach merged with a sea the colour of turquoise. Their magnificent villa was set on its own tiny island where privacy was assured, but Rio had informed her that more populated places lay only a short boat trip away on one of the thousand-plus coral islands that made up the Maldives nation.

'What's so fascinating?' Rio crouched down beside her to ask.

'The lagoon is like a giant rock pool,' Holly confided. 'It takes me back to when I was a kid and my aunt used to take me to the seaside.'

'Not your parents?'

Holly levered back on to her knees and collided with stunning eyes that reflected the golden sunlight. Three days into their honeymoon, her heartbeat was still hitting earthquake mode every time he got close—and that seemed to be *most* of the time.

'Dad could never get away from the farm,' she explained.

'You must miss your parents a great deal.' Rio made that observation with quiet understanding.

Holly nodded agreement. 'But hopefully not for much longer.'

His ebony brows drew together. 'I don't follow.'

'Once we've been married a couple of months, I'm going to tell Mum and Dad about us and then we can go and visit,' Holly outlined with a slight flush. 'That way there won't be so many awkward questions about how long we've known each other and so on.'

Rio dealt her an incredulous scrutiny. 'Are you telling me that your parents are still *alive*?'

It was her turn to look confused. 'What else would they be?'

'I thought they were dead. When we first met you told me that you had *nobody*,' Rio reminded her.

'I didn't mean they were dead!'

'But you didn't even mention the possibility of inviting your parents to our wedding! Of course I assumed they were gone. What else was I to think?'

Biting her lip with discomfiture, Holly averted her eyes from the level probe of his and released a rueful sigh. 'Mum and Dad were very upset when I got pregnant. They sent me to live with my aunt in Manchester. I was supposed to give Timothy up for adoption and then go back home again. But once he was born I couldn't do it, so that was that… I was on my own.'

'When did you last speak to your parents?'

'A week after Timothy was born,' Holly admitted

half under her breath. 'But I've written to them a few
times to let them know that I was all right—'

'But you *weren't* all right!' Rio cut in drily.

Holly ignored that reminder. 'I didn't give them an
address, though, because I didn't want them feeling they
had to get involved. It wouldn't have been fair. I made
my choice,' she completed gruffly.

Rio closed his hand over the taut fingers clenching
on her slim thigh. 'You made the right choice.'

'Well, until now it didn't seem like it…it seemed like
I was the most useless mother ever,' Holly admitted, her
throat thickening with sudden tears.

Curving a strong arm round her downbent shoulders,
Rio raised her up. 'You had a lot of bad luck.'

Holly looked up into the beautiful tawny-gold eyes
set in that lean, dark, devastating face. Suddenly, he was
claiming her lips with devouring hunger, crushing her
softer curves into his hard, muscular frame, giving her
all the reassurance she needed. Her heart pounded like
crazy beneath that surprise onslaught and she clung to
his broad shoulders to stay upright.

Rio lifted his dark head again with a ragged laugh.
'I should be cooling the wild passion. You might be
pregnant, *bella mia*.'

'I don't think so.' She had had a headache earlier
and only a minute ago she had almost succumbed to
tears, both of which were familiar signs to her of PMS.

'Why?'

'I just know—'

'But you didn't *know* when it came to Timothy, did
you?'

Holly reddened. 'I don't think I wanted to know—'

Rio stared down at her, shimmering eyes intense

above his hard cheekbones. 'I hope that isn't the case with *my* baby.'

'How could you think that?' Holly was taken aback by that undercurrent of dark suspicion in his response. 'But it would be better all round if I wasn't pregnant this soon...people will talk if I have a baby short of the nine-month mark.'

Rio gave a fluid shrug that signified his supreme indifference to such gossip.

'Well, maybe it doesn't matter to you,' Holly conceded tautly. 'But I wasn't exactly happy when I was carrying Timothy, and if I have another baby I'd like it to be different. I'd like to feel proud that I'm pregnant and not feel that people are judging me or sneering at me behind my back.'

In receipt of that frank speech, Rio groaned out loud and eased her close again. '*Dio mio*...of course you want it to be different, but believe me, whatever happens, it will be.'

Did Rio actually *want* her to have conceived his child? Holly wondered anxiously. As she was almost certain that she had not, she could not help worrying that perhaps his certainty that she would so easily fall pregnant again had thrust him into a marriage that he might just as quickly regret. That very evening, her period arrived. She was putting Timothy to bed when she chose to tell Rio that there was not going to be a baby.

Rio tensed, strong bone-structure tightening, and then he gave her the heartbreaking smile that always made her feel as if she was the only woman in the world for him. 'It's too soon for you anyway, *tesoro mio*. We should wait until Timothy is a little older.'

'Yes...' But, perverse as human nature was, Holly

then found herself wishing that she *had* conceived, for she sensed that with Rio a baby would be a major and welcome event. Timothy was undeniably enthralled by the tall, dark male who had become part of his life, and Rio was so good to him.

However, the world Holly was living in still did not feel quite real to her. Although she worked hard at hiding those stabs of insecurity from Rio, she could not help being scared that suddenly it would all be snatched away again. Had she been pregnant with his child, perhaps she would have felt safer, she acknowledged uneasily, ashamed of that lowering reality.

Holly watched while Rio tasted.

'This is sensational,' he breathed appreciatively. 'What is it called?'

'Somerset apple cake.'

'You're an incredible cook.'

'I started learning when I was four. Baking skills are a matter of pride in a farming community,' Holly told him with a rueful grin, light playing on her animated face as she sat cross-legged on the bed, clad in a colourful silk sarong. 'But to tell you the truth, Mum was really grooming me for the neighbour's son. She thought Robert was wonderful but I just didn't fancy him—'

'Did he *fancy* you?' His beautiful mouth slanted with vibrant amusement at the term.

'Well, just then I think he fancied anything female,' Holly confided, heart lurching predictably in receipt of that glorious smile of his. 'He was dating one of my mates when I left home and his parents didn't approve because she was a real townie.'

The phone by the bed buzzed and Rio answered it.

She listened to him talk in Italian and just watched him
while she melted into a hopeless puddle of love and
longing. They had been married for exactly twenty-
one days and already she could not imagine existing
without him, could not even accept that she could have
lived for twenty years on the same planet without being
aware that the love of her life was breathing the same
air. For that was what he was: Rio, this male who had
become so impossibly precious and important to her
every waking hour.

He was just...*perfect*. Entertaining, clever, caring.
He spoilt her like mad. He was always buying her loads
of stuff she didn't need, introducing her to fantastic
new experiences and somehow making every single
day seem special. She had learned to water-ski, snor-
kel and sail. He was also fantastic with kids. Timothy
was enslaved, and adoring Rio seemed to be good for
Timothy because her son was much more confident.
And a restaurant menu would never terrify her again
because they ate out most evenings and she was familiar with most of the terms now and quite happy to ask
if she came across anything she didn't understand. She
had also finally had her ears pierced, but her nerve had
almost failed her at the last minute and only a fear of
embarrassing Rio had got her through it.

Nobody was perfect, her more sane self cautioned,
so she worked hard at coming up with a flaw or two.
Rio didn't need much sleep. He was incredibly active,
but good diet and lots of exercise had increased her
own energy. He was naturally dominant, but when he
had been teaching her to water-ski that had been welcome because the first time she sank below the waves
she would have given up if he hadn't bullied her into

repeated efforts. She had ended up having a fabulous time, she reflected forgivingly.

Indeed, every morning she woke up in Rio's arms she felt as if she had won the jackpot. All her insecurity had evaporated. No man had ever treated her so well and no man had ever wanted her to the degree that Rio appeared to want her. Face warming, she scanned his bold, bronzed profile and the long, sexy, indolent slump of his lean, hard, muscular frame. There was something very reassuring about a bloke who could not keep his hands off her for longer than a couple of hours, she thought with a secretive smile. Obviously, he was pretty highly sexual, but he made her feel as though she was irresistible. The strong attraction between them was anything but one-sided. Was it any wonder that she was blissfully happy and more madly in love than ever?

So what if he didn't love her? There was time enough for that to come. He did do romantic stuff. He gave her surprise presents and held her hand and seemed truly fascinated by every mundane aspect of her previous existence. And in three long weeks they had not had a single argument. She didn't count screaming at him when he told her to get back on the water-skis and not act like a baby. Or that time he had dragged her out of bed before dawn to go fishing and cheerfully told her that she ought to stand up for herself more often. And when she had done so five minutes later he hadn't liked it at all.

'You're coming with me,' he had delivered in full command mode.

And much later, when she had been even more bored out of her mind than she had expected to be on that stupid boat, she had asked him why it had been so important that she join him.

'I just like you around,' Rio had murmured in some surprise that she should need to ask.

Only then had it occurred to her that a bloke who had been twenty-four hours a day in her company but who could still demand the twenty-fifth hour, figuratively speaking, was paying her quite a compliment.

Rio slung the phone aside with an impatient sigh. 'Business is intruding even before we fly home tomorrow. My mother's at the Priory and expecting to meet you but I'm afraid that I have to head for New York more or less immediately.'

'Oh…' Her heart sank at the prospect of the parting ahead, and then she scolded herself for being too possessive.

'I know it's far from ideal but I really don't think another raincheck would be acceptable. Do you think you could handle meeting her on your own?' Rio reached for her with the unquestioning self-assurance of a male aware that his attentions were always welcome, his question clearly rhetorical.

Seated on the edge of the bed, he set Holly down on her feet between his long, hair-roughened thighs while he proceeded to ease loose the knot on her sarong. At that moment, with her heart racing, he could have asked her to walk into a fire and she would have gone in blind faith. She trembled, reacting to the tiny flame already igniting deep in her pelvis, the delicious wave of anticipation already currenting through her. No matter how often he made love to her, it was always the same.

'I ache just looking at you…' Rio confided thickly as the sarong dropped to the floor and his appreciative appraisal settled on pouting breasts crowned by straining pink nipples.

'Me too…' She felt wanton, breathless, entirely in the grip of quivering excitement.

He touched her, toyed with her aching flesh and stripped off her bikini briefs to run a seeking hand down to the damp welcome already awaiting him. By the time he tipped her back on the bed she was a willing sacrifice. Straightening, he peeled off his T-shirt and shed his chinos, revealing the awesome thrust of his virile shaft. Liquid longing filled her and she pushed away an instinctive shame at her own powerful response to his bold masculinity. He laced long, indolent fingers into her hair, drawing her up, encouraging her to caress him with her mouth, an exercise that she had been stunned to discover raised her own level of arousal to an almost embarrassing degree.

'You're so incredibly sensual…' Rio breathed in a roughened growl of male satisfaction. 'I'll have to drag myself away from you tomorrow. You're turning me into a sex addict, *cara*.'

Certainly it wasn't very long before he tumbled her back on the bed with a groan of raw impatience and sank into her hard and fast and without ceremony, sending her excitement racing to such a peak that a strangled cry of joy was wrenched from her. And then there was nothing for her but the relentless rhythm of his lean, hard body over and inside hers and the intense pleasure that sent her rocketing to an ecstatic height with his name on her lips.

'Sex with you *is*…' Rio mused reflectively in the aftermath, making her tense a little, for she would have much preferred him to use a less earthy term and she was unsettled by the rather disconcerted light in his dark-as-midnight eyes, '…absolutely sensational, *bella mia*.'

'Good,' Holly mumbled, both arms wrapped round him tight as she revelled in the lean finger stroking her cheekbone and the kiss he dropped on her brow. She was far too sensitive, she told herself. So Rio didn't talk about his emotions, but could she consider that unusual? Even the day her own father had cried over her being pregnant the older man had uttered few words. Her male schoolmates had been more given to off-colour jokes and clumsy flirtation, and Jeff had never really talked about anything but himself.

'Go to sleep…' Rio urged lazily. 'We have a very early start in the morning.'

During the flight the next day, Rio was fully occupied with his laptop. Bored with watching the films on offer, Holly went to check on Timothy, but he was sound asleep and their nanny was catnapping too. With a smile at the picture they made, Holly returned to the main cabin and decided to entertain herself with the pile of glossy magazines which she had seen Sarah absorbed in earlier.

She leafed through the pages, pausing to admire the fabulous fashion, only to be bemused by the belated acknowledgement that she could now probably afford to buy anything she liked, courtesy of her incredibly generous husband. Shooting his darkly handsome profile at the other end of the cabin a tender lingering scrutiny, she settled down to read.

A full-page shot of a vaguely familiar beautiful blonde wearing the ultimate in country casuals caught her attention and she scanned the name below. Of course, she had known that face! It was Chrissie Kent, the model who had become a household name after doing an entertaining series of luxury car advertisements on television a couple of years earlier. Holly admired the handsome pair of springer spaniels seated at Chrissie's feet and thought that the model must be a genuinely nice person if she made time for pets in her jet-set existence. She then turned to the opposite page, only to be confronted by a far more familiar face.

Billionaire Italian tycoon, Saverio Lombardi, escorting his fiancée at the Cannes Film Festival.

A fevered pulse beginning to thump like mad at what felt like the foot of her convulsing throat, Holly read and re-read that single line and then fixedly studied the picture of Rio and Chrissie Kent together. Perspiration beaded Holly's short upper lip. She was in shock, so much shock that she just sat there for a long time. Rio had been engaged to Chrissie Kent?

Christabel...of course, Christabel. The woman was incredibly beautiful, pale blonde hair falling waterfall-straight either side of her stunning face. Her fantastic figure was sheathed in a daring cerise-pin satin gown slit to the thigh and so tight that only one in a million women could have got away with it. She even had legs that went on and on and on to the most abnormal but flattering length.

Tummy unsettled by the revelation that had burst like a bombshell upon her, Holly began to read the article and turned the page, only to see Christabel seated on a silk-upholstered sofa in the town house where she herself had once dared to sit. Without warning, Holly also remembered how she had posed and clowned for Rio while she paraded designer fashion and pretended to *be* a model. Instantly she wanted to jump out of his jet without a parachute. Instantly she felt humiliated beyond belief.

But what shook her most of all was that the magazine was not that old an issue. Only six weeks ago Rio had *still* been engaged and had *still* been committed to a summer wedding with another woman. Like a bloodhound on the scent, Holly began to leaf frantically through the remaining magazines in search of further information. But when she found the facts that she had believed she wanted in a weekly magazine of much more humble origin, she wished that she had missed seeing it.

The issue which announced the sudden 'shock' break-up of Rio and Christabel had come on sale only a week after Holly had first met Rio, and indeed also featured a small grainy photo of her own wedding and much speculation about her identity. There she was, posed on the church steps with huge scared eyes, hanging on to Rio with an extreme lack of cool. Wild curly hair was blowing round her in a messy tangle. She looked a total fright. She looked like the bride of Frankenstein...

CHAPTER EIGHT

'YOU'VE BEEN VERY quiet,' Rio told Holly in the limo that collected them from the airport to ferry them home to the town house. 'Are you feeling all right?'

'I'm fine.' Even to Holly's own ears, her voice sounded strained, but a more expansive response was impossible with Sarah and Timothy seated beside them.

In any case, Holly still had no idea what she planned to say to Rio when she did finally get him alone. She was still mentally reeling, her mind awash with a crazy cascade of ever more confused thoughts. The anger surging higher and higher inside her was no help to her concentration. Behind the anger lurked pain and fear and a terrifying sense of betrayal. Without the smallest warning, her confidence in what she had believed to be a happy marriage had been smashed to pieces. It seemed that their relationship was built on the proverbial shifting sands rather than on firm foundations.

Faced with such unpalatable and humiliating facts, what else *was* she to think? Rio had bedded her within days of breaking up with one of the most beautiful women in the world. Christabel Kent was an icon, every male fantasy combined, but, worst of all, she was ten times closer to being Rio's equal in looks, sophistication and importance than Holly could ever hope to be. Indeed, Christabel was exactly the kind of female that men like Rio Lombardi *did* marry: a trophy wife, famous in her own right.

Common sense told Holly that Rio had married her on the rebound, and that was *very* bad news, she thought wretchedly. Rio could not have been thinking straight when he swept her off to bed on a passionate impulse. Nor could he have seriously considered what he was doing when he then insisted that he wanted her to marry him.

Only now was Holly recalling Ezio Farretti's prophetic warnings. 'He's just not himself right now and you don't want to get your feelings hurt.' Older and wiser, and knowing the situation as Holly had not, Ezio had recognised the high risk factors at play. Holly's vulnerability, Rio's volatile temperament and simple proximity had been a dangerous combination.

After all, Rio must have been with Christabel for quite some time and breaking up with her must have been traumatic, Holly reasoned painfully. Hence Rio's short temper, his need for a distraction, his sudden startling susceptibility to a youthful redhead incapable of concealing her starry-eyed admiration. In the normal way of things, Holly reckoned that Rio would barely have noticed that she was alive.

'I'll be heading back to the airport in a couple of hours,' Rio reminded her as they entered the town house. 'I'm going for a shower.'

Before she could follow him she was held back by their nanny, who needed to discuss arrangements for the weekend off she was about to take. Agreeing that

Sarah could depart that afternoon, Holly then hurried off in Rio's wake.

He was in their bedroom, already half-undressed, his shirt hanging loose, a bronzed, energising slice of muscular, hair-roughened chest on view, his potent and entirely natural sex appeal pronounced. Holly came to a halt just inside the door, her heartbeat accelerating, her mouth running dry, no matter how hard she tried not to react to him. He was so gorgeous, from the crown of his proud, dark head to the soles of his bare brown feet, and she loved him as she had never known she could love anybody. But what she had learnt from those wretched magazines had ripped her apart, not least because she knew that she *should* have received that same information from him. And the very fact that Rio had *not* told her only made her feel that her every worst fear was justified.

Rio surveyed her with level dark golden eyes. 'There is no point throwing a three-act tragedy, *cara*. It won't change anything.'

Totally disconcerted by that statement, Holly stared at him. 'What are you talking about?'

Unimpressed, Rio slanted a dark brow. 'You've been in a hellish sulk ever since it dawned on you that I'm leaving you to your own devices for the next week,' he informed her drily. 'But you'll have to get used to the idea of getting by without me when I'm away on business.'

'Will I?' Something close to a hysterical giggle feathered in Holly's tight throat as she realised how he had interpreted her silence and how he had put his own rather demeaning spin on what lay behind her behaviour.

'It'll be a challenge for you at first because you haven't made friends yet. But by this time next year you won't be dependent on me for company,' Rio asserted with confidence, strolling closer and reaching for her hands. 'You'll learn to lead your own life while I'm abroad. My mother will support you. She knows a lot of people and you can get involved in the charities we support through the foundation or, indeed, in whatever else interests you.'

Her hands jerked in the warm hold of his. Her husband knew how besotted she was with him and he thought that her poor little heart was just breaking at the prospect of surviving an entire seven days without him. And the way he was talking about a future in which they led separate lives chilled her to the marrow.

As Holly yanked her fingers free of his hectic colour fired over her cheekbones. 'Is that what Christabel would have done?'

Rio's sculpted mouth tightened, eyes hardening at what he clearly translated as an ungenerous and potentially catty response. 'What *she* might have done hardly concerns us.'

'Are you going to tell me why I had to read a flippin' magazine just to find out that your ex-girlfriend is the world-famous model Chrissie Kent?' Holly demanded half an octave higher.

Rio went very still, golden eyes gleaming from below luxuriant black lashes. 'I don't quite understand the relevance of Christabel's public profile.'

'Like heck you don't!' Holly snapped, her temper provoked by that cool, snubbing response. 'You knew I had no idea. Couldn't you at least have told me that much about her?'

Rio expelled his breath in an impatient hiss. 'I knew you'd be intimidated. I knew you would beat yourself up making stupid comparisons. So, *no*, I wasn't in a hurry to ram that fact down your throat.'

At that disconcertingly honest response, Holly lost every scrap of her feverish colour. She felt as if she was standing there naked and as see-through as clear glass. She felt humiliated that he should understand her that well and face her with her own insecurity. 'Yes, it would be a very stupid comparison to even try to attempt…wouldn't it?'

'*Santo cielo*…that's *not* what I meant!' Now anger brightened Rio's gaze, tautened his lean, strong face. 'I just felt that you'd be better equipped to deal with all that after we'd been married for a while.'

Holly's hands coiled into hurting fists. 'Oh, you know me so well, do you? You think you can predict how I'm likely to react to everything?'

'It seems that on that particular score I was accurate.'

Holly refused to be squashed. 'But then your ex-girlfriend's public profile, as you called it, was only the tip of the iceberg, wasn't it? Like when were you planning to tell me just how little time passed between you breaking up with *her* and getting involved with *me*?'

Perceptibly, Rio's big, powerful frame tensed.

'I want a date,' Holly told him feverishly. 'I want to know how much of a time lag there was.'

'Believe me, *bella mia*…you don't,' Rio countered flatly.

'It was barely even a couple of weeks…I'm right, aren't I?' Holly persisted, determined to get the truth out of him. 'Going by the date on that magazine article, it couldn't have been much longer than a couple of

weeks since you'd broken up. Why else was Ezio warning me that you weren't yourself when I first met you?'

His darkly handsome features froze. 'Thank you,
Ezio. Tell me, do you make a habit of discussing me
with my employees?'

'Oh, I'll be sure to make a habit of it from here on
in. It seems to me I've got more chance of getting an
honest answer from *other* people than from you!' Holly
condemned, refusing to be embarrassed by his freezing disapproval and defending herself. 'I still remember
what you said when you asked me to marry you. You
said you had been engaged "until relatively recently".
Which hardly suggests a gap of less than a month—'

'Leave it,' Rio cut in with ruthless bite. 'I'm going
for that shower before this ridiculous argument esca-
lates any more—'

In incredulous, seething frustration, Holly watched
him resume stripping off his clothes. Clad only in his
Calvin Kleins, he headed for the bathroom.

'I could ask Ezio,' Holly threatened between gritted
teeth, although she knew that now that they were married she would never ever go behind Rio's back like
that, or indeed place the older man in such an awkward position.

'I parted from Christabel an hour before you walked
out in front of my limo.'

Holly blinked. Those words hit her as though they
were in a foreign language she could not fathom, for in
a self-protective act her brain seemed to throw up barriers to her understanding. And then, without warning,
she grasped what he had said and there was no hiding
from it, no avoiding the reality that what he had just

admitted was a hundred times more devastating than she had expected.

Rio swung round, scanned her pale, shattered face and swore in roughened Italian, but as he moved back towards her she backed away.

Holly parted dry lips. 'An...*hour*?'

Strong jawline clenching, he studied her with grim golden eyes. 'I don't see that the precise amount of time is material in this particular case...'

An uneven laugh was dragged from Holly as she collapsed down on the side of the bed, fearful her knees were about to give way under her. An hour. Only an hour had passed between him leaving Christabel and first meeting *her*, and forty-eight hours later he had hauled her off to bed. And he expected her to accept that there was nothing relevant in that super-shrunken timeline?

'You couldn't possibly have known what you were doing,' she said sickly.

No way did she need huge experience of men to make that statement. An hour. It was laughable, terrifying, outrageous. And only two days later Rio had proven that reality to her beyond all possible doubt by doing something that she knew in her heart had been quite out of character for him: taking her to bed.

He wasn't the sort of bloke who went in for one-night stands. He wasn't the sort of bloke who got a kick out of going to bed with some woman he hardly knew just for the sheer hell of it. There were men like that but Rio wasn't one of them. Rio had a real good-taste threshold. Rio had a conscience. Rio was not an oversexed teenager with out-of-control hormones.

But Rio had one quirk which had betrayed both her

and him: it would take torture to make him talk about his own feelings. He would probably sooner slow-roast over a hot fire than admit that he had been upset and off-balance after breaking off his engagement. In fact, that was an understatement, she recognised, and hadn't she seen the evidence of how he was feeling for herself? His emotions had been seething, but more than anything she had sensed anger…anger and bitterness. Anger against himself, anger presumably against Christabel, bitterness that their relationship hadn't worked out?

'I *always* know what I'm doing.' Rio made that claim as though it was etched in stone on his soul, a credo through which he lived his entire life.

But Holly wasn't convinced. She had often thought that she knew what she was doing and then later looked back and marvelled at how persuasive other promptings could be in overruling all caution and common sense.

'What did you do? Decide to turn round and marry the very first woman you met?' Holly demanded shakily, striving for an ironic note with that question, for she was not serious in asking it.

'Believe it or not, that thought did cross my mind,' Rio ground out fiercely.

Holly just stopped breathing altogether and gazed back at him in horror.

'Only to be just as quickly set aside because I am *not* a lunatic!' Rio continued with raw force.

'But that's just what you did. You married the first woman you met. Dear heaven…I could've been anybody!' Holly gasped.

'Don't be ridiculous. Do you think I would marry just anybody?' Rio roared back at her, visibly outraged by that suggestion.

Holly lowered her head and studied her tightly linked hands. She was more or less just anybody on her own terms. She was young, female and reasonably present-able but that was that. She was trembling. 'Maybe you would if you were angry enough. Tell me, did Chris-tabel dump *you*?'

'*Per amor di Dio...* I could snap my fingers and get her back right now if I wanted her!' Rio slammed back at her.

The silence sparked like hay threatening to whoosh into flame.

'I didn't say that...' Rio groaned out loud. 'OK...I said it but I shouldn't have.'

So now she knew who had done the dumping. But now she also knew something she would have been hap-pier *not* to know: that Christabel wanted Rio back and that he was well aware of the fact. That news was like a cold wind chilling her sensitive skin.

'Just tell me why you broke up with her,' Holly prompted dry-mouthed, her tummy churning at the terrible tension in the room.

'We wanted different things,' Rio said flatly.

'What kind of different things?'

'I think that's my business and hers.'

Holly paled as if he had slapped her. Then she got up and began to walk towards the door but Rio was ahead of her. He leant back against the door and trained smouldering golden eyes on her, his angry frustration unconcealed. 'This is *crazy*—'

'Get out of my way,' Holly demanded.

Instead, Rio closed strong brown arms round her and jerked her up against him. 'No,' he said, soft and succinct. 'I won't let you make Christabel a bone of contention between us.'

'You're the one doing that...' Holly condemned chokily, tears of stress and agonised confusion clogging up her vocal cords.

Long fingers swept up to frame her cheekbones. Her bright blue eyes evaded his. She was rigid, refusing to give an inch, but then he took her by surprise. He lowered his dark head and drove her lips hungrily apart with his own, his tongue delving deep into the moist interior. Angry, unhappy, confused, she fought her own response for the first time.

She shivered against him, insanely conscious of every hot, taut angle of his lean, muscular body, and she thrust her hand against his shoulder to push him away. But her enervated state of mind made her all too vulnerable and the sudden excitement burning like a betraying flame inside her was her undoing. Just as quickly, she was kissing him back with the same breathless fervour.

He lifted her up, brought her down on the bed, came down over her. He lifted her skirt and brought up her knees to deprive her of her briefs. And all the time he was taking her mouth time after time with the same drugging, demanding heat and her heart was racing like an express train, every fibre of her being madly aware of him and on fire.

By the time he slid between her parted thighs and entered her she was more out of control than she had ever been, overwhelmed by a wild, desperate craving which left room for nothing else. The excitement of release threw her to the heights and then dropped her down again lower than ever before.

'Now come join me for a shower,' Rio murmured

huskily, gazing down at her with a scorching satisfaction as he leant down to kiss her.

Sick at her own weakness, but outraged by his manipulation, Holly took him by surprise by twisting her head away and jack-knifing out from beneath him to roll off the bed. Clawing down her skirt, her face feverishly flushed and her eyes glittering like blue sapphires, Holly shot him a look of furious mortification.

'Do you think that's likely to solve anything?' she snapped in a voice that shook with the force of her disturbed emotions.

A wolfish and irreverent smile slashed Rio's darkly handsome features. 'There's nothing *to* solve, *bella mia.*'

The anger went out of her then, leaving her feeling hollow and miserable. The craven part of her wished she had not forced him to tell her even part of the truth. One hour, she kept on thinking, one hour between leaving Christabel and meeting her. *Of course* he had been on the rebound. How could their marriage have a hope of surviving? He would eventually wake up and feel trapped with her and Timothy, marvel at his own impulsiveness, his own failure to take a long-term view. Why would he stay with her when he didn't love her? Why would he settle for her when he could have Christabel Kent or her equivalent as a wife? Off with the old, on with the new...but life wasn't that simple. Sooner or later, Rio would regret marrying her.

As the door thudded shut on the bathroom Holly sagged. He wouldn't discuss Christabel. Why not? Loyalty? Or lingering feelings? And did he even care how she felt, knowing that Christabel would still take him back? A relationship that had lasted almost two years when she herself had only been with him for a month wouldn't be easily forgotten. Was she making herself unhappy over nothing? What, after all, had changed? Just twelve hours ago, she had been so happy.

Timothy was having a nap when she went into the nursery. She was chatting to Sarah when Ezio phoned to tell her that she had a visitor waiting downstairs. A Mr. Danby. Holly paled. Jeff? Jeff had come to see her? How on earth had he known where she was and what could he possibly want?

Jeff was in the drawing room. Slim and dark, he was more smartly dressed than she had ever seen him, but he had grown a goatee beard and a tiny clipped moustache that struck her as affected. And somehow he seemed much smaller than she recalled him being.

'Well, don't you look good?' Jeff remarked, studying the fashionable skirt and cashmere twin-set that fitted her slim figure like a glove. 'But then, why not? I suppose you have a whole string of credit cards now—'

'How did you find out where I was living?' Holly interrupted, hating the familiar way he had eyed her up and carefully keeping her distance.

'After seeing your wedding photos splashed all over the newspapers, I didn't need to hire a detective. You've fairly landed on your feet here, haven't you?' He glanced round the beautifully furnished drawing room and his full mouth twisted in acknowledgement of the staggering change in her circumstances. 'Well, more power to you. It's great that you've done so well for yourself—'

'What are you doing here?' Holly pressed unevenly, for every time she looked at him she remembered the shock of that fist coming into her face, the speed with which he had lost his head and attacked her.

'Obviously, I want to see my son,' Jeff informed her.

What colour remained in Holly's face drained away. 'Why would you suddenly want to do that?'

'A boy ought to know his father.' Jeff gave her a smug and pious smile, relishing her bewilderment and dismay.

Nausea stirred inside Holly. 'You said you'd make me sorry I was ever born if I told anyone that Timothy was your child. And when we needed you, where were you? You didn't want to know—'

'Things were awkward that day—'

'Awkward? Timothy and I ended up on the streets with nowhere to go! You didn't give two hoots about either of us. If you want to see the child you have the nerve to call your son, when are you planning to start paying towards his keep?' Holly demanded, her strained voice rising in volume. 'Do you think that you can just walk in here and—?'

An arm curved round her taut spine from behind, startling her, for she had not heard the door open, and then Rio murmured, 'It's OK, *cara.* I'll deal with this.'

'I'm afraid Holly and I didn't part best friends.' Jeff grimaced, moving forward with an insincere smile and extending his hand to Rio. 'I'm Jeff, Timothy's father.'

'Saverio Lombardi…'

Holly was appalled when Rio shook hands with her ex-boyfriend. It felt like a betrayal. She was equally appalled at the threat of being forced to trust a man with Jeff's temper around Timothy. She could not even bear to have Jeff inside their home. He brought back nothing but bad memories and regrets.

'I've seen a lawyer. Just so that I could check out my position,' Jeff hastened to explain. 'I'm going to ask for access visits and apply for joint custody of my son.'

Holly's heart sank right down to her toes.

'Of course. That's your right,' Rio responded equably.

'But Rio—' Holly began, not comprehending his failure even to proffer an argument or indeed understanding why Jeff, given that easy agreement, should look more startled than pleased.

'At the same time, however, any access visits would have to be supervised,' Rio continued.

Jeff frowned at Rio. 'Supervised? Why?'

'You assaulted Holly.'

'That was an accident!' Jeff protested vehemently, but even Holly could see that that reminder coming from Rio had severely disconcerted the younger man.

'My lawyers already have a statement from the woman whom you were living with at the time,' Rio told him with complete cool. 'She's quite prepared to testify that she saw you not only attack but also threaten Holly with further violence should she ever name you as her child's father.'

It was now Holly's turn to stare at her husband with shaken eyes, for only then did she recall the seemingly idle questions he had asked her in the Maldives about where she had found Jeff living when she had finally traced him to his girlfriend's apartment.

'You've got a statement from Liza?' Jeff was flushed with incredulous rage.

'Naturally you can still apply for access to Timothy and whatever else you like,' Rio pointed out. 'But it is only fair to tell you that I hope to adopt Timothy and that I will fight to do so, whether you have access or not.'

Jeff gave him a furious look of frustration. 'But I'm

quite happy for you to adopt the kid! I'm here ready to discuss a friendly arrangement with you—'

'Any arrangements or agreements required will be reached through the usual legal channels,' Rio asserted levelly.

'I've had enough of this!' Jeff stormed off to the door.

'You're still Timothy's father,' Rio said quietly. 'If you want to get to know your son I won't stand in your way.'

'Forget it!' Jeff yanked open the door, his eagerness to leave unconcealed. 'You're welcome to the yappy little brat!'

As her ex-boyfriend departed Holly was so ashamed of the way he had exposed his true nature that she could not meet Rio's gaze. 'Why did you keep on telling him he could see Timothy?'

'I won't let Danby use your son to threaten you or as a bargaining chip in some sleazy attempt to profit from the connection. But I needed to be sure that Jeff genuinely doesn't have any interest in Timothy.'

'What you said about Jeff's girlfriend, Liza…was that a bluff?' Holly mumbled.

'No. My lawyers do hold her statement. I felt that it was necessary to have proof of Jeff's violence to protect you and Timothy.'

'Has Liza broken up with Jeff?' Holly was still in shock at what she had learnt.

'Yes. I gather she caught him fooling around with one of her friends and she was more than willing to speak up on your behalf.'

Hell hath no fury, Holly reflected in a daze.

Level dark golden eyes scanned her pale, strained face and he caught her hands in his. 'I have to leave…

I'm already running late. You look exhausted. You should lie down for a while, *cara*.'

'Thanks…for sorting out Jeff,' Holly said jerkily.

'I'd have liked to do it with my fists,' Rio confided with unashamed male regret. 'But that could have put paid to any hope of adopting Timothy, and at the end of day Danby's not worth that risk.'

For a long time after Rio had gone Holly just sat beside Timothy's cot, watching over her son while he slept. Rio had derailed Jeff's motive with ease and she was very grateful, but she could not help thinking that he had not been half so successful at quieting her fears about the future. She was married to a bloke who truly believed that a rousing bout of sex answered all ills. And why did Rio imagine that? She had let him make love to her. And a sufficiently angry and alienated woman would have said no.

So why *hadn't* she said no? What she had learnt about Rio and Christabel had filled her with sheer panic. She loved him. She loved him so much. Wanting to kill him only went so far when she had felt that her whole world was under imminent danger of collapsing round her. She had started out all right when she first confronted him but then she had got too emotional and lost the plot.

When Rio came home she would make a more tactful and calm approach, and, one way or another, he was going to talk about Christabel whether he liked it or not, she swore to herself.

CHAPTER NINE

Two DAYS LATER, the limousine in which Holly was travelling drew up outside Marchmont Priory. The picturesque house was bathed in afternoon sunshine. Climbing out of the car, Holly breathed in deep and straightened her shoulders.

Holly had thought about calling Mrs. Lombardi in advance but she had been afraid that her offer to visit would somehow be put off. Although Rio seemed determined to cheerfully ignore all the signs that his parent was anything but happy at his sudden marriage to a stranger, Holly was not that insensitive. Naturally, Alice Lombardi would be concerned, but she was hoping that once Rio's mother actually met her she would realise that her new daughter-in-law was not as bad as she had feared.

She was ushered into the sunlit panelled sitting room, where a slim, still attractive blonde in her early sixties awaited her in an upright armchair. A closer and lengthier appraisal revealed the fine lines on Alice Lombardi's worn features and the pained stiffness of her movements.

'Please excuse me for not standing up to greet you,'

she murmured in her well-bred voice. 'My arthritis is particularly troublesome today.'

'I'm sorry. I should have phoned first—'

'Did Rio send you here?'

Holly reddened.

'I thought so,' Alice said ruefully. 'Rio can be very ruthless.'

'He wanted us to meet and I was glad of the excuse,' Holly responded awkwardly, backing down into the seat that was indicated.

'I may as well admit that Christabel is staying here this week,' the older woman replied. 'I shan't apologise for that. I can hardly turn my back on her simply because my son changed his mind about marrying her. She often visits me.'

'That's really none of my business.' But the news that Rio's ex-fiancée was on the premises was daunting and made Holly feel very much as though she had foolishly strayed into the enemy camp.

'If you say so...' Alice's gaze was as keen as her son's. 'How honest may I be?'

'As honest as you like.' Holly lifted her chin.

'Is your son, Timothy, my grandchild?'

Holly flushed. 'No.'

'And are you expecting a child now?'

'No, I'm not.' Holly supposed that those were fairly obvious questions to ask in the circumstances but she felt horribly like a little kid being questioned by a stern headmistress for unacceptable behaviour.

'I'm sorry if I've embarrassed you but I had to know.' The older woman now looked weary and defeated.

In the hiatus, a maid knocked and entered with a tray of tea. At a leisurely pace, fragile bone-china cups of heirloom quality were filled and delicate cakes were offered. Holly could not get a morsel past her tight throat and even to moisten her lips was a challenge.

'I don't know what has got into Rio,' Alice admitted tightly, tears glimmering in her strained gaze. 'Perhaps I am better not knowing, but if you have somehow contrived to trap him into marriage and your motivation was his wealth I will be your enemy and a most bitter one.'

Holly paled at that unhesitating assurance. 'I—'

'You have no career. You're penniless. How could my son even have *met* you?' Alice made no attempt to conceal her bewilderment. 'You're not from our world. Of course I'm suspicious of you. Rio won't tell me anything about you.'

Reminded of how poor she had been before her marriage, Holly was mortified. The smart outfit which had helped her confidence suddenly felt like finery she had no entitlement to be wearing. 'I really don't know why Rio sent me here—'

'Don't you? You're supposed to be ingratiating yourself. He's a typical man and he's planning to stay well out of the way until I've come to terms with you,' the older woman informed her drily. 'What age are you, for goodness' sake?'

'Twenty.'

'So now Rio's cradle-snatching.' Alice Lombardi was openly taken aback by the news that Holly was that young. 'I can only assume that my son is madly in love with you. There is no other possible explanation for his behaviour.'

Holly remained silent, unable to lie.

'Have you nothing to say?' Alice demanded in frustration.

'I love *him*,' Holly muttered fiercely and, setting down her untouched tea, she stood up, truly desperate to escape. 'I don't think there's much point me sitting here because I'm only upsetting you and I don't have the answers you want.'

'If Rio loves you, I don't need any answers.' The older woman studied Holly's troubled face with belated discomfiture. 'Nor will I interfere.'

'He doesn't love me,' Holly said bluntly. 'He likes me. He said he thought he could get fond of me but I'm not holding my breath.'

And with that confession, which appeared to startle her hostess, Holly slipped back out to the flagstoned hall and heaved a huge, craven sigh of relief. Only then did she see another woman poised by the massive stone fireplace.

'So you're Holly,' Christabel drawled with a scornful head-to-toe appraisal that would have left Holly squirming had Holly not been so intent on staring herself.

Sheathed in a fake-fur coat, a short dress the colour of cranberry and knee-length black leather boots, the blonde was so incredibly tall that Holly actually had to step back to receive the full effect. And the full effect of Christabel in the flesh was nothing short of spectacular. The shining fall of pale blonde hair, the startling green eyes, the voluptuous pink mouth. Then the lithe, shapely figure, the hand on the hip angled forward, the endless length of gleaming thigh presented by her taunting, aggressive stance.

'You look even better than your pictures,' Holly conceded helplessly.

'Are you trying to be funny with me?' Christabel spat, lips drawing back from her perfect teeth in a venomous flash. 'You've got some nerve, coming here to visit Alice. This is my turf. Don't you kid yourself that you've stolen my man. You only have him on loan!'

'*Extended* loan.' Holly threw her bright head back, bronze ringlets tumbling back from her pale heart-shaped face, clear blue eyes as steady as she could make them. 'If you were careless enough to lose Rio, that's your problem, not mine. But he's my husband now—'

'And how long do you think that's going to last?' Christabel loosed a shrill derisive laugh.

'As long as he wants it to. I don't want this bad feeling with you,' Holly admitted tautly. 'I'd nothing to do with you and Rio splitting up—'

'But if you hadn't come along we'd have got back together,' Christabel condemned. 'I'll break up your marriage if it's the last thing I do!'

'Christabel…*no*!' another voice interrupted, charged with censure.

Both young women spun. Leaning heavily on a stick, Alice Lombardi was several feet away, her thin features rigid with shocked disapproval as she stared at her house-guest.

All the way back to London, Holly thought of Christabel. Beautiful, angry, vindictive Christabel. She tried to tell herself that she wasn't worried. But a woman so flawless she barely looked human was hard to downsize in her memory bank. And if the gorgeous Christabel still hoped to get Rio back, even though he was now married, what did that tell her? Well, for one thing, it blew a large hole in Holly's dim assumption that something very serious had broken up their engagement.

Now she was no longer so sure. Christabel's declaration of war suggested that although Rio and the blonde might have had a major row when they had split up there had still been hope of a reconciliation.

And that new angle on the situation scared Holly, *really* scared her. For the first time Holly was afraid that Rio might have used her just to strike back at Christabel. Not deliberately, but reacting to a subconscious very male urge to level the score, might not Rio have turned to Holly and their marriage as a weapon? By nature, Rio was shockingly stubborn. He was also volatile and deep. What was going to happen if Rio woke up one day and realised that he still cared about Christabel? Already painfully aware that Rio had married her on the rebound, Holly could not see that as a farfetched fear. Rio didn't love her. Their marriage would not survive if he still had feelings for another woman, all too willing to take him back.

Forcing her thoughts to a halt at that point, Holly told herself that she was overreacting. Even so, after the afternoon she had endured it was impossible to feel good about either herself or her marriage. She needed to find a job, she decided in desperation, show some independence. Alice Lombardi thought that she might be a gold-digger who'd trapped Rio into marriage. Rio had also talked about the need for her to lead her *own* life. Maybe that was why he had hired a nanny to take care of Timothy. And, if their marriage did fall apart, she would be better off if she was already employed.

Rio phoned her every day, often twice a day. She lived for his calls, woke up every time she turned over in bed and found him missing and just counted the hours until he was due back. But, wanting to surprise him with actual results, she told him nothing about the Italian lessons she was already taking and kept her plans to find a job to herself. After signing up with a couple of office recruitment agencies, she devoted the remainder of the week to Timothy.

The evening of Rio's return, Holly went to the airport to meet his flight. It was a last-minute decision and the limousine had already left to pick him up, so she had to call a cab. The cab got caught up in traffic and, fearing that she had missed him, Holly had a frantic rush through the airport. Her heart leapt at first sight of Rio's lean, dark, devastating features as he strode into view with Ezio in his wake, and then, out of nowhere, it seemed, came Christabel.

Holly fell to a stricken halt as the beautiful blonde surged forward to intercept Rio and engage his attention. Holly stood there unnoticed, shattered by Christabel's sudden appearance and the suspicion that such an encounter could only have been prearranged.

With equal abruptness, Holly turned and walked away again. Still in shock, she went into a café, bought herself a cup of coffee and sat over it, determined not to go home until she had calmed down. Why had Christabel come to meet Rio off his flight? How had the other woman known where he would be? Furious anger welled up in Holly and festered into a rage like nothing she had ever known. Who was the wife? Who was the 'other woman'? All Holly knew as she finally set off home again was that throughout the week she had been made to feel more like Rio's mistress than his wife!

By the time that Holly finally arrived back at the town house it was getting late. As she crossed the hall

Rio appeared in the doorway of the library. Shorn of his jacket and tie, his black hair tousled, he looked rather less smooth and self-assured than he had when she had seen him earlier that evening. His lean, strong face was taut. His dark golden eyes scorched over her like a flame thrower's.

'Where the hell have you been all evening?' Rio's opening demand disconcerted her, for she had lost track of time while she had seethed at the airport.

'Out…' Awarding him the most minimal glance, Holly threw her head high, her gaze feverishly bright.

'Sarah told me that you went to meet me at the airport.'

'Well, I won't be making that mistake again,' Holly informed him from between gritted teeth. 'Tell me, is this house a Christabel-free zone or can I expect to trip over her here as well? After all, she appears to be welcome everywhere else, certainly more welcome than I am!'

Rio tensed. 'So you *did* see Christabel with me at the airport.'

'My goodness…you are *so* quick on the uptake!' Holly fired back at him.

Rio straightened to his full commanding height, narrowed golden eyes pinned to her furious and flushed face. 'Do you realise how worried I've been about you?' he condemned, sidestepping the issue of Christabel with infuriating dexterity. 'I got in at seven. It's now eleven!'

'You're lucky I came home at all!' Frustrated rage was climbing so high inside Holly that she could hardly get the words out.

'Am I? I'm not going to stand here and argue with

you in the hall,' Rio breathed glacially, throwing wide
the door of the library in invitation.

'Is the room soundproof?' Holly enquired sar-
castically.

As Rio thrust the door closed he reached for her
hand. 'What on earth has got into you?'

Holly yanked her fingers free. 'I've had about all I
can take for one week. At your request I went to visit
your mother, and do you know who she had staying
with her?'

'I haven't a clue.' Winged ebony brows pleated as
he lounged in an attitude of outrageous cool against
the edge of his desk, Rio surveyed her in expectation
of receiving the answer.

'Your ex-fiancée, although there's not a lot of the
"ex" about her this week!' Holly snapped angrily. 'I
don't feel like your wife. Your mother's been entertaining Christabel as an honoured guest but I got the frozen
mitt, not to mention a lot of embarrassing questions that
you should have foreseen—'

'*Dio mio*…Christabel was down at the Priory?' Rio
queried in surprise.

'I want to know what she was doing at the airport
tonight!' Holly informed him.

'It was *my* fault that Christabel had to ambush me
like that,' Rio stated with flat emphasis, his beautiful
mouth compressing. 'I refused to accept her calls. But
certain matters did have to be resolved.'

'Like what?' Holly could have done without knowing
that Christabel had been bombarding him with phone
calls as well.

'She's living in an apartment I own and hasn't yet
found other accommodation—'

'She's living in an apartment you own…?' Holly was aghast at that news. 'But you broke up with her weeks ago. She's famous. She must earn a fortune as a model and you're trying to tell me she *can't* find somewhere to rent?'

'She hasn't had the time. She's been in Paris.'

'She should have been out flat-hunting, then, not sucking up to your mother for sympathy! I'll be in one of your guest rooms until you've thought up a better story!' Holly told him fierily, wrenching the door open. 'And you still haven't explained how she knew where and when to find you tonight.'

Rio released his breath in a long-suffering masculine hiss that set her teeth on edge even more. 'It's common knowledge that I was in New York this week…and I usually fly home on Fridays at that hour.'

Holly's usually generous mouth closed tight as a coffin lid and she set off upstairs regardless, her slender back rigid. Of course, Christabel would know his movements better than *she* did. The blonde had been in Rio's life a lot longer. But Holly was fed up with being wrongfooted by Christabel, first with Rio's mother, who had made it quite clear where her loyalty lay, and then with Rio himself. Rio was acting as if she was being unreasonable, but worst of all he had taken the blame for that encounter at the airport himself. Holly would have been much happier had he bestowed blame on his former girlfriend.

When Rio strode into their bedroom Holly was slamming through drawers in search of a nightdress.

'You're not sleeping apart from me,' Rio told her.

'Watch me,' Holly advised.

'Do you have any idea how much I was looking forward to coming home to you tonight?' Rio demanded in a roughened undertone.

Her eyes stung with sudden tears and she closed them tight. *Could* she believe that? She had devoted the entire afternoon to beautifying herself and getting all dressed up for his benefit. And then she had seen Christabel, gorgeous blonde mane trailing and legs as long as a racetrack on display, and she had known she could not compete. But also that she should not *have* to compete.

'Everywhere I turn she's there where she shouldn't be—'

'I'm amazed that Christabel had the nerve to visit my mother,' Rio confessed, his anger audible. 'That shouldn't have happened and, believe me, now that I know it has, it won't happen again, *bella mia.*'

Holly gulped. 'I don't know *what* to believe any more—'

Slowly Rio eased her round to face him and scanned her shuttered face. He ran caressing fingers down the taut line of her cheekbone, laced them gently into her hair and turned her strained gaze up to his. 'You have to learn to trust me. Christabel's in the past. I've started a new life with you and Timothy.'

Denying herself closer contact with the heat and strength of that hard, muscular frame of his, Holly drew in a slow, sustaining breath. 'I can only accept that if you promise me that you won't have anything more to do with her.'

'No problem...' Appraising her with smouldering golden eyes, sculpted mouth in a sensual curve, Rio backed her over to the bed with predatory determination and an innate sense of good timing. 'Why would I want another woman when I've got everything I want and need at home?'

Holly wondered why, if that was true, he still wouldn't talk about *why* he had broken off his engagement. But then, perhaps from Rio's point of view there had been no great drama involved and he genuinely had nothing more to say on the subject. Possibly he had known for some time that the relationship wasn't working out and giving up on it had not been a sudden decision on his part. Why hadn't that possibility occurred to her before?

Having dealt with her own anxiety and triumphed, Holly concentrated instead on the hammering acceleration of her own heartbeat and the knot of enervating anticipation tightening low in her pelvis. She only had to look at Rio to want him.

Rio laughed with vibrant amusement when she practically tore his shirt getting it off him. 'You missed me,' he told her with immense satisfaction.

'Maybe...'

'I want to hear you admit it...' He took her readily parted lips in a passionate demonstration of hunger and her senses leapt and her wanton body flowed and surged under the powerful masculine demand of his. 'Well?'

'Can't talk right now...better things to do,' she confided, running a provocative hand down over a taut, muscular male thigh, feeling him jerk with a satisfaction as old as time itself and a knowledge of her own feminine power.

'Who taught you to do that?' Rio groaned, straining against her with unconcealed sexual need and extracting her from her dress with more haste than cool.

'You did...'

Hours later, in the dawn light, she watched him sleep. Jet lag had felled him where nothing else could. Jet lag, added to a couple hours of insatiable lovemaking. Yes, he had definitely missed her. *In bed*. She squashed the snipey little voice that came up with that unnecessary addition. Instead she contemplated Rio, lying with one long bronzed, hair-roughened thigh clear of the crumpled sheet, six feet four inches of golden masculinity so gorgeous that she still could not quite credit that he was her husband. She kissed a smooth brown shoulder, rubbed her cheek there with sensuous pleasure, revelling in the familiar musky scent and feel of his skin.

Her own body ached and she smiled with sleepy pride in that reality. Christabel was history. He had convinced her. If seeing his ex-fiancée after so long had not upset him, what was she worrying about? He might not love her but he certainly seemed happy with her, and in the early hours he had *still* been demanding to know what she had been doing at the airport to get back to the house so late. He had been worried about her, worried that she had seen him with Christabel, worried that she, Holly, might be upset. He always liked to know exactly where she was. Why hadn't she noticed how possessive he could be, how protective?

When she woke up again Timothy was nestled up against her, fast asleep. Fully dressed in tight-fitting black jeans and a husky sweater, Rio absorbed her surprise at her son's presence from his stance at the foot of the bed.

'I heard him crying and he stopped the minute he saw me. Sarah had already fed him, so I brought him in here. I played with him for a while and then I took him into the bathroom while I went for a shower. Never again,' Rio groaned feelingly.

'What happened?'

'First, he yanked a towel down over himself and screamed the place down, then he pulled a drawer out and got his hand stuck in it…and, when I took a peek out of the shower because I thought he was being *too* quiet, he was trying to eat the box of bandages he must've sneaked out of the drawer!'

Unconcerned by the furore he had caused, Timothy slept on, looking angelic.

Rio came down on the side of the bed, lean, powerful face taut. 'He really scared me. Suppose he had got his hands on something dangerous or choked on the bandages?'

'But he *didn't*,' Holly soothed, touched that he had missed Timothy enough after a week's absence to bring her son back to their room to play with him. 'He's just at an age where he needs a lot of watching.'

'I'll be a lot more cautious in the future, *cara mia*,' Rio swore. 'But it's just as well for him that nature made him cute and appealing because I almost shouted at him.'

Holly killed a guilty smile at that assurance. She definitely would have shouted out of sheer relief that Timothy had not got hold of anything more dangerous.

Five days later, an hour after Rio had left for a meeting in the City, Holly received a call from one of the recruitment agencies she had signed up with. An insurance company was willing to interview her for a receptionist's position. As the first agency Holly had approached had pointed out the paucity of her qualifications, the implication being that she was aspiring too high, Holly was thrilled just to be in line for consideration.

The interview was set up for noon that day. But at a quarter to eleven when Holly was coming downstairs, elegant in a fitted black suit, Rio breezed through the door. 'How do you fancy going to the races, *bella mia*?' he enquired.

Holly sighed. 'If you mean right now, I've got an appointment.'

'Reschedule it,' Rio told her carelessly.

'I can't—'

'Oh, yes, you can. You haven't learned how to be a Lombardi wife yet.' Rio gave her a breathtaking smile of amusement that made her heart skip a beat. 'With the sole exception of Timothy, you should drop everything to be with me when I'm free.'

Holly worried at her lower lip for a second or two and hardened her heart to the sheer vibrant appeal of him. 'So what was all that about me needing to lead my own life when you're away on business?'

'I don't always practise what I preach. And you may not have noticed, Mrs. Lombardi, but I am *not* away. What are you fussing about?' Rio mocked. 'A hair appointment?'

'I wasn't going to mention it yet but I have a job interview…that's not something I can rearrange.' Holly gave him an apologetic smile.

Rio stilled. In fact, not only did he still, he also stared, dark golden eyes fixing to her as if she had announced an intention of going bungee-jumping with a frayed rope. 'An interview for a…*job*? If this is a joke, where's the punchline?'

Holly stiffened. 'Why would it be a joke?'

Rio regarded her levelly. 'I don't want you to work. Why would you look for a job? It's not just a question of what I want either. What about Timothy?'

'Women work,' Holly replied defensively. 'Anyway, the position is only part-time.'

'Not my wife. What is this job?'

'Receptionist.'

'Are you even remotely aware of how wealthy we are?' Rio prompted in a charged and incredulous undertone.

'I'm not wealthy...*you* are.'

'It would be quite inappropriate for you to take an employment opportunity from someone else who really needs it, and that's my last word on the subject.'

'Well, it's not mine.' Holly's temper fired. 'I got the interview on my own merits and I'm proud of that and I intend to show up—'

His lean, dark, devastating face set hard. 'But I said no.'

Holly smoothed an unsteady hand down over her skirt but kept her chin high. 'Don't I have the right to disagree with you?'

'Not when I know better. You're not making the Lombardi name a laughing stock by chasing after some menial job,' Rio decreed with cutting emphasis.

Holly paled. 'So let's get this straight...if I was a brain surgeon or something snobby or important you would have a different attitude. But, as I'm only capable of work that you consider *menial*, I have to stay home to conserve your dignity.'

'As you're not a brain surgeon, I don't think we need discuss that angle. Come on,' Rio urged ruefully. 'Go and change into something livelier for the races.'

'No.'

'In a minute you're going to be chaining yourself to the railings outside the house like a suffragette fighting for the vote,' Rio countered very drily. 'Be sensible. I work very long hours. When I'm around, I want you around too—'

'Did anyone ever tell you that you can be very domineering? And the sort of bloke who has to control everything around him?' Holly paused and then went on, 'If I want to work, I will work.'

'Is that your last word?'

Holly nodded without hesitation.

Rio surveyed her with a level of brooding dissatisfaction that would once have filled her with instant wholehearted panic. Then, swinging on his heel, he mounted the stairs and left her standing there.

An hour later, while Holly waited her turn with the other applicants called for interview, she began to wonder exactly what she was doing there. Was she happy to leave Timothy solely to Sarah's care for half of every week? Hadn't she neglected to take into account the other demands on her time? Was she going to drop out of her Italian lessons?

In addition, Rio led a busy social life. They had already dined out once that week, with the directors of the Lombardi Foundation, an occasion that had not been half so intimidating as she had feared. And that very evening they had a big private party to attend. As Rio's wife she had to look good at such events and that meant more than running a last-minute brush through her hair and wearing the first thing that came out of her wardrobe.

Suppressing a rueful sigh, Holly decided that there

was no point whatsoever in putting herself through an interview for a job she did not even want. Only pride and the suggestion that she might be a gold-digger had sent her off in search of a job in the first place. Indeed, she had stood up to Rio purely on principle and she knew that her stubborn refusal to give way had shocked him.

Evidently, the husband who had told her that she would have to lead her own life hadn't really meant it. She started to smile then. Just as he had once carelessly admitted, Rio was spoilt. Alice adored her only son. Holly imagined others of her sex had added to that spoiling even by the time Rio became a teenager. He was drop-dead gorgeous and rich and absolutely charming…as long as he got what he wanted. Which, most of the time, he did. And why not, when he made her so happy?

Arriving back home, she was disappointed to learn that Rio had returned to his office at Lombardi Industries. Around three she went to get her hair done. Sly, the owner of the salon, who had long since grasped the fact that Holly was not Rio's imaginary cousin, Fiammetta, and had done so with very good grace, always gave Holly her personal attention.

'I hear Christabel didn't get that big cosmetics contract she was up for,' Sly remarked when she began trimming Holly's hair. 'But then, let's face it, she's not getting any younger…'

After telling herself that she was about to do the decent thing and change the subject, Holly heard herself saying instead, 'What age is she?'

'She's got to be over thirty…' Sly lowered her head to continue more confidentially, 'She's supposed to be pretty difficult to work with. A lot of people in the business don't like her. It makes you think that some of the juiciest rumours about her *have* to be true.'

'Rumours?' Holly was ashamed of herself, deeply ashamed, but she was as hooked as a fish on a line to the other woman's every word.

'The big cosmetics companies are very careful of their image and they expect the model they select as a figurehead to have a *clean* reputation...and Christabel, well, I've heard that she does— Oh, excuse me.'

As a stylist interrupted Sly with a query the brunette broke off what she had been saying and left Holly seething with curiosity. But the minute of reflection that followed sobered Holly and made her face burn. It was truly awful of her to be listening to gossip about Christabel. Rio would kill her. Rio would expect better of her. For goodness' sake, didn't she expect better of herself?

'Can we change the subject?' Holly asked when Sly returned to her.

'But we were having so much fun doing down Christabel,' Sly pointed out in amazement.

'I'm sorry...I know I encouraged you, but talking about her makes me feel bad.'

'That's what I keep on *telling* people about you. Sweet sincerity shines out of you. I bet Rio was blinded by the comparison between you and that female we're not going to mention again. My final word on the subject? Rio had an incredibly lucky escape.'

On the drive home Holly gathered her courage and stopped off at the same designer outlet where Rio had once taken her shopping. She wanted to buy an outfit that Rio hadn't seen before, something that he hadn't chosen for her. And she found it: a strappy short dress that was wholly feminine in design and made of glo-rious fabric that shone like pure, opulent gold beneath the lights.

Clad in her new lingerie, a daring combination of gossamer-thin lace-topped stockings, oyster silk pant-ies and a matching strapless bra, she was putting the finishing touches to her make-up, which she had la-boured long and hard over, when a knock sounded on the bathroom door.

She opened it, focused on a silk tie and automatically tipped back her head to connect with the dark golden eyes she loved, saying, 'Be honest...does this eye-shadow make me look like a panda with a hangover?'

'*Santo cielo...*' Rio murmured huskily.

'That bad?' Holly groaned in frustration. 'I've wiped it all off once already and I'll die if I have to do it again!'

'You look totally fantastic just as you are, *bella mia*,' Rio said very slowly.

Comprehension sinking in, Holly watched her hus-band literally trail his hotly appreciative gaze over her scantily clad body and she reddened and threw the mas-cara wand in her hand at him. 'My *eyes*, Rio!'

He caught the wand in one lean brown hand and threw back his arrogant dark head, raw amusement dancing in his dark-lashed gaze, a slashing smile of shameless acknowledgement on his mouth. 'Gorgeous... all of you, absolutely gorgeous. How long do we have before we have to leave?'

'Rio...' Her breath caught in her throat at the smoul-dering glitter in his scrutiny. His effect on her was in-stantaneous. A slow simmer of heat rose inside her, spread at wanton speed to sensitive places. Her nipples tingled and tightened and pushed against the cups of her bra and a tiny tightening sensation pulled deep in the pit of her stomach and made her press her thighs together.

'We have more important things to think about,' Rio imparted rather raggedly.

'Have we?'

'I was a real bastard earlier. How did the interview go?'

'The…interview?' Holly coloured, averted her gaze, not yet ready to admit that she had dropped out in advance of it. 'OK…fine.'

Rio spread his hands in an expressive motion. 'I personally feel that the wisest solution is for you to work somewhere in the Lombardi empire. Now, before you start saying that's nepotism, listen to the pros and cons…'

'Pros and cons…' Holly parroted, hugely taken aback by his suggestion.

'Your hours would be negotiable. So if I want us to take off somewhere for a break at short notice, or even have you accompany me on a business trip, there won't be a problem.'

'I see…'

'Of course, you will *have* to do some business courses first, and some of our company courses are quite demanding. But, when you're so keen to have a career, I can't see that being a problem. You just haven't had the opportunities before but now you do,' Rio informed her with satisfaction.

The silence lay, a silence of expectancy.

Holly was aghast. She was seeing demanding business courses stretching interminably into her future and cringing from the prospect. But after all the noise she had made about working, how was she supposed to turn round and tell him she had changed her mind? Especially when he had made such an effort to alter his own outlook on her behalf. Why were men so obtuse sometimes?

'Holly?' Rio prompted.

Holly swallowed hard and forced a weak smile. 'You're being really supportive. I'll think the idea over.'

'I have a surprise for you, *cara*. Put out your hand and close your eyes,' Rio urged.

Her mascaraed lashes clogged together. She felt him slide something onto her left hand and she untangled her lashes to look.

'Six-week anniversary present,' Rio imparted.

A fabulous sapphire and diamond ring now sat next to her wedding ring. Her throat closed over. When he went on a guilt trip, he really worked hard at it, she reflected, tears stinging her eyes. 'It's just gorgeous…' she said in a wobbly voice.

'What are you crying for?'

'I'm not crying,' she swore chokily. 'Look, I'd better get dressed.'

'Spoilsport,' he murmured huskily.

She had had to fall like a ton of bricks for him to discover that sometimes she loved him so much it literally hurt to think about it.

The party was held in a huge town house by a very fashionable middle-aged couple. The decor seemed to have a gothic theme, or maybe it was just the party theme, Holly thought, but there was a giant mural of dragons adorning one end of the vast main room and the lights were dim and the air heavy with the scent of incense. Huge mirrors hung on the walls and veiled marble statues lurked in dim corners.

'You've got some strange friends,' Holly told Rio.

'Frank and Lily are very conventional but they slav-ishly follow every fashion trend,' Rio informed her with amusement. 'The next time you visit it will all have changed.'

Holly saw Christabel make her entrance, could not really have missed it even had she tried. Wearing a shimmering, extremely short white dress that caressed every curve of her perfect body, Christabel turned every head in the room, both male and female.

As Holly sat there frozen by dismay and an instant sense of being under threat, Rio drawled softly, 'I'm afraid that on some occasions you will have to get used to seeing her around.'

'Did you *know* she was going to be here?'

'I didn't even think about it,' Rio countered in a de-cided tone of exasperation.

Holly then noticed that Christabel had a very pre-sentable male companion in tow and the sight soothed her. She knew what Rio was telling her and wished she hadn't commented. Christabel had a perfect right to go where she liked.

An hour later she watched Rio's ex-fiancée putting on a stunning exhibition of salsa dancing and generally becoming the life and soul of the party. By her side, Rio got quieter and quieter. When he had asked her to dance she had said no. She didn't know how to do salsa but now everyone was doing it and doing it with real style.

While Rio was at the other end of the room chatting to their host his cousin, Jeremy strolled up. 'Would you like to dance?'

'No, thanks.'

'You shouldn't let Christabel get you down,' Jeremy said bluntly.

'Oh, is she here? I hadn't noticed.' Holly knew she was sulking and feeling sorry for herself but she was unable to stop. She felt so plain, so colourless in comparison to Christabel. Why had Rio become so silent? Maybe he was jealous. Maybe seeing Christabel with another man annoyed him. How could it not annoy him, for goodness' sake? Christabel was just so unbelievably gorgeous, she conceded miserably.

Jeremy drifted off again and Holly watched Christabel giggle in company with their hostess, Lily. And then something happened. The older woman's face froze and she turned on her heel and stalked over to her husband and Rio. Christabel returned to her table and lifted her handbag to rifle through it. Then the dancers screened her from view.

But when Holly glanced back at Rio for the first time she saw him looking in Christabel's direction, lean, strong face taut, his tension unmistakable. Suddenly Holly's heart felt as if it was thundering at the base of her throat and threatening to choke her. As if in a dream, she watched Rio cut a path across the crowded floor, making a beeline for Christabel. Then she saw her husband standing with his ex-fiancée in the circle of his arms and she couldn't believe it. Her very worst nightmare was coming true before her eyes but she could *not* believe it.

But Christabel's head was down on his shoulder, her hair trailing across his dark jacket like a blonde banner. Some people had even stopped dancing to stare. The taste of bile in her dry mouth, Holly watched sickly as

Rio, with a supportive arm wrapped round Christabel, walked her out of the room.

Holly sat very still, just staring into space, eyes burning in her sockets, tummy cramping with nausea. She was horribly conscious of the surge of comment washing round the room in a tidal wave. She couldn't hear it because of the music but she could see and feel it: the heads moving together, the clumping up of couples into bigger groups, the agonising moment when she accidentally collided with a speculative glance.

Jeremy appeared in front of her. 'Rio called me on my mobile. He asked me to keep you company.'

Rio had phoned Jeremy? Rio had actually *left* the party with Christabel? Her husband had just walked out and left her stranded in front of an audience? Well, *where* did you *think* he was going with her? she asked herself numbly.

'I want to go home.' Holly got up, legs trembling, wanting some magic process to transport her outside, away from the watching eyes and the clattering tongues. Never in her life had she felt more humiliated. Never had she dreamt that Rio would do such a thing to her.

There was no sign of their host and hostess, which was a relief. Jeremy tucked Holly into a cab as if she might shatter into pieces if he wasn't careful. He climbed in beside her.

'There's no need for you to come with me,' Holly said woodenly.

Jeremy's phone started playing some ludicrously upbeat tune. He handed it to her. 'It's Rio…'

'Holly, I'm really sorry but I honestly didn't have a choice,' Rio breathed in bleak undertone. 'Look, we'll talk later.'

Later? *Never*, Holly told herself, returning the phone to Jeremy, blanking out his questioning appraisal. What was there to talk about? Rio had said he hadn't had a choice, but in actuality he had made his choice. Of course he was sorry. He had a conscience. But when push came to shove he just hadn't been able to resist the woman he really cared about.

'Rio's a very decent guy,' Jeremy asserted forcefully. 'He's my cousin. I know him. OK…I didn't see what actually happened but I'm certain there's nothing for you to get upset about.'

'Are you?' Holly held back an hysterical laugh at that plea on Rio's behalf. Decent guys don't walk out on their wives at parties. Only besotted ones did.

'There has to be some explanation. Christabel was acting weird and her antics were embarrassing Frank and Lily. Her date didn't stay long.' Jeremy lowered his voice to a constrained mutter. 'You know, she wasn't wearing anything under that dress.'

Slut, Holly thought, aghast and shocked, tears welling up in her aching eyes. Christabel had got to him with sex. Real brazen-hussy stuff. She was going to burn her stupid lace-topped stockings. Waste of time. She should have known better than to try to appeal to a bloke on that level. Especially when it was now painfully obvious that she was literally still in the nursery league in that department.

An hour later Holly wrote the ubiquitous note.

It was really great while it lasted but now it's over.

Dry-eyed, she packed her plainer clothes and then called a taxi. Hadn't she always known it wouldn't last? It *had* been wonderful while it *had* lasted, she reminded herself doggedly. And he had never said he loved her and she had never said she loved him. But he had given her a wedding ring and only hours ago he had given her a second ring that looked very much like an engagement ring. And suddenly she hated him with a hatred that tore her apart and she was sobbing into her suitcase, stabbed to the heart at the image of him with Christabel. It took her a good ten minutes to plaster herself back together again.

Striving not to waken their nanny in her room next door, Holly crept about her son's room, gathering up essentials. Timothy was going to miss Rio so much, she reflected wretchedly. But what could she do about that? Why was it that at the most awful moments of her life she always felt powerless and guilty, as if everything that went wrong was her fault?

No, she caught herself up on that thought. She was making her own decisions, *not* waiting on him. She was leaving him. She was going to divorce him for adultery too. If he was expecting civilised forgiveness, he had no hope. She might even make him wait the full three years before she agreed to a divorce. Not that a hussy like Christabel was likely to be put off by the prospect of living in sin. Stop it, *stop it*, her saner self intervened. Let him go, let him have her if he loves her, and to behave as he had he *had* to love her…

CHAPTER TEN

'WHAT HAVE YOU done to that pastry?' Mary Sansom demanded in dismay. 'It looks like you've been torturing it!'

Holly stared down at the shredded pastry and then glanced across the kitchen at her mother, a sturdy little woman with iron-grey hair, wrapped in a floral apron. 'I'll make some more.'

'I'll see to it.' The concern in her parent's steady blue eyes filled Holly with guilt.

She had been trying so hard to be cheerful, but putting a happy face on her misery was a challenge she had yet to meet. It had been almost three weeks since she had left London. By the end of her first day home she had been hoarse from explaining everything that had happened to her since Timothy had been born. And there had been tears, rebukes and regrets, but a lot of love too. That her parents could forgive her for all the grief she had caused had been a tremendous comfort to Holly, as was her mother and father's loving acceptance of their baby grandson. So she felt that they deserved more than the continual sight of her drooping like a wet rag.

Yet, as the days dragged by, her mother or her father

would often come up with some statement that unsettled Holly. 'Is this bloke you married a fool, then?' her father had asked, infuriating her with that mere suggestion. 'I reckon only a right fool would wed one woman when he still fancied his chances with another.'

'You just never think before you act,' her mother had lamented. 'But marriages have to be worked at and you should have talked to your husband. He was good to you. Why would he suddenly take off with this other shameless piece? I can tell you, your father would have no chance with a female like that,' her mother had told her with staunch and touching pride. 'No decent man would want a woman who carried on that way.'

Holly went up to bed that night and feared that the generation gap was yawning. She lay in her pine bed and felt the tears trickling again. She felt as if half of her had been brutally ripped away. She missed him with every breath she drew. She turned a dozen times a day to tell him something before she remembered that he wasn't there any more. She ached for him and despised herself and kept on wanting to phone him but could not begin to imagine what she could possibly say.

Two days later Mary Sansom announced over breakfast that the house needed 'a good going-over'. Knowing well that a thorough cleaning session was intended, Holly suppressed a groan. By teatime even the battered kitchen range shone from industrious polishing. Her parents were attending a church social that evening and Holly noticed that her mother seemed unusually quiet and anxious.

'You know, Dad and I...we always want what's best for you,' the older woman remarked without warning as Holly carried cake tins out to the car for her. 'It's not as though you've done so well on your own.'

Hurt by a comment that she was none the less well aware her mother had grounds to make, Holly retreated back indoors and got on with putting Timothy to bed. 'Da…Da?' he asked in a small mournful voice, from which hope had pretty much gone.

Eyes overflowing with tears of regret, Holly was on the stairs when she heard the back-door knocker sound. Assuming that her mother had overlooked something in her rather flustered departure, she hurried to answer it.

It was Rio. Stunned, Holly gaped at him, her tear-streaked face pale as a ghost between the tangled bronze ringlets tumbling round her shoulders. He gazed down at her with dark golden eyes that glittered below the heavy fringe of his black lashes and it was as if he had yanked a panic button in her heart, setting off a chain reaction that went right through her slender body in a stormy wave.

She parted dry lips. 'How…how did you find me?'

'Finding you down here was easy. Unfortunately I wasted over two weeks on the assumption that you'd taken some job and stayed on in London,' Rio admitted. 'Are you planning to invite me indoors?'

At that pointed question, Holly coloured and stepped back. Clad in fitted black jeans, a cream sweater and a loose-cut black fleece-lined jacket, Rio cut a powerful figure, dominating the homely kitchen, his dark head reaching within a couple of inches of the overhanging rafters.

'Watch out for the doorways,' she said automatically. 'They're lower.'

Poised with his back to the low-burning fire, Rio was

staring at her. As his incisive gaze wandered intently
over her she realised what a mess she must look, for her
hair needed to be tidied and she was wearing ancient
jeans and an even more ancient sweatshirt.

'You look about sixteen…' Rio murmured huskily.

Picturing Christabel's glittering sophistication, Holly
paled and tore her gaze away. She stared out instead at
the sleek red Ferrari parked in the yard. 'How did you
get that car up the lane?'

'Slowly.'

She could feel his tension as much as her own. It
was as if he didn't know how to talk to her any more.
She marvelled that she had ever convinced herself that
she could avoid a final meeting with him. But, oh, how
she wished that that had been possible when he stood
only feet away and she was aware of his presence with
every screaming fibre of her being. She was a mess of
conflict: hurting and hating and hungering all at once.

'How could you just walk out of our home with Timothy?' Rio asked with raw-edged abruptness.

'It wasn't difficult after what you did at the party,'
Holly replied tightly.

'You don't trust me at all…'

Holly said nothing. Her experience of his sex had not
taught her trust. When she had first given her trust Jeff
had broken it, and more than once. With Rio, she had
lived each day as it came, protecting herself by trying
not to look too far ahead but secretly always expecting
disappointment and heartbreak. That the worst had ultimately happened had come as no surprise. It was as
if she had been waiting for it all along.

'You want me to talk about Christabel…'

The nasty bit of her wanted to tell him not to bother,

as it was a bit late in the day for explanations. But common sense told her that, no matter how much hearing the truth might hurt, some day in the future she would be grateful that she had heard him out.

'OK...' Rio conceded, but the silence still dragged on like a hangman's rope threatening to snap tight at any moment.

Is it the sex? That was what *she* wanted to ask, what she was forcing herself to hold back because it would reveal too much. Only a woman eaten up with jealousy would even consider asking such a thing. A woman in love, desperate to reduce the breakdown to the lowest common denominator in the hope that it would somehow make it more bearable.

'Where do you want me to start?'

Holly spun right round in frustration. Rio was raking a not quite steady hand through his luxuriant black hair, pallor spread below his usually vibrant complexion and accentuated round the tight line of his sensual mouth. For the first time she noticed that his dark, devastating features had harder angles, as if he had lost weight. She was delighted that he looked so downright miserable and strained. Evidently life with Christabel was not one of unalloyed joy and frolics.

'*Dio mio*...maybe I should have rehearsed this first,' Rio breathed, his jawline clenching hard. 'Christabel and I had a long-distance relationship. Sometimes a month or more would go by without us seeing each other. Her career took her all over the world and I had similar commitments. I may well have spent more actual time alone with you than I ever spent with her.'

Surprise assailed Holly, for she had not expected to hear that.

'When we were together we usually had company. The less I saw of her, the more I thought I loved her.' Faint dark colour burnished his spectacular cheekbones. 'It's taken me a long time to work that out.'

'Work what out?'

'That, when the chips were down, I didn't know Christabel at all. What we had was superficial but I would've married her without ever appreciating that,' Rio admitted grudgingly.

'So what changed?' Holly almost whispered.

A faint sheen of perspiration overlaid his bronzed skin and he turned pale again right before her eyes. 'The night I met you, I let myself into her apartment to wait for her coming home. She wasn't expecting me… surprise, surprise,' Rio framed grittily, his dark, deep drawl slowing and tautening. 'When she came back she wasn't alone…'

Comprehension came to Holly in a surge. 'She had another man with her?'

'I need a drink,' Rio said hollowly.

Holly was ready to poison him. He had *forgiven* Christabel for carrying on with some other man? Incandescent rage at such injustice flamed through Holly. Her parents were virtually teetotal but brandy was always kept for emergencies. She poured him a glass and set it on the table so that he would have to reach for it. Rio drained the measure in one gulp.

The silence came back then, thicker and heavier than ever.

Rio threw back his proud dark head. 'I should've told you weeks ago but I didn't want to talk about it. She wasn't with a man…she was with a woman.'

Holly's lips parted company and stayed parted while

she attempted to compute that rather more shocking slant to her inner picture of infidelity and betrayal, but no matter how hard she tried she could not fit Christabel into that context. 'Are you serious?'

Rio dealt her bemused face a sudden exasperated appraisal. 'They were making love.'

'Oh...' Holly had no ready response to make.

'I promised her that I wouldn't talk about it...' Rio hesitated, intense eyes darker than she had ever seen them. 'But, let's face it, that's not why I kept quiet. I was shattered. I felt humiliated...sexually and in every other way,' he admitted in a raw undertone.

Holly could see what it was costing him to confess to that vulnerability and it hurt her even to listen. But her own thoughts were in turmoil as she tried to make sense of what he was telling her and make it fit more recent events. Unfortunately that attempt only left her more confused than ever.

Rio snatched in a deep, charged breath and gave her a bleak glance. 'Most guys like to think of themselves as studs. When you walk in on a scene like that with the woman you're planning to marry it's annihilating. I doubt that Christabel was ever faithful to me.'

'Then what do you still see in her?' Holly demanded in bewilderment. 'I mean...you're describing a situation most men couldn't forgive.'

'Christabel is so screwed up right now, I'd have to be a real bastard to walk by on the other side,' Rio countered grimly. 'Didn't you register what was happening at that party? Lily begged me to get her out of their house—'

'Our hostess, Lily...Frank's wife? *Begged* you?"

'By that stage, Christabel's escort had done a timely

vanishing act, probably out of embarrassment. She was out of her head on drugs—'

'Drugs?' Holly was totally disconcerted.

'Lily caught her in the act with cocaine and asked her to leave. Christabel refused,' Rio explained ruefully. 'Frank and Lily lost their eldest son to heroin a couple of years ago and Lily was very distressed. I agreed to help, not just for their benefit but also for Christabel's. She was out of control and making a total ass of herself.'

'But if you'd come and spoken to me first, *explained*—'

'You wouldn't have listened. You'd have lost your temper and I had to get Christabel out of there fast and without a scene.' Dark golden eyes rested on her in level challenge.

Holly swallowed hard, for there was a lot of truth in his forecast of how she would have reacted had he approached her first to warn her.

'The circumstances were exceptional.' His lean, strong face hardened. 'But I made the mistake of assuming that you'd understand that there was something really serious happening.'

'Yes...' Face burning, Holly gazed into the fire, no longer able to meet his scrutiny. 'Were you aware that she did drugs?'

'Before that party I'd no idea Christabel had a problem, but then she was too clever to take them around me. And that night I didn't want the responsibility, but she was part of my life for a long time and I felt that I *had* to help her,' Rio stated harshly.

'So what did you do with her?'

'I took her to the foundation hospital and contacted

her family. Two days after that Christabel signed herself into a rehabilitation clinic. She's still there.'

Recalling all the nasty thoughts she had had about the other woman, Holly felt sincerely ashamed. Christabel had genuine problems that she needed help to cope with and Rio had done the right thing in giving her his support.

'Did she go off the rails because you ditched her?' Holly mumbled uneasily.

'No. Her sister, Gwen, was able to tell me that her drug and alcohol abuse had begun well before she met me.' His darkly handsome features serious, Rio released his breath slowly. 'I did think she drank too much sometimes but I'm afraid I didn't recognise it as a problem and she didn't confide in me. However, her sister was very frank...'

'Did she blame you for Christabel's problems?'

'No, far from it. Apparently, Christabel was confused about her sexual orientation when she was a teenager. More recently, she was terrified that she was losing her looks and struggling to keep an increasingly heavy drug habit hidden,' Rio revealed.

'So where did you fit into her life?'

'According to Gwen, Christabel saw me as a financial security blanket for her future.' Rio grimaced at that tag. 'My defection faced her with realities she had refused to deal with and now she's *having* to deal with them. Her sister's a psychologist and she says that's much more healthy.'

'I heard that she had recently lost out on some big modelling contract as well,' Holly remarked uncomfortably.

'Gwen mentioned that too. Said there'd been rumours about Christabel's lifestyle. Naturally. People talk.'

Holly stood there several feet from him, struggling to face her own reality, but it was a daunting one. She had judged Rio without even giving him the chance to defend himself and she was ashamed that she had had so little faith in him.

'I'm sorry…I'm *so* sorry I just walked out the way I did,' Holly muttered shakily. 'I was really jealous of Christabel and what I thought you must've had with her. I felt like second-best, and then when I met her down at the Priory—'

'I *wish* you'd told me about that encounter—'

'She said she wanted you back and that I'd come between you, and that really upset me—'

'Of course it did because you don't think enough of yourself,' Rio breathed not quite steadily, reaching out for her hands and drawing her closer. 'And that's my fault—'

'No, it's not,' Holly sighed, her hands quivering in his. 'If I'd mentioned Christabel's threats then maybe you would've understood why I was so sensitive about her—'

'There was never any chance of a reconciliation. But if I'd been more honest with you you'd have found that easier to accept.' Brilliant dark eyes scanning her troubled face, his hands tightened their grip on hers. 'The truth is…I didn't know what hit me when I met you. I couldn't think of anything else *but* you and I told myself I was unsettled after what had happened with Christabel—'

'Naturally you were…I mean, that's OK,' Holly hastened to reassure him because she was so grateful he was holding her hands and still talking to her after the manner in which she had left their home.

'No, it wasn't OK, *cara*. I wasn't giving you what *you* deserved. I don't know when or how I fell in love with you but I was in deep very fast. You must've noticed that I couldn't let you out of my sight…did you think that was normal?'

'Normal? I felt the same way.' And all the time her mind was reaching back to what he had said just before that. 'I fell in love with you'. Had he really said that or had she imagined that he had said that?

'There was the most explosive attraction between us right from the start and the lust I could handle,' Rio asserted wryly. 'But I couldn't acknowledge that I was seriously involved because that would've meant admitting that I was this pretty stupid and potentially shallow guy who almost married a woman he didn't really love—'

'You didn't really love Christabel?'

'I believed I loved her but we were never close, not the way you and I are, but I didn't know what that closeness was until I found it with you, *cara*.' Rio confessed, dark golden eyes troubled. 'I got over Christabel too quickly. And it might seem strange to you but I was ashamed of that…and it made me very wary about what I was feeling for you.'

'Yeah…you told me you *liked* me—'

'But the cool-guy act went out the window when you disappeared,' Rio broke in feelingly. 'I was tearing my hair out. I was desperate. I couldn't work. I couldn't sleep. I was haunting homeless shelters…you just have *no* idea what I went through the first two weeks you were missing!'

But, gazing up into the over-bright shimmer of those

speaking dark eyes resting with such loving intensity on her face, she did have an idea and she ached for him even as the first stirrings of joy began to wing through her.

'*Dio mio*…I went to hell and back. I was worried sick. I thought I might never find you or Timothy again—'

'Eventually I would've gone to see a lawyer, but doing that and talking about a divorce…it would have been so final and I couldn't face it yet,' Holly confided chokily, her voice breaking up on her as she realised how near she had come to losing everything she cared about.

Rio wrapped his arms tightly round her and held her so close that she could hardly breathe, but at that instant it was what she needed more than anything else. 'I'd have fought a divorce. There's *nothing* I wouldn't have done to get you and Timothy back,' he swore above her head. 'I'd have begged you to come home. Don't you realise how happy I've been with you? Couldn't you feel that…*see* it?'

And she had felt it, seen it so often, she recognised with a shamed stirring of regret. He had been so caring, so tender and romantic, but without the words of love she had been afraid to simply trust in his behaviour. 'You said you liked me…and that bit about getting fond of me,' she reminded him. 'It was so unemotional and it was like you saying that you could never, ever fall in love with someone like me.'

Rio winced and looked down at her with more than a hint of embarrassment. 'I just didn't know what else to say to you. It wasn't meant the way you took it. I was very wary of that word "love" that soon after breaking up with Christabel—'

'And you deliberately misled me about that—'

'Yes, because I sensed you'd say no otherwise. Didn't you start wondering what planet I was from when I asked you to marry me only a few days after I had met you?' Rio muttered with rueful self-mockery. 'I jumped on the first excuse I got to hang on to you and Timothy. Where is he, by the way?'

'In bed…you can see him if you want.' Holly looked up at him, her heart in her eyes, for she was so happy with what he was telling her about his feelings. He wasn't trying to hide anything now. He was admitting that he had been confused and acting out of character but letting her know that his most driving motivation had been to keep her in his life. 'I love you so much.'

'I love you too, *tesoro mio.*'

Holly took him upstairs to see Timothy, who was still awake. His lashes lifted on sleepy eyes and he stared at them. Then her son sat up and with sudden startling energy tried to claw his way up the side of the cot into standing position. What was more, what he had often tried but never yet succeeded at, actually worked on this occasion.

'When did he learn to do that?' Rio demanded.

'That's the first time he's managed it.'

Clasping the cot bars, big blue eyes very wide, looking as surprised as a baby could be at finding himself fully vertical, Timothy gave them a huge grin. But then he made the strategic error of letting go of the top bar and he fell back onto his bottom with a howl of disappointment.

With a husky laugh of amusement, Rio lifted Timothy up into his arms. 'You were brilliant…Mum and I were really impressed!'

After that excitement, it took a while to persuade Timothy back into the notion of going to sleep but eventually tiredness won the day.

'Mum and Dad will be home soon,' Holly told Rio at the top of the stairs.

'No, they won't be. They're spending the night in a local hotel—'

Holly blinked in confusion. 'I beg your pardon?'

'I made my first visit here yesterday afternoon while you were out shopping with Timothy,' Rio confided rather tautly. 'Your parents invited me in and gave me the third degree. They suggested I visit this evening when they would be out, but they were worried that that wouldn't give us long enough to talk over our differences—'

'I don't believe this…Mum and Dad didn't breathe a word to me!' Holly gasped.

'It was spelt out to me that I was going to have a battle persuading you to come back to me, so I came up with the hotel idea—'

'Putting them out of their own home?' Holly exclaimed in dismay. 'They've never stayed in a hotel in their lives!'

'I know…they told me.' Rio smiled down at her with considerable amusement. 'And your mother was thrilled at the prospect.'

'You are *so* sneaky. You got them on your side—'

'We're quits. You've got *my* mother on *yours*.' Rio traded wryly.

'Like heck I have—'

'Is this your bedroom? Oh, I *love* all the flowers and the frills,' Rio teased, grasping her hand and tugging her inch by inch over the threshold and closing the door.

He meshed his fingers slowly into her bronze ringlets, beautiful dark golden eyes bright with adoring intensity as he gazed down her. He brought his mouth down with immense tenderness on hers and she trembled. Less patient, she pushed forward into the sleek, hard, familiar strength of his muscular frame. It felt so good just to be held but even more glorious to know that she was truly loved and to feel the unmistakable shudder of response that went through him as she kissed him back.

'You are so beautiful and I love you so much it hurts,' he husked against her reddened lips, his breath fanning her cheekbone. 'And every time I think that I might never have met you it terrifies the life out of me, *amore*.'

'I love you too,' she moaned, shamelessly eager to express that love, hands sliding beneath his sweater to glide over his hard ribcage, making him jerk against her and haul her even closer.

And then the excitement took over and clothes were shed with breathless energy between frantic bouts of kissing. There was a whole extra dimension to their loving, for they had spent three utterly miserable weeks apart, and being together again felt like a very special gift. In the aftermath of the passion, they lay locked together, full of peace and contentment.

Holly struggled to recall what they had been talking about earlier and blushed at the ease with which she had forgotten that conversation. 'What was that you said about your mother being on my side?' she whispered curiously.

'She came up to London because she was upset about the way she'd treated you, and that's how I found out that you'd met Christabel,' Rio explained lazily, propping himself up on one elbow to gaze down at her. 'So, when my parent discovered that you'd already walked out on me, all I got was a very humiliating lecture about how she wasn't at all surprised. How *could* you tell her that I said I might get fond of you?'

Helpless amusement filtered through Holly, for she was now remembering that Alice Lombardi had said that the only explanation for her son's behaviour was that he had fallen madly in love with her. 'Serves you right.'

Rio dealt her a rueful scrutiny. 'I never did apologise for letting you go down to the Priory alone. It's just that my mother does rather dramatise events, *bella mia*—'

'You told her nothing about me—'

'I told her *everything* in London. She had the smelling salts out, but you now stand high in her estimation as the female who rescued me from a scarlet woman and saved the family name from scandal,' he told her with a wicked grin. 'When she heard you'd been taking Italian lessons she was even more convinced I didn't deserve you—'

'How did you find out about them?' Holly gasped and then she groaned. 'Oh, no, I forgot to cancel them!'

'Relax. Your teacher phoned and I used the same excuse with her that I used for our nanny's benefit. Family emergency. I couldn't tell anyone that you might not be returning because I couldn't *face* that possibility,' Rio confided.

'If you'd told me the truth about your broken engagement it would never have happened...'

His darkly handsome features tensed. 'I didn't want you thinking less of me,' he muttered tautly.

'Think less of you? *How?*'

Dark colour now scored his superb cheekbones. 'I just thought you'd think less of me if you knew the truth. My fiancée turning to another woman… It may sound stupid to you, but I was afraid it might take the stars out of your eyes when you looked at me,' he finally completed in a distinct tone of embarrassment.

'And you liked the stars?'

Rio nodded in serious and steady confirmation.

'I still have the stars.' Holly linked her arms round him and loved him more than she had ever loved him for admitting that to her. So there he was, totally gorgeous and sexy and everything she had ever dreamt of, and yet he could suffer from insecurity too.

'I'm crazy about you, *tesoro mio*. You be sure to tell me if you ever find those stars blinking out.'

'You'll have to spoil me rotten…'

'No problem. Spoiling you usually means spoiling me too.' Rio gave her his husky, sexy laugh and eased her back into more intimate connection with him again.

Holly was entirely hooked on the message of loving intent in his possessive gaze. Just as well he didn't know how many stars there were…enough to last two lifetimes, she thought happily. And then he kissed her and the stars turned into fireworks again and she thought no more.

Eighteen months later, Holly glanced into the nursery at the town house to see Alice Lombardi literally swamped with young children. Seated between the twins' cots with Timothy on her knee, her mother-in-law was reading a story out loud.

Timothy was almost two and a half years old and, only the day before, Holly and Rio's dearest wish had come true. Jeff had not contested their application and the court had granted the adoption order. Alice had flown over from Florence simply to attend the hearing. Rio was now officially Timothy's adoptive father and Timothy had the same right to the Lombardi name as his baby sisters, Amalia and Battista. They had all celebrated with a special dinner the night before.

Three months earlier, Holly had given birth to the twins. It had been an easy but very tiring pregnancy and Rio had fussed over her to an almost embarrassing degree. He had also fainted dead away in the delivery room on the day of their daughters' birth, a reaction which he was still trying to explain away as the result of over-excitement. With three children in the household, Alice Lombardi was in her element when she visited. She adored children and that had been clear to Holly from the instant Timothy had crawled across the floor into the older woman's eagerly extended arms. Alice made no difference between Timothy and the more recent arrivals in the family, and Holly loved her for that.

Furthermore, although Rio's mother still had bad days with her arthritis, her health had improved a great deal. But then, Holly did not think Rio had ever understood quite how bored and depressed the older woman had been with her life prior to their marriage. But Holly had begun to understand as she watched Alice slowly lose her concept of herself as an invalid to become more active.

Leaving the older woman in peace to enjoy the children, Holly thought about how her own parents had also benefited from their marriage. Well aware of how independent his father-in-law was, Rio had not made the mistake of offering direct financial help, which would have been refused. Instead, her husband had invested in the farm, enabling her father to hire a worker to help out. Holly had had the pleasure of seeing her own father take on a new lease of life, no longer stressed by worry about how he would cope as he got older.

Yes, there was no doubt about it, Holly reflected as she changed into an elegant blue shift dress. Rio was one very special bloke, who went to endless trouble to help those he loved.

She respected him for what he had done for Christabel as well. Feeling that his former fiancée was having enough of a struggle getting her life back on track after leaving the rehabilitation clinic, he had asked Holly if she would mind if he simply signed that apartment of his over to Christabel. And no, she hadn't minded, and she had even been pleased when the blonde spoke to her months later at a charity function.

'Rio's a really great guy,' Christabel had proclaimed with genuine warmth and had then lowered her voice to groan, 'But, to be honest, he was way too good-living for me!'

Christabel's life had moved on too and she certainly seemed content. Having set up a successful modelling school, she had then caused a great stir with the announcement that she was bi-sexual and a reformed addict. That confessional session in front of the cameras had gained her enormous publicity but she had recently started dating men again.

Holly went to say goodnight to her children. Timothy was almost asleep and she straightened the bedclothes and removed half a dozen toy cars from the spread before dropping a kiss down on his smooth brow.

'Night…night,' Timothy mumbled and then revived

slightly as he focused on the tall dark male who had appeared in his bedroom doorway. 'Hug…Dad.'

During the hug, a whispered exchange took place. The toy Ferrari that Holly had removed from the bed was slid back under the covers but she turned a blind eye to that evidence of male complicity. Timothy was such a happy toddler, full of affection and little-boy liveliness.

'One down, two to go, *cara*,' Rio quipped as he curved an arm round her and accompanied her into the nursery. 'After having you around yesterday, I missed you at the office today.'

'I missed you too.' Holly smiled at the thought of how much her outlook on life had changed over the past eighteen months. She had never dreamt that she might end up doing a basic business course just to see what it was like and that she might enjoy it and want to learn more, but that was what had happened.

Right now, of course, with the children all so young, it wasn't possible for her to do much more than study part-time. That week, however, she had spent a morning with Rio at Lombardi Industries, actually seeing how the business world operated, and she had been fascinated by that insight into an average day in his life.

'If you were there the whole time I probably couldn't concentrate,' Rio confided, smiling appreciatively down into Amalia's cot. 'She's just beautiful when she's sleeping, isn't she?'

Holly tried not to laugh, but there was no denying that their eldest daughter had caused a lot of disruption in her first weeks of life by flatly refusing to sleep at almost any stage of the night. Holly had been darned grateful to have both a husband and a nanny. Mercifully, Amalia had recently settled into a more reasonable routine.

'And Battista…' Rio studied his younger daughter with touching pride. She had the same curly dark hair as Amalia, for their daughters were identical twins, but there the resemblance ended, since Battista slept like a log and seemed to have a more philosophical attitude to life.

Leaving the nursery, they went into their bedroom because Rio said he needed a shower before dinner.

'Same old routine. I don't know why I bother putting clothes on for you coming home,' Holly lamented in a long-suffering tone of teasing provocation.

Laughing, Rio threw back his darkly handsome head and then kissed her breathless anyway. 'What happened to those stars in your eyes?'

'Those stars are multiplying at an incredible rate,' Holly swore, gazing up into dark golden eyes that were full of love and appreciation and tenderness. He adored her and she knew it.

'I must be on a real winning streak, then, *tesoro mio*.' Rio locked her to his lean, powerful body with possessive hands.

'Not this evening, you're not,' Holly told him ruefully, striving not to quiver against him in an inviting way, although it was very difficult when her resistance was nil. 'Have you forgotten Alice is staying until tomorrow?'

'And dining out with friends,' Rio reminded her with a slashing smile of amusement as she let herself quiver and meld to him like a second skin, all restraint vanishing.

Holly gave him her starry-eyed look of love and saw

it beautifully reflected in his own gaze. She wound her arms round him, possessive and proud and dizzy with happiness, and it was a very long time before either of them thought of eating.

* * * * *

THE SPANISH GROOM

CHAPTER ONE

César replaced the phone, his lean, strong face taut, wide, sensual mouth compressed. So Jasper's health was failing. Since his godfather was eighty-two, the news should not have come as a shock...

Rising restively from behind his desk, César crossed his spacious office—a contemporary triumph of glass and steel, wholly in keeping with a minimalist building much mentioned in architectural digests. Formed round a series of stylish atriums embellished with lush greenery and tranquil fountains, the office block César had commissioned to house the London headquarters of the Valverde Mercantile Bank was as elegant and impressive as its owner.

But César was indifferent to his surroundings. His thoughts were on Jasper Dysart, who had become his guardian when he was twelve. He was a true English eccentric, a bachelor bookworm who had made rare butterflies his lifestudy, and the kindest old man imaginable. César and Jasper were mental poles apart. Indeed César and Jasper might as well have come from different planets, but César was fond of Jasper, and suddenly grimly aware that the only thing Jasper had ever wanted him to do remained undone and time now seemed to be running out...

A knock on the door heralded the entrance of his executive assistant, Bruce Gregory. Normally the very epitome of confident efficiency, for some reason Bruce chose to hover, a sheet of paper rather tensely clutched between his fingers.

'Yes?' César prompted impatiently.

The young blond man cleared his throat. 'The random security check has turned up a member of staff with financial problems.'

'You know the rules. Getting into debt is grounds for instant dismissal.' César frowned at the need to make this reminder when that warning appeared in all staff employment contracts. 'We deal with too much confidential information to take the risk.'

Bruce grimaced. 'This...er...person is a very minor cog in the bank, César.'

'I still don't see a problem.' The brilliant dark eyes were cool, unemotional, the hallmark of a hugely successful financial genius with neither time nor sympathy for those who broke the rules. César was contemptuous of weakness, and ruthless at exploiting it in business opponents.

'Actually...it's Dixie.'

César stilled. Bruce studied the wall, not wanting to see César smile at that information. Everybody know how César felt about Dixie Robinson, currently the equivalent of an office junior on the top floor. Dixie, quite simply, irritated the hell out of César.

She had not one single trait which *didn't* grate on her cool, sophisticated employer. In recent weeks, César had been heard to censure her sloppy appearance, her clumsiness, her friendly chatter, her constant collecting for obscure charities…and, it had to be admitted, a degree of incompetence at business skills that had raised her to the level of an office mascot. César, alone, was deflatingly untouched by the compensatingly warm and caring personality which made Dixie so universally well liked.

But then on a level playing field, Dixie Robinson would never have got as far as an interview at the Valverde Mercantile Bank: she had no qualifications. Jasper Dysart had *asked* César to give her a job. Personnel had jumped to the task, only to find themselves seriously challenged by Dixie's inability to cope with technology. Passed on from one department to another, Jasper's protegée had finally arrived on the top floor, a fact which had delighted her elderly sponsor but which had unfortunately brought Dixie into César's immediate radius.

César extended a hand for the computer printout. Bruce passed it over with perceptible reluctance.

Scanning down the sheet, César slowly elevated a winged ebony brow. Evidently Dixie Robinson led a double life. The list of her dissatisfied creditors included a well-known interior designer and the kind of bills that indicated some serious alcoholic partying. César was tickled pink, his even white teeth flashing in a derisive grin of satisfaction.

So her resolutely innocent front *was* a façade, just as he had always suspected it was. For a split second he thought how appalled Jasper would be—Jasper who broke out with a modest sherry only at Christmas and who fondly believed that Dixie Robinson was a thoroughly decent, old-fashioned girl with homely tastes.

'Obviously she's been really stupid. But if she's sacked, she'll sink like a stone,' Bruce pointed out gruffly. 'She doesn't handle anything confidential, César—'

'She has access.'

'I don't really think she's bright enough to use that kind of information,' Bruce breathed tautly.

César gave him a look of grim amusement. 'Got you fooled as well, has she?'

'Fooled?' Bruce's brow furrowed.

'Now I know why she always looks half asleep—too many late nights.'

In desperation, Bruce shot his last bolt in Dizzy's defence. 'I guess Mr Dysart will be upset not to find her here on his next visit.'

'Jasper's not well. It's unlikely that he'll be in London in the near future.'

'I'm sorry to hear that.' Bruce studied his employer's coolly uninformative face warily. Well, that was that, he acknowledged. He couldn't say he was surprised either. César was not a soft touch. And proof of such foolish extravagance had merely increased his contempt. 'I'll pass the information concerning Dixie on to Personnel.'

'No. I'll deal with this personally,' César contradicted without warning.

Bruce wasn't quite fast enough to hide his dismay.

'I'll see Miss Robinson at four,' César completed.

'She'll be very upset, César.'

'I think I can handle it,' César drawled, in the sort of tone that made the younger man flush and go into retreat.

Alone again, César studied that list of creditors, a smouldering look awakening in his narrowed gaze. Jasper was very fond of little Dixie Robinson. In fact, superficially Dixie was exactly the kind of young woman Jasper longed to have César produce as the future Mrs Valverde, the sort of girl who didn't intimidate an innocent old bachelor totally out of step with a world approaching the Millenium.

So there it was, out in the open. The admission that he *had* disappointed his godfather, César conceded with exasperated reluctance. Jasper's deepest and most naive hope had always been that César would marry, settle down and have a family. And live happily ever after, of course, César affixed, scornfully recalling his late parents. His volatile Italian mother and equally volatile Spanish father had between them stacked up half a dozen failed marriages before dying young and anything but happy.

Wincing at the very idea of marital togetherness with any woman, but with his conscience still causing him rare discomfiture, César brooded on the problem of Jasper's disappointment. Experience had taught César that there was no such thing as a problem without a solution. When shorn of the inhibiting factors of emotion and morality, the impossible could almost always become the possible…

No doubt Jasper fondly imagined that his veiled hints about what a wonderful wife Dixie Robinson would make some fortunate male had been too subtle to be recognised for what they were. In point of fact, Jasper had the subtlety of a sledgehammer, and when César had first picked up on his godfather's pointed comments on the subject of his protegée he had been anything but amused.

But now César grimly acknowledged that were he

to announce that he *had* got engaged to Dixie Robinson, Jasper would be overjoyed. César visualised Dixie with something less than joy, but Jasper thought the sun rose and set on her. And, as pleasing Jasper was César's only goal, there would be little point in persuading any other woman into playing his temporary fiancée. What Jasper wanted, César decided there and then, Jasper deserved to receive.

As he pictured how he might sensibly stress the need for a lengthy engagement between two such disparate personalities as himself and the office klutz, César began warming to the exercise. It would make Jasper happy. And Jasper, who could spend hours just choosing a single book, would scarcely expect his godson to leap straight from an engagement into matrimony.

And Dixie Robinson? Dixie was between a rock and a hard place. She would do as she was told. Around him, she was quiet and cowed, which was just as well because César was convinced he would strangle her if she behaved any other way. He would slim her down, smarten her up, do whatever it took to ensure that the fake engagement appeared credible. He would be nothing less than thorough...

'At f-four?' Dixie stammered, pale as milk as she stood over the photocopier, striving somewhat hopelessly to conceal the 'inoperative' sign flashing above a pile of discarded photocopies printed with impossibly tiny type. 'But why would Mr Valverde want to see me?'

Already conscious that his attempt to speak up on her behalf had taxed César's patience, Bruce did not dare utter a word of warning.

'Is it about that Arab guy whose call I cut off?'

Bruce tensed. 'He doesn't know about that.'

'That file I accidentally took out?'

Bruce paled at the reminder. 'You got it back from the bus company.'

Dixie gulped. 'I've been trying so hard to stay out of Mr Valverde's way…it's just he keeps on popping up in the most unexpected places.'

'César likes to be visible. What sort of unexpected places?' Bruce could not resist asking.

'Like the kitchen…when I was icing the cake for Jayne's leaving party last week. Mr Valverde went through the roof,' Dixie recounted, half under her breath, shuddering at the recollection. 'He asked me if I thought I was working in a bakery and I ended up spelling her name wrong. Then yesterday he walked into that little room the cleaning staff use and found me asleep…he gave me the biggest fright of my life!'

'César expects all his employees to make a special effort to stay awake between nine and five,' Bruce responded, deadpan.

Currently working two jobs just to keep a roof over her head, Dixie gave him an abstracted look, her eyes, so dark a blue they were violet, strained with anxiety and tiredness. Fear emanated from her in waves. Small though she was, she seemed to grow even smaller as she hunched her shoulders and bowed her head, the explosive mop of her long curly dark brown hair falling over her softly rounded face. She was terrified of César Valverde, had become acquainted with every hiding place on the executive floor within days of arriving there.

But then she had started out on the wrong foot, hadn't she? Her big mouth, she conceded glumly. While covering for the receptionist during her afternoon break,

Dixie had begun chatting to the gorgeous blonde seated in the waiting area. In an effort to make entertaining conversation, she had mentioned the world-famous model, Mr Valverde had entertained on his yacht the previous weekend. And then her employer had strolled out of the lift...

And without the slightest warning all hell had broken loose! The blonde, who it later transpired had actually been waiting for César Valverde, had risen to her feet to throw a jealous fit of outrage and accuse him of being a 'love-rat'.

Dixie's co-workers had very decently acknowledged that that charge might well have some basis in fact, but it was not an allegation César had expected to face within the hallowed portals of the bank because one of his own staff had been recklessly indiscreet. Indeed what César had had to say about Dixie's gossiping tongue had been, as one of the directors had frankly admitted while trying hard not to smile, unrepeatable. Since then she had been banned from manning Reception.

'Is César dating any nice girls at present?' Jasper always asked hopefully in his letters to Dixie, not seeming to appreciate that at the threat of what his godfather deemed a 'nice girl' César Valverde would undoubtedly run a mile. It was a well-worn joke in the bank that César's answer to commitment was escape.

But Dixie's troubled face softened at the thought of Jasper Dysart. He was a dear old man, but she hadn't seen him in months because he lived in Spain most of the year, having found the hot climate eased his arthritic joints.

Dixie had met Jasper the previous summer. She had been walking down the street when a thuggish bunch of

youths had carelessly pushed him aside when he didn't
get out of their way fast enough. Jasper had fallen and
cut his head. Dixie had taken him to the nearest hospital. Afterwards, she had treated him to tea and buns in
the cafeteria, because he had looked so poor and forlorn
in his ancient tweeds and shabby old overcoat.

They had been firm friends from that moment on.
She hadn't once suspected that Jasper might be anything
other than he appeared: an elderly academic living on a
restricted income. So she had been quite honest about
being unemployed, sharing her despair at not even being
able to get as far as an interview for a clerical job. She
had also told him how horribly guilty she felt about
being dependent on her older sister Petra's generosity.

They had arranged to meet up again, and Jasper had
escorted Dixie to his favourite secondhand bookshop,
where they had both promptly lost all track of time
browsing through the shelves. The following weekend
she had returned the favour by taking him to a library
sale, where he had contrived to buy a very tattered copy
of an out-of-print tome on butterflies that he had been
trying to find for years.

And then quite casually Jasper had announced that
he had fixed her up with an interview at the Valverde
Mercantile Bank. 'I put in a word for you with my
godson,' he had informed her cheerfully. 'He was very
happy to help.'

She hadn't had a clue that Jasper's godson was the
chief executive. And she had been utterly appalled to be
confronted by César Valverde that first day, and coldly
interrogated about exactly how she had met his godfather. He had made little attempt to conceal his suspicions about her motives in fostering such a friendship

with an elderly man, and had coolly enjoyed informing her that Jasper would be returning to his home in Spain at the end of September. Dixie had found that encounter deeply humiliating.

'César always had a head for figures...very clever chap with that sort of stuff,' Jasper had conceded vaguely when Dixie had later gently taxed him with his failure to tell her that his godson *ran* Valverde Mercantile and was, in fact, a super-rich and very powerful legend of thrusting success in the financial world. 'It's in his blood.'

Jasper was a genius at understatement. The Valverdes had been in banking for generations. César was the last of the dynasty, and reputedly the most brilliant. He also had very high expectations of his staff. All Dixie's colleagues had a university degree in financial management, economics or languages, and thrived on the cracking pace of a high-powered mercantile bank with an international list of hugely important clients and companies.

Dixie knew that she was a fish out of water at Valverde Mercantile, only fit, it sometimes seemed, to run messages, ensure the coffee machines stayed filled and perform the most humble of tasks. She worked really hard at keeping busy, but the kind of lowly work she did rarely produced results that other people could appreciate.

And Bruce Gregory's announcement had thoroughly shaken Dixie. The threat of a face-to-face meeting with César Valverde kept her stomach churning throughout the day. What had she done? What had she *not* done? Well, if she had made some awful mistake or oversight, she would have to grovel on her knees and promise to do better in the future; she had no choice.

Right now, the only thing keeping Dixie going through exhaustion was the knowledge that she had a steady salary coming in as well as what she earned working as a waitress several nights a week. That long talk she had had with the helpful lady at the Citizens' Advice Bureau had suggested that as long as she could prove an honest intent to pay back those creditors in instalments, her offer to do so should be acceptable, and would hopefully protect her from the threat of legal proceedings.

And, in the meantime, there was always the hope that her sister Petra would phone to say that she was back in funds again and able to send the money to clear her debts. Petra had always had terrific earning power as a model, Dixie reminded herself bracingly. All she herself was really doing was holding the fort until her sister could pick up the financial slack. Petra *had been* upset when Dixie called her to tell her about the bills she had neglected to pay before she flew out to Los Angeles in the hope of starting an acting career.

In the cloakroom, minutes to go before the encounter, Dixie freshened up and morosely surveyed her reflection. Plain and wholesome, that was her. The loose beige top and long grey cotton skirt at least concealed the worst of her deficiencies, she told herself in consolation. But as always it seemed particularly cruel to Dixie that she should have been endowed with hatefully large breasts and generous hips but only a height of five feet two inches.

As often happened at times of particular stress, Dixie drifted off into her own thoughts. Was it any wonder that Scott saw her as a good sport and a mate, rather than a possible girlfriend? Scott Lewis, handsome, extrovert and the love of Dixie's life. Momentarily, self-pity filled her to overflowing. And then she scolded herself for being so foolish. Hadn't she always known she didn't have a hope of attracting Scott?

She had met Scott at one of her sister's parties. Having just moved into a new apartment, he'd been giving a comic description of his less than successful efforts to get organised on the domestic front. His frank admission that his mother had spoilt him rotten had impressed Dixie, and before she had even thought about what she was doing she had found herself offering to come round and give him a hand...

When Dixie presented herself for her appointment, César Valverde's secretary, a svelte brunette in her thirties, gave her a pained look. 'It might have been a good idea to be on time, Dixie.'

'But I am on time.' Dixie checked her watch and then her face fell. Once again time had run on without her.

'You're ten minutes late.' The other woman didn't wince but she might as well have done.

Sick with apprehension, Dixie knocked on the door of her lofty employer's office and walked in, a band of tension tightening round her head, her mouth bone-dry and her palms damp.

César Valverde spun lithely round from the wall of glass which overlooked the City skyline and studied her. 'You're late,' he delivered icily.

'I'm really sorry...I just don't know where the time went.' Dixie studied the deep-pile carpet, wishing it would open up and swallow her and disgorge her only when the interview was safely over.

'That is not an acceptable excuse.'

'That's why I apologised,' Dixie pointed out in a very small voice without looking up.

There was really no need to look up. In her mind's eye she could still see César Valverde standing there, as formidable and unfeeling as a hitman. And close to him she always felt murderously awkward, not to mention all hot and bothered. Yet he was physically quite beautiful, a little voice pointed out absently inside her head.

He had the lean dark face of a fallen angel, blessed with such perfect bone structure that at first glance he knocked women flat with his spectacular sleek Mediterranean looks. Hair thick and glossy as ebony. Eyes the same colour as dark bitter chocolate, which blazed into the strangest silver in strong light. Mouth mobile, wide and sensual. A sensationally attractive male animal, but at second glance he had always chilled Dixie to the marrow.

Those stunning eyes were hard and cold, that shapely mouth rarely smiled, except at someone else's misfortune, and those sculpted cheekbones stamped his features with a quality of merciless unemotional detachment which intimidated. He might radiate raw sexuality like a forcefield, but Dixie still prided herself on being the only woman in the whole building who was repulsed by César Valverde. The guy could give a freezer pneumonia just by arching one satiric brow.

Belatedly conscious of the dragging silence, Dixie emerged from her own reflections and glanced nervously up. Her pupils dilated, her heartbeat quickening as she stared. A decided frown on his striking dark features, César Valverde was strolling in a soundless circle round her, his piercing gaze intent on her now shrinking figure.

'What's wrong?' she breathed, thoroughly disconcerted by his behaviour and the intensity of his scrutiny.

'*Dio mio*...what's *right*?' His frown deepened as her slight shoulders drooped. 'Straighten up...don't slouch like that,' he told her.

Flushing, Dixie did as she was told. She was relieved when he positioned himself against the edge of his immaculately tidy glass desk.

'Do you recall the terms of the employment contract you signed before you started work here?'

Dixie thought about that and then guiltily shook her head. She had had to fill in and sign an avalanche of papers at speed that first day.

'You didn't bother to study the contract,' César gathered with a curled lip.

'I was desperate for a job...I would have signed anything.'

'But if you'd read your contract, you would have known that getting into debt is grounds for instant dismissal.'

That unexpected revelation struck Dixie like a sudden blow. She stared at him in horror, soft full lips falling apart, what colour there was in her cheeks slowly, painfully draining away. César studied her the way a shark studies wounded prey before moving in for the kill. In silence he extended a computer printout.

With an unsteady hand, Dixie grasped at the sheet. Her heart felt as if it was thumping at the foot of her throat, making it impossible for her to breathe. The same names and figures which already haunted her every waking hour swam before her eyes and her tummy flipped in shock.

'Security turned that up this morning. Regular financial checks are made on all staff,' César informed her smoothly.

'You're sacking me,' Dixie assumed sickly, swaying slightly.

Striding forward, César reached for a chair and planted it beside her. 'Sit down, Miss Robinson.'

Dixie fumbled blindly down into the chair before her knees gave way beneath her. She was waiting for him to ask how such a junior employee could possibly have amassed debts amounting to such a staggering total. Indeed, in that instant of overwhelming shock and embarrassment, she was actually eager to explain how, through a series of awful misunderstandings and mishaps, such a situation had developed through no real fault of her own.

'I have not the slightest interest in hearing a sob story,' César Valverde delivered deflatingly as he lounged back against his desk again, his impossibly tall, lean and powerful length taking up a formidably relaxed pose.

'But I *want* to explain—'

'There is no need for you to explain anything. Debts of that nature are self-explanatory. You have a taste for living above your means and you like to party—'

Cringing at the knowledge that he knew about those shameful debts in her name, and her equally shameful inability to settle them, Dixie broke back into speech. '*No*, Mr Valverde. I—'

'If you interrupt me again, I won't offer you my assistance,' César Valverde interposed with icy bite.

Struggling to understand that assurance, Dixie tipped back her wildly curly head and gaped at him. *'Assistance?'* she stressed blankly.

'I'm prepared to offer you another form of employment.'

In complete confusion, Dixie blinked.

'But if you take on the role, it will entail a great deal of hard work and effort on your part.'

Sinking ever deeper into bewilderment, but ready to snatch at any prospect of continuing employment like a drowning swimmer snatches at a branch, Dixie nodded eagerly. 'I'm not afraid of hard work, Mr Valverde.'

Obviously he was talking about demoting her. Where did you go from office junior? Dixie wondered frantically. Scrubbing the floors in the canteen kitchen?

César sent her a gleaming glance. 'You're really not in a position to turn my offer down.'

'I know,' Dixie acknowledged with total humility, suddenly starting to squirm at the reality of how much she had always disliked him. Evidently she had completely misjudged César Valverde's character. Even though he had a legitimate excuse to sack her, he seemed to be willing to give her another chance. And if that meant scrubbing the canteen kitchen floor, she ought to say thank you from the bottom of her heart and get on with it.

'Jasper hasn't been well.'

The switch in subject disconcerted Dixie. Her strained face shadowed. 'By what he's said in his letters he still hasn't quite got over that chest trouble he had in the spring.'

César looked grim. 'His heart is weak.'

Dixie's eyes prickled. That news was too much on

top of all her other worries. Her stinging eyes overflowed and she dug into the pocket of her skirt to find a tissue. But the horrible news about Jasper did make sudden sense of César Valverde's uncharacteristic tolerance, and his apparent willingness to allow her to remain in his employment by fixing her up with another job. He might not approve of her, or of her friendship with Jasper Dysart, but clearly he respected his godfather's fondness for her. Presumably that was why he wasn't going to kick her when she was already down.

'At his age, Jasper can't hope to go on for ever,' César gritted, his unease with her emotional breakdown blatant and icily reproving.

Fighting to compose herself, Dixie blew her nose and sucked in a deep, steadying breath. 'Will he be coming over to London this summer?'

'I shouldn't think so.'

Then she would never see Jasper again, she registered on a powerful tide of pain and regret. The struggle to stay abreast of the debts Petra had left behind made a trip to Spain as out of reach as a trip to the moon.

'It's time we got down to business,' César drawled with perceptible impatience. 'I need a favour, and in return for that favour I'm prepared to settle your debts.'

'Settle my debts…what favour?' Dixie echoed, all at sea as to what he could possibly be talking about and stunned by the idea of him offering to pay off those appalling bills. A favour? What sort of favour? How could her staying employed in any capacity within the Valverde Mercantile Bank be any kind of a favour to César Valverde?

César moved restively away from the desk and strode over to the window, the clear light of early summer glittering over his luxuriant hair and hard, classic profile. 'In all probability, Jasper doesn't have long to live,' he spelt out harshly. 'His dearest wish has always been that I should marry. At this present time I have no intention of fulfilling that wish, but I would very much like to please him with a harmless fiction.'

A harmless fiction? Dixie's bemusement increased as she strained to grasp his meaning.

'And that is where you come in,' César informed her drily. 'Jasper likes you. He's very shy with your sex, and as a result he only warms to a certain type of woman. *Your* type. Jasper would be overjoyed if I announced that we had got engaged.'

'We...?' Dixie whispered weakly, certain she had missed a connecting link somewhere in that speech and beginning to stand up, as if by rising from the chair she might comprehend something that she couldn't follow while still sitting.

César wheeled round, a forbidding cast to his lean features. 'Your job would be to pretend that you're engaged to me. It would be a private arrangement between us. You would play the role solely for Jasper's benefit in Spain.'

A curious whirring sound reverberated in Dixie's eardrums. Her lungs seemed suddenly empty of oxygen. Disbelief paralysing her, she gazed wide-eyed across the room at César Valverde. 'You can't be serious... *Me*,' she stressed helplessly, 'pretend to be engaged to...to *you*?'

'Jasper will be convinced. People are always keen to believe what they *want* to believe,' César asserted with rich cynicism.

As yet uncertain that this weird conversation was actually taking place, Dixie moved her head in a negative motion. 'But nobody would believe *that*…that you and I…' A betraying tide of colour slowly washed up her throat into her cheeks. 'I mean, it's just so *un*believable!'

'That's where your upcoming hard work and effort will pay off.' Once again César studied her with that curious considering frown he had worn earlier. 'I intend to make this charade as credible as possible. Jasper may be naive, but he's no fool. Only when I've finished transforming you into a slimline, elegant Dixie Mark Two will Jasper be truly convinced.'

It crossed Dixie's mind that César Valverde had been at the booze. A slimline Dixie Mark Two? She snatched in a short, sustaining breath. 'Mr Valverde, I—'

'Yes, I expect you're very grateful,' César dismissed arrogantly, a scornful light in his brilliant dark eyes as he surveyed her. 'In fact I imagine you can hardly credit your good luck—'

'My good luck?' Dixie broke in shakily, wondering how any male so famed for his perception could be so wildly off course when it came to reading her reactions.

'An image makeover, a new wardrobe, all your debts paid *and* an all-expenses-paid trip to Spain?' César enumerated with cool exactitude. 'It's more than good luck…from where you're standing now, it's the equivalent of striking oil in the desert wastes! And you don't deserve it. Believe me, if I had an alternative choice of fiancée available you'd have been fired first thing this morning!'

'I was the *only* choice, wasn't I?' Dixie gathered in a wobbly voice. '*Your* type,' he had said minutes ago, the only woman liked by Jasper that César Valverde knew. A slimline Dixie Mark Two? How dared he get as personal as that? Didn't he even appreciate that she had feelings that could be hurt? But then why should he care, standing there all lean and fit and perfect, probably never having had to watch his appetite once in his entire spoilt rotten life!

'That's irrelevant. By the way, I want this arrangement of ours to stay under wraps.' César scanned her with threatening dark eyes. 'Do you understand the concept of keeping a secret, Dixie?'

Locked to those spectacular dark eyes, Dixie felt oddly dizzy and out of breath. 'A secret?'

'It's quite simple. If you open your mouth to another living soul about this deal, I'll bury you,' César Valverde murmured with chilling bite.

Dixie blenched. 'That's not very funny.'

'It wasn't meant to be. It was a warning. And you've been in here long enough. As soon as you walk out of this office, you can clear your desk and go home. I'll be in touch this evening so that we can work out the finer details.'

Dixie lifted her chin, her rarely roused temper rising at the arrogance with which he simply assumed that she would do whatever he told her to do, no matter how immoral or unpleasant it might be. 'Whatever decision I make, I can now consider myself sacked… isn't that right?'

'Wow, quick on the uptake,' César derided smoothly. 'Too dumb to safely operate anything with a plug attached, but reads Nietzsche and Plato in her spare time. According to Jasper, you have a remarkable brain. And yet you never do anything with it. You certainly never dreamt of bringing it into work with you—'

Her lashes fluttered over huge violet eyes. 'I beg your—?'

'But then that's because you're a lazy, disorganised lump, who contrives to hide behind the front of being a brick short of the full load! Only around me you won't get away with that kind of nonsense!'

Disbelief roared through Dixie as she reeled from the full impact of that derisive attack, even though on another level she longed to question him about Jasper having said that she had a remarkable brain. However, anger abruptly overpowered that brief spark of surprised pleasure and curiosity. 'If I can consider myself sacked, then I'm free to tell you exactly what I think of you too!'

César gave her a wolfish half-smile of encouragement. 'I'm enjoying this. The office doormat suddenly discovers backbone. Make my day… Only be warned— I will respond in kind.'

Teeth almost chattering with the force of her disturbed emotions, Dixie drew herself up to her full unimpressive height and hissed, 'You have to be the most unscrupulous, selfish human being I have ever met! Doesn't it even occur to you that I might have some moral objection to cruelly deceiving a sweet old man, who deserves better from a male he loves like a son?'

'You're right. That thought didn't occur to me,' César confessed, without a shade of discomfiture or remorse. 'Considering that you're currently on the brink of being taken to court for obtaining goods and services by fraudulent deception, I'm not remotely impressed by the sound of your moral scruples!'

Dixie shrank and turned white. 'Taken to c-court?' she stammered, aghast, her eyes nailed to him in the hope that she had somehow misunderstood.

CHAPTER TWO

'*Dio mio…*' César raised a winging ebony brow to challenge Dixie's stricken expression. 'Didn't you read that printout I gave you either? The interior designer, Leticia Zane, has instigated proceedings. Did you expect her to be sympathetic towards a client who took advantage of her services without the slightest hope of being able to pay for them?'

Numbly, Dixie shook her pounding head, her stomach curdling. 'But I haven't got any more money to give Miss Zane…I've already offered instalments.'

César Valverde shifted a broad shoulder in an unfeeling shrug. 'The lady may well have decided to make a public spectacle of you to deter other clients who are reluctant to settle up. You're a good choice—'

'A good choice?' Dixie parroted, scarcely believing her ears.

'You don't have socially prominent friends likely to take offence on your behalf and damage her business prospects.'

'But…but a court prosecution.' Dixie squeezed out those words, breathless with horror, utterly appalled by what he was spelling out to her. Her own naivety hit her hard. She stared down at the printout, belatedly reading the small type beneath the debt to Leticia Zane's firm. 'Prosecution pending', it said. Her blood ran cold with fear and incredulity. The interior designer knew very well that all the work on her sister's apartment had been done at Petra's behest. Dixie had merely been the mouthpiece who'd passed on the instructions.

'Delusions of grandeur have a price, like everything else,' César Valverde sighed.

'I can't think straight,' Dixie mumbled sickly.

'Sharpen up. I haven't got all day to wait for an answer that is already staring you in the face,' César breathed with callous cool.

Dixie gave him a speaking glance from tear-filled eyes and fumbled with the crushed tissue still clutched between her shaking fingers. 'I just couldn't deceive Jasper like that, Mr Valverde. I couldn't live with lying to him. It would be absolutely wrong!'

'You're being selfish and shortsighted,' César drawled crushingly, dealing her a look of hostile reproach. 'Getting engaged to you is the one thing that I can do to make Jasper happy. What right have you to say that it would be wrong or immoral?'

'Lies are always wrong!' Dixie sobbed helplessly, and turned away from him in embarrassment.

'Jasper won't ever know it was a lie. He'll be delighted. I plan to leave you with him in Spain for a few weeks…assuming he's well enough for me to leave, even temporarily,' César adjusted flatly.

'I couldn't…I just *couldn't*!' Dixie gasped strickenly, already plotting a weaving path towards the door, barely able to see through her falling tears but determined not to be swayed by his specious arguments. 'And it's wicked of you to call me selfish. How can you *do* that?'

'For Jasper's sake…easily. I'll call on you tonight to get your final answer. I think you'll have seen sense by then.'

Dixie hauled open the door with a trembling hand and shot him an angry, accusing glance. 'Go to hell!' she launched thickly as she walked out.

Only as she shut the door behind her did she notice the little clutch of staff standing with dropped jaws further down the corridor.

'And you OK, Dixie?' Bruce Gregory enquired kindly.

One of the directors put his arm round her in a very paternal way to walk her away. 'We'll get you sorted out with a job some place else.'

'Not in a bank,' someone whispered ruefully.

'Ever thought of cooking for a living?' another voice asked brightly. 'You're a great cook.'

'A restaurant kitchen could be very stressful, though.'

'And I drop things,' Dixie muttered, a sense of being a total failure creeping over her.

'Imagine you telling César to go to hell!' the director remarked bracingly.

'But he'll never let Personnel give her a decent reference now,' Bruce groaned as the older man slotted her into a seat in the office she shared with a couple of the secretaries. Just about everybody on the whole floor seemed to crowd around her then.

'He tried to blackmail me,' Dixie mumbled sickly.

'Say that again…' someone breathed.

Dixie reddened, and then turned very pale with fright at what she had almost revealed in her distress and buttoned her mouth. 'Don't mind me…I don't know what I'm s-saying,' she stammered fearfully.

And she registered then that her brain was in a state of complete flux. What César Valverde had suggested already seemed completely unreal, a figment of her own fevered imagination. A fake engagement to please Jasper? A fantasy slimline Dixie Mark Two, united even in pretence with César's icy sophistication? Did blue moons come up in pairs?

'I don't know what we're going to do for a laugh around here now,' someone lamented.

'You'll have to get your goldfish out of the fountain... wasn't the ideal environment for them anyway. César raised Cain when he saw you out there feeding them,' Bruce reminded her ruefully.

'There's only one now, and I don't even have an aquarium!' Dixie sobbed, because it felt like absolutely the last straw. To take her goldfish out of the fountain below César Valverde's office and never, ever come back into the building? Suddenly she felt completely bereft and cut adrift.

Across the room, her desk was being cleared for her. One carrier bag grew into three as books, knitting, fish food and sundry items were removed from the crammed drawers. Tissues were supplied and a glass of water was pressed on her.

'We're all going to really miss you, Dixie...so we had a bit of a whip round.' She was mortified when a large fat envelope was thrust by Bruce into her shoulder bag. She realised then that everyone had known even before she did that she was getting the sack, and had been waiting to comfort her.

'I'll give you a lift home with your bags,' Bruce volunteered.

The chipped china jardinière was filched from beneath the dying cactus on her desk, and the goldfish she had found abandoned at the bus stop in a plastic bag removed with some difficulty from the fountain and temporarily rehoused.

'I just can't get over how kind everyone's been,' Dixie confided as she climbed into Bruce's car in the basement car park.

She clutched the planter with careful hands, gazing down at the single handsome goldfish she had secretly christened, César. He had eaten his original companion, and even the one she'd actually bought for him, fearing that he would be lonely. César the fish was up near the surface, patrolling with fast flicks of his tail. Dixie gave him a loving and abstracted smile.

'César can be a real bastard. But the guy's a complete genius. You can't expect him to be human too. Try not to think about it. Go round and do Scott's washing…or whatever,' Bruce advised, striving to be upbeat. 'That always seems to give you a lift.'

Yes, it did, she acknowledged ruefully, only this evening she would be waiting tables. But doing anything for Scott gave her the feeling that she had some small personal stake in his busy life. And in the right mood, if Scott didn't have a hot date or wasn't eating out, he might suggest that she cooked some supper and stayed to eat with him. She *lived* for those infrequent invitations.

'You were in with César a very long time,' Bruce commented abruptly.

'We talked a little about Jasper.'

'Dixie…why did you say César tried to blackmail you?'

'I must've been trying to make a silly joke…'

Bruce sent her scared face a covert appraisal. 'He never did approve of your friendship with the old man. Can't think why.'

As soon as Bruce had carried her bags upstairs for her, he left to speed back to the office, long hours being a feature of his highly paid employment. Dixie unlocked the door of her bedsit. She transferred César the fish into a large glass mixing bowl and fed him, setting him next to the window in the hope that a view of the pigeons on the roof opposite would keep him entertained.

Locking up again, she went down the street to call in on a neighbour she often babysat for at weekends. In return the older woman kept her Jack Russell dog, Spike, during the day.

She took Spike for a quick walk in the park, and then nervously carried him back up to her bedsit for the night. She wasn't allowed to keep pets, but she had never had any bother sneaking Spike in after it got dark. Now that the light nights had arrived, she was really scared that she would be seen.

How on earth had her life got into such a terrible, frightening mess? she asked herself in a daze as she watched Spike wolf down his dinner. The future had looked so promising when she had first come up to London to share Petra's spacious apartment, certainly a lot brighter than it had seemed for many years beforehand…

Dixie's mother had died when she was five and her father had remarried the following year. It was hard to recall even now that Petra wasn't really her true sister but actually her *step*sister—the daughter of her father's second wife, Muriel. Already a teenager, Petra had had little interest in a child seven years younger, but Dixie

had always longed for a big sister and had adored blonde
and beautiful Petra. At seventeen, Petra had left home
on her first modelling assignment.

A year later, Dixie's father had died of a heart attack, and the year after that Muriel had shown the first
symptoms of what was to prove to be a long, debilitating terminal illness. Dixie had never managed to pass
any exams because she had been forced to miss so much
school. Whenever Muriel's health had been particularly
bad, Dixie had had to stay at home to see to her needs.
She had left school at sixteen.

Over the following four years, Petra had sent
money home regularly but the demands of a career
which took her all over the world had made it impossible for her to visit much. A year ago, Muriel Robinson had passed away, and Dixie had more or less
invited herself up to London to stay with Petra. Used
to living alone, Petra had understandably not been too
keen on the arrangement at first, but had soon appreciated that Dixie could look after her apartment when
she herself was abroad.

For her own convenience, Petra had opened a household account in both their names, and paid in sufficient
money to cover her bills, so that Dixie could easily pay
them for her. And when, soon afterwards, Dixie had
started work at Valverde Mercantile, she had had her
entire salary paid into the same account.

Dixie had frequently ordered expensive food and
alcohol for Petra's lavish parties. In the same way she
had dealt with Leticia Zane, after the interior designer's initial meeting with Petra, ensuring that all the
costly redecoration was done in exactly the way her
sister wished.

And then, about three months ago, Petra had suddenly announced that she was leaving the UK. Giving up the lease on her apartment, she had packed her bags and flown to Los Angeles. Dixie had moved into the bedsit. But within weeks the demands for payment had begun rolling in from her sister's creditors. Dixie had discovered that the joint account was not only empty of her own savings but also overdrawn. Only after the deputy bank manager had patiently explained it to her had Dixie understood that she herself could be held liable for Petra's unpaid bills.

She had immediately phoned her sister. After admitting that she was broke, but promising to help as soon as she could, Petra had rather drily reminded Dixie of all the money she had generously sent over the years that Dixie had been nursing her mother, Muriel. And Dixie had felt really guilty, because tough as those years had been they would have been intolerable without Petra's financial assistance.

But the next time Dixie had phoned that same number she had been told that Petra had moved on without leaving a forwarding address. That had been two months ago, and since then she hadn't heard a word from her sister.

The awful fear that Petra had not the slightest intention of getting in touch again, or of trying to satisfy her creditors, was now beginning to haunt Dixie. She felt so disloyal, thinking about Petra that way. Yet in her heart of hearts she was facing up to the harsh fact that her glamorous stepsister invariably put her own needs first.

And Dixie was terrified of being taken to court and appalled by the reality that she had no way of settling those dreadful bills. That was so unfair to the creditors concerned, and César Valverde *had* offered to pay them...

'Can I just run over this again?' Dixie asked the table of customers anxiously. 'That's one cheeseburger with pickles, one without dressing, a double—'

'How many times do we have to go over this?' one of the teenagers groaned. 'A double hamburger *with* pickles, a single cheeseburger *without*...'

Pink with embarrassment, Dixie hurried to amend her notebook as the girl ran through the entire order again. Beneath the jaundiced eye of the manager, Dixie thrust the order over the counter.

'Get those tables cleared,' he urged impatiently.

Scurrying over to her section of the busy café, Dixie began to load up a tray. She was so tired that she could feel her knees wobbling whenever she stood still. Wiping her damp brow with the back of her hand, she lifted the heavily laden tray. As she straightened, she could not help but focus on the tall, dark male blocking her view of the rest of the cafe. Dixie froze in shock and dismay.

César Valverde stood six feet away, emanating the kind of lacerating cool which intimidated. Brilliant dark eyes entrapped her evasive ones. As he lifted one ebony brow at her frazzled appearance and coffee-stained overall, Dixie simply wanted to curl up and die. Oh, dear heaven, how had he found out where she worked? And what did he want now, for heaven's sake?

But then had she really believed that César Valverde would take no for an answer? He wasn't accustomed to negative responses. His naturally aggressive temperament geared him to persist and demand in the face of refusal, she reminded herself. A workaholic, he thrived under pressure and lived for challenge. When César Valverde set himself a goal, he went all out to get it. She should feel sorry for him, she told herself. He really didn't know any other way to behave.

An exasperated male voice demanded, 'Where's our food?'

'It's coming…it's coming!' Dixie promised frantically, rudely dredged from her reverie. She fled without looking where she was going, as to look would have brought César Valverde back into focus again.

A shopping bag protruding from beneath a table was her undoing. Catching her foot, Dixie tipped forward, and the tray shot clean out of her perspiring hold. Eyes wide with horror, she watched pieces of food, coffee dregs, crumpled napkins, plates and cups go flying up in the air and fall in all directions. The noise of smashing china was equalled if not surpassed by the shaken exclamations of customers lurching from their seats in an effort to escape the aerial bombardment.

A deathly silence fell in the aftermath. Feverishly muttering incoherent apologies, Dixie bent down to scoop up the tray. The manager removed it from her trembling hands and hissed in her ear, 'You had your final warning yesterday. You're fired!'

Only yesterday, three entire meals complete with accompanying drinks had landed on the floor, because in an effort to speed up Dixie had overloaded a tray and then stumbled. Tears of mortification and defeat stinging her eyes, Dixie scuttled into the back of the café. Ripping off the overall, she reached for her cardigan and bag.

When she emerged again, the manager stuffed a couple of notes into her hand. 'You're just not cut out for waitressing,' he said ruefully.

A long, low and expensive sports car hugged the pavement outside the café. The driver's window whirred down. César surveyed Dixie with an enquiring brow.

'It's your fault I dropped that tray…you spooked me!' Dixie condemned unevenly.

'If you hadn't been so busy trying to ignore me it wouldn't have happened.'

'You are so smug and patronising. I hate you!' Dixie gasped truthfully, studying his staggeringly handsome dark features with unconcealed loathing. 'You always think you're right about everything!'

'I usually am,' César pointed out, without skipping a beat.

'Not about deceiving Jasper…so go away and leave me alone!'

Walking on past, Dixie struggled to swallow the aching thickness of tears in her throat. The car purred in her wake but Dixie was oblivious. In the space of one ghastly day a security that had at best been tenuous had come crashing down round her ears. Jasper was dying, she thought wretchedly, and she was going to end up being prosecuted like a criminal.

'Get in the car, Dixie!'

Having totally forgotten about César Valverde while she pondered her woes, Dixie nearly died of fright. She glanced round and saw the flash car only feet away. Sticking her nose in the air, she prepared to cross the road to the bus stop.

'Get…in…the car,' César framed as he climbed out, six foot three inches of towering bully.

'I don't have to do what you tell me any more!' Dixie
flung chokily.

A policeman crossed the road. 'Is there some problem here?'

'Yes, this man won't leave me alone!' Dixie complained.

'I saw you kerb-crawling,' the policeman informed
César thinly. 'Are you aware that kerb-crawling is an
offence?'

'This woman works for me, Officer,' César drawled
icily.

'Not any more, I don't!' Dixie protested. 'Why won't
you just leave me alone?'

'I don't like the sound of this, sir.' The policeman
appraised the opulent car and then the cut of César's
fabulous dark grey suit with deeply suspicious eyes.

'Look, that's my bus coming!' Dixie suddenly
gasped.

'Settle the misunderstanding, Dixie,' César com-
manded in a tone of icy warning.

'What misunderstanding?' she enquired in honest
bewilderment.

'This gentleman was kerb-crawling and employing
threatening behaviour. I think we should all go back to
the station and sort this out,' the policeman informed
her as he radioed in the registration of César's car.

César looked at Dixie. Eyes like black ice daggers
dug into her. It was like being hauled off her feet and
dropped from a height. She blinked, and then warm
colour flooded her drawn cheeks. 'Oh…you actually
think…my goodness, are you kidding?' she pressed
in a strangled voice. 'He would never bother *me* like
that…I mean, he would never even *look* at me like that!'

'Then what was this gentleman doing?' the police-man asked wearily.

'He was offering me a lift home…and we had a slight difference of opinion,' Dixie mumbled, not looking at either man in her mortification. This policeman had *genuinely* suspected that César Valverde had been kerb-crawling with an intent to…?

'And now she's going to get in my car and be sensible,' César completed stonily.

Dixie slunk round the sports car and climbed in. 'It's not my fault that policeman thought you might've been making improper suggestions,' she muttered in hot-faced embarrassment.

'Oh, don't worry about that. That *wasn't* what he was thinking. He thought I might be your pimp,' César gritted not very levelly, half under his breath, his accented drawl alive with speaking undertones of raw incredulity.

Dixie nestled into the gloriously comfortable bucket seat and decided that silence was the better part of valour. Flash car, flash suit. In this particular area César probably had looked suspicious.

'How *dare* you embarrass me like that?'

'I'm sorry, but you were annoying me,' she mumbled wearily.

'*I*…was annoying…*you*?'

He seemed to find that very difficult to understand. But then an enormous amount of boot-licking went on in César Valverde's vicinity, Dixie reflected, struggling to smother a yawn.

People shouldn't worship idols, but they did. Expose the average human being to César's intellectual brilliance, immense wealth and enormous power and influence, and they generally behaved in all sorts of

undignified ways. They toadied, they talked a load of
rubbish in an effort to impress, and went to ridiculous
lengths to please and be remembered by him.

As for the women—that constant procession of gorgeous females who paraded through his life, Dixie reflected sleepily. Well, he had the concentration span of
a toddler, always on the look-out for a new and better
toy. And he invariably had a replacement lined up before he ditched her predecessor. But he was never available during working hours, and those women who tried
to breach that boundary lasted the least time. Possessive behaviour was a surefire way to make César stray.

César shook her awake outside the building where
she lived. 'As a rule, women do not fall asleep in my
company.'

'I don't fancy you,' Dixie mumbled, barely half
awake, and then aghast at the sound of what she had
just said.

'Then you won't develop any ambitious ideas while
we're in Spain, will you?'

'I'm not going to Spain.'

'Then you can send Jasper cute "glad you're not
here" postcards from prison.'

Dixie sat up, full wakefulness now established, and
turned aghast eyes on him.

César gave her a faint smile. 'It's your first offence,
but who knows? Women often get weightier sentences
than men when they transgress.'

Her tummy tying itself into petrified knots, Dixie
whispered shakily. 'Maybe we should talk this over.'

'I think we ought to,' César agreed smoothly. 'A
female who said she was your landlady cut up rough

when I knocked on the door of your bedsit earlier and a dog started barking. She came upstairs to investigate.'

Dixie sat bolt upright, horror now etched on her face. 'Oh, no, she heard Spike and now she knows he's there!'

César released an extravagant sigh. 'And pets aren't allowed. I gather it's going to be a question of moving out or getting rid of the dog.'

Dixie shook her head in anguished disbelief. This was truly the very worst day of her entire life. 'Why did you have to knock on the door? You must've frightened Spike! He's usually as quiet as a mouse.'

'I think Spain's beckoning,' César remarked lazily. 'You have one very angry landlady waiting to pounce.'

'Oh, no...' Dixie groaned.

'Life could be so different,' César drawled smoothly. 'All those debts settled...no nasty hanging judge to face in court...relaxing trip to Spain...Jasper happy as a sandboy and the comforting knowledge that you are responsible for giving him the best news he's ever heard. *Wrong?* I don't think so. I don't think anything that could give Jasper pleasure at this trying stage of his life could possibly be wrong.'

Hanging on every specious word, Dixie watched him with a kind of eerie fascination. He was so damnably clever, so shockingly good at timing his verbal assaults. Here she was, her whole life in ruins and on the very brink of being thrown out on the street because she couldn't possibly give up Spike, and a living, breathing version of the devil was holding out temptation without shame.

'I couldn't...'

'You could,' César contradicted softly. 'You could do it for Jasper.'

Dixie's soft full mouth wobbled as she thought of Jasper dying and never, ever seeing him again. Her eyes began to prickle and she sniffed.

'You can pack right now. It's *that* simple,' César stressed in the same low-pitched deep, dark tone.

He sounded mesmeric. Dixie couldn't peel her wet eyes from him either. In the dusk light, his bronzed features were half in shadow, dark eyes glimmering silver beneath the sort of long, incredibly luxuriant black lashes that would drive any sane woman blessed with less to despair.

'My dog, Spike...' she muttered uncertainly, so very, very tired it was becoming an effort even to string words together, her mind a confused sea of incomplete thoughts and fears.

'Spike can come too. One of my staff will pick up the rest of your possessions tomorrow. You won't have anything to do,' César asserted gently.

At that moment, the concept of not having anything to do impressed Dixie like the offer of manna from heaven. 'I...I—'

César slid out of the driver's seat, strolled round the bonnet and opened the door beside her. 'Come on,' he urged.

And Dixie found herself doing as she was told, all the fight drained out of her. 'A harmless fiction', César had called it. A pretend engagement to make Jasper's last days happy. And it *would* make Jasper happy. She knew how much Jasper longed to see César on the road to creating the family circle that Jasper had never managed to create for himself. Maybe lying wasn't always wrong...

Her landlady emerged from her small flat on the

ground floor. As she broke into angry, accusing speech, César settled a wad of banknotes into her hand. 'Miss Robinson will be moving out. I hope this takes care of her notice.'

A phone was ringing somewhere horribly close to Dixie's ears. Struggling to cling to sleep, she sighed with relief when the shrill buzz stopped, but her eyes slowly opened on the dawning realisation that she didn't have a phone in her bedsit.

Her brain in a fog, Dixie surveyed her unfamiliar surroundings. For a moment she couldn't even remember where she was. Then her attention fell on the suitcase lying open with miscellaneous garments tumbling untidily out of it. And whoosh, everything came back in a rush; she was in César Valverde's London home.

The phone by the bed started ringing again. This time Dixie reached for the receiver. 'Hello?' she said nervously.

'Rise and shine, Dixie.' César Valverde's rich, dark drawl jerked her bolt upright in the bed. 'It's half-six and I want you in the gym by eight, dressed appropriately and fully awake.'

'The gym?' Dixie was aghast at the news that she was expected to be up before seven in the morning, particularly on a Saturday. Even Spike was still asleep in his basket. He was as fond of having a lie-in as his owner.

'I've engaged a fitness instructor to put you through your paces,' César completed drily, and rang off.

A fitness instructor? Dixie stared into space with wide eyes, picturing some giant, suntanned muscle-bound male standing over her like a bullying sergeant-major, bawling instructions liberally splattered with abuse. She shrank. Maybe the instructor would be nice and break her in gently. She tried to imagine César hiring someone nice. Hope dwindled fast. The fitness instructor would be tough and pitiless. César was, after all, the male who had called her a lazy lump.

Scrambling out of bed, Dixie roused Spike and left the bedroom. A short corridor beyond led out to a small enclosed courtyard.

On her arrival the night before, Dixie had been handed over to César's butler, Fisher, like a unwelcome parcel. The comfortable *en suite* bedroom she had been assigned on the ground floor was former staff accommodation. Dixie had understood the distinction being made. She was not going to be treated like an honoured guest in César Valverde's palatial Georgian mansion.

Having attended to Spike's needs, she went for a shower. Appropriate clothing? Dixie had never been in a gym in her life. A baggy pair of sweat-pants and an oversized T-shirt were all she had to wear. The unflattering combination made her look as wide as she was tall. A slimline Dixie Mark Two? But what if the exercise routine *worked*? a more seductive voice asked, and she dawdled by the mirror then, imagining Scott suddenly recognising her as a member of the female sex…

Her stomach growling with hunger, she was about to go off in search of the kitchen when a quiet knock sounded on the door.

Fisher appeared with a tray bearing a tall glass filled with some strange greyish green liquid. 'Miss Stevens faxed your diet plan to Cook yesterday,' the butler explained. 'I believe this is the lady's own personal recipe for an early-morning energy boost.'

'Oh…' In bewilderment, Dixie accepted the glass. *Diet plan?* She didn't like the sound of that. She was willing to exercise, but diet? And who on earth was Fisher talking about?

'Miss Stevens?' Dixie queried with a frown.

'Gilda Stevens, the fitness instructor,' Fisher supplied expressionlessly. 'Her instructions regarding your menus were most precise.'

At that point, Dixie's tummy gave an embarrassing gurgle. So her fitness instructor was a woman. Taking a sip of the noxious brew, Dixie tried not to grimace. A cruel woman. The drink tasted like dishwater with bits of floating weed, but, remembering her manners, Dixie drank it down and waited eagerly to be told when she might receive her first meal of the day.

'Mr Valverde will be in the gym in five minutes,' the butler informed her as he retrieved the glass and returned to the door.

'What about breakfast? Do I eat later…or something?'

'That *was* breakfast, Miss Robinson.' At her aghast look of disbelief, the older man averted his eyes.

'A drink…a drink is all I'm allowed on this plan?' Dixie breathed shakily.

In silence, the older man nodded.

Fisher gave her directions to the gym. On her way there she caught tantalising glimpses of magnificent paintings, marble floors and wonderful rugs. She was not surprised to walk into a superb purpose-built gymnasium worthy of the most élite health club.

At the far end of the spacious room, César was lounging elegantly back against a piece of machinery that looked like an instrument for torture. He was talking to a brunette wearing less clothing than Dixie wore in bed. Presumably Gilda Stevens. A tiny white crop top adorned the lady's dainty bosom. Skintight white shorts hugged her impossibly slender hips. Every inch of visible skin was tanned and satin smooth.

Oh, no, why does she have to be so gorgeous? Dixie thought, cringing from such a cruel comparison, such an impossible peak of feminine perfection.

Tall and supremely authoritative in a dark designer suit, sunglasses dangling from one brown hand, César spoke without turning his dark, arrogant head. 'Don't skulk, Dixie. Come and join us. Gilda's done us a very special favor in agreeing to devote her personal attention to you at such short notice.'

The very thin brunette studied Dixie critically as she walked towards her.

Dixie flushed, her soft mouth tightening with embarrassment. César swivelled round, as light as a dancer on his feet in spite of his size. His winged brows pleated as he took in her appearance with frowning dark deepset eyes. 'Haven't you got anything more suitable to wear?'

'Dixie would probably feel too self-conscious in more revealing garments. I've seen this so many times before,' Gilda Stevens informed them both. 'Fortunately, diet and exercise can work real miracles—'

'Look...' Dixie began. 'I'm not an inanimate object you can discuss—'

'I'll send out for some gear for you,' César cut in, lean bronzed features already distant as he strode towards the door.

Gilda gave Dixie a cool, assessing appraisal from glassy blue eyes, and a panicky sensation twisted Dixie's empty tummy. Before she could even think about what she was doing, she raced in César Valverde's wake. Suddenly he felt like her only friend.

'César!' she gasped strickenly.

At the door he wheeled round, brilliant eyes glittering with impatience.

'César…she's not a normal woman,' Dixie whispered almost pleadingly. 'When she stands sideways on she's only about six inches wide! I didn't know anybody could be that thin and still live…and of course I look enormous to her, but I can't help the shape I was born with!'

After a stunned pause, César threw back his arrogant head and burst out laughing.

'It's not funny,' Dixie hissed in severe mortification. 'When you talked about hard work and effort, you didn't mention depriving me of food and putting a stick-insect in charge of me. Did you see how she looked at me? Like I was the size of an elephant and she wanted to skin me?'

César pivoted round to the wood-panelled wall and braced one lean hand against it as he struggled to contain his mirth. Turning his head back to her, silvered dark eyes still vibrant with reluctant amusement, he murmured drily, 'It's the deal, Dixie. Gilda has an international reputation in the fitness field.'

'I'm hungry,' Dixie mumbled tightly, but, disorientatingly, she found that she couldn't take her eyes off him. With laughter dying out of his lean, strong face and his cool, dark brooding air of detachment banished, she glimpsed a different César Valverde. A devastatingly masculine male with megawatt charisma, she recognised in some shock. Colouring with discomfiture, she dragged her eyes from him and stared at the wall instead.

'Tough…no pain, no gain,' César rhymed without pity.

'Have you ever been on a diet, César?' Out of the corner of her eye she could see his classic profile, and she found her head easing round towards him again without her own volition.

'I'm too disciplined to over-indulge.'

Dredging her attention from a profile worthy of a Greek sculptor, Dixie decided it would be safer to study the natural wood floor.

'Don't *do* that…it always winds me up!' César imparted with startling abruptness. 'Look at me when I'm speaking to you!'

Blinking in hot-faced bewilderment that he had actually noticed she almost never looked directly at him, Dixie glanced up.

César's aggressive jawline eased only slightly. 'That's only one of your most annoying habits.'

As he turned away, Dixie cleared her throat awkwardly. 'What did you tell Miss Stevens to explain *why* you are hiring her for my benefit?'

Complete surprise flared in his stunning eyes. 'I don't explain my actions to anyone. Why should I?'

Why should I? The baseline on the way César Valverde lived his entire life, Dixie registered. He was so self-contained, so unapologetic about guarding his privacy. Naturally he wouldn't have the slightest inhibition about snubbing people who exercised their curiosity.

'Dixie…we'd better get started,' Gilda Stevens called. 'We'll begin with a weigh-in.'

Dixie hadn't been on the scales since she was sixteen, and inside herself she simply cowered.

'I'll see you tomorrow,' Gilda told Dixie.

Face-down on a mat, perspiring freely, Dixie tried to nod, but even that took muscle power and she decided not to bother. After all, at some stage she would have to get up, walk…well, maybe crawl, she decided. She was beyond caring about putting a proud face on her exhaustion.

'You're out of condition,' her torturer sighed as she took her leave. 'But now I've shown you the ropes you'll be able to follow through on your own every day.'

Every day. Dixie suppressed a groan but she forced a grateful smile. Gilda might be tough, pitiless and completely lacking in the humour department, but she had worked out alongside her and had been tireless in her efforts to ensure that Dixie did every single exercise correctly. Horribly, hatefully tireless.

Left alone, Dixie slowly slid into a comfortable doze. The sound of footsteps made her stir. Tipping back her head, she focused sleepily on Fisher's polished shoes.

'Where would you like to eat lunch?' the butler asked.

'Here will do.'

A tray was set on the floor. A plate piled high with salad greens and raw slivers of vegetable awaited her.

'I never liked salad,' Dixie confided guiltily.

'It's a detoxifying diet, I believe,' Fisher commented. 'You do get a whole grapefruit mid-afternoon.'

Dixie's tastebuds shuddered, but she was so hungry she munched at a piece of celery. 'I like starchy food. I like meat, pasta with lashings of cheese…chocolate fudge cake,' she enumerated longingly, mouth watering as she fantasised.

Another pair of shoes appeared in her field of vision. Italian leather casuals with handstitched seams. She froze.

'But you're not allowed to cheat,' César Valverde drawled.

'I thought you were at the bank,' Dixie said accusingly.

'I intend to keep an eye on this project. Just as well,' César condemned. 'Gilda's gone, and here you are lazing about like you're on holiday!'

'I'm so weak I can't move!' Dixie gasped in disbelief.

César crouched down to her level with athletic ease. Hard dark eyes assailed her dismayed orbs in a head-on collision. 'I checked your staff medical. You're healthy. There's no reason why you shouldn't follow a structured fitness regime. Why didn't you change into one of the exercise outfits I had sent over?'

They had all looked so incredibly small, and Dixie hadn't fancied struggling to squeeze herself into figure-hugging garments with Gilda around.

'You're over-tired because you let yourself get far too hot.'

'I need to eat to have energy,' Dixie muttered self-pityingly.

César dealt her a chilling glance of reproof. 'Your attitude to this is all wrong. In fact your attitude to life in general is your biggest flaw. You're so convinced you're going to fail you won't even bother trying!'

'I'll follow the schedule…OK?'

'That's not good enough. I want one hundred and five per cent commitment from you.' As César studied her with fulminating intensity, his jawline squared. 'Keep in mind what this is costing me. The sum total of your debts was considerable. And if you haven't learnt it yet, learn it now. There is no such thing as a free lunch.'

Having paled during that crushing speech, Dixie could no longer meet his ruthlessly intent gaze. 'I...I—'

'I paid for the right to expect you to stick to your side of this deal. Start slacking and you'll have me standing over you with a stopwatch! And if you think Gilda's bad, you ain't seen nothing yet!' César swore in unapologetic threat.

That evening, Scott's welcoming, 'Am I glad to see you!' was balm to Dixie's low self-esteem when she arrived on his doorstep.

Shyly pushing her heavy fringe off her brow, Dixie smiled up at him. Tall, slim and fair-haired, Scott responded with a matey punch that hurt her shoulder, and showed her straight into his kitchen.

'I had some friends staying for a couple of days. What a mess they left this place in!' he complained.

'I'll soon have it sorted out,' Dixie told him eagerly.

On his way back out again, Scott glanced at her and then frowned slightly. Pausing in the doorway, he stared at her. 'Have you done something to your hair or changed your make-up or something?'

Dixie tensed. 'No...I don't wear make-up.'

'It must be the colour in your cheeks. You look almost pretty.' Scott shook his handsome head over this apparently amazing development, frowned as if he was rather surprised to have noticed the fact, and departed, leaving her to the mounds of dishes stacked on every available surface.

Almost pretty. In real shock at the very first compliment Scott had ever deigned to pay her, Dixie hovered in the centre of his filthy kitchen with a dreamy look on her face. Colour in her cheeks? It was the effect of the exercise, it *had* to be! Maybe the detoxifying diet was starting to work already! Scott had finally noticed that she was female...

Suddenly feeling like a woman on a mission that might just miraculously transform her life, Dixie swore to herself that she would be up early the next day and into the gym to work out. Humming happily, she washed dishes, scrubbed the floor and cleaned the cooker.

'I don't know how you do it!' Scott exclaimed appreciatively as he paused by the kitchen door in the act of donning the jacket of a smart suit. 'What would I do without you, Dixie?'

Like a starved plant suddenly plunged into water and sunlight, Dixie blossomed and beamed at him.

'I'm off out now, but there's no need for you to hurry home,' Scott assured her. 'And if you could find the time to run the vacuum cleaner round the sitting room, I'd be really grateful.'

'No problem,' Dixie hurried to tell him. 'Is the washing machine fixed yet?'

'No, the mechanic's coming on Wednesday.' Scott grimaced. 'He says I must have one of those rogue machines.'

Dixie followed him to his front door with the aspect of someone walking on hallowed ground. 'Hot date?' she asked with laden casualness.

'Yeah. A real stunner too,' Scott chuckled. 'See you, Dixie!'

'See you,' she whispered, closing the door in his wake.

It was after ten when Dixie and Spike got back to
César Valverde's imposing home. She had to use the
front door and press the bell to gain entry. She just
hadn't been able to bring herself to leave Scott's apartment sooner, not until she had polished every piece of
furniture and vacuumed every inch of carpet. As Fisher
said goodnight to her, Dixie gave him a vague smile
and drifted away.

She was ludicrously unprepared for César Valverde
to stride out of one of the reception rooms off the lofty
ceilinged hall and demand harshly, 'Where the hell have
you been?'

'I…I b-beg your pardon?' Dixie stammered.

'I expected a report on your progress at six and you'd
already gone out,' César imparted grimly.

'Oh…I was with Scott.' Dixie studied him vaguely,
as if she couldn't quite manage to get him into focus.
In fact, she was striving to superimpose Scott's beloved
features onto César, to make him more bearable, but for
some strange reason the attempt wasn't working. And
instead she somehow found herself making all sorts of
foolish comparisons between the two men…

César was much taller, more powerfully built, his
skin a vibrant gold where Scott's was fair. César's luxuriant black hair was perfectly cut to his well-shaped
head, not endearingly floppy like Scott's…oh, heavens,
what was she doing, and why was she studying César
Valverde like this, noticing every tiny thing about him
where once she had been afraid to look at him?

An odd shivery sensation Dixie had never experienced before ran through her when she collided with
those striking dark eyes of his…so piercing, so brilliant, so *alive*. A definable five o'clock shadow rough-

ened his jawline, accentuating the wide, sensual shape of his mouth, the perfect whiteness of his teeth. And he still looked so incredibly, impossibly immaculate, she reflected in growing wonderment. How did he *do* it? Here she was, with wind-tousled damp hair, a stain of cleansing fluid on her T-shirt and shoes spattered from puddles.

'How do you do it…how do you look so perfect all the time?' Dixie heard herself ask wistfully, desperate for the magic secret, the miracle formula which might transform her appearance as well.

'Are we on the same planet?' César enquired with satiric bite.

'I don't think so.' Dixie reddened with sudden discomfiture.

'Who's Scott? A boyfriend?' César demanded with a chilling edge to his dark, deep-accented voice.

'Oh, I don't have a boyfriend… Scott's just…Scott… well, Scott…' Suddenly Dixie was having some difficulty in quantifying her relationship with Scott, because tonight she had rediscovered hope, and to write Scott off as merely a friend now felt like acknowledging defeat again.

'Scott?' César queried with an impatient flare of one ebony brow.

'Scott Lewis…' Her blue eyes became even more abstracted. 'I love him, but he hasn't really noticed me that way yet, but I think he might be on the brink—'

César clenched his even white teeth. 'I'm getting closer to the brink too—'

Dixie heaved a sigh, shoulders down-curving. 'So I suppose I still have to say that Scott's just a friend.'

'Dixie…I asked a straight question. I didn't request

an outpouring of girlish confidence,' César informed
her with withering cool. 'I hope you're more circumspect with him than you are with me. I don't expect to
find out that you've confided in him about our private
arrangement.'

'Scott and I don't have those kind of conversations.'
Inexplicably the happy shine on Dixie's evening was
now beginning to drain away, leaving her feeling rather
down on the dumps. 'Nothing deep—'

'He's got his head screwed on, then, hasn't he?'
César sent her a winging glance of burning exasperation. 'You're not grounded enough for a deep conversation. Inside that flighty, vacant head of yours, you're up
in the bloody clouds with the angels most of the time!'

But then there was no room for magic or love in
César Valverde's world. He was so grounded in reality he didn't know what it was to dream. Well, he was
missing out on an awful lot, Dixie decided, determined
not to be affected by his censure.

Without warning the door of the room César had
emerged from opened again. A gorgeous blonde in an
elegant strappy black dress peered out and frowned at
Dixie. 'Staff problems, César?'

Taken aback by the appearance of the other woman,
Dixie stiffened with discomfiture.

César dredged his frustrated attention from Dixie
and turned with a slashing smile. 'Nothing that need
concern you, Lisette.'

Lisette. Frisky name for a frisky lady, Dixie thought
nastily, and then was genuinely shocked by her own
bitchiness. Lisette was probably a very nice woman,
and was undoubtedly far too good for César Valverde.
He was a real rat, the kind of guy who didn't phone,

always put work first, cancelled dates last-minute and strayed without conscience the instant he got bored. Poor Lisette. She was more to be pitied.

Dixie went to her room and settled Spike into his basket. She fed César the goldfish, still feeling guilty about him being alone in his bowl. But he obviously preferred being alone. He was an aggressive fish. But possibly the two companions he had eaten had been the wrong sex, she reflected with a considering frown. Maybe he would be transformed by the arrival of a female fish... Could she risk adding to the body count?

As Dixie pulled on her shortie pyjamas, she struggled against the conviction that if she didn't eat some proper food soon her stomach would meet her backbone. After all, now she had a goal, a *real* goal. Scott was worth that one hundred and five per cent commitment César had demanded from her. She would throw herself heart and soul into Gilda's fitness schedule.

But hunger kept Dixie tossing and turning, unable to sleep. At one in the morning she rolled out of bed in sudden decision. An apple, a slice of toast, a cup of tea with the merest drop of milk...surely such a meagre snack wouldn't show on the scales?

As Dixie crept with a fast-bating heart towards the kitchen, the entire house was in darkness. She stubbed her toe on the edge of the kitchen door and went hopping round on one leg in the gloom, silently screaming until the worst of the pain receded. Then she folded down on her knees in front of the giant fridge. Tugging open the door, she sat there gently massaging her aching toe and contemplating the immensity of the temptation now available.

One little sin, she urged herself circumspectly. Just

one… A sandwich…she wouldn't butter the bread, she bargained with herself. Or what about a thin slice of cheese on toast with a dash of that salsa…or possibly…?

'Just what do you think you're playing at?'

At the sound of that raw-edged icy demand coming out of nowhere at her, Dixie almost had a heart attack.

CHAPTER THREE

WITH a strangled cry of fright, Dixie twisted round on her knees, her heart pounding so fast she couldn't breathe.

The lights beneath the units flipped on, framing César, barefoot and bare-chested, only a pair of close-fitting jeans hugging his long, powerful legs as he stood there surveying her with complete scorn.

'I only wanted a little snack,' Dixie whispered tremulously. 'I didn't think I'd wake anybody up!'

'When I go to bed, I switch on the alarm system. If anything moves down here, I know about it.'

Abstractedly still rubbing at her throbbing toe, Dixie studied him with huge violet eyes. Clothed he was intimidating; half-naked he was…he was *awesome*. The instant that thought occurred to her, she reddened with mortification and twisted her head away, terrified that he might read her face and somehow *know* what she'd been thinking. But in her mind's eye she still saw César. Wide brown shoulders, sleek strong muscles flexing beneath smooth healthy skin as his hand dropped back from the light switch, a magnificent torso with curling black hair hazing his pectorals, and a stomach as taut and flat as a washboard.

A frisson of strange heat curled in Dixie's stomach and then seemed to dart down somewhere infinitely more private and sort of twist in pleasure-pain. Her mouth felt as dry as a bone and she didn't know what was the matter with her. Spooked by his descent, and dying with embarrassment at being caught in the act of trying to cheat on her diet plan, it was all too much at once. Dixie parted her lips to explain herself, but to her utter horror a choky little sob escaped instead.

'Porca miseria!' César glowered at her in disbelief. 'You can't be *that* hungry!'

Seeing him through a haze of mortifying tears, Dixie dragged herself upright and turned away, struggling to get a grip on her seesawing emotions and hide her face.

She didn't read anything into the silence that followed, merely pictured him gripping his whiplash tongue between his teeth sooner than risk provoking her into a real crying jag. And she felt so hatefully childish. She had never been a crybaby, but he always made her feel so awkward, useless and silly.

'Madre di Dio...' César Valverde breathed incredulously. 'Who ever would have believed it? You've got the body of a men's magazine centrefold!'

Dixie's damp eyes slowly opened wide with bewilderment. Not even crediting that he could possibly have said what she thought he had said, she whirled round. She connected with stunned dark eyes engaged in a shockingly intimate appraisal of her lightly clad length. Having until that instant completely overlooked the fact that she was only wearing a pair of shrunken shortie pyjamas, Dixie crimsoned under that raking scrutiny and crossed her arms over herself.

'Don't!' César ejaculated forcefully, his seemingly

mesmerised attention nailed to the proud swell of her full breasts so clearly delineated by the clinging cotton jersey.

His transfixed gaze came to a halt at her tiny waist, and at that point keeping a distance became more than he could apparently bear. Striding over to her, he turned her round with one impatient hand. Like a male quite unable to believe the evidence of his own eyes, he scanned the highly feminine curve of her hips and the surprising length of her shapely legs.

'What…for heavens' sake…*what are you doing*?' she gasped in helpless confusion at his behavior as she attempted to coil away and conceal as much as possible of the body she loathed.

'I assumed you were overweight. I thought you were hiding a multitude of sins beneath those shapeless sacky clothes you wore. I didn't even know you *had* a waist! And *Dio*, all the time…all the time,' César slowly repeated in a roughened and dazed undertone that sent a curious quiver rippling down her taut backbone, 'You were covering up the kind of lush curves that keep teenage boys awake and fantasising at night!'

'I don't know what you're talking about!' Dixie pulled away, hugging herself with her arms, shaken and mortified by what he was saying and convinced that he was being sarcastic. But, whatever, it was obvious that in his eyes she wasn't anything like as overweight as he had evidently believed she was. So maybe she could now risk letting her breath out, because holding her stomach in was becoming painful.

César backed off a soundless step, brilliant dark eyes veiled, faint colour highlighting his slashing cheekbones. A shuttered look wiped all expression from his stunning dark features as he continued to survey her. 'I know you don't. And while obviously you have no idea how to maximise what you've got, *I* have,' he stressed with unconcealed satisfaction. 'We'll be in Spain within a few days.'

'Within a few days?' Dixie parroted in astonishment. 'But that doesn't give me enough time to—'

'You don't need time. All you need is the right clothes and something done with that hideous untidy mop of Raggedy-Ann curls.' César strolled gracefully over to the fridge, flipped the door wide and cast her a satiric glance. 'Eat your heart out! And go easy on the exercise. Conserve your potential. I intend to exploit every luscious inch.'

And with that smooth invitation, light gleaming over his thick dark hair and smooth brown back, César sauntered back out of the kitchen, exuding in waves the kind of self-satisfied aura that he usually reserved for closing a major deal.

Every luscious inch? In a total daze of disbelief, Dixie squinted down at the much despised bountiful bosom which had caused her such agonies of mortification during her teens. Both her stepmother, Muriel, and Petra had been naturally thin, and only minimally endowed in that department. Both had fully entered into Dixie's conviction that such generous curves were gross and only worthy of concealment.

And school had been a nightmare for Dixie. She had started to develop at an age when her classmates were still flat-chested. The cruel, thoughtless teasing from the girls and the crude comments of the rowdier boys had devastated Dixie's confidence in her own body. Her pronounced hour-glass shape had made her a target for ridicule. Times without number she had come home from school and gone up to her room to cry her heart out.

Muriel had bought her a big sloppy sweater which she could pull down over her hips, ensuring that the size of her breasts became instantly less likely to attract attention. And ever since then Dixie had relied on the same remedy and dressed accordingly.

And yet César Valverde had, incredible as it seemed to her, actually looked at her figure with stunned appreciation. No, not any kind of *personal* appreciation, she hurriedly adjusted, wondering how on earth she had contrived to pick up such an exaggerated false impression from him. He had only been acknowledging that she had the sort of over-generous curves that teenage boys liked, and that was certainly not news to Dixie. His appreciation had been of the entirely dispassionate variety. But what she had always considered a great disadvantage and a flaw, César somehow saw as an asset.

And suddenly he didn't think she needed to lose weight, or even exercise too much. But had she really stood there, letting him look her over when she was, if not quite half-naked, certainly only minimally clad? A hot tide of painful color swept up Dixie's throat at that belated awareness. He had taken her so much by surprise. Now she felt sick with chagrin, and all desire to eat had ironically evaporated. Slamming shut the fridge door, she returned to her room.

So César Valverde didn't think she was quite as unattractive as he had believed. Hadn't he noticed her tummy or the surplus flesh on her thighs and ribcage? She peered over her shoulder at the pronounced swell of her hips and slowly shook her head, his staggering change in attitude still a complete mystery to her. But then César Valverde treated her like a piece of meat, to be properly packaged for sale in a butcher's window, and after all, the only living person she had to impress was Jasper Dysart…

César walked into the sunlit gym with Gilda the next morning and then stopped dead. His sunglasses dropped out clean of his hand. Sheathed in a fitting one-piece dark green leotard, Dixie was doing her warm-up exercises.

She paused and connected unexpectedly with César's shimmering dark eyes. She fiercely resisted the urge to wrap her arms round herself like a self-conscious schoolgirl. The leotard was less revealing than a swimsuit, she reminded herself. As she gazed across the gym, unwittingly entrapped by that piercing silvered stare of his, so bright in that dark masculine face, she began feeling light-headed, and without even realising it slowly fell still.

A wave of startling heat slowly engulfed her from head to toe. Her eyes widened, her pupils dilating as for the first time she became aware of her own body in the most extraordinarily unsettling way. Her skin felt too hot and tight to encase her bones. Her breasts felt strangely heavy, stirring in their cotton casing with her every shortened breath and making her nipples ache with oversensitivity.

Gilda picked up César's sunglasses and extended them to him. With a slight frown he slowly dredged his attention from Dixie, and momentarily studied the sunglasses as if they didn't belong to him.

'I got up really early this morning.' Dixie blinked

rapidly, like a sleepwalker rudely awakened. She folded her arms tightly above her waist, face burning as she strove to work out what had happened to her there for a few seconds while seriously hoping it never, ever happened again because she had felt really peculiar.

'That's the spirit!' Gilda applauded in the incredibly tense silence.

Without comment, César strolled over to one of the tall windows, effortlessly elegant in pale, beautifully cut chinos and an aqua silk short-sleeved shirt. Dixie's gaze abstractedly followed him, taking in the tense set of his wide shoulders, the aggressive jut of his set profile and the dusting of darker colour delineating one carved cheekbone. He was so incredibly perfect, she conceded absently, still having a problem getting her brain into gear while she could not help but wonder what was bothering him. Business, no doubt, or perhaps irritation at her unwelcome presence in his home and the disruption of his own workaholic schedule.

Two days later, Dixie appraised her new hairstyle in fascination. Her mop of curls had been tamed by the talented stylist. Sleek, feathery layers curved back from her face, fanning down into casual waves just clear of her shoulders. Shorn of the chunky overhang of hair she used to hide behind, her cheekbones now lent fresh definition to her features.

The beautician was waiting for her in another part of the salon. Dixie had given up on make-up because she had always seemed to buy the wrong colours and had never been satisfied with the look she ended up with. But with an expert adviser on hand to select the right shades, she was delighted with the subtle effect contrived with a few light cosmetics.

Clutching a beauty case crammed with items, as per
César's explicit instructions, she finally emerged and
walked back to the waiting area. She was astonished
to see César there, talking into a mobile phone while
glancing broodingly at his watch and studiously ignoring the many languishing female glances coming his
way from both staff and customers.

Dixie's steps slowed. Look at me, she suddenly
wanted to shout. *Notice* me! The shock of that instant
desire to impress was profound, but she soon explained
it to her own satisfaction. Five minutes after she had
arrived for her appointment at the salon, César had descended without warning. So wasn't it only natural that
he should now be keen to see the end result, and equally
natural that she should expect to be noticed?

After all, hadn't he told the stylist exactly what he
wanted him to do with her hair? Hadn't he warned
the beautician that he didn't want her covered in what
he had bluntly described as 'a two-inch deep layer of
goop'? She smiled helplessly at the memory.

'You've got to have a tongue in your head in a place
like this,' César had informed her drily before he departed again. '*You'd* give them a free hand, but they
need limits.'

And Dixie hadn't been the slightest bit embarrassed
while César was domineeringly engaged in setting those
limits, because two most unexpected compliments had
indirectly come her way. No, Dixie would not require
highlights, lowlights or any other kind of lights in her
dark brown hair. Dark brown hair was elegant, César

had stated, and also, since Dixie had flawless skin, why cover it up?

Now, when she was about six feet away from him, César's smooth dark head turned in her direction. He stilled, appraising her with unreadable dark-as-night eyes. Her breath fluttered in her throat, her heartbeat quickening as she waited for his reaction.

'Major improvement,' César commented as he retracted the aerial on his mobile and strode towards the exit, having awarded her little more than an assessing glance.

The wobbly smile of anticipation on Dixie's lips fell away as she rushed to keep up with him. 'Yes, it is, isn't it?'

'What?'

'An improvement?' Dixie reminded him wistfully, encouragingly, as they emerged on to the crowded street outside. 'I can't believe I look so much smarter.'

'Only from the neck up. Your wardrobe is still a disaster area,' César pointed out, thoroughly deflating her as he stood back for her to step into the rear of his chauffeur-driven limousine.

'No, you first,' she urged uncomfortably, still very conscious of what she felt to be his superior status.

'Move, Dixie,' César gritted in her ear.

In haste, Dixie scrambled into the limousine, sending a file sitting on the back seat flying. As documents spilled out, Dixie groaned and bent down to clumsily gather them up again. 'I didn't expect you to take the trouble to come into the salon this morning,' she admitted, squinting down at the documents and realising that there was no way she could even try to put them back in order when they were written in a foreign language.

'I didn't expect to have to take the trouble either,' César confided almost to himself, his attention lingering fixedly on the mess of confused papers now being apologetically slid on to the seat between them. 'I was in the middle of a board meeting before it dawned on me that I couldn't trust you alone in a place like that. You might go overboard and emerge looking totally unrecognisable—'

'I've always sort of wanted to be blonde,' Dixie mused absently, now engaged in hurriedly cramming the documents out of sight within the file. 'My sister's blonde—'

'—or you'd sit there in a total daydream and let them do whatever they felt like doing to you. It was too big a risk.'

'I'm sure this has all been very inconvenient for you,' Dixie muttered ruefully.

'You're not joking, but we'll get the clothes problem sorted today too. We're flying out to Spain the day after tomorrow.'

'That soon?' Dixie sighed. 'Spike's going to miss me terribly.'

'The dog? I haven't laid eyes on that dog since the night you moved in,' César remarked, with belated awareness of that surprising fact.

'Oh, you have, you just haven't noticed him. Spike hides when there are people around. He was very badly treated by his first owner. The lady he used to stay with during the day was a volunteer at the animal refuge, but he'll have to stay in your house while I'm away because I couldn't ask her to keep him for so long.'

'Couldn't...er...Scott keep him?'

'Spike is terrified of men. Anyway, Scott's at work

all day, and often out at night as well. I'm going to miss him too… Do you think I'll be in Spain long?' she asked rather guiltily.

'What does Scott do?' César enquired, without answering that question.

'He's a stockbroker with a City firm called Lyle and something…'

'Makes sense,' César said softly.

'What does?'

'That the smartass who has you acting as an unpaid skivvy would be a broker. Brokers are wheeler-dealers. He saw you coming.' César flicked her a narrowed glance of complete exasperation.

'You don't know what you're talking about…Scott is *not* a smartass!' Dixie had turned very pink, highly disconcerted as she was by that uninvited opinion coming from such a source.

'He knows that you're infatuated with him and he uses it to his own advantage.'

'I didn't ask you what you think and I don't want to know either!' Her hands tightly linked on her lap, Dixie stared unseeingly out the window at the heavy traffic. 'How did you find out that I help out with his housework anyway?' She suddenly had to know.

'I heard two of the secretaries talking about what an idiot you were weeks ago.'

Dixie trembled. It took that much effort to hold in the surge of angry humiliation now eating her alive.

'You don't seem to know any of the tricks other women are *born* knowing. Doing the guy's washing doesn't seem to be getting you very far,' César said with scathing cool.

'I hate you…do you know that?' Dixie jerked round to look at him, violet eyes pools of angry, hurt reproach.

'For telling you the truth? If you had any decent friends they'd have broken the news and given you a few useful hints long ago.'

For a split second meeting those stunning dark eyes on the level deprived Dixie of both breath and concentration. Her lashes fluttered in confusion and her head whirled. She sucked in oxygen and hurriedly turned her head away again, her heart slamming hard against her breastbone. She felt really shaky in the aftermath of that exchanged glance, and blamed it on her over-taxed emotions.

'You think I'm wasting my time, and yet you don't know Scott and you don't know me. What sort of "useful hints" do you think I need?'

'*Dio*…I'm not an agony aunt,' César drawled, boredom oozing from every honeyed accented syllable.

'Jasper spoilt you terribly…' Dixie's chagrined reaction to that snub leapt straight on to her tongue. 'That's why he worries about you so much. He feels responsible for the way you've turned out!'

The silence that rewarded that startling speech positively reverberated in her ears. Realising that she had been inexcusably blunt on the worst possible subject, Dixie glanced up in stricken apprehension.

Outraged dark eyes filled with rampant incredulity were trained to her.

'I'm sorry. I was too personal…but it's just you can be so very rude, and it doesn't seem to bother you that other people have feelings that can be hurt,' Dixie completed shakily.

'Is that a fact?' César drawled, with a sardonic smile that utterly dismissed her comments.

But Dixie was not fooled. She had drawn blood. His fabulous bone structure was rigid, his eyes glittering hard as diamonds. Dixie bent her head, shaken that she had spoken up to censure him and conscious that she had struck a very low and inappropriate blow in revealing that his godfather had actually discussed such very personal concerns with her.

She was thoroughly ashamed of herself. How could she have been so thoughtless? How could she have betrayed Jasper's confidence? And even though he had never been known to show them, César *had* to have some feelings! Naturally she had hurt César by voicing Jasper's guilty conviction that he had made serious parenting mistakes while he was his guardian.

Jasper had told her that César had always inhabited another plane from his peers. Intellectual brilliance had set him apart at an early age and made him intolerant of those less able. That whiplash tongue had made people very scared of César Valverde. If they weren't super-careful they lost face in César's presence; scorn was infinitely more humiliating than a straightforward rebuke or criticism.

'I should never have said those things,' Dixie whispered valiantly, desperately needing to try and put right any damage she might have done, particularly to Jasper's standing in César's highly critical eyes. 'And you mustn't get the idea that Jasper discussed you with me—'

'Where would I get an idea like that?' César countered, with such tacit scorn that she paled with even greater dismay and guilt.

'But it wasn't like that!' Dixie protested frantically. 'You remember all the publicity there was about that actress you dumped last summer? The one who was rushed into hospital with an overdose—?'

'Not an overdose. Alcoholic poisoning.'

'Oh…w-was it really?' Dixie floundered at that immediate contradiction.

'I dumped her because she was never sober,' César returned icily.

'Jasper didn't kn-know that, and he was upset at all the furore in the papers,' Dixie stammered. 'And that was when he said just a few things *unthinkingly*,' she stressed feverishly, 'about the way he had brought you up not having been the best—'

'*Accidenti!* I only knew the woman a few weeks.' Black eyes assailed hers in remorseless challenge. 'She had a problem long before I met her, but I persuaded her to accept professional help *and* I arranged for her to stay in a special unit where she received all the counselling and support she needed.'

'J-Jasper would've been so relieved to know all that,' Dixie mumbled weakly, treading now on ground she wished she had never dared to set a single toe upon.

Indeed, now squirming with embarrassment over her own clumsy misapprehensions, Dixie felt ten times worse. When she climbed out of the limo in César's imperious wake, she put an anxious hand on his sleeve. From his lofty height, he studied her small hand as if it was a gross invasion of his personal space.

Her nerveless fingers slid off his sleeve again as though she had been burnt. 'I didn't mean to hurt your feelings.' Sincere concern shone from her scrutiny.

'Hurt my feelings?' César echoed in disbelief. 'Where the hell do you get the idea that—?'

'You're a not very easy person to apologise to…are you?' Dixie was appalled to see bitter anger flaming in his burnished dark eyes. 'I just seem to keep on digging myself into a deeper hole with you. Every time I open my mouth, I put my foot in it.'

'A vow of silence would be welcome,' César spelt out grittily.

She got on his nerves, she conceded, her shoulders slumping.

'Don't slouch.' A lean hand squared over her spine to brace her upright again.

He really disliked her, Dixie thought morosely. Everything she did and said irritated him. She wasn't used to being disliked. Presumably that was why she felt so absolutely awful all of a sudden. Her usually sunny nature reacted to the endless night of his like oil on water. They were such incompatible personalities. He was so cold, so unfeeling, so critical, and that made her more nervous, more likely to say and do the wrong thing. She had always found it totally impossible to concentrate around César Valverde. It was as if her brain went on holiday.

César stole an undeniably apprehensive glance down at her tremulous lip line.

'I'm not going to cry…I'm *not*!' Dixie swore.

'You're not convincing me.'

Her wide eyes shimmered.

'*Dio*…you have really stunning eyes,' César breathed in an abrupt and roughened undertone, staring down into her face as if she was the only woman in the universe.

In severe shock, Dixie gazed back up at him, even her breathing arrested. That deep, sexy, accented drawl rippled down her sensitive spine and made her shiver in reaction. Locked into the dense darkness of his amazing eyes, it was as if the world had stopped turning for her, sentencing her to paralysis. Not a single thought filled her blank mind. And yet on another level she dimly recognised the desperate yearning surging up inside her like a hungry, terrifying beast. That sensation scared the living daylights out of her, but still she couldn't have moved, couldn't have spoken, couldn't have broken the spell that held her fast.

César did that. While she gazed at him, her heart beating so fast it felt as if it was about to burst from her chest, his spiky glossy black lashes lowered, setting her free from the cage of her own suffocating excitement. And as she watched, trembling, utterly disorientated by what was happening to her, she saw him breathe in very slowly and deeply, like a male tasting life-giving air after a long time asleep. A black frown line indented his brow, his striking features broodingly tense for a split second.

'I just got this really creepy feeling,' Dixie confided helplessly, tottering away from him to cannon blindly into a group of shoppers and stop to splutter unsought apologies while still blocking their path.

'Really...creepy...feeling?' César framed expressionlessly as he reached out a lean brown hand and tugged her out of harm's way and back towards him.

'I'm not feeling very well.' Her body still running alternately hot and cold like a broken boiler, her head spinning, her legs weak as matchsticks and her breasts throbbing in the most mortifying and uncomfortable way, Dixie focused on his burgundy silk tie with big bewildered eyes. 'I hope it's not the flu…or maybe I'm upset because I'm not likely to see Scott again for ages.'

A vague frown of recall on her flushed face, she looked up at César, surprised by the intensity of his piercing gaze. 'Why did you say that about my eyes?'

'I was trying to distract you. It worked like magic.' His eyes were as remote and icy as the Himalayas.

Distract her? From what? Oh, the tears. He had thought she was about to burst into tears and embarrass him in public. Naturally the bit about her eyes being stunning had been a whopper. It was a wonder he had managed to keep his face straight while he said it.

César urged her through the gilded doors of the hugely impressive store they had been standing outside. One step inside the doors, he abandoned her. The silence of an élite clientele and very expensive merchandise intimidated Dixie.

Her attention stayed with César, now in close conversation with a svelte older woman who appeared to have been awaiting their arrival. César had the most weird effect on her, she mused. That almost sick sensation of excitement she could only equate to her never-to-be-forgotten terror on a rollercoaster ride as a child. And he had treated her like an overwrought child.

He strode back across the floor to her, looking every inch what he was. A very, very rich and powerful man, a highly sophisticated male, superbly elegant in a formal pinstripe suit that accentuated every powerful line of his lean, magnificent length. He stopped a good four feet from her, rather as if he was in the presence of potential contagion. His expression was cold and hard as stone.

'Mariah will select your clothes. Regard them as

props and don't question her judgement. She knows what I want.'

And with that icy assurance he took his leave. Dixie stared after him with a perplexed frown. What had she done to deserve the deep freeze treatment? Just been herself, she decided glumly. Tactless, clumsy and embarrassingly emotional. Three flaws that César would never suffer from.

The evening of the following day, Dixie cast a dubious glance at herself in the bedroom mirror. Was that really her? The blue chambray skirt and fitted jacket showed an awful lot more of her body than she was used to seeing. As for the silk T-shirt she wore beneath, every time she looked down she was confronted by a view of her own cleavage. The strappy stiletto shoes had perilously high heels and she found it hard to walk in them.

The phone by her bed buzzed and she answered it.

'I want to see you in the drawing room in ten minutes,' César drawled coolly.

'Gosh, you nearly missed me. I was just on my way out to Scott's,' she confided cheerfully.

'It's going to take me a while to get the hang of these heels,' she carolled as she stumbled in the drawing room doorway and had to snatch at the doorhandle to steady herself.

In the act of lifting a brandy goblet to his lips, César froze. Dixie froze too. He was wearing a white dinner jacket that fitted him like a glove, the light colour throwing his vibrant golden skin and black hair and dark eyes into exotic prominence. He looked so devastatingly attractive Dixie's soft mouth fell open.

And for some reason César was staring at her too.

Suddenly self-conscious, and mortified by the way she had gaped at him, Dixie got all hot and bothered. 'Is this going to take long? I don't want to miss Scott.'

'*Dio mio*…he's unlikely to miss you.' Brilliant dark eyes scanned the fit of the T-shirt, the skirt outlining her tiny waist, then dropped to the shapely legs on display outside the gym for the first time. 'That bloody stupid woman!' he grated abruptly. 'You look like a bimbo! That neckline's too low. That skirt is too short.'

In frank dismay and surprise, Dixie gazed back at him. 'The skirt's only three inches above my knee—'

'Totally inappropriate for Jasper…and even more inappropriate for doing Scott's washing,' César completed with withering bite.

'I wanted him to see my new look.' Dixie's face had fallen like a disappointed child's.

César elevated a winged ebony brow, and suddenly such a desire seemed pathetic on her part. She flushed miserably.

Feeling both over and under-dressed, Dixie relinquished the colourful fantasy of Scott taking one look at her and instantly realising that she was the woman for him. She would put on her usual clothes and remove the make-up. Suddenly she was grateful that César had spoken up. She didn't want to make it obvious to Scott that she was trying to attract him. That might wreck their friendship and scare him off altogether, mightn't it?

'A jeweller is coming to show us a selection of engagement rings.'

'Oh…' Dixie said.

'Whatever you pick you can keep,' César informed her carelessly.

'No. When I get a *real* engagement ring, I'd like it to be my first. I'll just look on this one as being on loan.'

The jeweller arrived. By then, Dixie was hunched on the sofa, looking very self-conscious. She so wished she had had time to get changed. César was a real sophisticate, and if he thought she was showing too much flesh obviously he had to be right. She was ashamed that he had had to tell her what she should have realised for herself. And yet she had seen loads and loads of perfectly respectable young women wearing what she had assumed were similar clothes.

But now her jacket was buttoned to her throat, to conceal the offending T-shirt, and her restive fingers were constantly tugging at the hem of the skirt which felt indecently short.

'So choose,' César invited in the increasingly tense silence.

'Diamonds are very cold,' Dixie sighed. 'Pearls and opals are unlucky. Some people say green isn't very lucky either. I don't know anything bad about rubies, *but—*'

'So pick a ruby.'

The jeweller, who was keeping his head down, hurriedly extended the appropriate tray.

'Rubies are supposed to stand for passionate love,' Dixie completed in an apologetic undertone. 'A diamond might be more suitable.'

César breathed in very deep. With an unerring eye, he reached down to select the most opulent diamond ring. 'We'll have this one.'

The cluster was so big it looked like a fake out of a Christmas cracker. Dixie was relieved that she didn't like the ring. She felt it kept everything on a comfortingly impersonal basis.

As soon as the jeweller had checked the size of her finger, Dixie was on her feet. 'Can I go now?'

'Please don't let me keep you,' César drawled acidly.

Thirty minutes later, Dixie rang Scott's doorbell. She was totally taken aback when the door was answered by an unfamiliar man.

'Looking for Scott?' he said helpfully.

Dixie nodded.

'We work together…he said I could use this place while he's in New York.'

'New York?' Dixie stressed in a shaken tone, certain she must have misunderstood.

'Temporary secondment. Scott only got the offer yesterday. A chance like that, he didn't waste any time. He flew out this morning.'

Dixie was in shock. 'How long is he likely to be away?'

'A couple of months, I should think.'

CHAPTER FOUR

'MR VALVERDE is waiting,' Fisher informed Dixie with suppressed urgency.

Tears welling up in her eyes, Dixie settled Spike into his basket.

'Cook's going to bring Spike into the kitchen every day. He doesn't mind her,' the older man told her kindly. 'We'll spoil him rotten if he lets us.'

Nodding, because she didn't trust herself to speak, Dixie focused on the aquarium sitting on the chest. César the fish was at one end, his new lady companion, Milly, at the other. Neither seemed to venture into the other's territory. A bit like her and César Valverde, she conceded ruefully. She lived in his house but saw him only by rare and reluctant invitation.

'I'll take the aquarium down to the kitchen too,' Fisher promised.

'I talk to them every day.'

'Cook could talk the hind leg off a donkey.'

César was pacing the front hall. Lean, mean and magnificent in a lightweight charcoal-grey suit, burgundy shirt and silver-grey silk tie, he surveyed Dixie with glittering dark eyes of enquiry.

'I've kept you waiting...I'm sorry.'

As his attention lingered on her, Dixie smoothed an uneasy hand down over the skirt of her chic green summer dress.

César fixedly studied the ragged, uneven hem of the garment from which several stray threads still hung. 'What have you done to that dress?' he demanded.

Dixie had hoped he wouldn't notice. 'After what you said last night, I thought it might be a bit too short too… so I let the hem down, but it didn't go down the way I thought it would—'

'So why didn't you wear something else?'

'Fisher had already taken away my case.'

In thunderous silence, César gritted his even white teeth. Crossing the hall, he proceeded to hunker down and pluck away the hanging threads with impatient fingers.

'You see, I needed something to occupy me last night. Scott's been sent to New York for a while…I didn't even get to say goodbye…' Her voice trailed away as she absently watched a shard of sunlight glance over César's gleaming blue-black hair and then marvelled at the incredible length of his inky black lashes as she gazed down at him.

'Life's little cruelties toughen one up,' César advised with an outstanding lack of sympathy as he vaulted back upright. He pressed her towards the front door. 'And now, while you're in Spain, you won't have the distraction of thinking of Scott being back here in London.'

'I guess not…and it's a great opportunity for him.' Dixie gave a determined smile. 'Scott's boss must think very highly of him to offer him such a chance.'

César turned to her once inside the limo. 'You have blue shadow on one eyelid and green on the other.'

'Is it noticeable?'

'It's screaming at me.'

Dixie nodded, dug a tissue out of her bag and removed the shadow without resorting to a mirror. She then dug out a paperback and proceeded to read. This obvious solution to coping with César, who would sooner she was seen but not heard, had occurred to her the night before. If she dug her nose into a book he wouldn't feel he had to talk to her, and she wouldn't find herself inadvertently trying to chat to him.

An hour and a half later she hurried up the steps of his private jet, her excitement unconcealed. 'I've never been on a plane before,' she told the flight attendant without hesitation. 'I've never been abroad before either!'

'Sit down and behave like a grown-up,' César growled in her ear from behind.

Reddening, Dixie dropped down into the nearest seat.

'You sit with me.' César had the embattled air of a male restraining his temper with the greatest of difficulty.

Dixie wondered what she had done wrong. She hadn't spoken to him once, not once, and she'd assumed he would be delighted to be able to forget her existence. She'd had a great chat with his chauffeur on the way through the airport, and then there had been that lovely old lady she'd got talking to in the VIP lounge. Yet far from appreciating the space and privacy she had awarded his natural reserve, César had become tenser and colder by the minute.

As the jet taxied down the runway, Dixie started getting nervous at the prospect of her first take-off. In an effort to distract herself, she turned to look at César, where he sat to her right, a file open in one lean hand. 'What did I do that annoyed you?'

His hard profile clenched. He looked at her broodingly, shimmering dark eyes glinting from below semi-lowered lids. 'You're everybody's best friend. You have no dignity, no normal reticence. You told my chauffeur about Scott—'

'He told me about his daughter's marriage breaking up.'

'That's the point. He's an employee. I didn't even know he *had* a daughter!' César condemned as the engines whined and the jet began to race down the runway.

Dixie turned a whiter shade of pale and clutched at the arms of her seat with protruding knuckles. 'Oh, golly, I feel sick I'm scared...this is really frightening... I don't think I want to fly *anywhere*!' she suddenly wailed, jerking loose her seatbelt and starting to rise.

She was tugged back safely into her seat by a restraining hand. As she attempted to catch her breath, César took one look at the sheer panic etched on her face and, meshing lean fingers into her hair, held her fast and kissed her.

Dixie forgot she was on board a jet. She forgot she was afraid. She even forgot to be afraid of *him*. In shock, she felt the hard male heat of his mouth prying apart her lips. Like lightning suddenly unleashed inside her, that kiss zapped out every sane thought and burned her up with excitement. Without realising it, she clutched at him. As the tip of his tongue expertly invaded the moist sweetness of her mouth she shuddered, as if she was in a force ten gale, and pushed the fingers of one hand ecstatically into the springy silk of his hair.

He felt so good she wanted to sink into him and lose herself for ever in the frantically seductive tide of physical sensation assailing her. She was wildly, madly aware of every throbbing cell in her own body. Fierce energy and urgency was penned up inside her, fighting for release. She never passed the point of temptation. She got one taste of temptation and simply succumbed.

Without warning, César jerked away, long fingers dropping to her forearms to set her back from him. Dixie opened her eyes, blinked, and focused on his lean strong face, the feverish glitter in his brilliant dark incisive eyes. She couldn't see his anger, yet somehow she could *feel* his anger, silently striking out at her in the unbearably tense atmosphere.

'Did I do that wrong as well?' she asked, struggling to come to grips with the devastating reality that César Valverde had actually kissed her.

His incredible lashes dropped down over his eyes. He released her, but the silence continued to seethe.

'Of course you only did it because I started to panic about flying.' Dixie twisted her head away and tried to stop shivering.

'Even Jasper is likely to expect an engaged couple to exchange the occasional kiss,' César imparted very flatly.

Dixie swallowed hard on that assurance. She would have thought Jasper would be shocked rigid if they exchanged a passionate kiss in front of him. *Passionate?* No, not for César, she decided, her tummy muscles tightening with sudden extreme discomfiture. For César it had obviously just been a casual kiss, something in the nature of a reluctant rehearsal. He was probably affronted that she had thrown herself into that kiss as if they were Romeo and Juliet.

'You think I enjoyed you kissing me too much.' Looking anywhere but at him, Dixie was extremely embarrassed but determined to clear the air. 'You took me by surprise… I guess with your experience you're used to that kind of overboard response, but it was more of an experiment for me—'

'I think this may well be one of those deep conversations better shelved.'

Unexpectedly, Dixie turned back to face him, a sunny smile of anticipation slowly curving her reddened mouth. 'You don't understand. If *you* can make me feel like that, I can hardly wait to find out how Scott can make me feel!'

The silence refused to break. Indeed, the silence sat there like a huge brick wall barrier.

César stared steadily back at her, dark eyes black as a stormy night, not a revealing muscle moving on his strong dark features.

As the tension crackled sky-high, Dixie frowned in bewilderment. 'I just wanted to reassure you that I wasn't being silly and feeling attracted to you or anything like that… I mean I just *couldn't* be attracted to you…you're so…' She faltered to a halt in the pin-dropping quiet greeting that impulsive explanation.

'So…*what*?' César invited, with the most lethally intimidating smile.

Dixie gulped, an odd, thrilling chill running down her taut spine, as if she was dicing with death on the edge of a precipice. 'So…so far removed from me—'

'That's not what you were about to say.'

'I was getting too personal again,' Dixie back-tracked in haste.

'*So what*, Dixie?'

Mesmerised by the full onslaught of his dark stare, she whispered, 'So cold, so self-absorbed, so inhuman…'

'And you are so refreshingly, dangerously…honest,' César murmured.

Dixie had stopped breathing without understanding why. Then at that moment the bright voice of the flight attendant broke the spell. 'The captain wondered if Miss Robinson would like to visit the flight deck, sir.'

César rested his arrogant dark head back. 'I should think Miss Robinson would be delighted. Don't touch anything, Dixie…don't fall against anything either.'

The flight attendant giggled.

Dixie went pink as she rose from her seat, well aware that César hadn't been joking.

By the time Dixie got out of the jet at Malaga, her cheerful outlook had vanished. Reality had dug in and dug in hard.

Until now she had cravenly avoided thinking about the masquerade that loomed at journey's end. She had concentrated her thoughts on simply spending time with Jasper again. That was in itself a most pleasurable prospect. She was intensely fond of Jasper and refused to dwell on the idea that he might be seriously ill. What could not be cured had to be endured. Dixie had learnt that lesson at an early age.

Only now, as she wandered in César's purposeful wake through the airport, was she becoming miserably, guiltily aware that she was about to take part in a deception which went against every principle she had been raised to respect. She had been in the depths of despair when César had approached her with his proposition. Sick with worry about Petra's debts, and exhausted by the strain of working two jobs, she had been further devastated to learn of Jasper's failing health…

And she remembered sitting in César's Ferrari later that same evening, listening against her will to his silver-tongued assurance that their pretend engagement would be the best news Jasper had ever heard. César had made it all sound so simple, so harmless. He had even made her feel that to refuse would be selfish and cruel.

But the imminent prospect of lying to an old man as sincere and trusting as Jasper made Dixie feel sick with nerves and guilt. She stumbled round a baggage trolley and stood gazing into space. How could she look Jasper in the face and lie?

'Dixie!' Striding back to intercept her for about the fourth time, César snapped an imprisoning hand over her shoulder to turn her in the right direction again. *'Accidenti!* Didn't you even notice you'd lost me?'

'No…'

Outside, César pressed her into a chauffeured limo with the driven aspect of a male who had valiantly herded an entire flock of wandering and wilful sheep through the crowded airport.

Dixie emerged from her uneasy thoughts to find César doing up her seatbelt. Jawline hard as a rock, he tightened it the way a medieval jailer might have tightened a chain on a prisoner likely to try and escape. 'Now just stay there…don't move.'

Lashes fluttering, Dixie gazed up at his lean, dark,

devastatingly attractive face in total bemusement. 'Where would I move to?'

'And you can ditch that miserable expression. Agonising over Scott is forbidden!' Grim dark eyes scanned her startled face without remorse. 'You have a part to play, and although I don't expect your performance to qualify for an Oscar, I *do* expect you to look reasonably happy.'

'But I wasn't agonising over Scott. If you must know, I was worrying about lying to Jasper—'

'Leave the lying to me.'

'Yes, you'll be so much better at that than I could ever be,' Dixie conceded reflectively.

Flames of gold flared in César's incredulous gaze. 'I don't know how I've got you this far without strangling you,' he confessed in a shaken undertone. 'I have reserves of restraint I never knew I had.'

Dixie snatched in a stricken breath. 'That's a horrible thing to say…what could I possibly have done to deserve that?'

César spread the fingers of his two clenched brown hands very slowly. 'You want to know…you *really* want to know?'

He was truly angry, Dixie realised in shock and perturbation, violet eyes very wide.

'One…' César gritted, like a male about to embark on a very long speech. 'You have the attention span of a flea. Two…you wandered through the airport like a headless chicken. Three…you're still acting like the office junior. Exactly when are you planning to psych yourself into the role of my fiancée? While you were giggling like a schoolgirl with my cabin staff and trying on their hats, I heard you refer to me three times as *Mr* Valverde. Four…you're emotionally manic—'

'M-manic?' Dixie parroted tremulously.

'Either you're acting euphoric or you're on the brink of tears! There is no happy medium, no nice quiet level of normality.'

'My life hasn't *been* very normal recently,' Dixie pointed out, her throat thickening.

'Point five,' César growled rather raggedly as her violet eyes shimmered in helpless reproach, 'I do not like being ignored.'

Like a spoilt child, convinced that the entire world revolved around him, was Dixie's first thought. Fortunately she didn't say it out loud, but she was tempted to remark that she didn't recall him showing any sign that he wished to speak to her himself. Surely he didn't expect her to sit beside him in total silence, like a glove puppet waiting for an empowering hand?

'I wasn't ignoring you. I thought you preferred me to keep a low profile—'

'A *low* profile?' César echoed in a tone of rampant disbelief.

Dixie reddened and clasped her hands tightly together on her lap. 'You have so many hang-ups—'

'Hang-ups?' César ejaculated rawly.

'You're not a people person. And just having fun is beneath you. That brain of yours just never stops ticking and dissecting things…you are so deadly serious all the time. It's unnerving.'

'I find you equally unnerving,' César imparted after a staggered pause.

Involuntarily, Dixie collided with eyes that were silvered by a stray shard of sunlight filtering into the car, eyes that were dazzlingly beautiful in that lean, dark, brooding face, and her heart jumped and her tummy twisted and her conscience smote her all at once. In confusion she turned her head away, but in her mind's eye she was now seeing the unhappy, far too bright and knowing little boy whom Jasper had once sadly described to her. A cynic at the age of five, with a deep distrust of adults.

A wealthy young mother's fashion accessory only while he was still at the cute baby stage, César had been the pretty much unwelcome result of an impulsive and short-lived marriage. His parents had parted before he was even born. His playboy father had wanted his estranged wife to terminate her pregnancy, and when she'd failed to follow his advice had considered himself absolved of any further responsibility, other than financial, towards his son.

Finding a toddler's needs more of a nuisance than she had envisaged, César's youthful mother, Magdalena, had regularly left him with an ever-changing succession of nannies for weeks on end. As soon as she could she had put César into an English boarding school, and had often found it more convenient to simply leave him there during the long vacations.

'Magdalena was very immature. Her own parents were dead, so she had no support. She often had good intentions but she was hopelessly selfish,' Jasper had explained heavily. 'forever promising to visit César at school but always letting him down. One of his stepfathers encouraged her to make more effort for a while, but he was soon out of the picture again.'

So it was no wonder that César was a complete loner, Dixie conceded tautly, already deeply regretting her censure. She had been unjust and unkind. César couldn't help being the way he was. By the time Jasper had got hold of him, at twelve, the damage had been done. César had walled up his emotions. He had never had a real home, never had a proper family or even siblings to tease him, never been loved just for himself... except by Jasper.

'Why are you looking at me like that?' César demanded in sheer frustration as the limo drew up at a private airstrip where a helicopter awaited them.

Shaking her head in mingled emotion and embarrassment, Dixie made no response. But she had suddenly appreciated that César might talk about Jasper in that cool, offhand way of his, but that Jasper Dysart was probably just about the only person in the whole world whom César actually cared about.

And if anything happened to Jasper, César was in all probability going to be absolutely devastated. Jasper was César's one weakness. And suddenly the extravagant lengths César was prepared to go to in his determination to make Jasper happy struck Dixie as the most touching, telling thing ever...and the tears welled up.

'OK...' Tensing, César raised expressive lean brown hands in an attempted soothing motion that did not come naturally to him. 'You don't fancy the helicopter, but the alternative is hours of driving through the mountains and spending the night in a hotel.'

Dixie tore her shimmering gaze from César and said chokily, 'Actually I was thinking about you.'

'Don't think about me. I really do not *want* you thinking about me.'

Dixie nodded jerkily.

César reached for her knotted fingers, straightened

them out and threaded on the opulent diamond engagement ring.

'I'll do the best I can to convince Jasper…I promise!' Dixie swore feverishly. 'I'll act just the way he would expect me to act if I was in love.'

'What's that likely to entail? No, no, make it a surprise,' César advised as he edged her by subtle motions out of the car.

'I'll try to think of you the way I think of Scott…' Dixie confided very seriously.

'That could be dangerous. You might fall in love with me instead.'

Dixie sent him an arrested look full of such astonishment that César stared back at her, hard black eyes narrowing and glinting, fabulous bone structure tautening. Quickly her mind went empty, and it was suddenly so hard to breathe, so impossible to look away.

Abruptly, César removed his intense gaze from her. 'I may be a cold bastard, but I don't want this charade to cause any lasting damage. A woman who cries her heart out over a cannibalised goldfish has to be more than usually vulnerable. In fact when I saw you leaning over that fountain asking the survivor how he could have stooped to eating his only friend, I decided you were totally off this planet.'

'I get very fond of my pets, but there is no danger that I would *ever* get fond of you!' Dixie retorted in fierce self-defence, and she scrambled into the helicopter without a backward glance.

For the duration of the flight over the snow-capped sierras of Andalusia, Dixie was deep in her own thoughts. She was reliving that whirling other-worldly sensation that overwhelmed her whenever she met César

Valverde's eyes. It was terrifying, embarrassing, and yet weirdly thrilling. And she had finally worked out what was the matter with her...

César was gorgeous. Undoubtedly she was reacting to his intense sexual charisma. It was not that she was mentally attracted to him, she reasoned, it was that she was *bodily* attracted to him. Like when she was peckish and the vision of a tempting dessert formed inside her head. Foolish, harmless and meaningless, she told herself, resolving to keep a tighter rein on herself now that she understood the problem. And putting César on a level with chocolate fudge cake made her feel a lot less threatened and self-conscious. She would soon get over such silliness.

When the helicopter began to descend, it was dusk. As the craft tilted, Dixie gazed down into a thickly wooded hidden valley, a silvered road snaking like a ribbon through it into the distance. A beautiful hacienda clung to the steep forested slopes. The seemingly endless stretch of pale walls and red-tiled roof glimmered in the fading light. The helicopter set down on a helipad within the perimeter walls.

César sprang out and stretched in a hand to assist her. Dixie grasped his fingers, her eyes brimming with surprise. '*This*...is where Jasper lives?'

'What did you expect? A little cottage complete with butterfly net in the foothills?'

Dumbly, Dixie shook her head. It was a simply huge house, with all the elegant opulence that only the very, very rich take for granted. As they crossed an exquisitely landscaped courtyard, with a softly playing fountain to the side entrance, César reached down and closed his hand over hers. 'Let's get the big announcement over with.'

A smiling middle-aged woman awaited them in the vast tiled hall. As she spoke, a frown instantly indented César's brow.

'What's wrong?'

'Jasper's not here.' César dropped her hand again—there now being no necessity to pretend he wanted even that small amount of physical contact with her, Dixie assumed. 'His housekeeper hasn't a clue where he is either. Typical Jasper! And in his state of health what on earth is he doing running about the countryside?'

'Maybe you should have phoned him to tell him we were coming.'

'I wanted to surprise him.' César sent her an impatient glance. 'Out of character for me, but exactly the kind of impractical impulse that Jasper would expect from a newly engaged couple!'

Dixie stared at him, not quite grasping the connection.

César's wide, sensual mouth twisted. 'I thought the very sight of me arriving with you unannounced would make us look more convincing…like I couldn't wait to show you off!' he pointed out in exasperation as he strode back to address the hovering housekeeper in fluent Spanish again. 'Ermina will show you up to my room. I'll need to make some calls to run Jasper to earth!'

An older man laden with their luggage was already heading up the ornate wrought-iron and stone staircase. Dixie followed the housekeeper up to the first landing, briefly stilling with an uncertain frown. She flushed. No, she must have misheard him. César couldn't have said '*my* room'. He couldn't possibly be expecting her to share his bedroom!

But minutes later Ermina showed her into a very large and luxuriously furnished bedroom, where her luggage and César's sat together like a statement. Dixie surveyed the bed, with its massive intricately carved headboard. It was an extremely big bed. No, she was being ridiculous. This was some silly misunderstanding. After all, Jasper was very old-fashioned, and rather fond of muttering about the appallingly lax moral habits of modern youth.

Tilting her chin and striving to suppress her discomfiture, Dixie went downstairs again to find César. She located him in a magnificent library, and for a split second her awed and eager appraisal of all those tempting shelves of books made her still in wonderment.

César was on the phone, talking in Spanish. His dark, deep drawl sounded so...so sexy, Dixie reflected dimly, listening to all those fluid rolling vowels with instinctive appreciation, a curious little quiver fingering down her spine. She studied him. Even after hours of travelling, César retained his incredible elegance, and he paced the room with the prowling sure-footed grace of a leopard.

Turning his arrogant dark heard, César finally chose to acknowledge her presence in the doorway. 'If you're hungry, Ermina will fix you some supper.'

It was her cue to depart again. Staying put took courage.

'There's been a bit of a mix-up.' Dixie shuffled her feet restively. 'They've gone and put my stuff in with yours...in the same room, I mean, and I don't have the Spanish to explain that...well, you know—'

'No, I don't know.' César elevated one satiric black brow with daunting cool. 'Naturally we have to share a bedroom. Jasper's not an idiot. If we slept apart he would never believe this engagement was for real!'

CHAPTER FIVE

OPEN-MOUTHED, Dixie stared back at César, heated colour rising in a slow tide beneath her pale skin. 'You really expect me to share your room?' she whispered in disbelief.

César cast aside the cordless phone. 'Where are you coming from on this? Clarify the problem for me.'

The weighted silence pulsed.

Recognising the chill hardening his brooding dark features, Dixie drew in a sustaining breath. 'I couldn't possibly sleep in the same bed. I didn't bargain on anything like that when I agreed to this arrangement.'

'Didn't you? You sold your immediate future to me for a price. I've paid that price. You were up to your throat in debt, and scared witless of being dragged into court to answer for your dishonesty. You are not in a position to call the shots here,' César warned with icy bite, studying her as if she had crawled out from beneath a piece of furniture and was in dire need of being thoroughly squashed. 'And you are *far* from being the little innocent you like to pose as for Jasper's benefit!'

That full frontal attack came at Dixie out of nowhere and she was quite unprepared for it. She gaped at him. 'I'm not dishonest, and—'

'You *are* dishonest. You ran up debts you hadn't a prayer of paying. You are no better than a thief.' César's eloquent mouth curled with contempt. 'You should've faced up to that by now. And when you start trying to pretend to be something you're not with me as well, it's time to call a halt to your fantasies!'

'Fantasies…?' Dixie repeated weakly.

'The big parties? The ludicrously expensive trappings for a rented apartment? What else but fantasies? Maybe you were trying to buy friends. But I don't have the slightest pity for you,' César informed her without hesitation. 'I know you have a brain, and I *know* you had to know exactly what you were doing—'

'But those parties weren't mine…and neither was the apartment!' Dixie broke in helplessly.

'I think you assumed that Jasper might pick up the bills for you. What a shock it must've been to learn that Jasper is as poor as a church mouse!' Brilliant dark eyes like lasers probed her shattered expression for a betraying response. 'Did you really think I wouldn't work that possibility out?'

Pale as milk and trembling, Dixie was appalled by his suspicions. 'I honestly don't know what you're talking about, and if you'd let me explain about those debts in the first place, you'd have known that—'

'You worked your way into Jasper's soft heart and stupidly assumed he was loaded?' César incised with stinging scorn. 'I'm not a fool. First the friendship, next the extravagant spending spree, and then no doubt you wrote to Jasper, anxiously confiding that you had got into some financial hot water—'

'No…no, that's crazy!' Dixie was falling into deeper shock by the second.

'And then possibly Jasper wrote back saying how much he would've liked to be able to help you…but unfortunately, since his trust fund was embezzled by a crooked accountant over ten years ago, he has been wholly dependent on me!'

'I wouldn't *do* anything like that…wouldn't have dreamt of worrying Jasper with my problems!' Dixie's eyes were stricken as she moved her head in a negative motion. 'You have such a hateful opinion of other human beings, César. You're always looking for the bad, never, ever the good.'

Unimpressed by that pained condemnation, César continued to survey her from his towering height, eyes as cold as black ice. 'Oh, I acquit you of real evil, but I'm certain that at some stage you must've attempted to fish yourself out of trouble by approaching Jasper for a loan.'

'Then perhaps you ought to ask him for my letters,' Dixie countered with as much dignity as she could muster. She lifted her head high, her mouth tightly compressed with the effort self-control demanded of her. 'And perhaps you ought to get your facts right too.'

'And where could I possibly have got them wrong?' César traded very drily.

'My sister threw those parties—'

'You don't have a sister. You don't have a single living relative.'

'I'm talking about my *step*sister, Petra Sinclair. She's made quite a name for herself as a model. The apartment was hers. When I first came to London I lived with her, and because she was away so much she opened this bank account so that I could settle her bills. Then everything went wrong… *somehow*!' Dixie shook her

aching head again, her forehead furrowing, as if she
was still trying to come to grips with how everything
had gone so very wrong.

'Petra...*Sinclair*?' César queried, with the oddest
stress and a look of surprise.

While sensing something not quite right, either in
his intonation or in his narrowed stare and hardening
jawline, Dixie was far too involved in telling her story
to let his curious reaction to her sister's name register
with her for more than a second.

'Petra decided to go to Los Angeles and become an
actress, and she's still over there...I don't know where.
Well, you see, the deputy bank manager...who was just
incredibly *nice*,' Dixie stressed, and then fell into a
somewhat erratic explanation about the joint account
and the way she had often ordered goods and services
on Petra's behalf.

'If you're telling me the truth, Leticia Zane would've
been well aware that *Petra* was her client.'

'Of course she was,' Dixie confirmed wearily. 'But
once Miss Zane realised that Petra had left the UK she
was furious. I don't think she believed me when I told
her that I didn't have an address for Petra—'

'Probably not. I can check all this out,' César warned
her, but for some reason the warning emerged almost
as an afterthought, the suggestion being that he had already decided that she was telling the truth.

'Go ahead. I've got nothing to hide.'

He asked her several more probing questions. The
set of his mouth grew more grim. 'I take back what I
said about your brain,' he breathed. 'It's weak on sur-
vival skills and common sense.'

'You don't understand. Petra was terribly upset about

the whole thing too, but by then, with the expense of moving to LA, she was really broke. If you only knew how terrific she was when my stepmother was ill—'

'She *was*?' For some reason César sounded very surprised to receive that assurance.

'Petra was absolutely wonderful, and I was very grateful. She really is a great person—a little thoughtless sometimes, but very generous and kind with everything she's got…when she's got it, I mean,' Dixie concluded rather limply.

'Generous…kind,' César echoed, as if he had never heard the words before, his deep, forceful drawl having for some reason sunk to the level of a constrained whisper.

Dixie looked up worriedly, drained by that outpouring.

César was studying her as if she was some strange life-form he had never come across before. An uncharacteristic mix of reluctant fascination and suppressed disbelief mingled in his brooding dark features. 'I imagine you're extremely *fond* of Petra?'

Dixie nodded in confirmation. She wasn't blind to César's incredulity, but, unlike him, she believed in taking people as they were. Petra's faults did not detract from Dixie's affection for her stepsister. Nor had Dixie ever resented the lack of hands-on help she had received during her stepmother's long illness. Petra and her mother had never got on, and Petra could not have coped with that caring role. In contrast, Dixie had loved her stepmother very much, and had wanted to do everything she could to repay the woman who had taken her into her heart as if she were her own child.

César stared steadily down into Dixie's clear blue

eyes, opened his mouth and then finally closed it again. Then curiosity seemed to get the better of him, and he breathed, 'For how long did you take care of your step-mother?'

Dixie told him.

César braced a taut hand on the edge of the hand-some library table beside him. 'Quite a slice of your life,' he remarked grimly.

'It's not something I'll ever regret.'

César expelled his breath in a slow hiss and glanced away from her. 'Even I can now accept that you would never have tried to coax money out of Jasper,' he conceded heavily. 'I got the wrong idea. I thought you'd been leading some kind of double life. Now I know that what you see is what you get with you...and that is spooky.'

'Spooky?'

'Let's just say that we don't have a great deal in common.' César flashed her a veiled look. 'Only very rarely am I forced to appreciate what I have by a terri-fying glimpse of an alternative lifestyle and outlook.'

Recognising that he no longer believed that there was any truth in those dreadful suspicions he had cherished, Dixie sagged with relief.

'I owe you an apology,' César stated grittily.

'It's not important. You were sure to come up with a really nasty scenario. You can't help the way your mind works,' Dixie said forgivingly. 'Have you had any luck finding Jasper?'

'No...for all I know he's out camping somewhere under the stars!' César's profile tautened with a con-cern he couldn't hide.

Dixie cleared her throat awkwardly, deciding that

now that César was more approachable she should return to the prickly question of sharing a bedroom. 'César, I really do think Jasper would take a very dim view of coming back home to find us in the same bedroom—'

'Don't be ridiculous,' César countered with careless cool. 'We're not living half a century ago.'

'Jasper has very strong Christian beliefs,' Dixie pointed out very gently, conscious that César was sure to believe that he knew best where his godfather was concerned. 'He lives very much in his own little world, and it dates back more than half a century. I honestly believe he would be very shocked and offended at us sharing a room under this roof.'

César dealt her an impatient frown. 'You haven't a clue what you're talking about. Jasper has never questioned what I do in my private life.'

Did you bring your private life into his home? she badly wanted to ask, but couldn't bring herself to that controversial brink. César's notoriety as a ruthless womaniser was a source of very genuine concern and mortification to Jasper. But possibly Jasper had never dared to admit that to César. Indeed, it was hard to picture Jasper standing up to César, of whom he stood in considerable awe.

César swept up the phone again, indicating that the subject was closed.

'César…I'm just not comfortable with this bedroom arrangement,' Dixie persisted valiantly, her mind boggling at the prospect of sleeping in the same room as César, never mind the same bed.

'Quit while you're ahead, Dixie. Allow me to know my own godfather better than you do. Act like I'm

Scott,' César suggested with a satiric glance of finality as he strode out of the library.

Dixie made a beeline for the books. An hour later, she climbed upstairs with a towering pile of rather dusty hardbacks, it having proved impossible for her to make a smaller selection. Her cases had already been unpacked for her. Eager to get to bed now that she had her books, she went back downstairs, found the kitchen and helped herself to a glass of milk. Then, back in the bedroom, she located one of the ridiculously glamorous new nighties she had been endowed with and hurried into the beautifully appointed bathroom with its fleecy towels. Stripping off on the spot, she got under the shower.

She was far too strait-laced, she told herself then. César would never dream of making a pass at her! They would each sleep on their own side of what was admittedly a very generously sized bed. There was an adjoining dressing room and with a little mutual care and consideration it needn't be that embarrassing an exercise.

Five minutes after reaching that seemingly sensible conclusion, Dixie was tucked up in bed in the enthusiastic hold of a weighty tome on eighteenth-century philosophy, her shapely figure fetchingly sheathed in palest green silk. When César walked through the bedroom door she was mental miles away, and she didn't hear him.

So when she groped out blindly for her milk, and then was forced to tear her attention from her book and actually look for the glass, she was quite transfixed to suddenly notice César casually peeling off his shirt about ten feet away.

She took in that magnificent expanse of golden brown male flesh and flexing muscles and just gaped.

'Ignore me,' César drawled with supreme casualness, a strange silvered challenge in his dazzlingly bright eyes, his expressive mouth twisting.

Barely breathing, Dixie ducked her head down again, heartbeat racing, mouth dry. The printed page swam. She could see nothing but César, could hear nothing but the rushing in her own eardrums and, preternaturally loud, the soft rasp of a trouser zip. He does this all the time, a dry little voice said inside her head. He's used to sharing a bedroom, a bed. Don't embarrass yourself by reacting in any way. She could breathe if she tried, *couldn't she*? Well, possibly, if she cleared her disobedient brain of wanton images of César Valverde completely unclothed.

Warmth like heated honey pooled in the pit of Dixie's stomach and made her quiver. She wanted to watch him undress. That awareness shook her rigid, but it still took real physical restraint not to lift her head again and peek.

When the bathroom door closed behind César, she drank in oxygen in great needy gulps, her face hot as hellfire with shame. Was this what sexual curiosity felt like? She couldn't ever remember being tempted to spy on Scott. Thank heaven, she thought, genuinely loathing the secret burn of guilty excitement which César's mere presence now unleashed in her. Continued exposure to César's deeply unsettling aura of raw animal sex appeal had finally decimated her natural defences.

César strolled back out of the bathroom. Without the will to stop herself, Dixie peered surreptitiously out from behind her book, glimpsed long powerful thighs lightly dusted with dark curling hair, what might have been the hem of a pair of black silk boxer shorts, and felt as if she was about to have a heart attack.

'I see you hit the library hard.' With easy grace, César swept up a book and glanced through it.

In studious silence, Dixie nodded without looking at him. She didn't trust herself to look at him any more. She was really ashamed of herself. Out of the corner of her eye, she saw him pull back the sheet and slide into bed.

'To think I assumed you would cover yourself from head to toe to share this bed with me,' César confided, in a low-pitched murmur that was terrifyingly intimate.

Her tension shooting up to megawatt heights, Dixie slowly turned her head to register shimmering dark eyes lingering on the ripe curves cradled by sheer silk. A heady surge of colour blossoming in her cheeks, Dixie pressed her book against the swell of her full and now tingling breasts. 'I never thought—'

'There's too many things you never think about...' César mused in a thickened undertone that growled through the beating silence like a warning.

Already fiercely preoccupied with the mortifying throb of her tightening nipples, Dixie was striving to sink herself beneath the more decent concealment of the sheet that had fallen to her waist. Yet colliding head-on with silvered eyes as mesmerically bright as stars in that lean, dark face, she stilled, paralysed by the sudden greedy burst of excitement flaming through her disobedient body.

'Whereas *I* never stop thinking, except in bed, where other more natural instincts take over,' César imparted in a whisper as rich as thick velvet. 'So cold, so inhuman, but *not* in the bedroom, *cara*.'

Dixie found herself leaning over him slightly without even recalling the move that had sent her into that dangerous and inexplicable change of direction. It was like being drawn by a force stronger than she was, to the heart of a fire that might burn but still blazed a cruel attraction for her. 'César...?' she queried shakily, her tongue cleaving to the roof of her dry mouth.

In an almost involuntary motion César lifted a lean brown hand, hard colour accentuating the feverishly taut slant of his high cheekbones. And still Dixie was held there by those stunning silver eyes, fighting to get a grip on a mind that had shut down even as César dropped his hand again, clenching his long fingers into a fist in the humming, dragging quiet. Her soft pink mouth opened, the tip of her tongue creeping out to moisten her generous lower lip.

And with a sudden, driven groan of surrender, César reached for her with two powerfully impatient hands and dragged her down hungrily into his arms. Lightning struck between one second and the next. One moment Dixie was hung on the agonising brink of a craving she did not even fully comprehend, and the next she was lost without hope of recovery.

Her whole body exulted in the ferociously hard demand of César's sensual mouth crashing down on hers. Anything softer would have been cruel disappointment. As he rolled over and pinned her beneath his weight, his tongue stabbing into her mouth to plunder the sweetness within, she was overwhelmed by the rawness of his passion and the shockingly aggressive surge of emotion rising within herself.

Her wondering fingers glossed over his broad, smooth shoulders and then speared convulsively into his luxuriant black hair, to curve to his skull and imprison him. Welded to every sleek muscle in César's big powerful frame, she felt the hot hard thrust of his all-male arousal against her quivering stomach. The responsive heat that burned up inside her reduced her to a mindless jelly.

'Why does this feel so incredibly good?' César ground out accusingly against her reddened lips as they fought in concert to get breath back into their lungs.

César was holding Dixie so tightly that breathing remained more of a challenge than a likely possibility. Hazily studying her own fingers, which were now possessively welded to his cheekbones, Dixie parroted weakly, *'Good?'*

One hand meshed into her thick silky hair, César gazed down at her, brilliant eyes lambent silver pools of fierce frustration. 'This is not the time to think of me as a trial run for Scott—'

'Scott?'

As if he couldn't concentrate long enough to listen, César let one questing hand smooth down over the swell of one full breast. As every skin cell in her shivering body jumped in electrifying reaction, any hope of sanity reasserting itself was quickly lost. Dixie gasped out loud, eyes dilating, head tipping back to expose her throat as she trembled with a hunger as fierce as it was ungovernable.

César breathed something rough and fractured in Italian, his entire attention melded to his own hands as he lifted them to her slight shoulders to brush down the straps that concealed her from his almost reverent

gaze. A husky, sexy hiss that was almost agonised escaped him.

'You are *so* gorgeous…' he gritted not quite evenly
as the glistening sheer fabric slid down the proud upper
slope of her full breasts, catching on prominent pink
buds already swollen with excitement.

And in the same self-conscious moment that Dixie
tried to cover her wanton flesh, César touched her where
she had never been touched before, and the entire world
vanished in the violent surge of her own overpowering
response. 'César…' she moaned.

'Madre di Dio….' César husked, with the self-absorp-
tion of a male wholly bent on seduction.

He shaped her tender flesh, his thumbs glancing over
the sensitised rosy peaks, making her jerk and squirm
helplessly. And then he bent his dark head to a straining pink bud and laved it with his tongue, with the kind
of sensational expertise that sent her temperature rocketing to fever-point and wrung strangled sounds from
low in her throat.

Her back arched, a tight maddening ache spiralling
up between her thighs, sending every inch of her mad
with uncontrollable desire. Shuddering in the circle
of her arms, César closed his hungry mouth over hers
again. She didn't hear the door opening, wasn't aware
of anything before Jasper's well-bred voice, raised in
a tone of delighted surprise and welcome, interrupted
them. 'My dear boy, *when* did you arrive?'

César jerked his head up and Dixie looked past his
shoulder in sudden horror and confusion. Jasper was
hovering like a small portly Santa Claus suddenly told
that Christmas had been axed. Dixie was too shocked

even to be grateful for the fact that César was blocking all but her face from Jasper's aghast look of recognition.

'We'll discuss this downstairs, César,' Jasper announced in a deeply shaken and pained tone of censure as he turned on his heel.

CHAPTER SIX

PARALYSED by Jasper's swift entrance and even swifter exit, and the situation she now found herself in, Dixie studied César, who was still staring at the space Jasper had briefly filled, his bemusement doubtless the result of being addressed as though he was a misbehaving teenage boy.

'Porca miseria!' Suddenly coming back to life, César pulled free of Dixie's loosened hold, thrust back the rumpled sheet and sprang out of bed. 'Jasper looked at me as if he hated me!' he exclaimed with the glancing rawness of shock, pushing a not quite steady hand through his wildly tousled black hair, dark, deep-set eyes full of fracturing emotion.

Frantically engaged in righting the bodice of her nightdress, a sob of distress in her voice, Dixie whispered jaggedly, 'I t-told you Jasper wouldn't approve!'

'I wasn't expecting him to return this late and walk right in on us! This is scarcely how I planned to make our announcement. But when I tell him that we're engaged, he'll calm down,' César forecast with frowning conviction.

Unable to look at him any longer, and wishing she shared his confidence, Dixie rolled over on her stomach and stared at the headboard with strained eyes full of deep regret and shame. What had she been doing with César? What had he been doing with her? Her wretched body ached from the severance of his. Cold little shivers of reaction now rippled through her, but deep down inside herself she was hatefully aware that the physical craving which had reduced her to such a level still lingered on like her worst enemy.

'Jasper chose an opportune moment to interrupt us,' César continued with meaningful cool as he banged through the storage units in the adjoining dressing room, evidently in search of clothes. 'Next time you get into bed with me, cover yourself from head to toe.'

'There won't *be* a next time,' Dixie responded in a chagrined undertone. 'I wasn't expecting anything like that to happen.'

'But now you have reassuring proof that I *am* human. Throw a sexually active male into bed with a scantily clad woman putting out provocative signals…and he'll fall from the path of rectitude so fast your head will spin!' César slashed back with defensive bite.

Dixie rolled over and sat up. 'I wasn't provocative,' she protested in dismay and bewilderment at such a charge. 'I was reading my book…I was minding my own business! You just pounced on me!'

Emerging from the dressing room, only halfway into a shirt, César sent her an incredulous look, eyes splintering a silvered challenge. 'You were *begging* for it!'

'I don't even like you…I wouldn't beg you for anything!' Dixie flung back in increasing turmoil.

'No? Very much against my will and my intelligence, I am sexually attracted to you.' As he made that grudging acknowledgement César slung her a brooding look, his darkly handsome features rigid as stone. 'It's really getting on my nerves, but unlike you I'm prepared to be honest about it…I'm not telling the whole world every hour on the hour how much I'm in love with someone else!'

In a complete daze in the aftermath of that gritty confession, Dixie surveyed César with very wide eyes. He was attracted to her? *Personally* attracted to her? Since when? A rosy blush slowly lit her cheeks. 'You're attracted to me…?' she parroted, suddenly feeling very short of breath.

'It's lust, Dixie…pure naked *lust*.' César stressed in sizzling contradiction. 'A complication we can do without…and do without it we will.'

As his brilliant eyes glittered like ice shards, Dixie was mortified. Bowing her head, she pulled her knees up under the sheet and hugged them. She got the distinction, and the message he had gone out of his way to make. Nature was playing the cruellest kind of joke on them both. The sexual chemistry was there, but nothing else, and César was relieved that Jasper's arrival had concluded their intimacy. Dixie was still feeling too embarrassed to feel relieved. Indeed, she could never recall experiencing such intense emotional turmoil.

Anger, resentment, pain, regret. The extent of her own confusion destroyed her ability to think straight. César had left the room before it occurred to her that she ought to go down to see Jasper as well. One didn't avoid dear friends, no matter how awkward the situation might be. Jasper had been embarrassed, and that was her fault. She shouldn't have allowed César to overrule her misgivings about sharing a room. And now it was her duty to soothe and reassure alongside César. It was time to act like one half of a couple…

As she hurriedly pulled on a light cotton robe, she thought fiercely about Scott. She knew Scott so well. His faults, his strengths. He might take her for granted, but she knew he genuinely liked and respected her as a friend. Beneath the city slicker image he worked so hard to maintain, Scott was a country boy with a love of home cooking. He was always very even-tempered and cheerful. And she did love him, she really *did*, had known the very first night she met him that he was the man for her. Scott's image finally glimmered into being inside her mind's eye. True, his features were a little blurred, but she let her breath escape with relief.

César was right. She hadn't appreciated his bluntness but he had been right, she told herself urgently as she ran a brush through her hair. Those mindless dislocated-from-planet-earth feelings she got every time she looked at César were sheer lust. And staggeringly beautiful looks and magnetic sex appeal were all César had to recommend him. He was impatient, quick-tempered, manipulative, sarcastic, critical and essentially cold…except in the bedroom.

Satisfied by that summing up, Dixie left the room. Of course, she then acknowledged, César was impatient because he liked everything perfect. And he was sarcastic and critical because he was so much cleverer than most people, and it had to be frantically frustrating always having to wait for others to catch up with his reasoning. Being so very rich and powerful had spoilt him, but he couldn't really be blamed for that either, could he? And if he was cold, well, he had endured the most heartbreakingly loveless childhood, and he was extremely fond of Jasper—indeed had seemed positively shattered in receipt of what could only have been a disapproving frown from Jasper...

Hearing the dull murmur of distant voices when she reached the main hall, Dixie followed them and found herself outside an ajar door. She was just about to sound a light knock and announce her presence when she heard Jasper speak in a grim voice she had never heard or even imagined she might hear from so gentle a man.

'So you gave my poor little Dixie a ring to seduce her,' Jasper was saying with harsh distaste. 'Here she is, compromising her own most deep-felt beliefs and doubtless innocently trusting that you *will* eventually marry her! But I don't share her faith, César.'

'*Dio*, I—'

'You tell me you're engaged to her, but not one word do you say about *loving* her,' Jasper broke in stiffly. 'Nor is there any mention of when this hypothetical wedding is to take place!'

'We've just *become* engaged,' César stressed in a driven undertone, sounding just a little desperate and equally unlike himself.

'You finally met a woman who wanted no part of your kind of loose living. You couldn't take no for an answer, so you offered her an engagement ring. A couple of months from now, when you've lost interest in Dixie, you'll throw her back out of your life again without any consideration for the damage you've done,' the older man condemned curtly.

'*Accidenti!* You've got completely the wrong idea—'

'I *know* you and I *know* Dixie,' Jasper contradicted heavily. 'I imagine she's hopelessly in love with you—

and I should've seen this coming. For months she's been telling me about everything you do in her letters. Why couldn't you have left her alone, César? It will be a long time before I can forgive you for this. Dixie's very dear to me. She's gentle and caring and kind…yet you didn't even have enough respect for her not to embarrass her in this house!'

'Let's sit down and talk this over calmly, Jasper,' César replied fiercely.

Outside the door, Dixie slowly retreated. Shocked and distressed by the bitterness of Jasper's censure, she could not immediately see what she could do to sort out such a ghastly mess. This was not the sort of discussion she could play a part in. Jasper would not speak freely with her present, and César would certainly not welcome her interference. And after what Jasper had witnessed in that bedroom it would be difficult to confess the truth about their fake engagement.

'No, I've already told you how I feel,' Jasper was saying tightly. 'I want you to leave this house right now, César. I'll send your clothes after you. If you're going to break Dixie's heart, get it over with when I'm here to look after her.'

'OK…I'll set a date for the wedding,' César drawled flatly.

'Next year?' Jasper suggested, audibly unimpressed by that offer.

'Next *week*!' César suddenly gritted explosively. 'Dixie and I will get married next week!'

Dixie almost fell over her own feet. In her disbelief, she stared wide-eyed at the door.

Complete silence had fallen between the two men.

She imagined Jasper was as shocked by that startling announcement as she was.

'That puts quite a different complexion on matters, doesn't it?' Jasper sighed with perceptible relief. He sounded much more like himself, but very weary and oddly breathless. 'So you do love her, even though you can't show it… Well, can't have everything…couldn't make a better choice than Dixie…'

'What's wrong, Jasper?' César exclaimed with raw abruptness. *Jasper!*

Reacting instantly to the current of alarm in César's exclamation, Dixie pushed open the door. Jasper was lying unconscious in a chair, looking terribly small and old and ill.

César was bending over him, frantically trying to revive him.

'Get a doctor!' Dixie urged.

César strode across the room to snatch up the phone. He was ashen pale beneath his bronzed complexion, and his dark eyes were blank with shock. He made the call, but for its duration he watched Jasper with appalled intensity, drawing in a shuddering breath of unconcealed relief when he saw his godfather begin to revive and mutter.

'Eduardo Arribas is a friend…he lives just outside the village,' César imparted as he replaced the phone.

Jasper was still confused and rather dizzy. César wanted to carry him up to bed, where he would be more comfortable, but Dixie thought it was better not to move him before the doctor's arrival, and she sent César to get a glass of water for him instead. She patted Jasper's hand soothingly.

'Heart, you know,' he complained weakly. 'Never passed out before…'

'You're tired…that's all. You should've been in bed hours ago.' Dixie reached for the glass César extended, noticing in some surprise that César couldn't hold it steady because his hand was shaking. She pressed the glass gently to Jasper's lips.

'Glad you're here,' Jasper mumbled. 'Both here… Suppose I'll have to face that wretched operation after all—'

'What operation?' César broke in with a sudden frown.

'I'm a silly old duffer…never liked hospitals,' Jasper muttered. 'Eduardo says I need one of those pacemakers fitted.'

Dr Arribas came very quickly. The two men helped Jasper up to bed, and Dixie then sat with him until he fell asleep, quietly reflecting on what she had overheard outside that room downstairs before Jasper's collapse gave all of them something rather more important to worry about.

César had actually promised to marry her next week! César, usually the most rational and cool of males, had been so shaken by his godfather's angry demand that he should leave that he had made a really crazy promise sooner than explain that the situation was not quite as it might have appeared. But then telling his godfather the truth would have been a considerable challenge after Jasper had seen the two of them sharing the same bed. Had César then admitted that their engagement was a complete fake, Jasper would have been even angrier.

Well, fortunately for César Jasper's state of health would protect César from being expected to keep to that insane undertaking to immediately marry her. Jasper would now be scheduled for surgery as soon as possible, and when he was convalescing no doubt César would confess that their supposed engagement had been a well-meant but foolish pretence. And César would just have to brace himself to explain that nothing whatsoever had really happened in that bedroom. *Nothing*, Dixie stressed for her own benefit. Nothing she need ever think about again, she told herself urgently. A moment's weakness, best forgotten.

When Dixie emerged from Jasper's room, she was surprised to find César waiting outside in the corridor.

'You should've come back in after seeing Dr Arribas out...' Her voice trailed away as she met César's haunted dark eyes and registered the strain which had indented harsh lines between his nose and mouth. 'Did Dr Arribas give you bad news of some kind?' she asked anxiously.

'No,' César said stiltedly, turning his head away, his strong profile clenching hard. 'In fact the prognosis is very good. Jasper may have told me that his heart was failing but I gather that was something of an exaggeration. Apparently he was just very much afraid of the idea of having this pacemaker fitted.'

'I can understand that. He's never had to go into hospital before.'

'When Eduardo first diagnosed his condition last year, Jasper buried his head in the sand and refused to consider surgery. He also told Eduardo that under no account was I to be informed,' César shared in a constrained undertone, digging his balled fists into the pockets of his well-cut trousers and moving restively away from her, a powerful tension etched into the taut set of his wide shoulders. 'Jasper *knew* that I would put pressure on him to have the operation…'

'Of course you would've. It's the only sensible option.' Dixie was bewildered by the depth of emotional reaction which César was visibly struggling to contain and conceal from her.

'He was afraid I would bully him into it,' César breathed with suppressed savagery.

'That faint Jasper had tonight has done the trick for you,' Dixie said consolingly. 'He's accepted now that he needs surgery.'

'But he'd never have had that attack tonight if it hadn't been for me!' César suddenly raked back at her, every syllable of that roughened assurance raw with stark guilt and self-loathing. '*Madre di Dio*…I damn near killed him!'

Really shaken by that outburst, Dixie protested instantly, 'That's not true, César. Dr Arribas himself said that this could've happened at any time—'

'*Accidenti!*' César's striking dark features were set with bitter self-condemnation. 'Don't feed me that sentimental bull! Jasper was extremely upset tonight…I've never seen him that upset about anything! Who caused that needless distress? *Me!* Me and my smartass ideas!' he completed savagely.

Shimmering dark eyes raw with angry pain and regret, César spun on his heel and strode away without another word, leaving Dixie standing with a deeply troubled frown.

She breathed in deep and swallowed hard. Every natural urge prompted her to follow César and reason with him. He was being far too hard on himself. She would never have allowed anyone else to walk away in such a state without trying to offer some comfort. But she forcibly restrained herself from such a move.

César, who let his guard down with nobody, had just let his guard down on a positive flood of self-recrimination. A few hours from now he might well look back on that emotional outburst and despise it as an act of weakness. He would, very probably, be most annoyed that she had witnessed that brief loss of self-discipline. He *was* a very private man. And he didn't like it when she got too personal, wouldn't thank her for her interference, she reflected, pained by that knowledge, suddenly finding herself hating the awareness that she couldn't reach out to César.

César was a perfectionist. He had started out with good intentions, buoyant in his confident belief that their fake engagement would delight Jasper. And then it had all suddenly gone horribly wrong. Jasper had been shocked and upset. Jasper had revealed a very hurtful lack of faith in his godson. César must have been shocked enough by that. He certainly hadn't needed to see Jasper collapse in front of his eyes as well.

She slipped back into Jasper's room and sat by his bed watching him sleep. At about three in the morning, his housekeeper, Ermina, came in, her kindly eyes full of concerned affection as she gazed down at her elderly employer and indicated that she would like to take Dixie's place.

Dixie wandered back to the bedroom she had vacated earlier and found herself pacing the floor while she anxiously wondered where César was. Had he simply moved into one of the guest rooms? In the frame of mind he had been in, Dixie didn't think it very likely that César would simply have gone back to bed.

After a certain amount of hesitation, she left the room again and went downstairs. There was still a light burning in the elegant sitting room where César and Jasper had had their unfortunate confrontation earlier. Dixie opened the door. César was slumped in an armchair. He had been drinking. A half-empty brandy decanter sat on the sofa table beside him, and he still had a glass clasped in one taut-fingered hand. He looked at her with curiously unfocused dark eyes.

'*Dio...*' César slurred with brooding wit. 'It's everybody's best friend!'

Dixie's soft heart still went out to him. She was tempted to tell him that he was his own worst enemy. He just could not cope with what had happened tonight. He was trying to drown the nasty unsettling effect of his own emotional turmoil in alcohol. And, since alcohol was a depressant, it had only made things worse.

'You'll feel much better tomorrow if you get some sleep now.'

'Proper little ray of sunshine aren't you? Tell me, how does it feel to know that you got it right and I got it *all* wrong?'

'Got what right?' she prompted uncertainly.

'You said lies were always wrong. You were right. You said I'd be so much better at lying than you. You were *wrong* about that,' César gritted, thrusting long fingers roughly through his black hair. 'When Jasper confronted me, I completely blew it—'

'His attitude upset you...you weren't prepared for it.'

'He hates my guts now.'

Dixie knelt down by his feet and looked up at him with concerned blue eyes. 'Of course he doesn't. It was a storm in a teacup.'

'A storm in a teacup,' César repeated unevenly, gazing down into her wide eyes and blinking slightly.

'You take everything far too seriously. Jasper was taken aback…the bedroom bit was very unfortunate, and then, instead of reassuring him, I bet you got on your high horse—'

'My high horse…?'

Dixie gently removed the glass from his hold and then linked her fingers with his. 'César…look on the bright side.'

'The bright side?'

'All right, I use a lot of clichés but clichés are often spot-on,' Dixie pointed out as his hand closed round hers. 'Here you are, feeling really miserable—'

'Guilty,' César contradicted harshly.

'But when we came here you thought Jasper was dying. Now you know that he has every hope of making a complete recovery.'

'True…' César frowned, as if he hadn't quite absorbed that message yet.

'He'll probably live until he's at least a hundred,' Dixie added bracingly. 'And staying away from him now has only made you feel worse.'

'The sight of me might have upset him again,' César breathed darkly. 'That's why I kept my distance.'

'There you are again, thinking the very worst. Jasper loves you,' Dixie scolded softly. 'He just isn't as naive as you assumed. Because he was so surprised at the idea of us being engaged, he suspected that—'

'I had dishonourable intentions?' César grimaced.

Dixie slowly stood up and tugged suggestively at César's hand, in the hope of getting him upright.

'What are you doing?'

'You need to go to bed.'

César rose with something less than his usual inbred grace, and swayed ever so slightly. Dixie smiled at him. Shorn of his icy reserve, he had such tremendous humanity. His ridiculously long lashes swept down, closing her out for a split second, and then he looked at her again and gave her an almost boyish smile that made her heart give a violent lurch.

'You're so nice—you make me feel very bad sometimes,' César shared.

Dixie's smile died. 'I irritate you.'

'No…it's more like meeting my conscience face to face. I'm getting used to it.'

Dixie's smile glimmered again as they reached the bedroom door and she opened it. 'Do you feel better now?'

'Not so as you'd notice.'

'You were only trying to make Jasper happy. You had good intentions,' Dixie assured him warmly.

César gazed down at her with those stunning silvered eyes, a curious stillness freezing his facial muscles as if some sudden revelation had struck him. As he studied her with bewildering intensity, Dixie entirely forgot the rest of what she had intended to say. He slowly lifted one lean hand and stroked a long forefinger very, very gently along the generous curve of her mouth. Her heart jumped and her breathing arrested, a trail of fire tingling where he had touched.

'Never trust my intentions,' César husked, the accented words velvet-soft. 'I invariably calculate everything right down to the final full-stop.'

'You probably can't help yourself…'

Dixie found it impossible to concentrate when she

looked up into that lean, dark fallen-angel face of his.
Instinctively she hovered, without acknowledging either
her own fierce reluctance to be parted from him or the
fact that César had actually tightened his grip on her
hand. Indeed, all of a sudden it was as if the world was
standing still, and in the interim every sense magically
sharpened. She was incredibly aware of each breath
that she drew, of the surging pulse of her own blood
through her veins…

'I feel…I feel like I'm tipsy,' she confided.

'Least it's not a "really creep feeling" this time…'
César muttered almost dazedly as his dark head slowly,
steadily lowered to hers.

And she stopped breathing, sanity drowning in his
brilliant magnetic gaze. As his mouth found hers, with
a sweetness that was almost unbearable, she felt her
knees start to give. He caught her up into his arms and
cannoned backwards into the door to close it. 'Stay
with me…I don't want to be alone tonight,' he confessed raggedly.

And then he kissed her again, hard, hungry, drugging kisses that blew her mind and melted her to liquid
honey. He might have spoken again. But every time he
tried to stop kissing her Dixie held him fast. The wanting had escaped like a damburst inside her, carrying
all before it. So powerful was that need she could not
resist it.

With an erotic expertise she was defenceless against,
César let his tongue delve deep, emulating a far more
intimate possession. Sealed in his arms, she trembled
violently, heartbeat racing, pulses thrumming. Bringing her down on the bed, he knelt over her, releasing
the tie on her robe, tugging it down out of his path as he

pressed his mouth hotly to the sensitive skin at the base of her throat, and she jerked and whimpered out loud.

That betraying sound made César jerk up his head. He gazed down at her then, and stilled, tension snaking through every muscle of his lean, powerful body. 'No, I'm not sober…this shouldn't be happening, *cara*,' he began with breathless urgency. 'I'm not in control.'

'Why should you be?' Dixie asked helplessly.

Disconcerted by that unexpected response, César stared down into her starry eyes, and he dragged his hands from her slender forearms like a male fighting himself every step of the way. A long shudder racked him. 'Stop looking at me like that,' he urged unsteadily.

Dixie was fascinated. 'Like what?'

With a stifled expletive, César closed his eyes and snatched in a jagged breath of restraint. *'Accidenti!'* he groaned. 'I want you so *much*…I've never wanted a woman as desperately as I want you right now!'

That acknowledgement of her feminine power was like a shot of adrenalin in Dixie's veins. It was a power she had never dreamt she might possess. There was no rational thought in the manner in which she reached up to César and found his wide, sensual mouth again for herself. An intoxicating sense of joy surged up inside her, lending a fevered edge to the fierce pulse-beat of desire thrumming wildly through her.

César reacted to that invitation by flattening her to the bed. As he connected with her shapely curves he growled deep in his throat with all-male pleasure. They exchanged searing, scorching kisses while Dixie tried stubbornly to unbutton his shirt without disconnecting herself from him.

César made one last attempt to get a grip on the situation. 'We *can't*...' Resolution failing as she spread her hands appreciatively over his magnificent torso, he raised her up in his powerful arms and struggled as clumsily as a teenager to extract her from her night-dress, while letting the tip of his tongue dip between her parted lips before he groaned in belated completion, 'Can't do this...'

'Shut up...' Dixie sealed her lips wonderingly to a smooth, hard shoulder. Like an addict, she drank in the scent and the hot salty taste of his bronzed skin. Everything about him felt so good, so right, so perfect. She started to work steadily downwards, in love with every sensation she shared with him, overwhelmed by a glorious sense of freedom.

'Say my name...' César breathed jerkily.

'César...'

'Again,' he purred, like a big hungry cat, trembling as she reached the flat, taut muscles of his stomach.

'César...César...César,' Dixie sighed voluptuously, engaged in following her every sensual instinct, smoothing exploring fingers down over his long muscular thighs, discovering the distinctly shocking bulge of his pronounced arousal, but only for a split second.

With a broken hiss of impatience, César wrenched at his zip and started kissing her breathless again. Her heart sang; her whole body blazed. As he fought his way out of his clothes he found her breasts, and it became even more of a struggle to undress and make love to her at one and the same time. Dixie had never even imagined such explosive passion could exist, and she revelled in it. She couldn't get close enough to him. He couldn't get close enough to her.

'You were made for me, *cara*...' César closed his

mouth reverently to a rosy pink nipple and laved the straining bud with his tongue.

Her spine arched and she panted with helpless pleasure, hands biting into his shoulders. The illusion that she was in control was gone by then, but she didn't care. He dragged her down into a frantic hot well of excitement, where all she could do was feel and react to the incredible intensity of sensation. Her skin felt as if it was burning over her bones, super-sensitive to his every caress, and she just couldn't stay still.

'You meet my passion with your own,' César muttered with intense appreciation. 'You make me burn for you, *cara.*'

He traced the length of a slim trembling thigh, and the throbbing ache at the heart of her suddenly surged to screaming proportions. As he sought out the moist heat of her most sensitive flesh, she flung her head back and writhed. The surging excitement was almost intolerable. Her temperature was rocketing, her body electrified.

'I can't bear it…I can't bear it!' she suddenly gasped wildly.

César crushed her reddened lips under his again and made her bear it, hot, timeless moments of bittersweet pleasure that drove her crazy. And then he shifted over her, sliding between her thighs, pushing up her knees. In her fevered state, she understood only that at last the unbearable ache of emptiness might be satisfied.

'*Dios…* I can't wait any longer,' César growled.

And she opened her eyes and looked up at him, absorbing the feverish flush on his high cheekbones, the silvered intensity of his eyes, the sheer hunger all for her, and it made her feel that she was flying as high and free as a kite.

As he arched over her, the hot, hard surge of his hungry invasion took her by surprise. The sensation was so new to her she froze in astonishment, and then he thrust deeper, and a sharp, piercing pain dragged a startled cry from her lips.

César stilled in bemusement. 'I'm the first...?' he exclaimed, thunderstruck.

As the pain receded she shifted helplessly beneath him, unable to think, not wanting to speak, longing only to luxuriate in the incredibly intimate feel of him inside her. And that one tiny movement of hers destroyed whatever shred of self-control César had gained from his shock at her innocence. With a ragged groan he thrust deeper still, with passionate urgency, no more able than she to detach himself from the driving demands of his own body.

All awareness of self fell away as he engulfed her in his stormy rhythm. Wild and mindless pleasure controlled her. Her heart thundering against her breastbone, she rode that storm with him. All that mattered was that he shouldn't stop, shouldn't deny the remorseless craving he had unleashed within her. And he drove her to a frenzied climax that made her cry out in ecstasy, her body convulsing in what felt like a thousand pieces as he slammed into her one last time.

Afterwards she felt as if she was falling and falling, down into endless layers of soft cotton wool. And although later she would dimly recall César trying to rouse her to speech, she just couldn't stay awake in the hold of the most seductive contented peace she had ever known.

CHAPTER SEVEN

DIXIE woke up only when a maid pulled open the curtains. Blinking sleepily, she began to sit up, only then realising that she was no longer in César's bedroom.

'Lunch will be ready in one hour, *señorita*,' the smiling maid informed her in perfect English. 'Señor Valverde asked me to wake you.'

A Technicolor replay of what she had been doing shortly before dawn with César assailed Dixie. Shock reeled through her in waves. She could not understand how a mere few hours ago making love with César could have seemed so right, so natural and so inevitable.

César had been drinking, far from his usual unemotional and rational self. But even in that state César had attempted to call a halt. In fact he had tried to be the voice of reason more than once, Dixie remembered. With a sinking heart she recalled ripping him out of his shirt. Colour ran like a banner of shame into her cheeks. She had taken advantage of César...

How could she have done that? He had kissed her first, hadn't he? He had started it...but he had also tried to stop it. But she had wanted him, craved him, shamelessly clung. High on the discovery of the power a woman could have over a man, she had discarded every inhibition. Oh, dear heaven, was there the remotest possibility that she could ever look César Valverde in the face again?

As the maid carried in her clothing and proceeded to hang each garment in the built-in wardrobes, Dixie was frozen by ever-deepening panic to the bed. She was picturing César as he had been in the early hours, César as she had never seen him before. César, unusually vulnerable, knocked for six by Jasper's collapse and his own guilty conscience.

In kissing her, he had surrendered to a moment's temptation. And she had entirely misread the situation. César had really just been seeking the reassuring warmth of human contact, but, being César, he had expressed that need in the form of a sexual invitation. What she should have done was give him a hug or talk to him…or something.

It was all *her* fault. How could she blame him? According to the magazines she read, men weren't good at withstanding temptation. The average single male was programmed to say yes every time. No way could César be held accountable for what she had wantonly encouraged him to do!

He had been so shocked when he'd realised that she was still a virgin. Dixie groaned. She had even gone to sleep while César had presumably been trying to talk to her about what they had just done and why they shouldn't have done it! Within five seconds that speed-of-light intelligence of his would have homed in on the fact that he had made a major mistake. Suddenly she was very grateful that César had shifted her out of his room and slotted her into a guest room bed.

Sliding off the bed, she went for a shower. Then she

put on an elegant blue skirt and matching sleeveless top. With every passing minute her inner turmoil simply increased.

Why *had* she cast away every principle and just seized César along with the moment? She hadn't thought of Scott once! But then she had never got past friendship with Scott. And clearly she had a more physical nature than she had ever appreciated. That was obviously why she had lost control with César.

Last night's events had upset her equilibrium as well, but she hadn't recognised her own vulnerability. She had succumbed to what César had earlier bluntly described as 'pure naked lust'. She winced at the label, but there it was. César had awakened the sexual side of her nature.

Better to face that mortifying fact head-on rather than make silly sentimental excuses for herself and begin imagining that she was now falling in love with César! Hadn't that stupid thought been in the back of her mind as she'd drifted blissfully off to sleep in his arms? Yes, it had been. Her subconscious already trying to provide a more acceptable excuse for her behaviour.

But she was *not* falling in love with César. She loved Scott…or did she? She was no longer so sure of that fact. From the moment César had come close she had begun thinking less and less about Scott. Suddenly she didn't know what was going on inside her own head any more. But she badly wanted to see Scott again, and reinforce her feelings for him. Loving Scott from afar was safe; loving César would be emotional suicide. How many times had César already warned her not to get too keen on him?

As she sat at the dressing table, feverishly brushing her hair, a light knock sounded on the door.

In the mirror, she saw César's tall dark figure. Paralysis set in instantaneously.

In beautifully cut chinos the colour of toffee and a black polo shirt, César looked drop-dead gorgeous. All bronzed and dark and dangerous. Her heart lurched and she quivered in dismay.

'Let's not talk about earlier,' she heard herself say tautly. 'We should forget it ever happened.'

'Dixie, I—'

'Please don't say any more,' Dixie broke in at frantic speed.

'I can't forget it ever happened.' The assurance was harsh.

'Work at it…you'll be surprised. I always think mistakes are forgotten the quickest, but maybe you don't make enough mistakes to know that the way I do,' Dixie muttered rather limply, fiddling with the hairbrush, avoiding even his reflection now, because even his reflection sent her heartbeat crazy. 'How's Jasper?'

'He slept late. I haven't actually seen him yet, but I gather he's fine. It was Ermina who told me he would be coming down to lunch,' César proffered with audible impatience. 'We *have* to talk about this, Dixie. I need to know what you're trying to say to me.'

Paling, Dixie breathed in deep. 'It was an awful mistake. We were both upset. You'd been drinking. I was concerned, trying to comfort you…things just got out of hand. What more is there to say?'

'Are you telling me that you went to bed with me because you felt *sorry* for me?' César prompted with wrathful incredulity.

Dixie moved her head in a helpless gesture of confusion. 'I don't know… Apart from the obvious, I don't *know* why I did it!' she finally confessed.

'"Apart from the obvious"? What does that cover?' César demanded suspiciously.

'The lust bit,' Dixie whispered, marvelling that he hadn't grasped that for himself. 'I just get really carried away when you kiss me.'

The thunderous silence pulsed.

César settled his lean hands to her shoulders, raised her upright and turned her round. His stunning eyes locked into her mortified gaze like guided missiles. He bent his arrogant dark head and kissed her. Stars exploded in the darkness behind her lowered eyelids. Fireworks blazed up in a shower of sparks inside her. Her legs went hollow; her mind went blank.

César held her back from him, retaining a steadying hold on her slight shoulders. Deceptively indolent dark eyes surveyed her bemused expression. 'It's the sort of problem we need to work on together, Dixie.'

'I thought you'd be furious with me for taking advantage of you when you weren't quite sober,' she admitted in bewilderment.

César tautened, lashes dropping very low over glinting eyes. 'I'm not remotely sexist, and I'm remarkably resilient.'

Still struggling to understand why he had kissed her, Dixie tensed when he reached for her hand. He slid the diamond engagement ring on to her finger. 'You left it in my bathroom. Jasper will be expecting to see it.'

And only then did she realise why he had kissed her and why he wasn't furious. They still had to pretend to be engaged for Jasper's benefit. So when César closed a seemingly possessive hand over hers on the way down-stairs she wasn't surprised. It was all part of the act.

'I didn't like to mention it before,' she confided. 'But I overheard you and Jasper talking—'

César glanced at her enquiringly. 'How much did you hear?'

Dixie looked awkward. 'Enough to know that it was going badly. You let Jasper back you into a corner—'

'I did…did I?'

'Well, you know you did,' Dixie pointed out ruefully. 'Telling Jasper that you'd marry me next week could've got us into a very difficult situation!'

Dark colour sprang up over César's spectacular cheekbones. He opened his mouth as if he was about to say something really cutting, and she stiffened. Then something strange happened. He looked at her. He sealed his lips again, veiled his eyes and simply shrugged a shoulder, expressively conceding the point.

'We'll have to tell him the truth when he's recovering from his op,' Dixie sighed. 'I think he'll understand why we did it.'

César's lean fingers gripped hers rather more tightly. 'Slight change of subject here, before we join Jasper,' he murmured smoothly. 'When we made love—'

Dixie bristled like a cornered animal, suddenly finding the hunter on her trail again. 'I thought we weren't going to discuss that again!'

'Just this once…' César studied her with broodingly intent and incisive dark eyes. 'I had this weird and wonderful idea that it might be something *more* than lust.'

Dixie reddened, humiliated by what she read into that admission but determined to assure him that she was not so foolish. 'You really don't need to worry about that, César.'

'I...don't?'

Dixie stared miserably down at their linked hands, thinking what a joke they were. 'I'm not silly enough to think that being physically attracted to someone is the same as being in love. Scott's still the only guy for me,' she swore vehemently.

César dropped her hand and bit out a sardonic laugh. 'You were with *me*, not him!' he derided.

'I'm pretty ashamed of that,' Dixie mumbled chokily.

'So you should be,' César confirmed in a suddenly savage undertone. 'Let me tell you, if you were in love with me I'd have an armed guard on you at all times. I wouldn't trust a woman as dippy and disloyal as you out of my sight!'

'But I don't even have a relationship with Scott yet,' she protested in her own defence.

'And if *I* have anything to do with it you never will!' César shot back at her chillingly.

Bemused by that assurance, Dixie finally worked up the courage to look up. César looked outraged. She was nailed to the spot by silvered eyes as piercing and threatening as knives.

'You used me,' César condemned fiercely. 'I don't let anybody do that.'

'How did I use you?' she gasped strickenly, seriously out of her depth and fighting to comprehend how she had angered him to such an extent.

'*Santo cielo*...like a bloody dry run for Scott! And to think I was worried about the fact that I hadn't taken any precautions!' César sent her a glittering look of what could only be described as pure loathing.

'Precautions?' Dixie was still working through the astonishing concept of César being some sort of sexual experiment, and not doing very well.

'Of course you're already on the Pill, prepared for Scott,' César assumed with even greater scorn. 'The last thing you were going to risk was an accidental pregnancy, and I'm grateful…don't think I'm not! But when this fiasco is over I want you out of my life like you were never there in the first place!'

Dumbfounded by the number of contradictions, unexpected attacks and freewheeling assumptions coming her way, and hopelessly confused, Dixie watched César stride off, aggression radiating from every taut line of his lithe, powerful frame. She followed at a slower pace. She *wasn't* taking the contraceptive Pill. The risk of a pregnancy hadn't even occurred to her. Confronted with that daunting reality, she went into even deeper shock.

Without warning, César wheeled round and strode back to her. Closing his hand back over hers again, he released his breath in a fractured hiss. Grim dark eyes gazed down into hers. 'I'm sorry…I had no right to attack you like that.'

Shaken by the gruff apology, Dixie muttered in a stifled voice. 'It's OK. I understand.'

'I don't think you do,' César said flatly.

But she did, she thought wretchedly. Over the past twelve hours everything had gone haywire. Sudden intimacy had brought down the barriers between them, and now the barriers had to be raised again. But no wonder César had been so on edge when he was worrying about whether or not he might have got her pregnant. Right then she decided to let him continue believing that he didn't need to worry about that possibility. She told herself that it was unlikely that one rash act would lead to the conception of a child, and stamped down hard on her anxiety. This morning she had to smile like a woman in love and newly engaged. Not one hint of the divisions between them could be revealed in Jasper's presence.

Jasper was waiting for them in a sunlit courtyard beneath the shade of a giant casuarina tree. With a wide smile on his creased face, he rose to his feet. 'Now don't tell me that I should've stayed in bed. Father Navarro is joining us for lunch.'

In the act of settling Dixie into a chair behind the beautifully set table, César stilled. 'Father Navarro?'

'So that we can set a date for the wedding. I gave him a call this morning. We haven't got time to waste. Eduardo wants me into that clinic within the next two weeks!' Patently unaware of the bombshell he had dropped on them both, Jasper sank back down into his seat, exuding an air of happy complacency.

CHAPTER EIGHT

As JASPER cheerfully suggested that César pour the wine, Dixie struggled not to visually betray what a shock she had just received.

'Don't look so disapproving, César,' Jasper scolded gently. 'One glass of wine won't do me any harm. This is a very special occasion.'

'Jasper...I seriously doubt that you need the excitement of a wedding night now.' César filled the crystal glasses with an admirably steady hand.

'Nonsense. I don't want you both feeling that you have to put things off until *after* my op! I'm fit enough for a quiet family affair.' A slight frown of strain formed on Jasper's worn features as he studied them both. 'Oh dear, have I taken too much of a liberty in contacting Father Navarro?'

César gave him an amused smile that impressed Dixie to death. 'Of course you haven't.' He glanced fleetingly at Dixie. 'Jasper and the village priest are old cronies, *cara*. He was sure to share our news with him first.'

Jasper relaxed again. 'You'll throw a big reception for all your friends once you're back in London, but a private ceremony here is much more your style, César.

You won't be bothered by any paparazzi in this neck of the woods.'

Dixie suddenly grasped two things. Jasper was throwing himself into this wedding idea to take his mind off his coming surgery. He was also very much afraid that he wasn't going to survive the operation.

'You'll be fine. Apart from this little heart thing, you're in great condition for a man of your age,' she told him, as if he had spoken his fear out loud.

'Dixie reads me like a book,' Jasper told César rather smugly.

'You think a lot alike,' César remarked, without any expression at all.

And then the village priest arrived. For the two older men it was a jovial meal. Dixie kept on finding her mind drifting off the dialogue. She watched César, in awe at his self-control, his ease of speech, his ability to hide his horror at the situation in which they now found themselves. She kept on waiting for him to casually produce some clever reason which would regrettably make such a wedding out of the question in the near future, but César made not the slightest attempt.

Indeed, throughout that meal she could not drag her attention from César. That lean, strong face, the shard of sunlight that gleamed over his blue-black hair every time he threw his well-shaped head back, the warmth in the beautiful dark eyes she had once thought so cold when he looked at his godfather. He was putting on the show of the century for Jasper's sake.

By the time Father Navarro took his leave, a date only five days away had been settled on for the ceremony. Jasper went indoors for a nap. As his quiet footsteps receded, Dixie suddenly rose from the table and walked away, dragging in great gasps of the hot, still air as her tension slowly drained away, only to leave her in a state of disbelief.

Standing by the wall bounding the courtyard, she looked beyond the gorgeous terraced gardens spread out below to the magnificent view of the lushly wooded mountains. And she thought, Now César is about to tell me that we have no choice but to get married.

César paused several feet away, studying her with veiled dark eyes. 'You're furious with me.'

Dixie turned a strained profile to him, shaken reproach in her troubled blue eyes. 'You got us into this. Somehow I assumed you'd magically get us out of it again.'

'If I'd argued Jasper would've suspected I was having second thoughts about marrying you, and then he would've been upset. I couldn't risk it.'

'I care very much about Jasper, but I don't want to go to the lengths of a church wedding to placate him!' Dixie admitted starkly.

'We can get an annulment later.' César moved soundlessly closer, his brilliant eyes silver-bright slivers beneath his lush ebony lashes. 'I know you didn't bargain on this, and I'm not about to try and browbeat you into it. I realise that I'm asking you for a really huge favour.'

Her attention locked to his strikingly serious features, the stark tension etched into his fabulous bone structure, and something inside her just began to melt like butter left out under the sun.

'César, I—'

'*Please*…I need you to do this for me,' César breathed with roughened sincerity.

Dixie collided with his eyes, and a wave of such physical craving consumed her that it was a literal agony not to be in his arms. Shocked by that awareness, she trembled and twisted her head away. 'OK… it'll just be for a few weeks. Then we'll be back in London and we can just tell Jasper that it didn't work out.'

'I swear you won't regret this decision.'

Involuntarily, Dixie stole a glance at him. A slashing charismatic smile had driven the tension from his startlingly handsome features. As a burst of heat ignited in the pit of her stomach she lowered her gaze again, appalled by the power he had to disturb her. A power he wasn't even trying to exercise, a natural power he had simply been born with.

'There's just one thing you could do to make things a little easier,' she heard herself say stiffly.

'Name it.'

'Could we try and avoid each other as much as possible?'

For a split second César looked stunned.

Conscious that she had been clumsy, Dixie dropped her head and added, 'I just think it would make us both more comfortable.'

'You didn't seem particularly uncomfortable over lunch,' César remarked very softly. 'In fact you never took your eyes off me once.'

There he was again, seeking reassurance that she wasn't getting keen on him, Dixie reflected in mortification, her cheeks flaming. 'I was acting.'

'I should've thought of that. So you were imagining I was Scott?' he prompted in a roughened undertone.

Too embarrassed to look at him, Dixie interpreted that fracturing intonation as one of immense amusement. 'What else?'

* * *

Dixie's reflection in the tall cheval mirror took her breath away. Three days earlier César had had a selection of wedding dresses flown in, complete with a seamstress to make any necessary alterations on the spot. Just another prop for Jasper's benefit, Dixie had gathered. But seeing herself in full bridal regalia now, on her wedding day, was somehow something else entirely...

Jasper had insisted on loaning her a diamond tiara that had belonged to his mother. The jewels glittered like a wreath of stars in her upswept hair. And the gown? The gown was a perfect dream. Ivory silk enhanced by delicate embroidery skimmed her breasts, hugged her tiny waist and fell softly down to feet sheathed in gold embroidered shoes straight out of *Cinderella*.

Over the past five days Dixie had scarcely seen César, except in Jasper's presence. On César's side, keeping up an act had demanded little more than an impressive air of concerned interest in her wellbeing, and circumspect walks in the grounds after dinner.

'Jasper doesn't trust us to be alone,' César had gritted with a flash of outrage while his godfather strolled about in the courtyard above them like an eagle-eyed chaperone. 'What does he think I'm about to do? Drag you under the trees like a randy teenager?'

Recalling that incredulous outburst the previous evening, Dixie could not help smiling as she was ushered out of her room by Ermina, who had insisted on helping her to dress. Dear Jasper, she thought fondly. He didn't trust César an inch on the moral restraint front. Her smile slowly ebbed. Jasper really had nothing to worry about. That fateful night of passion would never be repeated.

Jasper watched Dixie come down the stairs with immense pride. 'You look superb, my dear.'

He handed her out into the waiting car as if she was a queen, and the run down the steep mountain road to the tiny church on the outskirts of the village slumbering in the heat of midday took only minutes. Jolted by the appearance of a photographer, to record her entrance on Jasper's arm, Dixie was a bundle of nerves when she mounted the shallow steps clutching her beautiful bouquet.

As the ceremony began, César finally turned to look at her. His dark, deep-set eyes flared silver, and he didn't turn away again. Eduardo Arribas, standing up as best man, had to give him a suggestive nudge when it was time to put the ring on her finger. Dixie was conscious of nothing but the quiet words of the service and César, devastatingly tall and sensationally attractive in an elegant charcoal-grey pinstripe suit.

She was leaving the church before she remembered to remind herself that it was all just a masquerade and not real at all. The photographer made them pose, and when they finally climbed into the car that would waft them back to the house for the wedding breakfast, she expected César to say something very cynical along the lines of, I'm glad that charade's over!

'You look absolutely incredible in that dress,' César breathed huskily instead.

'You don't have to pretend when we're on our own.'

'I'm not pretending—'

'Yes, you are. You know you are…like when you told me I had really stunning eyes,' she reminded him ruefully. 'You can switch off the act until we have to get out of the car again.'

In receipt of that dauntingly prosaic assurance, César murmured almost aggressively, 'You *do* have gorgeous eyes.'

Dixie sighed. 'Why are you carrying on like this?'

César met her frankly reproachful gaze with shimmering dark eyes that blazed a heat trail of intense sexual awareness through her. Dixie quivered. The atmosphere was suddenly so raw with leaping tension she couldn't breathe. Her mind filled with wanton imagery of their brief intimacy only days earlier. The hot, drugging glory of being in his arms. The wondrous, incredible sensation of that lean, powerful body moving over hers. In the grip of such memories, Dixie shifted on the seat, stabbed by guilty excitement.

And when César curved a lean-fingered hand to her waist and drew her close memory and reality converged, and there was not a thought in her head that she shouldn't do what she so desperately wanted to do. He crushed her soft mouth under his with devouring hunger. With scant ceremony, Dixie speared her hands possessively into his thick black hair and pulled him to her. Her thundering heartbeat merged with his and slowly, very slowly, they disappeared below the level of the car windows until they were lying full-length on the back seat.

Some timeless period later, after a bout of fevered kissing that left them both struggling for oxygen, César raised his head. 'The car's parked,' he remarked with a slight frown. 'The driver's gone.'

As César raised himself, taking her with him, Dixie surfaced, almost senseless from the depths of an all-encompassing passion and with her tiara askew. With deft hands César eased the tiara free, straightened her tumbled hair and slotted the tiara back into place.

'I think we'd better make our entrance…you can't have a wedding breakfast without the bride and groom, *cara mia*.' A heartbreaker of a smile curved César's wide, sensual mouth. As her heart gave a violent lurch, that smile set Dixie back at least five minutes in the recovery process.

César handed her out and smoothed down the folds of her gown as if they had all the time in the world. Then, before she could even catch her breath, he bent down and swept her up into his arms. 'What—?'

'Tradition, *cara*. Relax,' he teased, reading her anxious face with instant understanding and amusement. 'If you ever went on a diet, I'd forcefeed you with chocolate fudge cake every night.'

Dixie had never heard that teasing intonation from César before. It poleaxed her. And she was even more taken aback by the revelation that César could do something as distinctly uncool as kiss her breathless in the back of a car while their few guests waited for them to emerge.

In a decided daze, she let him carry her into the house, for all the world like a real bride on her wedding day. Hovering in the imposing shaded entrance, Jasper watched them approach with unconcealed contentment.

As they drew level he smiled, and said in a cheerful undertone, 'Bruce flew in with your mail, César. He also brought an unexpected visitor, whom I'm sure will be very much appreciated. I haven't shared your news yet. I love to surprise people!'

And indeed, as César strode into the comparative dimness of the hall, Dixie's beautiful ivory gown trailing across him like a banner, Jasper certainly succeeded in his wish to see people surprised.

César's executive assistant, Bruce Gregory, moved forward first, focused on Dixie in her wedding dress and fell still with a dropped jaw.

'Close your mouth, Bruce,' César murmured gently to the younger man. 'You look like one of Dixie's fish.'

The unexpected visitor pushed past Bruce. A very glamorous blonde wearing an eye-catching leopard print skirt and matching crop top that exposed her exotically jewelled navel. She let her breath escape in a startled hiss when she saw the bride and groom. Momentarily, her beautiful face was a study of complete disbelief.

'Petra?' Dixie exclaimed in delighted amazement. 'César, this is my sister, Petra!'

Brilliant dark eyes narrowing, César came to a halt and surveyed the now brightly smiling blonde. 'Hello, Petra,' he drawled smoothly. 'What a shame you had to miss the ceremony by such a narrow margin!'

'Petra…this is César…César Valverde,' Dixie announced, with considerable pride in her ability to introduce her famous sister to someone she felt to be worthy of her notice.

'Everybody knows who César Valverde is,' Petra Sinclair remarked with a patronising look of amusement she attempted to share with César, but César simply stared steadily back at her, not a muscle moving on his darkly handsome face.

'How did you find out where I was?' Dixie demanded, still in César's arms and momentarily blinded when the photographer stepped forward to take a flash photo of their entrance.

'You left a forwarding address, darling. And when I showed up at César's house and ran into Brucie, I persuaded him to let me hitch a ride out here with him.'

'Brucie' angled a somewhat weak and apologetic smile in his employer's direction. César sent him a flashing glance that made him tense. 'Congratulations, César,' he managed, nonetheless. 'And Dixie, my very warmest good wishes. I have to confess...I didn't see this development on the horizon.'

'You said it first,' Petra said, rather shrilly. 'But don't you just love weddings? I know *I* do!'

César slowly lowered Dixie to the floor. 'Excuse me, *cara*,' he murmured in a quiet aside. 'I have an urgent call to make.'

Petra crossed the hall and closed an arm round her much smaller stepsister. 'I really have missed having you around,' she confided, while Jasper looked on with warm approval of such sisterly affection.

Surprised by Petra's unusual demonstrativeness, Dixie glowed. 'I've missed you too. How was California?'

As Jasper moved away, Petra dropped her smile and gave a petulant shrug. 'It didn't work out, and then I landed back in London, expecting you to be able to put me up—'

'Oh, *no*!' Dixie was dismayed.

'And then when I realised you were in Spain, with dear old Jasper, I just crossed my fingers and *prayed* there'd be room for an extra house guest!' Petra studied Dixie's concerned and guilty face with cool green eyes. 'As I'm really broke right now, I had no choice.'

'No, *of course*, you didn't,' Dixie agreed fervently, hoping that César and Jasper wouldn't mind Petra staying on while she herself looked forward to an opportunity to catch up with all her sister's news.

César returned to her side, and Dixie noticed that Bruce was now welded to a phone on the far side of the hall.

Although Dixie would have appreciated a few minutes to talk to her sister in private, she could see it wasn't possible when everybody was waiting for their meal. At the table, she had Jasper on one side of her and César on the other. Petra ended up beside Father Navarro, who seemed to be rather heavily into talking about the joys of early matrimony and large families. Unfortunately Petra made several rather inappropriate comments, and then sank into a silence punctuated only by large yawns.

'I'm just so pleased Petra is here,' Dixie shared shyly with César as he put his hand over hers to cut the beautiful wedding cake. 'Obviously she's really tired, and she's not too comfortable with men of the cloth, but isn't she just gorgeous?'

'So that's the shade of blonde hair you hanker after? It wouldn't suit you at all,' César informed her in a charged undertone. 'You're not hankering after the butterfly tattoo and the body piercing as well, are you?'

'Well, I must say—'

'All that stuff hurts like hell. You'd be in real agony,' César interrupted, watching Dixie pale. 'Your stepsister must be very brave.'

'Yes, she is. Things didn't work out for her in California, but she's just taking it on the chin.' Dixie sighed, full of sympathy.

After the meal, Dixie went to the cloakroom to tidy

her hair. When she emerged, Petra was pacing the floor outside, an angry look on her face.

'I nearly fell asleep over that meal...I thought the punishment was never going to end!'

Curving a determined hand over her arm, Petra herded Dixie into the nearest empty room. Closing the door, her blonde stepsister rested back against it, widening her cat-green eyes meaningfully. '*You* and César Valverde married?' she questioned with a rather high-pitched laugh. 'I am gobsmacked—and obviously it changes my plans. I can hardly stay here when you've just got hitched!'

Dixie stared at her in surprise. 'Why ever not?'

'Use your brain, Dixie,' Petra said thinly. 'This is Jasper's house, and now you'll be taking off on some extravagant honeymoon trip. I can scarcely plonk myself down here and wait for your return. I wouldn't want to anyway. I've never met so many pontificating old bores in one spot in my entire life!'

'This is actually César's house, Petra. It belonged to his late father, but Jasper has lived here for years.' Disconcerted as she was by such scorn, Dixie couldn't help being relieved that Petra wasn't instantly subjecting her to a barrage of awkward questions as to how she and César had contrived to get together. She really didn't want to lie to her sister. 'And since Jasper hasn't been too well, César and I won't be taking off anywhere.'

'Rather you than me. I can't stick nurse-maiding old folk, but I can see that this time it's paid off *very* well for you!' Sullen resentment flashed in Petra's eyes. 'Look, why don't you do me a favor and just give me a loan so that I can hightail it back out of this rural place and leave you to enjoy the fruits of your stupendously *good* marriage?'

In receipt of that pointedly derisive speech, Dixie frowned in growing bewilderment, wondering what had got into Petra, who was usually the life and soul of every social gathering. 'A...*loan*?'

'You just married an entire bank,' Petra spelt out with a curled lip.

Uneasy colour lit Dixie's cheeks. 'Petra, I couldn't possibly ask César to give you money—'

'Why not? Is the catch of the century tight with his mega-millions?'

'César settled the bills that you overlooked when you flew out to California,' Dixie countered uncomfortably, disturbed that her stepsister had yet to make any reference to the debts she had left behind her.

Petra stiffened. 'So César knows about all that?'

'Yes.'

Petra reddened angrily. 'It wasn't my fault that I got in such a mess!'

'No, I know it wasn't.' But Petra seemed to have a very cavalier attitude to other people's money, and that did trouble Dixie.

Soothed by Dixie's agreement, Petra sniffed. 'Well, if you'll excuse me for saying so, I've got no desire to hang around here playing gooseberry to my kid sister!'

'If you stayed, it wouldn't be like that... I mean...' Dixie floundered '...our marriage isn't like that.'

But as soon as she said that she recalled the heated embrace she and César had shared in the car. She flushed. Had César been acting for Jasper's benefit again? Or was César just not very good at maintaining a platonic relationship? Or was it even remotely possible that César could still be as tempted by her as she was by him? She discounted that third possibility and opted to believe the first. He had just been *acting* passionate.

'What is that supposed to mean?' Petra demanded very drily.

'César only married me to please Jasper. It's really just a pretend marriage to keep Jasper happy until he gets over his coming surgery,' Dixie heard herself confess tautly. 'So there would be no question of you needing to feel like a gooseberry.'

Petra gave her an arrested look, green eyes gleaming with sudden satisfaction. 'Now that does make more sense to me. After all, what the hell would a guy like César Valverde see in a little dowdy dumpling like you? No offence intended,' she added carelessly as Dixie paled, 'but let's face it, you're no oil painting, and he *is*—'

'Yes,' Dixie cut in tightly, really hurt by that 'dumpling' label.

'The guy is absolutely gorgeous,' Petra continued, carefully examining her own striking reflection in a nearby mirror. 'He's a hunk and he's loaded. Much more my type than yours.'

'I guess he is,' Dixie responded not quite evenly, studying the carpet, feeling very round and very small and horribly plain for the first time since César had worked what she had fondly imagined was a transformation of no mean order. You thought a new hairstyle and some fancy clothes could pull off a miracle? a little voice sounding remarkably like Petra's sneered. Are you for real?

'And César has got to be bored witless stuck here with you and that bunch of old fogies! And you really don't count, do you?' Petra said reflectively, as if her thoughts were far away. 'You're quite right. In the circumstances, there's no reason why I shouldn't stay. It might be fun to spend some time with you.'

Dixie focused on her stepsister's exotically embellished navel, shocked and concerned to discover that from the instant Petra had pointed out that she herself was much more César's type she hadn't really wanted her to stay any more. She was appalled by such a mean-minded prompting.

'And...have I got a surprise for you!' Petra continued, digging a hand into her fashionably tiny bag to produce a crumpled envelope.

At that point the door opened, framing César. Tall and dark and smiling. Even so Dixie sensed an oddly charged quality to his stance. His attention immediately went to her troubled face.

'Your ex-landlady passed it on to me.' Petra handed the letter to Dixie and sidestepped César with a vibrant smile to walk out of the room.

'What's that?' César demanded, striding forward.

Dixie's attention fell on the handwriting. 'Oh, my goodness, it's a letter from Scott!'

Eyes glittering like ice shards, César reached out a hand and snatched it from her again.

Dixie gave him an aghast look of complete bewilderment.

'Dio...' César scanned the postmark. 'He posted this from the airport!'

Bruce's voice intervened quietly from the doorway. 'Everything's organised, César.'

One of the maids chose that same moment to enter with a tray of coffee.

'Can I h-have my letter back, please?' Dixie stammered.

'Be my guest.' César returned the letter with precise cool and strolled across the room to join Bruce. 'Would you like some coffee? Help yourself. I need somebody really grounded around me at this minute, because whether you realise it or not, the most major event of my bride's day is now taking place. And this thrilling, unexpected joy, so thoughtfully provided by my stepsister-in-law? A letter from Scott.'

'He's never written to me before, César!' Not really listening, believing that he was teasing her again, and Bruce's presence quite passing her by, Dixie was busy tearing open the envelope. 'Oh, *no*!'

'He's dead?'

'Don't be silly, César. Scott wanted me to go round to his flat so that the repair man could fix his washing machine.'

'New York wasn't far enough,' César mused reflectively.

'But he's actually given me his phone number over there!' Dixie shared in genuine surprise. 'Imagine that!'

'The computer's using every line in the house at the minute,' César delivered flatly. 'And it costs a *fortune* to ring New York.'

'You're right. And then there's the time difference,' Dixie muttered vaguely, automatically glancing at César, as if she expected him to clarify that seeming technicality for her.

'Time differences confuse the hell out of me. You'd have to look it up…haven't a clue where. Get the hell out of here, Bruce,' César raked softly to his convulsed executive assistant, who, having emerged from sheer incredulity, was now struggling desperately hard not to laugh.

'I'd really have liked to know how Scott was getting on with his new job,' Dixie sighed, re-reading her three-line letter rather forlornly.

'He'll be having a whale of a time. New York is a very exciting place,' César murmured, evidently in an attempt to be comforting. 'It's full of sophisticated, gorgeous, unattached women.'

'Knowing Scott as I do,' Dixie mused absently, 'he's sure to be making the most of the experience.'

She was lost in her own thoughts. She no longer believed that she was in love with Scott, and was rather embarrassed by that reality now. How could she have known herself so little and contrived to assume so much?

Over the past week or so she had learnt a lot about herself, and grown up a fair bit too. While she'd been nursing her stepmother she simply hadn't had a social life. And when she'd arrived in London men hadn't exactly beaten a path to her door. So she'd developed a crush on Scott, a harmless but rather juvenile infatuation that had given her more pleasure than pain. After all, she'd enjoyed daydreaming about Scott and discussing him endlessly with anybody willing to listen. Not having a boyfriend hadn't seemed to matter while she had Scott to focus on, and goodness knows she had had nothing much else in her life, she conceded ruefully...

In the stretching silence, César watched Dixie like a hawk. Looking pale and unbearably sad as she inwardly acknowledged the end of an era, Dixie crushed the letter slowly between her fingers. For a normally sunny personality, the gesture seemed redolent of real drama.

'OK…you can phone Scott tonight.'

Emerging from her reverie in some surprise, Dixie encountered the full onslaught of César's penetrating dark eyes and struggled not to shiver in reaction. She wondered why he looked so tense, so…*guilty*? She immediately discarded that fleeting impression. What, after all, could César have to feel guilty about, today of all days? Jasper was happy as a sandboy.

'Thanks…I'd like to wish him well,' she admitted.

'I'm afraid we'll have to leave soon. And, beautiful as that dress is, I imagine you'll want to change,' César continued with supreme cool.

That statement certainly grabbed Dixie's attention. 'Leave?' she queried. 'Leave to go where?'

'We'll be spending the next few days at another location.'

'Like…like on a honeymoon?' Dixie prompted in undisguised horror, quick to catch his drift in spite of his avoidance of that emotive label. 'But I assumed that with Jasper unwell—'

'Eduardo Arribas will be staying while we're away. Jasper naturally expects us to *want* to spend time alone together.'

Colliding with César's stunning dark eyes, Dixie reddened and looked away. 'But it's going to be so awkward…being alone, I mean.'

'Pack plenty of books,' César advised bracingly.

While Dixie was getting changed, Petra came upstairs to find her again.

A bright smile suggesting a considerable improvement in her mood, her stepsister breezed into her room and broke straight into speech. 'Since you *are* going away, César's offered me the use of a condo in an exclusive development on the coast! I've decided to take him up on it. He knows it's too quiet here for me.'

Dixie smiled as she slid her feet into shoes. 'That was really kind of him.'

'Kind? Oh, I don't think it was just that—and I'm so relieved you told me the truth about this marriage of yours *because...*' As Petra fulminatingly scrutinised Dixie, in her scarlet designer sundress with its flirty hem, her green eyes sparkled with more than a hint of malice. 'I think César fancies me like mad!'

Dixie's stomach turned over sickly. The colour drained from her face and she turned away to hide her reaction.

'I can always tell when a man wants me,' Petra continued with conviction. 'When César first saw me downstairs he just froze; he didn't show any reaction at all. Of course he *couldn't*, could he? Not when it was supposed to be his wedding day! And he's clever, isn't he? Good at concealing things...'

'Yes, he is,' Dixie acknowledged gruffly, her throat closing over. And suddenly, with a sinking heart, she knew exactly why she was hurting—but not why she was so shocked by Petra's announcement. After all, most men were attracted to Petra. Her stepsister wasn't just glamorous and sexy; she was a fun person to be with. So why had she got the idea that César was less than impressed by Petra? Had that been wishful thinking?

'In fact, I think César's already regretting getting himself into this crazy charade with you just to keep the old boy content!' Petra opined drily. 'Still, like you said, that'll be over soon, and César will be free to do as he likes...and I'll certainly be free to do it with him!'

CHAPTER NINE

DIXIE never once asked César where they were to spend their brief honeymoon. In a melodramatic mood, new to her experience, her sole concern was getting César away from Petra as fast as possible. She could not have borne the strain of seeing them together, watching her stepsister flirt, watching César cloak his eyes, shutter that lean, dark, fallen-angel face to conceal his desire to respond in kind…

She had never dreamt she could feel so sick with jealousy or be torn by so many deeply unpleasant emotions. Nothing could have prepared her for the shameful knowledge that for a split second she had actually felt she hated Petra, and had wished her stepsister would vanish in a puff of smoke like the wicked fairy!

But within an hour of their departure Dixie's anger was directed solely at herself. She had fallen head over heels in love with César, but she had cravenly refused to confront that reality. Stubborn denial hadn't protected her, it had just left her out of touch with her own emotions and defenceless. The pain she had tried to evade she was feeling now. César was never going to love her back.

Her love had been an accident waiting to happen. His

sheer animal sex appeal had overwhelmed her, and then she had started thinking about him and worrying about him and caring about him. All common sense had deserted her and she had ended up in bed with him, foolishly risking pregnancy and even greater heartbreak.

If she had never experienced that incredible intimate closeness with César she would have been less vulnerable. Whereas *now*… Dixie reflected with intense shame, she couldn't even look at that lean, powerful body of his, exquisitely packaged by superb tailoring, without feeling quite sick with longing and desire.

The helicopter delivered them to the airport, where they boarded the jet. Dixie pretended to doze during the flight. Put aboard a second helicopter in Athens, she was merely grateful that conversation was impossible, but was surprised that César had chosen to travel so far afield when a more convenient location would surely have satisfied Jasper's expectations.

When they had made a final landing, César lifted Dixie out of the helicopter. They were only yards away from a golden stretch of sand and surging sparkling blue sea. The pilot loaded their luggage into the beach buggy parked above the quay.

'It's a private island,' César divulged with considerable satisfaction. 'And we have it all to ourselves.'

Of course, Dixie thought without surprise. He wouldn't want other people around. He wouldn't want to have to pretend they were normal honeymooners, all over each other like a rash and deliriously happy. Parting her lips, she said as much before she could think better of it.

'You've got a point,' César agreed, studying her

strained profile and the down-curve of her lips. 'Delirious happiness is not a realistic goal at this point in time.'

As Dixie climbed into the beach buggy she flushed guiltily. 'I've been a real drag all the way here, haven't I?'

'No,' César countered steadily. 'You've just been quiet.'

Dixie frowned, trying to recall when she had last really spoken to César. They had been leaving the house. 'You would've found Petra much better company,' she heard herself say tightly now. 'Maybe you should've dropped me at the condo on the coast and brought her here instead. Jasper wouldn't have known any different!'

That outburst took César as much by surprise as it did Dixie. Clamping her hand to her mouth, she stared at him in horror over the top of her fingers. 'Just joking!' she added abruptly.

His brilliant dark gaze narrowed and gleamed as if he had suddenly struck gold. 'Where did you get the idea that I was interested in your stepsister?'

Dixie stiffened, lashes concealing her stricken gaze. 'Most men are.'

'I'm not most men.'

But he *was*. Long tall blondes with a lot of temperament were his trademark. And for the few minutes it had taken them to say their goodbyes and depart Dixie had carefully observed César's behaviour. He had more or less ignored Petra. Men did not simply ignore Petra when she was smiling and being genuinely amusing. Such a complete lack of reaction had convinced Dixie that César was indeed very much attracted to her stepsister but determined to hide the fact.

In the shimmering silence that rewarded his assurance that he was *not* one of the common herd, César's wide, sensual mouth suddenly clenched hard. Breathing in deep, he sent the buggy up the hill at a roaring pace and drew it to a grinding halt outside an amazing house that was, until the very last bend, all but concealed by a magnificent belt of specimen trees and wild lush planting.

'Oh, this is really lovely,' Dixie whispered shakily, knowing that men didn't relish comments on their driving skills.

His bronzed profile taut, shimmering eyes veiled, César sprang out, hauled out all their luggage in one go and strode to the door with it, ferocious tension splintering from every movement.

All too well aware that she should have kept quiet about her suspicions, Dixie followed him at a slower pace into the cool tiled hall. What had possessed her? she asked herself miserably. Naturally César would not wish to confess that he was attracted to Petra when he had already more or less accidentally shared a bed with Dixie and there wasn't the slightest chance of him getting together with her stepsister in the near future.

'I had hoped to avoid admitting it,' César breathed in a driven undertone. 'But I disliked Petra on sight. It was instantaneous.'

Falling still, Dixie gazed at him in astonishment.

'In fact there is a five-letter word that sums up my exact opinion of your stepsister, who wasn't under my roof an hour before she began causing trouble!' César slung in raw-edged addition.

'A f-five-letter word…?' Dixie stammered.

'But out of respect for your affection for her I would prefer not to use it.'

He couldn't mean... But, absorbing the icy glitter of his eyes, Dixie registered that he did mean exactly that, and she reeled in shock. But out of the shock emerged the most giddy sense of relief she had ever experienced.

'Right now,' César murmured with sudden surprising intensity, 'I don't have another woman in my life, and—'

At that precise moment, his mobile phone buzzed.

With an expressive sound of impatience César answered it, and immediately tensed. Dixie was close enough to recognise the pitch of a woman's voice. Dark colour accentuated César's slashing cheekbones. He glanced around himself like a male in dire need of an escape hatch, and finally strode out through the front door again with something less than his usual cool. 'It's not very convenient for me to talk at this moment,' she heard him confide grittily.

He leant up against the side of the beach buggy, wide shoulders rigid, his entire attention fiercely pinned to Dixie, who was lugging her case noisily upstairs one step at a time.

'Here, let me take that,' César insisted when he caught up with her. 'That was Lisette on the phone. I...I told her I'd got married.'

'I suppose it's as good an excuse as any you'll ever have.' Dixie surveyed him with reproachful eyes. 'But couldn't you have come up with something kinder?'

'Kinder?' César repeated, very much as though he wasn't quite getting the response he had expected.

'What an awful shock for the poor woman! One minute you're having an affair with her, and the next—'

'The relationship hadn't progressed as far as the bed-room…and now it's over, OK?' César cut in, ruthlessly blunt in his exasperation.

Embarrassed, Dixie reddened and averted her eyes. 'I really don't think that's any of my business, César. I'm sorry, I shouldn't have said what I did,' she told him apologetically. 'It's so confusing, this pretending and then not having to pretend…after a while pretending begins to feel like the real thing, and before I know where I am, I'm being too personal again.'

'Maybe we should just keep on pretending. It might be more interesting…' César cast wide the single door off the landing.

Dixie was already puzzled by the absence of any other doors in so apparently spacious a villa. 'Interest-ing? My goodness!' she gasped after one astonished glimpse at the vast and luxurious bedroom stretching before her.

Maybe there was another bedroom downstairs. She turned round. César had already gone down to get the rest of the luggage. On the ground floor, Dixie discov-ered an incredibly opulent reception area, an elegant dining room and a superb kitchen with a fridge full of food. She finally accepted that there was only one bed in the entire house.

César rejoined her and helped himself to a rather large brandy. Dixie took a deep breath. 'César, when I was upstairs I just couldn't help…er…noticing that there's only one…'

While she had been speaking César had downed the brandy in one unappreciative gulp. He straightened his shoulders and angled a shuttered look at her. 'I think this would be a good time for you to ring Scott,' he said flatly.

'Oh…yes, right,' Dixie muttered, distracted by that suggestion.

Five minutes later she dialled the number, and was delighted when Scott answered immediately. Scott was surprised to hear from her, but really, really pleased.

'You're homesick? Oh, Scott, how awful!' Dixie sighed with loads of sympathy, while watching César ram back the sliding patio doors with what struck her as quite unnecessary force. 'Tell me about the New York office… But you're really smart too, Scott, don't let people intimidate you,' she urged supportively as César hovered several feet away with the most strange aura of controlled menace, his lean, strong face rigid, bright eyes mere slivers of silver. 'Of course you'll cope. I know you'll be absolutely brilliant. I have every faith in you. I always have had. You can do *anything* you want to do!'

César suddenly strode past her into the kitchen. The door slammed. Dixie flinched. She heard a dulled thud, a muffled oath and then an unholy silence stretched. She stared in real dismay at that closed door. Was César OK? Had he fallen and hurt himself? The door opened a crack again and she relaxed slightly.

'Yes, I'm still here, Scott,' Dixie continued a little weakly.

'You're such a special person, Dixie. I feel better already,' Scott told her gratefully. 'I'll take you out to dinner when I get home.'

'Dinner? Oh I'd love that,' Dixie assured him, rather eager to get off the phone now.

'Can you give me your number?'

'Well, I'm in Greece right now,' Dixie explained uncertainly.

'What are you doing there?' Scott sounded aghast. 'Are you on holiday?'

'A sort of working holiday.' As the kitchen door crashed shut again, Dixie concluded her call.

She sped into the kitchen. Ashen-faced and breathing rapidly, César was leaning back against the units, blood dripping from a cut on his left hand. 'Oh, your poor hand!' Dixie moaned in instant agony for his suffering.

Reaching straight for the first-aid kit prominently displayed, Dixie broke into it. 'Let me get that cleaned up—'

'Don't fuss…it's just a graze!' he grated.

Dixie hauled over a chair and dragged him down into it. He looked as if he was about to faint. It was his thumb, quite a deep slash. 'This might need stitches—'

'Nonsense…it's nothing.'

'How on earth did you do it?'

'I…*bumped* into something on the wall,' César advanced, with brooding grimness and eyes as unreadable as a black wall.

'Do you feel dizzy?'

'No,' he growled.

Dixie dealt with the cut with great efficiency.

'I suppose you were a girl guide.'

'Yes…' Dixie studied that lean brown hand, so dark against hers, and without the slightest warning was just overcome with strong emotion. He would have submitted to death by torture sooner than admit up-front that the sight of blood seriously challenged his ability to stay upright. Without even thinking about it, she pressed her lips softly to the back of his hand.

César tensed, but when she tried to pull back he held on to her. 'I have a confession to make.'

Drowning in a wave of appalled mortification at the rather revealing liberty she had just taken, Dixie bowed her head.

'*I* had Scott sent to New York.'

'S-sorry?' Dixie stammered with a frown.

'The minute you told me about Scott I was worried that you might be tempted to put being with him ahead of Jasper,' César revealed harshly. 'So I called in a favour with a partner in his firm and arranged to have him sent abroad. All it took was a two-minute phone call.'

Genuinely horrified by that level of cold-blooded calculation, Dixie lifted her head and gazed into fathomless dark eyes.

'And I'd be lying if I said I was sorry,' César completed.

'I'm just…I'm just so shocked by this…' Registering that it didn't seem quite right to still be holding hands with César after such a revelation, Dixie tugged her fingers free with a tearing sense of loss and confusion she despised. 'You are, without doubt, the most dreadfully selfish person,' she told him unsteadily. 'I can only hope that this temporary transfer at least benefits Scott's career, because so far he is not enjoying himself over there!'

'I think I'm beginning to feel sorry,' César remarked thoughtfully. 'Not sorry I did what I did, but sorry I succumbed to the disastrous desire to confess.'

'That doesn't surprise me in the slightest,' Dixie said unevenly. 'Don't you *ever* think of people as individuals?'

'I'm getting the image of an exceedingly *wet* individual where Scott's concerned,' César shared very drily. 'I hand him the opportunity of a lifetime and he gets homesick after a week in one of the most exciting cities in the world!'

'That's not the point,' Dixie protested. 'People are more than just puppets you can manipulate!'

'Isn't it strange that I always had this sentimental belief that a free confession won an instant pardon?' César drawled as he rose to his feet with controlled grace.

Dixie leapt up, her cheeks colouring at that response. There was a certain truth in that comeback. If César hadn't chosen to tell her what he had done, she would certainly never, ever have found out. She followed him back into the sitting room. 'Yes…well, actually I   '

'I think I'll go down to the beach for a while.' His darkly handsome features shuttered, César murmured drily. 'I need no mystic powers to divine that this is unlikely to be a wedding night to remember!'

Technically, it *was* their wedding night, Dixie recalled numbly. And she guessed that so far César hadn't found it very entertaining. On the trip here she had been a real wet blanket, and not much more fun since their arrival. In less than an hour she had preached at him twice. 'I'm sorry you're bored,' she whispered tightly, just as he reached the doors that led out to the grounds.

César stilled. 'I'm not bored.'

'Are you hungry?' Dixie pressed hopefully, guilty discomfiture and a very strong desire to keep him with her making her powerfully keen to feed him. 'I could make you something to eat.'

Against the backdrop of the magnificent sunset, César shook his arrogant dark head in apparent wonderment at the offer. 'I'm not hungry for food.'

Her brow indented. César turned back to her. Silhou-
etted against the strong light, broad shoulders sheathed
in the finest pale linen, lean hips and long powerful
thighs accentuated by expensive tailoring, he was achingly beautiful. Bronze skin, black hair, glittering dark
eyes silvering as he tipped his proud head back. Her
tummy twisted and her heart jumped, tension snaking through her as she succumbed to the compulsive
need to stare.

'I'm hungry for you…' César murmured.

'For…for me?' Dixie's shaken voice was strained.

'Famished, ravenous, starving,' César extended, not
quite levelly, dazzling eyes glinting over her like laser
probes.

Her tummy flipped sky-high, her legs turning hollow.

'Just thought I'd mention it… You see, what was an
awful mistake for you *wasn't* an awful mistake for me,'
César spelt out very carefully.

Dixie couldn't take her eyes off him. She was paralysed to the spot. 'It…wasn't?'

'*I* thought the experience was sensational,' César
confided huskily.

Dixie shivered as her full breasts stirred, their rosy
peaks swelling into almost painful sensitivity. 'Possibly because you had been drinking—'

'No…and don't do that—don't sell yourself short!'
César censured, bright eyes blazingly intent on her bemused face, his mouth twisting. 'A man can't fake his
response to the woman he wants.'

And as she stared at him and divined his meaning,
and involuntarily lowered her gaze, a soft little sound
of sheer surprise escaped her parted lips. His arousal

was boldly etched, and as she met his eyes again the devouring hunger there made liquid heat burn up between her slender thighs. In fact, so intense was that physical sensation she stumbled back a step in dismay.

'You couldn't trust me within a yard of that bed with you in it,' César admitted with unashamed candour. 'I would definitely pounce! I'll sleep down here.'

As he swung away, Dixie's face fell a mile. Yes, he really wanted her...well, sexually. The lust bit again. *Sensational?* A wanton tingle ran down her spine and her legs quivered. He was walking out of the door...why wasn't she stopping him? Sex for the sake of it—what he was used to, *all* he was used to, and the most he had ever required from a woman. But not enough for her. All wrong for her! She loved him too much already, was too vulnerable, too painfully aware that within weeks Jasper's recovery would lead to a complete separation.

But as César disappeared into the lengthening shadows he flung Dixie into emotional turmoil. She was so tempted to snatch at what he offered. What did she have to lose? She wanted him so much. More than pride, more than principle. And at that instant it was César's own ruthlessly cutting drawl which flooded her memory. 'You're so convinced you're going to fail, you won't even bother trying!'

Right, Dixie decided, her adrenalin fairly leaping to that challenge. Just for once she was going to take a risk and break all her own rules. She plucked the magnum of champagne from the ice bucket in the fridge, dug out a corkscrew and started down the hill to the beach, plotting every step of the way. He was scared of commitment, so she would have to set him free at the outset rather than give him the faintest hint that she was hoping for anything other than a casual affair. That way he would relax…

César was on the shore, staring out to sea. Kicking off her shoes, Dixie padded across the sand with a fast-beating heart, wishing he would hear her and turn round, but the soft rush of the surf concealed her approach. She trod right up to him and pressed the champagne bottle into his hand.

He spun with a startled frown.

Dixie planted the corkscrew into his other hand and addressed his chest. 'I thought it was sensational too… and I don't see any reason for you to sleep downstairs on a stupid squashy floral sofa—'

'Scott?' César almost whispered.

'He's in New York!' Dixie responded, quick as a flash. 'He's like—'

'Out of sight…out of mind?' César slotted in with rich cynicism.

'It's not like that, César—'

'*Dio mio*…why am I arguing?' César demanded in a raw undertone as he suddenly dropped both champagne and corkscrew and swept her up into his arms with devastating strength and enthusiasm.

'Absolutely no strings,' Dixie told him breathlessly, the warm, achingly familiar scent of him washing over her as she wrapped her arms round his neck and pushed her face against his shoulder. 'I'm not a committed sort of person,' she added, in case her first statement hadn't been enough to release him from any subconscious anxiety that she might be more clingy than his usual kind of lover.

César lifted her higher and crushed her soft mouth with fierce hunger under his. She went weak from head to toe. Urgently prying her lips apart, he kept on kissing her, but the whole tenor of the embrace changed. He went from passion to unexpected tenderness, running his mouth lightly over her swept down eyelids, her damp cheeks, before recapturing her reddened lips with a sweetness that was almost unbearable, his breath mingling with hers. And then, very slowly, he slid her down over his powerfully masculine frame until her bare feet hit the sand again.

As she looked up at him with unwittingly enquiring eyes, César framed her hectically flushed cheekbones with two big hands. 'Sand gets everywhere,' he murmured teasingly.

And he knew that. Of course he did. Nine years older than her, he was a lot more than nine years ahead of her in experience. But Dixie discovered that she didn't want to think about the other women César had had in his life, or of how very different she was from those other women. Not glossy, not glamorous, not sophisticated, not even blonde. She didn't fit the mould, and that scared her.

When they arrived in the bedroom she felt horrendously shy. She hadn't had to think about what she was doing the last time, hadn't had to take responsibility. But César reached for her with a knowing light in his beautiful dark eyes and drew her close. With deft hands he unzipped her dress, gently brushed the straps from her shoulders and let the garment fall to her feet.

His burnished gaze gleamed with rich appreciation over the strapless ivory silk bra and matching lace panties she wore. 'You're exquisite, *cara mia*,' he murmured very softly.

'You say all the right things…practice, I suppose,' Dixie conceded tautly.

A wolfish grin illuminated his mobile mouth, brilliant eyes glinting. 'You're so perfect for me. Nothing I do impresses you!'

'Oh, it does…' Dixie contradicted instantly, dark blue eyes anxious that he should think that, even as her susceptible heart lurched beneath the onslaught of that wonderful smile.

Catching her up in his arms, he laid her down on the magnificent canopied bed. Her breasts rising and falling with every shortened breath, she watched him peel off his clothes with fluid cool. Her heart pounded in her ears as the surging tide of longing dug deep, warming her cheeks, clenching her fingers in on her palms. His lithe, sun-darkened body had the balance and flow of a classic statue suddenly cloaked in living flesh and muscle, but no statue had ever been so rampantly male in his arousal.

'I just can't believe this is us,' she whispered, as a mental image flashed into her mind of César as he was at the bank. Ruthlessly cold, remote, reserved. The memory terrified her.

'Believe it,' César urged huskily, surveying her opulently feminine curves with reverent anticipation.

'But it's not really us…it's like time out of time…'

Lacing his fingers possessively into her tumbled hair, César tugged her into his arms. Suddenly she was trembling helplessly, shot through with need, shifting against his lean, hard length with leaping hunger. Moth to a candle-flame, she thought fearfully, and then, as he freed her breasts from their silk confinement and expertly caressed the tormentingly sensitive tips, she gasped, and the glory of simply feeling stopped all thought dead in its tracks.

'*Dio*...I love your body, *cara mia*,' César confessed with passionate intensity, and as he cupped her ripe curves he bent his dark head and let the tip of his tongue travel down between her proud breasts, licking the perspiration from her skin.

Her tummy contracted, excitement pulling at her. 'I never knew I could feel like this...' she gasped achingly.

His sure hands curved over her hips as he lifted her up to him and kissed her with unrestrained hunger and all-male dominance. Her every sense sang. He traced a slender trembling thigh to its apex, groaned with eloquent appreciation as he discovered the hot dampness even her panties couldn't conceal. He pressed his mouth hotly to the tiny pulse going crazy at her collarbone and gritted feverishly, 'Jasper was right to patrol the courtyard all those endless evenings...never had so many cold showers in my life!'

She kissed the top of his head, loving the silky density of his hair, the smell of him, the smoothness of his cheekbones below her palms, the interesting roughness beyond, and all the time the heat was pooling inside her, driving her increasingly crazy. 'Want you so much,' she moaned.

'How much?' César demanded with sizzling bite.

In the state she was in as he stripped away the silk and lace barrier still separating him from her she couldn't quantify such a thing. At that moment he was everything, the planet around which she spun like a satellite. 'Too much...'

'Not possible, *mi amore*.' He strung an enervating line of darting kisses over her squirmingly restive body, finding erotic places she hadn't known existed before, letting his fingertips smooth through the damp dark curls screening the hot core of her.

And then he relented and traced the silken flesh crying out for his touch, and her breath caught on a rising pant of sensual shock and she threw her head back, spine arching as the shameless pleasure took her in uncontrollable waves. She ached and she needed him with every screaming fibre of her wanton body.

He came over her and she folded round him, exulting in his heat and his hardness and his weight. And when he surged into her with primal force the wild burning excitement of his possession drove her out of her senses. He sent her flying with every thrust, until she reached an incredible peak and the expanding ache inside her could no longer be restrained. Then she cried out in ecstasy with him, her body convulsing beneath his before she drowned in the sweet aftermath of satiation.

Encircled in his arms, she felt so safe, so supremely, crazily happy.

'You're always surprising me, *cara*,' César drawled softly above her head, and yet there was something in that light almost lazy intonation which made her tense. 'I really didn't think you'd share a bed with me again.'

Long, elegant fingers turned her flushed face up to his. 'Didn't you? You're like chocolate fudge cake…I can't resist you,' she muttered ruefully.

'The oddest thing is…I rather respected those principles of yours.'

Feeling suddenly very naked and under attack, Dixie pulled out of his arms and rolled over. She was caught in a trap of her own making. It wasn't the pleasure which had seduced her, it was the love, the hungry, overriding need to be as close to him as his skin, and to take what she could for as long as she could.

'And sex on a no strings basis?' César mused in a suspiciously smooth tone bordering on the sardonic. 'I've got to hand it to you. For a female who was a virgin only a few days ago, you learn fast.'

Dixie dug her hot face into the pillow like a hedgehog going into hibernation.

'And possibly it's my incurably suspicious mind at work again, but does your sudden change of heart relate to the fact that now that we've consummated this marriage of ours we can no longer go for an annulment?'

Slowly Dixie raised her head and turned over, dragging the rumpled sheet defensively round herself. 'I don't understand…'

Eyes as keen as silver daggers held hers by sheer force of will. 'We'll have to go for a divorce now. You could make a huge alimony claim.'

Her colour evaporating at that suggestion, her dark blue eyes pained, Dixie simply stuffed her head back in the pillow and turned her back on him.

'No comment?' César probed icily.

So now she was a gold-digger, willing to sacrifice her principles and jump into bed with him purely out of greed! Dixie just sagged, deeply hurt and really angry with him. He could be so stupid when it came to the things that really mattered. He couldn't take anything at superficial value. Didn't he know her at all? How could he have possessed her body with such fiery tenderness while that over-developed brain of his was coming up with such a nasty scenario?

'Does everybody try to rip you off?' she whispered.

'Rarely do I put myself at risk.'

Dixie lifted her head, her dark blue gaze gleaming into chilling, dark, formidable eyes that might have belonged to a stranger. That hurt even more, but she rammed back the pain and tilted her chin. 'Stop worrying. Your bank balance is safe…I'm just using you for sex!'

A stunned light flashed in César's intent stare. 'You didn't say that—'

He looked shocked rigid, and somehow that pleased her. 'Oh, I did. And, blunt as it was, it's really all I've got to say on the subject.'

'You don't mean it…' César released a sudden husky laugh. 'Of course you don't. We're married…you're my wife!'

'You wouldn't accuse your wife of sleeping with you for the sake of money…well, maybe you would,' Dixie conceded, his stock being very low in her eyes at that moment. 'In fact you just did.'

César curved his arms round her rigid, resisting body. 'You changed your mind so suddenly. I have a logical mind. I need to know your motivation.'

'I've just explained that, and will you please let go of me?'

'No.' César planted a kiss at the nape of her neck.

'We're not really married and you know we're not,' she murmured heavily. 'I don't like you saying that we are.'

Instantly, he released her. 'Fine…'

He left her alone then, and she didn't like that either, could feel the stormy tension emanating from him in perceptible waves.

'*And* you owe me an apology,' Dixie muttered miserably.

'I don't apologise to one-night stands,' César breathed witheringly.

The silence stretched and stretched.

'OK,' César ground out tautly. 'I should've reserved comment on a potential alimony claim until it actually happened. Since I asked you to marry me, *and* I asked you to share this bed, my suspicions were unreasonable and unjust.'

There was a definite sense of waiting expectation in the silence which followed that admission of fault, but unfortunately, in relieved receipt of that apology, Dixie just fell asleep, worn out by a very long and emotional day.

Hours later, Dixie lay watching César sleep as the dawn light filtered through the slats of the tall shutters that screened the balcony. Having pushed off the bedding, he lay on his stomach in a relaxed sprawl, his blue-shadowed jawline resting on a brown forearm, ebony lashes gleaming above a slightly flushed cheekbone. He looked younger, less intimidating, incredibly sexy, not an inch of that lean, muscular bronzed body out of condition.

Some time during the night they had collided again, and clung and made love with such frantic intensity she blushed just thinking about it. And she wondered, indeed marvelled that César could desire her as much as he evidently did, and still she couldn't begin to understand it. Sex was clearly very important to César, and hadn't he told her that himself? Bed being the one place he let himself go. Oh, she had already divined that when he had said back in London that she had the kind of shape which kept teenage boys awake and fantasising at night he was talking about himself at that age.

But it didn't mean anything, did it? Physical release, fleeting pleasure on his terms. But she wasn't going to think like that, she scolded herself. She was going to live for the moment.

'Magdalena…my mother, she had tremendous charm and I was very fond of her,' César admitted rather tautly as he lay back against the tumbled pillows like a lithe, bronzed pagan. 'But she was a total airhead. I worried more about her than she did about me.'

'Did you ever meet your father?'

'Once. I was ten. He was curious…that was all,' César admitted without a shade of censure.

'And how did it go?' Dixie prompted.

César grimaced. 'I unnerved him, *cara*. I was a real little nerd at that age, and I had a pretty smart mouth. Yet he left me everything he possessed when he died the following year—probably because I was his only child.'

'So how did you end up going into the family bank?' Dixie asked curiously.

'My father was a playboy all his life, but he expected something more from me,' César conceded with wry amusement. 'He stipulated in his will that I could only inherit his shareholding in Valverde Mercantile if I started at the bank at the bottom and worked my way up.'

'Your first serious girlfriend?' Dixie questioned daringly.

'I was eighteen. I found her in bed with my best friend. I think I can safely say that she was my *only* serious girlfriend.' César leant forward to refill her wine glass.

'You must've been so hurt!' Dixie muttered fiercely.

César smiled at her, a surprisingly tender and amused smile. 'I survived. So tell me about Scott,' he invited.

Dixie blinked. 'What about him?'

'I'm just curious.'

'He likes football and cars. He's twenty-two on his next birthday...' César winced without her noticing as she ran an abstracted fingertip round and round the rim of her glass, wondering why on earth he wanted to hear about Scott. 'He's not a smartass,' she said carefully. 'But he would really love to be called one. Everybody he admires at work seems to be like that, so he wears the same clothes and drives an old Porsche he really can't afford.'

'You're describing a very immature personality.'

'Yes...well, you can't expect him to know everything yet.' Her affection for Scott warmed her smile. 'He's really quite sweet.'

Taking her by surprise, César pulled her into his arms and crushed her soft mouth with fierce, almost angry urgency under his, making her world spin on its axis. 'I'm not sweet...'

Feeling giddy, she scanned the lean strong face above hers with a secretive light in her eyes. She found some of the strangest things sweet when she found them in César. His grizzly bear reaction to her walking away down the beach and getting lost in a book for three hours and totally forgetting about him. His energetic need to be *doing* something every second of the day. His sudden bursts of passion at the most inopportune moments...like when she was in the middle of making a meal or trying to change the bed.

In a week of incredible contentment and happiness, Dixie had learnt a lot about César, and had fallen even more deeply in love with the complex male behind that dark fallen-angel face. He could be so incredibly tender, so honestly affectionate, but always in a hit and run fashion, retreating again fast. Her dog, Spike, had been a bit like that at first, she mused. Full of distrust and unease, afraid to respond to her overtures or express affection.

'What are you thinking about?' César probed, at the wrong moment.

Dixie reddened, knowing he absolutely did not want to know that she had been comparing him to a dog who had been mistreated by a cruel owner in his early years.

'No, don't tell me.' César's bronzed features shuttered as if he had thrown away the key and locked her out.

But she knew what to do when that happened now. She closed her arms round him tight and shut her eyes, as if she was too unobservant to read his signals, and kissed him regardless. He tensed, and then with a hungry driven groan he kissed her back with ravishing need.

'We're leaving the day after tomorrow.' Over an hour later, Dixie was still in César's arms. She was anxious about Jasper's coming surgery, but sad that they had to leave the island.

'No, we're leaving tomorrow.'

'But you said we were flying back on the thirty-first.'

'It'll be the thirty-first in less than five minutes,' César informed her wryly. 'You need a calendar. Somewhere you've lost a day.'

And out of nowhere, as Dixie thought about calendars, something that she had tucked right to the back of her mind struck her. She had always had a twenty-six-day cycle, and today her period should have started, but it hadn't…

So she was late. Perhaps her system had been upset by the change in diet and climate, she told herself feverishly. But what if it wasn't that? What if she had conceived César's baby that very first night?

CHAPTER TEN

'I WANTED to gag Jasper when he started telling us what was in his will!' César confessed, pacing the elegant waiting room like a caged lion and shrugging back his sleeve to consult his slim gold Rolex watch for possibly the fourth time in as many minutes. '*Accidenti!* If I ran a merchant bank the way they run the surgical unit here, I'd be a pauper!'

'Jasper will be fine,' Dixie told him with soothing conviction.

'How can you be so calm?' César demanded, almost accusingly.

'My stepmother was in Intensive Care several times towards the end.'

A veil of dark colour accentuated César's spectacular cheekbones. He breathed in deep and swallowed hard. 'The queen of the gentle put-down, *cara mia*,' he murmured with a wryly apologetic twist of his beautiful mouth. 'I walked smack bang into that one, didn't I?'

'Jasper will come through with flying colours. It's a straightforward procedure.'

César flung himself down on the seat beside her, only to fly upright the instant the door opened. It was the surgeon. His reassuring smile told Dixie all she needed to know, but César talked at length to him. Dixie watched César with her heart in her eyes. He was being very Italian, or was it very Spanish? She smiled. Whichever, he was in a volatile, highly expressive mood, his lean hands moving to illustrate his speech. Not a side of his nature he had ever shown at the bank, where formality and reserve as chilling as ice had always ruled him.

And how would César respond if she chose to tell him that she was carrying his child? Probably with ice. Dixie lost colour, her eyes shadowing with strain. After Jasper had checked into the clinic on the busy outskirts of Granada yesterday, Dixie had mentioned that she had some shopping to do and had slipped away for an hour. She had bought a pregnancy testing kit, and early this morning she had used it. Within minutes the simple test had confirmed that she was pregnant. The shock had hit her hard. Had César not been so worried about Jasper's surgery he might well have questioned the extent of her preoccupation.

How on earth *could* she tell César? He wasn't even aware that there had been cause for concern. She had let him assume that she was taking the contraceptive pill, and since the wedding César had ensured that they took not the smallest risk. Regardless of what she had allowed him to believe, he had still chosen to use protection. Such scrupulous care told Dixie that César was determined not to accidentally father any woman's child.

But it had already been too late. She was carrying César's baby and she didn't feel it was his fault; she felt it was all her fault! And when, as had happened throughout the day, rosy images of a little girl or boy with César's eyes had strayed into Dixie's mind, she felt even guiltier, and more foolish than ever for being so happy with César on the island. In spite of reminding him on their wedding night that their marriage wasn't a real marriage, she had ended up behaving as if it was. Yet their brief but intense relationship was already existing on borrowed time, and within a few weeks would end entirely.

They spent the following day at the clinic, quietly taking turns to sit with Jasper. By that evening, however, César was in an ebullient mood. Being a dire pessimist, having feared the very worst might happen either during surgery or in the crucial recovery period which followed, César's relief at his godfather's continuing steady improvement now knew no bounds.

Back in their luxurious hotel suite, he pulled a full-length gold evening gown out of the closet and dropped it on to the bed. 'Dress up. We're going out to celebrate!'

Had Dixie done her own packing she wouldn't even have had a suitable dress to wear, because it would not have occurred to her that they might go out anywhere special while they were staying in Granada.

Emerging from the shower twenty minutes later, a towel wrapped round his narrow hips, César dropped Dixie's wedding and engagement rings down on the dressing table beside her. 'You leave them absolutely everywhere. Every opportunity you get, you take those rings off and forget about them. Sooner or later they'll be lost or stolen!'

'I'll try to be more careful,' Dixie said in a small voice.

'Sometimes it's like you're trying to make some kind of statement with those rings,' César murmured grittily, but the sight of Dixie rising from the stool, clad only in a highly feminine peach lace bra and diminutive panties, set his mind in what was becoming a very predictable direction.

'*Porca miseria!*' he breathed raggedly. 'You look fantastic!'

As she turned round self-consciously, her cheeks warm, she encountered brilliant dark eyes and felt the wicked weakness and heat he could evoke so easily flood through her trembling body.

'*Dio*…how I want you, *cara*!' César loosened his towel and reached for her in practically the same movement.

He crushed her into the hard, muscular heat of him and she shivered violently, every pulse-point reacting instantaneously. But, for the first time in over a week, a new voice in her head screamed no. Momentarily, she stilled in confusion at that negative prompting, but César's power over her wanton body was greater. Snapping free the bra and casting it aside, he raised his hands to shape her achingly responsive flesh and she was lost, moaning helplessly under his hungry, sensual mouth as he backed her down on to the bed.

It was wilder than it had ever been between them. Raw and sexy and frantically exciting, even shocking in its intensity. He didn't have to wait. She was ready for him. And the instant she felt him inside her she was out of control, reaching a height of intolerable excitement so fast she raked her nails down his back in shaken reaction and he had to smother her scream of release with his mouth.

And then it was over and she was in a complete daze and César was gazing down at her with unconcealed satisfaction. 'It gets better every time,' he said with a very male wolfish grin, sliding off her and then hauling her up into his arms to carry her back into the shower with him.

Only somehow this time she felt embarrassed and ashamed. No longer was it possible to pretend that theirs was a normal relationship. It was really just a casual affair, she told herself. But while she stood under the shower, getting her hair wrecked, knowing it would be wildly curly and unmanageable after a second soaking, an even more disturbing thought occurred to Dixie. It wasn't even an affair. The truth was far less presentable. By settling those debts César had bought her, like a can of peas off a supermarket shelf, and here she was *sleeping* with him as well.

César folded her into a big fleecy towel as if she was a small child. 'I keep on forgetting how new to all this you are,' he drawled softly as he surveyed her evasive eyes and tense mouth. 'But at the same time I like that knowledge. It makes everything so special between us—'

'Does it?'

'Of course it does.' He rested his hands on her taut shoulders, ebony brows drawing together in a frown. 'The last forty-eight hours have been very stressful…we just blew away all that tension in bed and it was electrifying. That's nothing to feel awkward about.'

But Dixie was not in the mood to be comforted. She felt like one of those stress-busting toys businessmen kept on their desks for relaxation. And when César turned away she saw long parallel scratches marring his smooth brown back and just about died a thousand deaths on the spot. She scuttled out of the bathroom to get dressed, feeling hot tears burning the back of her eyes, all her emotions in upheaval at once.

She knew why she was upset. What could be more brutally realistic and impossible to overlook than an unplanned pregnancy which would infuriate the man she loved? Her days of closing her eyes to harsh facts were at end. It wasn't possible to live for the moment with new life growing inside her womb.

César took her to a really fancy restaurant for dinner by candlelight. Dixie wondered out loud why people would want to have to squint at the menu. César requested another candle.

Vintage champagne was brought with a flourish. Dixie asked for mineral water.

César translated the entire menu for her. Then she said she just wanted a salad and played with it.

César had pre-ordered chocolate fudge cake as a surprise. She said she wasn't hungry enough to eat it.

He told her the coffee was a speciality. She told him it tasted metallic and funny.

She left her rings on the sink in the cloakroom. This necessitated a return to the restaurant from the very doors of the nightclub they had been about to enter and twenty-five minutes sitting in a traffic jam. Dixie gave the restaurateur a glum smile of apology and put the rings back on again.

César gave her a brooding look of censure. 'I'm amazed that diamond wasn't stolen.'

'I'm not,' Dixie said, without a shred of remorse for all the inconvenience she'd caused. 'It looks like it fell out of a Christmas cracker!'

César's teeth visibly clenched. 'OK…I've finally got the message. You don't like your engagement ring.'

'It's not mine, it's yours…so what does it matter what I think of it?' Dixie snapped pettishly, shocked at herself, indeed shocked at the way she had been be-having all evening, but quite incapable of controlling the stormy promptings of her own flailing insecurity. And hating César, oh, yes, absolutely hating him as the evening had worn on. Hating him for every smile and every woman who stared at him. Hating him for forget-ting about precautions the one time he couldn't afford to forget. Hating him for making her love him and not loving her back...

'*Dio!* What is the matter with you?' César suddenly launched at her halfway back into the limousine. 'Why the hell are you acting like this?'

As she saw his chauffeur swiftly step back in discom-fiture, Dixie reddened fiercely and twisted her pound-ing head away, her true self recoiling from the blunt bewilderment César expressed in spite of his anger.

'You've been like that little girl in the nursery rhyme. You know the one,' César asserted sardonically. 'When she was good, she was very, very good, but when she was bad, she was horrid!'

'I just don't feel like pretending any more.' She wanted to bite down on her tongue but she couldn't; she just couldn't hold the bitterness back.

The silence seemed to scream.

'And what's that cryptic utterance supposed to mean?' César's rich, dark drawl was suddenly cool as ice, and it had been a very long time since he had used that tone with her.

'You're making me feel bad about myself.'

'Using men for sex has its disadvantages,' César in-cised very drily. 'I thought that was a stupid joke, but now I'm starting to wonder.'

Dixie drew in a breath so deep she was surprised she

didn't burst. The bright lights of the city streets flickered in her eyes. 'It's a lot worse than that…'

'Tell me this is a mini-breakdown after all the stress we've had and I'll take a deep breath too and all this bull is going to wash over me while I embrace saint-like restraint!' César shot back at her in a roughened warning.

Dixie desperately wanted to keep quiet, but she couldn't. Now all those feelings had foamed up inside her, she had to let them out. 'What we've got is very sordid—'

'I didn't hear that.'

'You bought the right to tell me what to do when you paid those debts. You said that yourself,' Dixie reminded him shakily. 'And I could just about live with that if we hadn't ended up in bed—'

'When we made that deal there was nothing between us. We've gone way beyond that level since then!'

'Well, I still really hate you for what you've done to me!' Dixie told him wildly. But even as she slung those bitter words she knew that she wanted him to pull her into his arms and tell her she was talking rubbish and make her feel safe again, not just sit there like an insensitive stone watching her tear herself apart!

'OK.' César stared at her, lean, strong face ferociously taut, eyes a bright lambent silver as unreadable as a mirror, and then he lifted the phone to communicate with his chauffeur. Minutes later, the limo drew out of the traffic and purred in at the front of their hotel.

'I'll see you tomorrow at the clinic,' César breathed without inflection, and a moment later the passenger door beside Dixie opened for her to get out.

'*Tomorrow?* Where are you going?' she demanded helplessly.

'I don't think that's anything which need concern you now.'

It had never once occurred to Dixie that César might just walk out on her and the argument she had begun. It felt like the cruellest kind of punishment. Appalled into silence, she climbed out and watched the limo pull back into the flow of traffic.

She already knew she had made a dreadful mistake. She had wrecked the relationship they did have. Getting a grip on her wildly fluctuating emotions, she sat up waiting for César to come back. At that point she was absolutely convinced that in spite of what he had said he would return to the hotel. But at three in the morning she went to bed and fell into an uneasy doze, only to wake up still alone at dawn, and feel very scared.

He had probably just gone back to the hacienda for the night. It was only an hour's drive away, she reminded herself. They were only in a hotel because it was more convenient while they were spending so much time with Jasper.

Experiencing a very real need to talk to someone about the mess she had made of things, Dixie toyed with the idea of ringing Petra, where she was staying on the coast. But the nagging awareness that confiding in her stepsister on her wedding day had given her nothing but grief held her back. And César, who wouldn't dream of confiding anything private in anybody, even under torture, would be furious if she was indiscreet.

So Dixie buttoned up her desire to unburden herself, but ended up succumbing to the temptation to ring Scott for another chat, just to fill in the time until she could go to the clinic and sit with Jasper. Scott was much more cheerful. He had been told that he would be free to return to London within a fortnight. Emboldened by that news, he had ventured out to explore New York, but only got as far as the car showrooms. He spent most of the call talking at length about a car he had fallen in love with.

More clued up about Corvettes than she had ever wanted to be, but relieved Scott was happier, Dixie took a taxi to the clinic around ten. It was distinctly humiliating to arrive with Jasper and discover that although César had not been in touch with her he had already sent a message to his godfather. It did not occur to her that she had stayed on the phone to New York for well over an hour because she hadn't the slightest idea that the call had actually lasted that long.

'Such a shame that you and César have to be separated so soon after the wedding,' Jasper sighed with sympathy.

'Sorry?' Dixie prompted uncertainly.

'This stockmarket crisis…César having to rush back to London,' Jasper filled in gloomily. 'Said he'd call in on the way to the airport. You should go with him. You shouldn't be sitting about here with me.'

Stockmarket crisis? What stockmarket crisis? César was rushing back to London? In receipt of that devastating news, it was a challenge to summon up a sunny reproving smile, but Dixie managed it because she cared so much about the old man anxiously watching for her reaction. 'I *love* sitting about here with you!'

Jasper's forlorn look evaporated. 'I expect César will be far too busy to spend time with you over the next few days anyway,' he conceded. 'He's a terrible workaholic.'

César was returning to London. César was leaving her behind in Spain, just the way it had always been planned, Dixie reminded herself numbly. César had already been away from Valverde Mercantile for more than two weeks. Soon Jasper would be able to go home to convalesce, and she would stay on to keep him company and ensure he didn't try to do too much too soon.

She chatted to Jasper, and only when the sound of answering silence finally penetrated did she appreciate that he had fallen asleep. She couldn't even recall what she had been talking about. Feeling the need to stretch her legs, she slipped out of the room, only to stop dead again.

César was striding down the corridor towards her. In a fabulous light grey pinstripe business suit teamed with a white shirt and silver silk tie, he was no longer the relaxed and smiling male she had come to expect. As he drew to a halt a couple of feet from her he looked cold, distant and unbelievably intimidating.

Meeting those chilling dark deep-set eyes, she felt as she had that very first day she had gone into his office, to be faced with the computer print-out listing Petra's debts. The shock of that realisation made Dixie shiver in disbelief. It was as if everything that had happened between them since then only existed in her own imagination.

'Jasper's asleep,' she muttered unevenly.

'He needs all the rest he can get. I'll call him this evening.'

Dixie breathed in deep and braced herself to say what she knew needed to be said. 'César, I'm really sorry about the way I acted last night—'

'Forget it,' César cut in with dismissive, deflating cool.

Her tension screamed up another notch. It was as if

a terrifying wall of impenetrable glass separated him from her. It was as if they had never made love, never laughed together, never shared anything. 'I *can't*…I didn't mean it when I said I hate—'

'I don't want to talk about this.' He was cold as ice, his impatience unhidden.

Involuntarily, Dixie's eyes just filled with tears.

With a soft, succinct expletive, César splayed a hand over her spine to press her another few yards down the corridor into the empty waiting room. He didn't close the door, though. As he walked over to the window a nurse walked past, her footsteps an audible reminder that they didn't have privacy. Then Dixie sensed that César didn't want privacy, didn't want to speak to her in depth, didn't want to be with her one second more than he had to be. The completeness of that rejection savaged her like a physical blow.

And, suddenly feeling dizzy, she sank heavily down into a chair. 'You're dumping me…' She hadn't meant to say that, hadn't even thought of saying that, but somehow that was what emerged from her bloodless lips.

Ferocious tension radiated from every inch of César's rigid back view. He dug coiled fists into the pockets of his well-cut trousers, tightening the fine fabric over his long powerful thighs, but he didn't turn round and he didn't respond.

'Where did you go last night?' Dixie whispered shakily, desperate to talk just to keep him with her, because her whole world felt as if it was shattering around her.

'The beach.'

'Wh-what beach?' she stammered, completely thrown by that admission, as Granada was a long drive from the coast.

'A beach…OK? What does it matter *where* I went?' César gritted in a driven undertone.

'I was worried about you…you told me once not to do that.' Dixie recalled in a sick daze.

'I've settled the hotel bill.' César half turned towards her and then swung back to the window again, but not before she had seen the fierce tautening of his strong profile. 'You'll be more comfortable staying at the hacienda. Jasper's chauffeur will run you back and forth. In a couple of weeks you can come back to London. We'll sort out the rest then.'

If there was a right moment to tell César that she was carrying his baby, Dixie acknowledged painfully, this was definitely not it, here where they could be interrupted at any time or overheard.

César finally spun round. He treated her to a glittering diamond-hard appraisal, not a revealing muscle moving on his darkly handsome face. Then, slowly elbowing back his superbly tailored jacket, he removed something from the inner pocket. 'You might as well have *this*…' He tossed the tiny item with studied casualness down on her lap. 'I'm never going to give it to anybody else.'

In complete astonishment, Dixie gazed down at the exquisite ruby ring, the sunlight gleaming over the beautiful jewel's rich gleaming density of colour.

'Throughout this whole thing you've been really great.' César hovered uneasily halfway towards the open door, like a male being painfully pulled in two different directions, lines of deep strain engraved between his nose and compressed mouth, brilliant eyes screened. 'I should've told you that first…but I wasn't in the mood. You should sell that ring. Scott may not know it yet, but keeping you in washing machines will probably be more of a challenge than keeping a Porsche on the road!'

Scott? Why was César suddenly talking about Scott? Dixie's brain refused to function. Why was he behaving so unnaturally? Was he reminding her about Scott in the hope that she would pick up on that prompting and stop being so embarrassingly emotional?

'Yes,' Dixie muttered flatly. 'But it won't be a Porsche. It'll be a Corvette.'

'Sorry, am I interrupting?' a bright familiar female voice exclaimed from the doorway.

Dixie's head flew up and she gaped, utterly taken aback by the sight of her stepsister standing there, her sleek brown torso and endless long legs on show in a white lace top and brief flirty skirt. 'Petra...?' she breathed in bewilderment.

'I thought César was going to bring you down to the car to see me, but I got fed up waiting.' Petra flicked back her stunning golden mane of hair, a distinctly petulant look on her lovely face. 'I feel like I've spent the whole morning in that blasted car *waiting*!'

César frowned at Dixie. 'Sorry, I forgot to mention that your sister had decided to fly back to London with me.'

'Forgot?' Petra repeated thinly, but then she plastered a wide, bright smile on her lips and shrugged. 'This guy is just so bad for my ego!'

Dixie just looked through the two of them, refusing to focus on either as she struggled valiantly to conceal the most sick sense of betrayal. So, César had gone to the beach. And who had been staying by that beach? She understood now, wished she didn't. So much for his impressively stated dislike of Petra! Last night César had walked away from her and deliberately sought out her beautiful stepsister's company.

'It's time I got back to Jasper.' Pale as death, Dixie scrambled upright, eager to escape both her companions. 'Have a good trip back to London!'

'Dixie...?' Halfway down the corridor César caught up with her, but he only succeeded in halting her by catching hold of her hand.

Unwillingly, Dixie spun back. *'What?'* she demanded baldly.

César gazed down at her with charged dark eyes, and then very slowly let go of her hand again. 'Nothing... nothing at all!' he breathed fiercely, and strode away.

Dixie leant back against the wall until she had stopped trembling, and as soon as he was out of sight dived into the cloakroom to be ingloriously and horribly sick.

CHAPTER ELEVEN

THREE weeks later, Dixie arrived back in London.

Every evening for those three weeks César had phoned her. After she had given her daily bulletin on Jasper, César had then questioned her in astonishing detail about what she did every day, right down to what she was reading. And every evening she had just talked and talked about nothing in particular, just so that she could keep on hearing the sound of that rich, dark drawl. Not once had either of them referred to their marriage, their once intimate relationship, or the divorce that now had to be on the cards.

Indeed, César's constant calls had utterly bewildered Dixie, until she had belatedly worked out that he was behaving exactly as Jasper would expect a newly married husband to behave when he was separated from his wife. Naturally there would be no necessity for such pretences once she was back in London.

Dixie was a complete bag of nerves by the time César's chauffeur met her off her flight. She hadn't been sleeping well, and keeping up a sunny façade for Jasper had been a strain. And three long endless weeks away from César's enervating presence had forced her to face too many depressing realities.

What they had briefly shared was over. For César, it had been a casual sexual affair. For her, it had been the most wonderful but ultimately the most traumatic experience of her life. And right now she still felt that she was never, ever going to recover. She had known César had a very low tolerance for the kind of scene she had thrown that night in Granada, but she still felt that even he could have practised sufficient consideration not to make it obvious that he was planning to replace her with her own stepsister.

But she was equally aware that she couldn't afford to wallow in her squashed ego or her misery. She was pregnant. She was broke. She was unemployed. To save face she would very much have liked to vanish out of César's life with a cheery smile, but as matters now stood that wasn't an option open to her. It was time she told César about the baby. She had been tempted to just blurt the news out on the phone, but had decided that that would be the coward's way out.

It was afternoon when Dixie trekked wearily in the chauffeur's wake towards the limousine parked outside the airport. She wasn't expecting to have to face César before evening. So when the passenger door suddenly opened and César climbed gracefully out she was completely unprepared, and an expression of unconcealed dismay froze her face.

And that dismay merely concealed a whole host of humiliating and all too personal reactions. César looked so impossibly gorgeous. Black hair gleaming in the sunshine, stunning dark eyes just zooming in on her susceptible heart and stealing it back again. Feeling the tarmac literally rock beneath her feet, Dixie came to a halt, just staring endlessly at him, wondering with a

deep sense of injustice why he had to look so fantas-
tically sexy and exotic in an incredibly elegant cream
designer suit. And here she was, a make-up-free zone,
hair curling and wearing the first outfit she had pulled
out of the wardrobe.

'I'd have met you off the plane, but Spike doesn't
like being left alone in the car...' César began tautly.

'S-Spike?'

An agonised whine sounded from the back seat.
César bent down and reached in and emerged with
Spike, his little short legs pedalling in the air with ex-
citement, pleading brown eyes prominent.

Dixie just dived at Spike. Reaching him out of
César's arms, she scrambled into the car to take part in
an ecstatic reunion with her pet. By the time Spike had
been restored to order the limo was a long way from
the airport, and Dixie was grateful for the distraction.

'I can't believe he came with you.' Dixie watched as
Spike arranged himself between them, like a dog trying to stretch himself to three times his natural length
so that he could be in contact with both. 'My goodness,
he's not the slightest bit scared of you!'

Spike made that comment somewhat redundant by
giving Dixie's hand an apologetic lick, then squirming round and sneaking in the most grovelling fashion
imaginable across the back seat to settle down beside
César and look up at him with worshipping eyes.

'He's quite friendly,' César conceded in modest understatement, stroking Spike's tufty ears and reducing
the Jack Russell to a mindless heap of bliss.

'I just never thought...I mean, he was so *terrified*
of men!' With difficulty, Dixie mastered her astonishment. 'It took me ages to win his trust, but obviously

you have the magic touch…only…' She bit her lip anxiously. 'He's going to be very upset if he loses you now.'

'Yes, I feel it could really traumatise him,' César agreed reflectively. 'You'll have to try to detach him from me by easy stages.'

'Yes, of course.'

'I shouldn't think you'll be able to consider moving out of my house in the near future,' César sighed.

Dixie continued to survey Spike with wondering eyes. Welded to César's thigh, he was the very picture of intense doggy devotion. 'I guess not…'

A slow smile nudged at the corners of César's once tense lip-line. 'I have to confess I've spoilt him.'

'He needed spoiling.'

Silence fell. Dixie watched Spike as though her life depended on it. He was a great ice-breaker, she thought ruefully. And she couldn't help but be touched to see César being so kind to her distinctly scruffy little pet. She had really been dreading seeing César again after that emotionally devastating final meeting at the clinic. Unfortunately even Spike wasn't likely to be much use as a diversion once she told César what she had to tell him…

'When we get back to the house,' Dixie began, deciding that César deserved some warning of what was coming his way, 'we'll have to talk. I'm afraid I've got something really serious and shocking—well, *very* shocking to confess, and you're not going to be very happy about it… In fact, I think you're likely to be really annoyed, and I want to say now in advance that that is understandable—'

'Scott flew out to Spain and you sneaked out and slept with him…' César slotted in rawly.

Dixie's lashes fluttered up on incredulous dark blue eyes. She couldn't have responded to such an outrageous suggestion had her life depended on it.

'*Madre di Dio*…anything of that nature, keep it to yourself, because "annoyed" won't cover it. I'll *kill* him!' César swore in a voice that fractured between visibly clenched teeth.

'What's the matter with you? Have you been drinking…or something?' Dixie enquired tautly.

'No, but I badly need a large shot of alcohol,' César confided jaggedly as he leant forward and wrenched open the drinks cabinet.

'Scott has not been in Spain.' Hot, mortified colour now bloomed in Dixie's cheeks. 'And I can't imagine why you think he would've been, or that I would do what you suggested. Perhaps you think I behaved in a rather impulsive fashion with you, but believe me, I've learnt my lesson.'

César thrust shut the drinks cabinet without succumbing to temptation. He drew in a deep, steadying breath. 'I had nerves of steel until I met you.'

'I was just trying to prepare you for what I have to tell you,' Dixie muttered ruefully.

'Relax. I'm cool as ice,' César informed her with glittering dark eyes of probing enquiry that made it very hard for her to breathe. 'Battle-hardened, unshockable, and ready to cope with anything you want to throw at me.'

The limo drew up outside the house. Dixie smiled at Fisher as he opened the imposing front door.

'Welcome home, Mrs Valverde,' the butler said with immense warmth.

'Oh, no, who told you we were married?' Dixie

gasped in dismay, looking worriedly at César. 'It's a really big secret!'

'It's all round the bank too,' César told her apologetically.

Dixie's eyes got even bigger. 'Bruce didn't keep quiet? Oh, how awful for you, César!'

'I'm bearing up surprisingly well. And I wish I could tell you that it was a seven-day wonder, but it's a story set to run and run, and that in itself has created certain problems you may not have foreseen,' César confided, curving a determined arm over her spine and walking her fast towards his study, Spike at their heels.

'Problems?'

'Wedding presents, invitations out as a couple—'

'*Wedding* presents?' Dixie exclaimed in horror.

César slammed shut the door, leant back against it with squared shoulders and breathed. 'OK...give me the really serious, very shocking bad news. Don't keep me in suspense...'

Dazed by the revelation that their marriage was now a matter of public knowledge, and feeling rather light-headed from the effects of stress and tiredness, Dixie surveyed César with open misery.

'I just wish I hadn't been foolish enough to let you think what I let you think... You see, I'm not and I've never been taking the contraceptive Pill,' she admitted tightly, and waited for César to leap to the obvious conclusion.

His lush black lashes dropped very low over his fiercely intent eyes. 'What's that got to do with anything?'

A wave of dizziness ran over Dixie. She swayed slightly.

'You've gone white!' Striding forward on that exclamation, César steadied her with two careful hands and backed her down gently on to a leather couch.

'I'm pregnant...' Dixie told him flatly as he dropped down on a level with her.

'Pregnant,' César repeated, as if he had never heard the word before.

'That night Jasper collapsed...' Dixie added in a helpful whisper, wondering when the awful truth was going to sink in.

'You're pregnant...' César's eyes suddenly silvered and flashed. 'All of a sudden I feel...almost dizzy,' he completed, not quite levelly.

Dixie just couldn't bear to watch his next reaction. She bowed her head over her tightly clasped hands and waited for the storm to break. In the circumstances, he would have to be superhuman not to lament such bad luck.

'You've got my baby inside you...' César framed with audible difficulty, his dark deep drawl roughening.

'After just that one time,' Dixie sighed shakily.

César unlaced her fingers with gentle force and wound them into his palms. '*Dio*...just that one time, *cara mia*,' he swore in the strangest tone.

'You're very shocked. I don't blame you. You were so careful every other time...' Her voice trailed away in embarrassment.

'The hand of fate is definitely operating here,' César remarked, sounding buoyant in what she could only assume to be his evident determination not to hurt her feelings or cause offence in any way. 'But I'm much inclined to think this is only what you call a storm in a teacup—'

'A storm in a teacup?' Dixie parroted in disbelief.

'Obviously you're not looking on the bright side,' César censured silkily. 'We're married—not that anyone would guess that by the ringless state of your hands.'

'I took the rings off as soon as I said goodbye to Jasper. I thought our marriage was to stay a secret,' she explained, mystified by the turn the conversation had taken, still apprehensively fearing a more painful response to the revelation that she had conceived.

Vaulting upright, César bent down and lifted her slowly into his arms. 'You need to lie down. You're very tired.'

'We need to talk about this now.'

'When you're more comfortable.'

Supporting her with one powerful arm, César opened the door and strode across the hall to mount the stairs. 'This isn't where I sleep,' she protested.

'It's just not the done thing to keep your wife in the servants' quarters.'

'I was very comfortable there…I really don't want to intrude,' Dixie said miserably. 'You've got marvellous self-discipline, haven't you? You still haven't said one thing that I thought you would say.'

'It's a mistake to try and second-guess me. And I don't want to be discouraging, but because your mind works on a different plane from mine you don't read me very well,' César declared ruefully.

He settled her down on a magnificent canopied bed in a spacious room that had a distinctly masculine decor of burgundy and dark green. Several other doors led off from it. It was a truly massive house. Slipping off her shoes, he helped her out of her light jacket, paus-

ing with amusement to scrutinise the price label still
attached to the garment.

'So, say what you have to say,' Dixie urged anxiously.

'After you've had a nap, *cara*.' César sank down on
the side of the bed, lean bronzed features arranged in
an expression of unbelievable calm. 'You came close
to fainting downstairs and you're still very pale. We've
got plenty of time to talk.'

Dixie pushed her face into a pillow. 'Stop being nice,'
she pleaded in a pained voice. 'It just makes me feel
more of a nuisance. I know you don't really feel nice...
it's just you hide your true feelings better than I do.'

César smoothed one of her curls down, watched it
spring back rebelliously and smiled. 'Go to sleep,' he
murmured softly. 'If it's any consolation, I used to think
I could read you like a book, and then I discovered that
there's nothing logical about the way you think. It's all
gut reaction and impulses with you, thrills and spills...'

'Not true,' she mumbled, just loving him being
there, too exhausted even to despise herself for being
that weak. She might as well enjoy it, she thought. He
wouldn't be there for much longer.

Dixie slept until almost seven that evening. When she
wakened, she went for a shower and thought about
César. He had been really kind. Why had she expected
anything else? He was too sophisticated and too self-
disciplined to react like a scared teenager trying to escape his responsibilities. But would kindness ultimately
prove to be any easier to bear?

Fisher came to the door to inform her that dinner
would be served at eight. She put on an elegant black

sleeveless dress. She had worn it on the island, but the
new fullness of her breasts gave the dress a tighter fit.
Already her body was changing shape, an ever-present
reminder of the tiny life forming inside her.

In the formal dining room, Fisher had set out magnificent silver candelabra and the very best china and crystal. Poor Fisher, Dixie reflected ruefully. He couldn't
have a clue how inappropriate the romantic approach
was for this particular occasion.

César joined her in the doorway. She turned. Tall,
dark and devastatingly attractive, he made her outra-
geously aware of her own femininity.

'Do you think you can tolerate candlelight for one
meal?' César enquired lazily.

Recalling that dreadful evening in Granada, Dixie
went pink. 'I was really awful that night, wasn't I?' she
groaned. 'I'd just found out I was pregnant and I went
into a sort of tailspin—'

César frowned in surprise. 'You knew about the baby
that far back?'

Dixie nodded.

'No wonder you were upset,' César settled her down
into her chair.

Fisher served their meal. It was delicious, and she
was hungry, but she couldn't have said what she ate.
Afterwards, they had coffee in the drawing room, and
her tension started to rocket again.

'Can we get the rest of this discussion over with?'
Dixie asked, rising restively from her seat and beginning to wander aimlessly round the room. 'I don't understand how you can just make conversation as if
there's nothing wrong!'

Slumbrous dark eyes rested on her. 'The obvious

answer to that is that as far as I'm concerned there *is* nothing wrong. I want this baby,' César countered with incredible cool.

Dixie didn't see that that was necessarily the slightest bit obvious. 'But it was an accident—'

'No, and don't ever use that expression again.' César's mouth twisted as he moved forward to steady a tall lamp which she had brushed past. 'Take it from one who knows, tiny babies grow into adolescents who do not want to live with the news that they are the result of an accidental lapse in birth control!'

Dixie flushed and backed into a chair before setting off in another direction. 'I know that, but—'

'I can't believe that you would want a termination.'

'I don't.' Dixie stiffened defensively. 'But I thought you might.'

'That's not something I need to think about. My father tried to deprive me of the right to be born,' César reminded her with wry distaste. 'I could never feel like that about my own child. I don't just *want* our baby, I also intend to be a good father right from the start.'

Both those sweeping statements of intent left Dixie bereft of breath. Not once had she even hoped for that level of acceptance or commitment from César. 'That'll be difficult when we're living apart…divorced, I mean,' she finally pointed out awkwardly, coming to a halt as she met with another obstacle.

Helpfully, César removed the entire jardinière from her path. 'I'm afraid this is where *you* have to be very brave and self-sacrificing, *cara mia*.' He surveyed her with glittering dark eyes full of expectation.

'I don't understand…'

César spread fluidly expressive hands in a gesture of finality. 'It's goodbye to Scott time.'

'Goodbye to Scott?' Dixie marvelled at the way poor Scott seemed to intrude in all sorts of places where he didn't belong.

'If we both want to do what is best for our child, we won't even consider getting a divorce now,' César asserted with complete conviction, watching her turn in little circles in the centre of the room.

Wildly disconcerted by that announcement, and giddy at the mere thought of it, Dixie breathed, 'But—'

'So we stay together, but Scott's *out* of our lives,' César stressed tautly. 'You have to accept that.'

'But Scott's just a friend—'

'You spent one hour and forty-two minutes on the phone to New York from our hotel in Granada,' César cited in a low-pitched growl of censure, making no move to protect her from stubbing her toe on the edge of the marble hearth. 'That was at least one hour and thirty minutes of what I call excessive friendship!'

Dixie studied him wide-eyed and then stumbled over the hearth. She righted herself with a bracing hand on the superb fireplace and slowly shook her head. 'Oh, my goodness...was I really on the phone that long? How on earth do you *know* that?'

'I paid the hotel bill before I came to the clinic,' César reminded her grittily.

He really was obsessed with Scott. She couldn't think how she had failed to notice that before. And he was genuinely angry that she had chatted that long to Scott on the phone. Was he jealous? Jealous of Scott? And being Dixie, in the grip of an astounding idea, she instantly asked him outright.

Dark colour accentuated César's fantastic cheek-bones, lashes sweeping down on bright slivers of silvered outrage. '*Porca miseria!* Don't be ridiculous!'

Dixie flushed, and now saw no reason to add that she had long since got over her conviction that Scott was ever likely to be anything other than a friend. 'Sorry. I just—'

As she wandered back near the lamp table, César put his hands on her slight shoulders and directed her down on to a sofa. 'You're making me dizzy. Stay put,' he instructed. 'All I am saying is that there is only room for two people in this marriage. You and I.'

'What about Petra?' Dixie almost whispered, knotting her fingers together.

Strong face clenching, his expressive mouth curled. 'I can put up with her in small doses, but if you could persuade her that covering up a little more flesh would make her look less like a hooker, I'd be grateful.'

Stunned by that sardonic response, Dixie studied him fixedly from below her lashes. 'But you went to see Petra the night you left me at the hotel—'

'No, I did not go to see her. I ran into her…to be exact, she ran into me the following morning,' César contradicted with careful clarity, seemingly quite unaware of Dixie's extreme tension. 'I do own the block of apartments she was staying in. I used one myself that night. Petra saw the limo, invited herself over for breakfast and expressed a desire to return to London with me. I could hardly refuse.'

César drew a perfectly possible scenario. Yet no matter how badly Dixie wanted to believe him, newly learnt cynicism assailed her. César was so clever. Would César tell her a truth that would hurt her now that he was talking about staying married to her? If he had been attracted to her stepsister, if he had followed through on that attraction, it would be very foolish of him to confess it now and drive an uneasy wedge between Dixie and Petra.

All Dixie knew was that she still couldn't quite follow what had been going on with César, either that night or the following morning. He had come to the clinic armed with a fabulous ruby ring as a kind of goodbye gift. Petra had been unusually brittle and awkward, exactly as she might have behaved had she got 'close' to Dixie's supposed temporary husband.

'You created a problem there,' César drawled, as if he could read her mind. 'You should never have told Petra that our marriage was a fake.'

Dixie stiffened. Her second mistake had been stopping short of complete honesty. Had she confided that she and César were rather more than platonic partners, her stepsister would surely never have admitted or acted on her interest in him. So if anything *had* happened between César and Petra that night on the coast it was partly her own fault, not least for saying all those ghastly things about their relationship and tearing it apart.

'Did she tell you where she'd be staying in London?' Dixie asked uncomfortably.

'No, just that she'd be with a friend.'

'I'm sure she'll be in touch soon.'

'I shouldn't think we've seen the last of her,' César remarked quietly.

Dixie's thoughts were on her stepsister. It made her unhappy to acknowledge that the wedge between herself and Petra already existed, in the form of her own insecurity. And she knew then that she would have to talk to Petra before she could put those secret and undoubtedly quite foolish fears away.

As soon as Dixie had decided that, she was then free to appreciate how very happy she actually was. There wasn't going to be a divorce. César was determined that their child should have the stable background and support he himself had been denied. A little of her happiness ebbed on her next acknowledgement: if she hadn't been pregnant, César would have been discussing their divorce right now.

'I'm not sure you could cope with being married to me for years and years,' Dixie remarked ruefully.

César tensed. 'Why not?'

'You get bored awfully easy.' All her doubts showed in her eyes.

'How could I possibly get bored with you? I never know what you're about to spring on me from one minute to the next!'

'The trouble is, I also know you're not very good at being faithful.'

'Try me! *Dios mio*,' César rhymed, visibly shaking at having that thrown in his teeth. 'You seem so soft and trusting, but when it comes to me you're really tough and suspicious!'

Dixie thought about that and decided it was very true. 'You wouldn't respect anything else,' she pointed out helplessly.

'Tell me, were you like this with Scott?'

'No. He's not very clever and ruthless—'

'I forgot…he was really sweet,' César breathed with derisive bite.

Fisher knocked on the door to mention an urgent call.

After waiting fifteen minutes, and deciding that César might well be absolute ages, Dixie walked back upstairs at a sedate pace. With a gentle hand she shut the bedroom door. Then she took an undignified leap on to the wellsprung bed, punched the pillows with exuberant energy, rolled over again to kick off her shoes and gasped, 'Yes...yes...*yes*!'

The door that led into the connecting sitting room was ajar. Slowly it spread wide to frame César. Lounging back against the doorjamb, an unholy grin slashing his dark features as he absorbed Dixie's paralysed expression of appalled chagrin, he cast aside the cordless phone in his hand.

'So, I must be pretty good at doing something, *cara mia*,' César remarked with sexy sibilant softness. 'Downstairs, I would never have credited that you had the slightest enthusiasm for staying married to me. But here you are celebrating all by yourself. Fancy that.'

'I...I—'

César shimmied his shoulders fluidly out of his jacket and pitched it on a nearby chair. Tugging loose his tie, he surveyed her widening eyes and the colour building in her cheeks.

'Yes, now you *know* when I want you!' César carolled with satisfaction. 'That has to be a step in the right direction.'

And Dixie just couldn't control her response to the atavistic leap of boundless excitement tearing through her. He came down beside her on the bed with a brilliant smile that tore her heart from its moorings. Heat pooled deep inside her and made her tremble, and yet beyond that she was conscious of the most powerful ache of tenderness. Gosh, he just looked so really happy, even happier than he had been on the island. The first thing she did was hug him tight, straining against him as the last of her tension drained away in the circle of his arms.

'I've really missed you...' he groaned raggedly.

In bed, she translated.

'I've even been thinking about you when I'm at the bank,' he confessed.

Thinking about the frustrating emptiness of the bed, she translated.

He curved his fingers to her cheekbones and kissed her breathless, so much hungry need in his stunning dark eyes she couldn't stop staring, still marvelling at the miracle which had made this elegant, cool, often cold guy seemingly burn with endless desire for her uncool and never elegant self.

'I got used to you being there...now you're here,' he completed, with a wealth of relief in his roughened intonation.

Back in the bed, she translated, but she ached with love for him, and told herself she wasn't going to want any more than he was able to give her. And tomorrow she would put on the ruby ring. Bit of a joke, that, she conceded. César had given her a ring that symbolised *her* passionate love for *him*, just because rubies were the only jewels she had seemed to have no reservations about...

'So I want to see Scott one last time,' Dixie concluded in the simmering silence. One glorious week had passed since her return to London, and this was their first difference of opinion.

'No,' César said flatly.

'Just to explain that I've got married and that that's

why I haven't been in touch,' Dixie repeated for the second time.

'I don't want you anywhere near him. I think that's perfectly reasonable,' César drawled.

'Well, I don't,' Dixie muttered ruefully. 'I don't think it's reasonable at all. Nor do I think that you should behave as if I need your permission.'

'You're my wife,' César breathed chillingly, like a domestic tyrant. 'You should *care* about what I think.'

These days Dixie wasn't as easily chilled as she had once been. 'It's not like Scott's an ex-boyfriend or anything. I would understand if you were jealous—'

'I'm *not* jealous!' César gritted with predictable ferocity. 'Jealousy would imply that I regard him as a threat. Why would I consider an immature twenty-two-year-old car fanatic a threat?'

'I used to imagine I was in love with Scott, but I got over that ages ago,' Dixie remarked with studious casualness.

The silence hung there, throbbing with undertones.

'OK.' César flung the *Financial Times* down across the breakfast table and stood up. 'You can meet him somewhere public for an hour.'

'I'll call him today…' Dixie returned to her book and her coffee with an aura of complete tranquillity.

César reached the door at an unusually slow pace, and then swung back. 'I could come too,' he suggested abruptly.

Without lifting her head, Dixie muttered, 'Not much point you meeting him now. Anyway, he'd be so in awe of someone like you he wouldn't be able to relax.'

'I should hate to be a third wheel.'

Dixie laughed at that idea, knowing that César would simply take over.

'Why don't you ring Scott next week, when Jasper's here?' César suggested then, as he hovered by the door. 'I'm sure Jasper would love to meet him.'

'No, I don't want to leave it that long.' Dixie looked up and gave him a sunny smile, finally registering that he was about to leave. 'Will you be home for lunch?'

The brooding look on his lean bronzed face evaporated like magic. 'I'd really love to, but lunch at home exhausts me.'

Dixie coloured.

'Actually, I'm down for a very boring diplomatic do at lunchtime today... I'd much rather be with you,' César murmured, still lingering while she went back to her book.

In bed, she was thinking. Typical. But she warmed up inside with the wonderful safe feeling she was beginning to experience around César now. Sexual desire might have got him involved with her in the first place, but he was turning out to be so surprisingly wonderful in other ways.

According to Fisher, César had gone to fantastic lengths to win Spike's affection. Spike had been lured from his various hiding places with chocolate drops, doggy bones, choice treats from the dining table and toys. With a patience and a determination that had quite dumbfounded his butler, César had inched and pushed his way into Spike's scared little heart. And Dixie was incredibly touched that a male who had never had a pet in his life had made such a big effort. Initially he could only have done it to please her, but now he had been doubly rewarded by Spike's devotion.

Then there was the custom-built pond her goldfish now rejoiced in. César the fish hadn't eaten his companion, Milly, and they swam around together occasionally now. It would be too much to call them inseparable, but who knew what the future might hold?

Indeed, the only thing that troubled Dixie was that César hadn't yet offered to try to help her locate Petra. She still didn't know where her stepsister was staying. She had thrown out loads of hints, but either César hadn't picked up on them or he preferred that her stepsister remain out of touch. And Dixie had worked out that that was either because he genuinely couldn't stand Petra or because possibly something *had* happened between them which he didn't want Dixie to find out about...

But that was the only current cloud on Dixie's horizon. Next week, when Jasper arrived to spend the rest of the summer with them, they were having a belated wedding reception with five hundred guests. Dixie felt married now. Every time she woke up in the morning in César's arms she felt jubilant. It was the little things that mattered. The way he phoned her from the bank on what sometimes seemed the slimmest pretext. The way he had laughed at the sight of Spike trying to drag a bone nearly as big as himself upstairs. The way he talked about the baby, as if he or she was already here and part of their lives.

Dixie rang Scott at work mid-morning and told him she had got married. He reacted as if he was really shocked, and was surprisingly keen to make an arrangement to meet up with her that evening. She had rather thought he mightn't want to bother.

And then, at lunchtime, without the smallest warning, Dixie's world fell apart again. Bruce Gregory phoned to ask her where César was lunching.

She frowned in surprise. 'He mentioned an embassy thing—'

'No, he cancelled that to meet with your stepsister, and he must have his mobile switched off. I assumed he'd be back with you, at the house, but Fisher said not. So, do you know where they are?' Bruce prompted hopefully, quite unconscious of the bombshell he had dropped. 'The chairman of the Osana Corporation wants to speak to César urgently.'

Dixie's lips moved to frame conventional words before she could find her actual voice. 'I'm sorry, I didn't pick up on where they were planning to go.'

Bruce rang off, leaving Dixie sitting there in shock. César was with Petra? All this time César had known where her stepsister was? Well, obviously he had, if he was lunching with her! And yet he hadn't mentioned it to Dixie, even when he knew how worried she was that Petra hadn't been in touch?

Dear heaven, were they having an affair? If Dixie hadn't conceived, their marriage would have been over now. Yet César hadn't been acting like a male trapped in a marriage he didn't want! Or had he been? Had she just been too dumb and too much in love to see the obvious? Although if César was involved with Petra, why was he dragging Dixie off to bed early every night?

Half an hour later, Fisher opened the door of the drawing room. 'Miss Sinclair, madam.'

And before Dixie could even catch her breath, Petra erupted into the room, tear-stained and almost hysterical.

'I've done something dreadful, and you're going to

hate me, but you're the only person who can help me!' her stepsister gasped before Fisher even got the door closed behind her.

'Help you?' Dixie was already rising from her seat.

'I made an awful mistake. I tried to blackmail César!' Petra ran a trembling berringed hand through her tumbled blonde tresses and groaned. 'How could you marry a ruthless bastard like that, Dixie?'

Dixie had slumped heavily back into her seat. Blackmail? So she had been right. Something *had* happened that night on the coast.

Her stepsister lit a cigarette with a hand that was still shaking so badly she could hardly get the flame near the tip. 'César said I'd never work again if I stayed in the UK. He said I was a spiteful, nasty harpy and I wasn't fit to polish your shoes, and that if I hurt you he'd be after me like a shark in a feeding frenzy...and the worst thing is...it was *all* true!' Her face crumpling on that final wail, Petra sobbed in very real distress.

'You slept with César...' Dixie gulped, feeling as if she had been smacked in the face by a brick, trying to be big enough to come to terms with such a betrayal and finally doggedly forcing herself upright to offer comfort. Whatever Petra had done, César had no business intimidating her to such an extent.

'Slept with César? Chance would be a fine thing!' Petra hissed through her falling tears. 'I threw myself at him that morning in Spain and he told me to *wise up!* He wasn't even tempted. In fact, do you know what the worst thing was?'

Not even tempted? Dixie suddenly found her sympathy gushing a lot more freely and closed her arms round her much taller stepsister to bring her down on to the sofa beside her. 'No…what was the worst thing?'

'César *knew* I was going to make a pass at him and he tried to head me off, and then, when I sort of moved close…' Her stepsister's tremulous voice faltered and she burst back into tears.

'What?'

Petra emerged from her hair, looking pathetic. 'He said he got this really creepy feeling when I did that, so could I please stop it?' she howled. 'And I just felt so *ugly* and *horrible* then!'

Dixie patted her shoulder soothingly. 'I can understand that…'

'Then he left me sitting in that limo on my own most of the morning…like I was just nobody!' Petra wept. 'First he went into this jeweller's, and I'm sure he was in there an hour, and then he went into the hotel, and he was away even longer, and when he came out he was in this really freezing hostile mood and he ignored me. I was really starting to *hate* him by then—'

Dixie broke into that self-absorbed flood. 'So what did you try to blackmail César about today?'

'I called him up out of the blue this morning and told him he'd be really sorry if he didn't agree to see me,' her stepsister revealed shakily. 'And when he showed up I threatened to tell Jasper Dysart that your marriage was just a big empty nothing!'

Dixie turned pale. 'Oh dear…'

'It was my way of trying to get my own back,' her stepsister whispered shamefacedly. 'I'd never have done it. But if I ripped off some money from César, I thought I would feel better about him humiliating me!'

'I don't think César meant to humiliate you, Petra.'

'It was *very* humiliating when he burst out laughing at my threat and told me that you were pregnant!' Petra protested, shredding a tissue violently between her thin fingers. 'And then he got really cold and heavy and scary and said he'd *pay* just to get me out of your life, and I felt even worse then!'

Trying very hard not to smile, Dixie comforted her distraught stepsister. All Petra's real problems came tumbling out then. How she'd stopped getting modelling assignments in London because she was getting older. How nobody had shown the slightest interest in her bid to become an actress in Los Angeles. And Dixie finally began to see what had really been bothering Petra when she'd arrived in Spain.

'I was just so jealous. I just couldn't credit you had got hitched to this mega-rich, gorgeous guy, and there was me, trying so hard all these years and never even getting close to the altar!' Petra pointed out chokily.

'I encouraged you by telling you that our marriage was a fake—'

'It wouldn't have mattered. I was so desperate to prove myself more fanciable than you I'd *still* have tried to poach him!'

'I know.'

'He said he was going to come straight home now and tell you *everything*...so I had to get here first, because I really don't want to lose you, because you're always there for me...' Petra mumbled tightly. 'Nobody else ever is.'

At that very moment the door flew open. Petra cringed into the sofa. Dixie stood up. César got only one aggressive step into the room.

'I'm really grateful you found Petra for me, César,'

Dixie delivered with a determined smile. 'And now that she's told me everything we're mending fences.'

'Mending fences?' César gritted incredulously, a fulminating toughness clenching his darkly handsome features.

'So you're a bit sort of superfluous here at the moment,' Dixie mentioned, very apologetically.

César backed off with extreme reluctance.

Dixie got Petra calmed down and tucked into a taxi.

César was waiting behind the front door for her. 'I should've been straight with you about Petra right from the start,' he announced darkly. 'The minute you said her name the night you explained about those debts, I recognised it. She's notorious! A publicity-grabbing, free-loading, prom—'

'I know,' Dixie interceded gently. 'Did you honestly think I didn't?'

César took an unusual split second to close his mouth again.

'I lived with her for quite a while,' Dixie reminded him. 'But I always try not to judge other people just because they're from a different mould. Petra's always been very insecure.'

César parted his lips, looked deep into Dixie's reproachful blue eyes and subsided again, like a volcano with a lid suddenly crammed forcibly down on its fiery destructive flow.

'I'm very fond of her and you really don't need to protect me from her. You certainly don't need to bring out any big guns. She'd never have carried out that stupid threat. She's just been going through a rough patch and her self-esteem is very low.' Dixie sighed with compassion. 'She got used to relying on her looks to get her everything she wants. Now she needs support and understanding so that she can make some changes—'

'*Accidenti!* If you think she's going to change—'

'She will, but not overnight.' Quiet confidence backed that assurance from Dixie. 'She really has no choice. She can't run around dressed like a teenage raver for ever. And it's all right. She won't want to visit when you're around,' she told him soothingly. 'She really doesn't fancy you a bit now.'

Dumbfounded by that decidedly upbeat conclusion, César watched Dixie head for the stairs. 'Where are you going?'

'I'm meeting Scott for a drink after he comes out of work.'

César froze.

'You said it was OK.'

'I lied.' He said it so quietly Dixie almost didn't hear him.

Dixie gazed down at him where he stood in the hall.

César strode up to the landing and dug clenched fists into the pockets of his well-cut trousers. He didn't look at her. 'I really don't want you to go,' he breathed in a ferociously taut undertone. 'I'm scared that if you see him again you'll realise you're still crazy about him.'

'I'm scared'. Knowing how much that admission must have cost him, Dixie just melted. 'I'll cancel, then. You didn't need to worry,' she murmured gently. 'I've loved you to bits for weeks now.'

Having dropped that news because she felt he deserved it, Dixie continued on to the bedroom to call and cancel her arrangement with Scott. Would she regret telling César that she loved him later? She didn't think so. It got harder and harder to conceal her own emotions.

César followed her into the room. 'You said you loved me...' he prompted, not quite levelly. 'Does that mean you're just sort of very *fond* of me, or that you're as keen on me as you were on Scott?'

Her heart just overflowed. He sounded so vulnerable. She turned round with a helplessly tender look on her face. 'I was just infatuated with the idea of being in love with Scott. That was only the tiniest shadow of what I feel for you.'

His strained dark eyes blazed into brilliance. 'I thought it was still Scott—'

'You pushed him out, but I didn't want to face that at first...because I didn't think we had any future.'

César reached down and took her hands and drew her to him. 'I've been praying we had a future ever since the night Jasper was taken ill.'

Dixie's eyes rounded. 'That soon? Our very first night together?'

'*Dio!* It was really weird. I just looked down at you outside the bedroom door and it was like being hit with a brick,' César imparted gruffly.

Dixie was hanging on his every word. 'Painful?' she probed worriedly.

'I'd just realised I was in love with you, and I didn't want to let go of you in case you got away,' César revealed, a dark flush emphasising his taut cheekbones. 'And then I felt terrific the next morning, until you shot me down by saying it was a mistake and how Scott was the only one for you—'

'Oh dear...I thought that was what you wanted to hear. I really did.' A sort of heavenly chorus was sounding in Dixie's bemused head at that moment. César *loved* her. He'd felt as if he had been hit with a brick, which suggested a moment of stunning self-revelation. Suddenly those words acquired the hue of a deeply romantic and touching confession.

'What I *wanted* to hear? Are you kidding?' César demanded, a full octave higher, keen to tell her just how wrong she'd been in that assessment. 'I was already sick to death of the guy's name, but that morning I wanted to wipe him off the face of the earth! Every time I turned round there he was, like an invisible presence!'

Dixie stretched up and framed his furious face with two adoring hands. 'I'm sorry I upset you like that. I wouldn't have done it for the world if I'd known how you felt about me.'

Thoroughly consoled, César seemed to recollect himself then. His stunning dark eyes shimmered. He curved his mouth into the centre of one of her palms and then he started kissing her fingers in the most shockingly erotic way, and she got all out of breath and her knees wobbled. With the sense of good timing that always distinguished him, César got the message and lifted her up into his arms.

Later, she didn't remember how they'd got to the bed, and their clothes had sort of melted away. And after they had made wild, passionate love, with the new sweet knowledge that lay between them and joined them closer than ever, they were able to talk again.

'So there I was, feeling very rejected,' César relived feelingly, back on the topic of the morning after their first intimacy.

'And you're not used to feeling rejected,' Dixie slotted in tenderly, stringing a line of little sympathetic

kisses across a wide brown shoulder which tensed unexpectedly. 'So it must have really hurt.'

'You're always shooting me down out of the sky.'
César turned up her face and smiled with so much love
down at her. 'I was really panicking when we went out
to join Jasper for lunch—'

'Panicking?' Dixie looked dubious.

'As far as I could see you were still clinging to Scott,
and I wasn't going to get another opportunity to change
that!' César extended ruefully. 'So when Jasper dropped
the news that he was getting organised for our wedding,
it was like a last-minute rescue. I reckoned the minute
I got a wedding ring on your finger I'd be in a position
to stage an all-out war on your affections—'

'You really wanted to marry me?' Dixie gasped, and
then she recalled the rough sincerity with which he had
persuaded her to go ahead and marry him, and knew
she was hearing the absolute truth.

'*Per meraviglia!* Of course I did. I'd never have let
Jasper push us that far if I hadn't!' César stressed. 'I
could have given him two dozen different reasons why
we shouldn't get married that quickly—not the least
being that you deserved the chance to have the enjoy-
ment of planning a proper wedding.'

'But it was a lovely wedding,' Dixie assured him.
'And we had a terrific honeymoon.'

'After your stepsister arrived, I couldn't get you away
fast enough,' César confided, without a shade of remorse. 'One glance was enough to tell me she was out
to cause trouble.'

'I didn't see that until it was too late. She told me she
thought you were really attracted to her—'

'In her dreams,' César growled like a grizzly bear.

Dixie told him that Petra wasn't really as bad as he seemed to think. He didn't look madly impressed by the news, but at least he wasn't arguing any more. Some unanswered questions continued to worry at Dixie, and she was eager to make further inroads into César's wonderfully new and welcome willingness to explain his own feelings and motivations.

'So, if you were so fed up with the idea of Scott, why did you encourage me to ring him on our wedding night?'

'You just looked so lost and unhappy after getting that stupid letter he sent...' César grimaced. 'I felt guilty. I felt I didn't have the right to deny you contact with him—'

'Oh, César, if you loved me that was really sweet and unselfish of you...' Dixie's eyes misted over her view of his broodingly handsome and tense features.

'It was a buck stupid impulse!' César countered. 'And when I heard you oozing care and compassion on the phone to him I just wanted him dead and buried! So I went into the kitchen and smashed my fist against the wall and hit the blasted can opener...'

'Oh, d-dear.' Dixie's voice wobbled betrayingly in spite of her attempt to hold back her sudden amusement. 'Your poor thumb.'

'I was just eaten with jealousy.'

He had finally admitted it. She kissed his thumb in reward.

'And then after that I thought I was in with a real chance, because I never believed you were just using me for sex, *mi amore*,' César revealed, curving her close with two possessive hands and studying her with even more possessive eyes.

'No, I knew I was in love with you by then, but I didn't want to scare you off…and then I did that anyway, in Granada,' Dixie lamented.

'You really shocked me, *cara mia*,' César agreed. 'I just had to get out of the city and sort everything out in my head. Once I'd done that, I realised that I couldn't really expect you to feel any other way when I hadn't admitted how I felt about you. Then Petra arrived for breakfast and really wound me up.'

'I know…let's forget about that,' Dixie urged.

'I was coming back to the clinic to tell you that I loved you and I bought the ring on the way. I remembered you saying that rubies stood for passionate love… *What's wrong?*'

'I've really misjudged you.' Dixie sighed. 'And now I understand it all. You saw that hotel bill and knew I'd been calling Scott—'

'That shot the ground out from under me, and I was too proud to tell you how I felt then,' César admitted. 'But I'd cooled off by the time I got back to London, and I tried to keep the lines open between us. I also grovelled to Spike to get him on my side. I was ready to do anything it took to hang on to you…'

Such confessions were music to Dixie's ears. 'So the baby really was good news?'

'The *best*!' César grinned at her with wolfish satisfaction and smoothed a rather smug hand over her tummy. 'I really struck gold. I was ready to play a thousand violins about the baby needing a father.'

'I was so happy when you said you didn't want a divorce.' An expression of dismay suddenly crossed Dixie's features. 'Gosh, Bruce was trying to get hold of you to tell you that you had to call the chairman of the Osana Corporation—'

'Relax, I picked him up on the car phone.'

'Oh, no…and I've just stood poor Scott up!' Dixie registered in horror as she realised what time it was.

'Happens to the best of us. You can ask him to our wedding reception, but tell him he must bring a partner. You're very much spoken for,' César reminded her, watching her edge surreptitiously off the bed to let Spike in because he was whining piteously outside the door.

'Just for a little while…he gets awfully lonely.'

'Just like César the fish… A *fish*!' César emphasised without warning as Dixie turned, wearing a gobsmacked look. 'How could you christen a goldfish with my name?'

Sidling back into bed, Dixie breathed, 'Because he was always eating other fish. How did you find out?'

'Fisher couldn't resist letting me know. I didn't think it was really sweet either. There's comparisons and there's comparisons, and a manic goldfish—'

'No, he's got a partner now, and I think he's settling down…and you had that beautiful pond built just for him—'

'I was very tempted to stick him in with a very large and hungry carp to teach him the rules of the jungle!'

'Only you didn't.' Dixie ran an appreciative hand over his magnificent torso, feeling him tense in instantaneous response, revelling in the glow of love in his intense dark eyes, feeling she should have worked out long ago that her warmth would almost inevitably draw him to her. 'You're changing…'

'No, I'm still the cold, critical, inhuman guy you fell

madly in love with,' César rushed to assert, somewhat apprehensively. 'I'm not going to change!'

'Spike, get down off this bed!' Dixie called in a shocked aside. 'He's never been allowed on a bed in his life…what's got into him?'

César looked slightly uneasy.

Dixie surveyed him in mute disbelief.

'He was crying like a baby. He was really missing you. He'd have dug compassion out of a stone!' César protested in his own defence.

Dixie concealed a tender smile against his shoulder. She just loved him to death, and he loved her, and he loved their unborn child, and he even loved her dog and tolerated her goldfish. For a once commitment-shy male, he had made tremendous strides, and she was planning to spend the rest of her life ensuring he never had cause for a single regret.

* * * * *